ROMULUS BUCKLE
& the
Engines of War

ROMULUS BUCKLE

& the
Engines of War

RICHARD ELLIS PRESTON, JR.

47NORTH

The characters and events portrayed in this book are fictitious. Any similarity to real persons, living or dead, is coincidental and not intended by the author.

Text copyright © 2013 Richard Ellis Preston, Jr.

Published by 47North
PO Box 400818
Las Vegas, NV 89140

ISBN-13: 9781477807682
ISBN-10: 1477807683
Library of Congress Control Number: 2013935320

For my parents,
Richard and Janet,
with love.

Part One:

THE PHOENIX AND
THE IRON CROSS

-I-

THE MOUNTAINS OF TEHACHAPI

Captain Romulus Buckle was a zeppelineer, and zeppelineers, with their instinctive affinity for air machines, never felt entirely at home on the steaming back of a horse, especially a horse scrambling up a precarious path cut into the icebound face of a mountain. Buckle grumbled curses, uncomfortable and random, into the mothball-musky wolf fur of his parka hood. Ice particles pricked inside his nose. Through the tunnel of his hood, the trail appeared to jerk back and forth as the horse clambered upward. Now and again a snap of freezing air punched in and stung the still-feeling edges of the otherwise numb skin on his cheeks and nose.

Buckle's goggles had frozen over a while before, leaving him near blind, but the fur lining insulated a good chunk of his face; the hoary lenses transformed the world into a bouncing shimmer. His horse, a coffee-colored brute named Cronos, was experienced on the trails—Cronos knew every cleft and cranny, according to Buckle's hired guide, Pinter— and Buckle had been told to leave the horse be and let him mountain-goat the treacherous heights the way he knew how to climb them.

Putting his life in the keeping of an aggressive horse he did not know did not please Buckle. But if he wanted to scale the mountain now, this was the only way he could do it. Dog teams would be useless on this kind of terrain.

"Time to wake up, Captain!" the glassy wobble that was Pinter shouted back over the rump of his horse, five paces ahead. "We're headin' over into the soft stretch of the traverse now, you hear? Into the pass. The wind don't bother to be so cantankerous there. But keep yer musket handy—we're ramblin' into saber-tooth territory!"

Buckle lifted his chin out of the wolf fur and shouted, "Aye!" He barely trusted the fidgety mountain man—with his gaunt features, uneven head, and half-wild eyes—but Pinter was a reliable guide, and one of the few who might, for a sizable payment, be crazy enough to take him high up the mountain in the Bloodfreezer storm season. It was the possibility of the Bloodfreezers that had kept the *Arabella*, the *Pneumatic Zeppelin*'s two-hundred-foot launch, moored in the town below, not far from the ruins of the old Crankshaft stronghold, and forced Buckle to make his ascent on horseback. Despite the frowns from Chief Navigator Sabrina Serafim and Chief Engineer Max, Buckle had insisted that he make the journey alone. He was not about to risk the launch and the lives of his crew to prove a theory—to pursue an obsession—of his own.

Buckle clamped his stiff fingers around the stock of his blackbang musket—something of a feat in thick gloves—and lifted it out of its sheath, laying the heavy weapon across his lap and flipping the pommel flap over its middle to protect it from the cold. A wrapping of oily rags kept the firing mechanisms from freezing solid—a necessity that also promised some delay if he ever needed to bring the firearm into action quickly.

Buckle grunted. He had three blackbang pistols holstered inside his parka—their wooden butts poked his kidneys as the horse bounced—and he trusted his own pistols and saber more than a clunky musket in a scrape, in any case.

The horse lunged up the steep path, delivering a whack to Buckle's spine that made him miss the smooth glide of his airship. The *Pneumatic Zeppelin* was moored in the dockyard of the Devil's Punchbowl stronghold, fifty miles to the southeast, undergoing repairs to the extensive damages she had suffered rescuing his father, Admiral Balthazar Crankshaft, from the City of the Founders over three weeks before.

Once freed from the clutches of the Founders, Balthazar had been busy: he and the Crankshaft council dispatched messengers to every corner of the land, each carrying an invitation to a secret parley with the purpose of forming an alliance against the Founders. Many clans had responded—Imperials, Alchemists, Tinskins, Brineboilers, and Gallowglasses—promising to send their ambassadors. Suspicions ran deep in the blood between the clans, but if the rumors were true, if the Founders and their Grand Armada were gearing up for a mass invasion, then to stand alone meant annihilation. And they all knew it.

In the meantime, Balthazar had begrudgingly given Buckle leave to take the *Arabella* up to Tehachapi in search of a shipwreck. On the night of the Tehachapi Blitz, more than a year before, Buckle had seen one of the attacking Imperial airships suffer a fatal hit—a Crankshaft cannonball had struck home, causing a multichambered hydrogen explosion that had lit up the sky—and the burning sky vessel, ripped wide open, her engineering gondola obliterated, had yawed wildly to starboard and drifted northeast into the mountains.

Buckle wondered if any of the men aboard the crashed enemy airship had survived; they would be long gone by now, over a year later. But it was not flesh and blood, nor even bones, that concerned Buckle—he'd be damned happy if each and every one of the attackers had burned alive—but rather the artifacts of the airship itself. The body of the fallen machine would most certainly provide evidence of its owner, the murderer of the Crankshaft clanspeople.

Buckle had seen the Imperial iron crosses on the sky vessel's flanks as she burned, but the Imperial chancellor, Katzenjammer Smelt, had sworn upon his life that his clan had not attacked the Crankshafts. Buckle did not trust Smelt, but he had to know for sure. And if the airship was not Imperial, to whom did it belong? Buckle's first instinct was to suspect the Founders: it could only benefit them and their treacheries if they could sow the seeds of conflict between the clans they planned to invade and conquer. Someone was stoking the engines of war, Balthazar had said. If the airship proved to be a Founders craft, then Buckle knew where to begin his search for his sister, Elizabeth, if she was alive. She had disappeared during the Tehachapi Blitz, leaving not a trace, and everyone assumed that she had been incinerated in the bomb blast that had obliterated much of Balthazar's house. But the word, whispered by the zookeeper Osprey Fowler and confirmed by Balthazar himself, was that Elizabeth was alive, and if alive, she had been taken by someone.

And Buckle would burn heaven and earth to rescue her.

With a jerk of his gallows-tree head, Cronos reached the crest of the trail. He turned in to a crevice in the wall, a gap barely as wide as man and horse, which quickly opened to an interior ravine where the sky crushed down upon a plunging, high-walled valley. Buckle pulled his parka hood back, the ice-rimed fur lining swamping his neck. The cold air bit his ears despite his pith helmet and its fur havelock flap, but it was very still and it was bearable. Buckle yanked his goggles up over the front of the helmet and squinted. The weak sunlight reflecting off the snow packed an uncomfortable level of glare, but it was a small price to pay to be able to see properly. The sky was gray as old iron, rippled with clouds. Caves dotted the steep walls of the valley, their irregular mouths dark and menacing, half-hidden by dense clutches of fir and pine—the needles glittered with ice and danced with black-and-white chickadees that chirped as they knocked little avalanches of snow from the branches.

Cronos rocked up and down, humping through the deep snow, though his work was eased by following Pinter's big brown horse as it broke the trail. Buckle coughed; a cloud of vapor burst in the air in front of his face and vanished.

Pinter jerked the reins of his horse and stopped, the bottoms of his stirrups leaving troughs in the deep snow, and turned in the saddle to peer at Buckle. "Best to be quiet as a mole up here, sky dog," Pinter whispered through vocal cords roughened by cold and gin. "The sabertooths, they tend toward the night, but it would be prudent not to announce the servin' up of horseflesh on their doorstep, if you catch my meaning, sir." Pinter smiled, stretching his skin, leathery and large-pored, over a long, narrow jaw.

"Aye," Buckle replied. The blanketing silence of the ravine muffled sound. His voice barely made it to his own ears. The landscape was oppressive. Not enough sky.

Pinter grinned, a sudden tightening of the muscles around his mouth, exposing two stumpy yellow teeth wobbling in purple gums. He drew two torches from his saddlebag. At his waist he carried a hollow bull's horn that glowed a yellow-cream color with the fire carried within it, fed by slow-burning snake grass. Fire horns were vastly more reliable than a match or tinder on the windswept mountain, a place where torches proved the best defense against the beasties that lurked there. Pinter had given a fire horn to Buckle, and he had laid its long leather strap across his shoulder so the horn was cradled at his waist.

"Just in case, just in case," Pinter muttered as he pressed the mouth of the horn to each torch in turn, igniting the tar-soaked wrappings at their heads. "The beasties don't like tar. They shy away from the flame and stink. So they tend not to swallow ye if yer holdin' one." The man laughed at his little joke, a rattling, bronchial chuckle.

"I know about sabertooths," Buckle said, annoyed at the volume of Pinter's noises. "Keep it down, will you, mate?"

Pinter's laugh choked off and his eyes narrowed. He thrust one of the torches into Buckle's hand before whirling his horse around in the snow.

"Then you know enough to keep movin'," Pinter barked in a whisper. "Keep moving, eh?"

Cronos jerked forward, following Pinter's lead without a need for spurring.

Buckle did not have any affinity for Pinter. No affinity at all. But the mountain man knew where the wreck of the mysterious airship was located—at least, he claimed he did.

And right now that had to be good enough for Romulus Buckle.

But he did not have to like it.

–II–

SHIPWRECK

THE SNOWDRIFTS IN THE RAVINE shallowed, making the movement of the horses smoother, and within twenty minutes, Buckle and Pinter crested the northeast end of the ravine. Buckle found himself overlooking a wide, gentle slope leading down into a snowbound valley curving between two craggy peaks. Even if he was as odd as a square peg, Pinter proved, pointing his heavily gloved finger, that he was no liar. For there, nearly in the center of the valley floor, flattened except for one towering stretch of her starboard-side girders, lay the sprawling wreck of a gigantic airship that once had been nearly the size of the *Pneumatic Zeppelin* herself.

"There she lies in her grave," Pinter announced, lifting his canteen for a swig of something unlikely to be water. "Dead as dead as dead be—but the dead always be a mystery."

Pinter offered his canteen, but Buckle shrugged it off. It took him a moment to find his voice in his tightened throat. "No thanks, Pinter," Buckle rasped. "You are a poet as well as a scout, I see."

"Sometimes I rhyme, perhaps. But only by a happy accident, sir—a strange tripping of the brainpan," Pinter said as he screwed the cap back onto his canteen, thought better of it, unscrewed it, and fired back another swig. Buckle caught a sharp whiff of the gin.

Buckle heeled Cronos in the ribs, and the big horse accelerated into a gallop. It did not take much coaxing—the animal was happy to run: the open slope, where the wind had scoured away all but a small crust of snow, was a relief after the deep drifts of the ravine. Pinter released a sudden snort, as if he had been caught off guard by Buckle's taking of the lead, and spurred his horse behind, awkwardly attempting to replace his canteen cap while balancing a burning torch and the musket across his saddle.

Buckle found himself grinning: it felt good to be aboard a horse at speed, even if he was somewhat uncertain of the huge animal, and the air was bracing and clear. Drifting snowflakes occasionally sparkled here and there, floating down from the sky, falling with such ease and curling gyre that they resembled snow fairies of lore, denizens of the mountain, wafting in to see what machinations consumed the mortal men below.

As he closed the distance to the shipwreck, Buckle's heart began to pound. The enemy airship had come down brutally, out of control and apparently tail first—the port-side superstructure collapsing upon impact, splitting apart every hydrogen cell that had not already been afire, igniting the volatile gas, and gutting the machine in a final conflagration. Half of the iron superstructure, the starboard flank, still pointed at the sky; its black girders, curved like the ribs of an animal, were wrenched and scorched and painfully reaching for their port-side sisters, which now lay in jumbled, icebound heaps on the ground among the ruin. It was difficult to see the entire wreck as a whole now that Buckle was so close: the tail section had been blasted and flattened beyond recognition, and the crash had displaced the port side of her frame from nose to stern.

Buckle remembered the old zeppelineer's "Tale of Woe."

If down to twisted wreck
My wretched fate so be,
Bury not my bones
Nor weep nor moan
Nor tear thy hair to mourn me.

Rather set to bended knee
Gather up my scattered scree
Hammer and nail
To the Bosun's rail,
And set my sail to eternity.

Buckle spurred Cronos to the left, circling the collapsed nose of the wreck to swing around on the starboard flank, where the fabric skin still clung in great swaths to the ribs. He wanted to find at least a shred of the clan emblem—the iron cross he had seen that terrible night of the raid. And he wanted to discover the airship's name. Even if the arch board was gone, the name should be everywhere—engraved on the captain's door, chiseled into the prows of the gondolas, inked in the logbook, and painted on the midshipmen's plates and mugs. Still, it might be difficult. The gondolas were crushed under the girders, and nearly every inch of machine was charred black, but surely some evidence remained.

The air on the slope was crisp and unnaturally full of echoes. The sounds of Cronos's hooves across the snow and the jangle of his tack seemed as loud as a charge of cavalry. Buckle could not escape the impression that he was circling the remains of a great monster, fallen facedown upon the earth, its innards incinerated and bones scorched in a death by fire, felled by a lightning bolt cast down from the heavens.

Buckle yanked back on the reins with a sudden jerk, and Cronos released an indignant whinny as he slid to a halt, working his bit. Towering over them, nine stories high, loomed the partially buckled midsection of the airship, where the skin still clung to the girders, ripped and burned but somehow largely intact, and there, black against the fire-seared, light-gray canvas, loomed the Imperial iron cross.

Exhilaration rose in Buckle: now he would prove Katzenjammer Smelt a liar. "Here!" he shouted back at Pinter as he slid out of the saddle, his feet landing hard on the snow. He wound Cronos's reins around a twisted girder, securing the snorting horse.

"I'm on yer tail, boy!" Pinter called out as he galloped up. "But mind yerself! The ground is spoilt with cutting jags! And mind yer musket, there!"

Buckle heard the mountain man's warning, but he did not heed it. He was already at full stride through the jumbles of twisted iron and frozen ropes and wires, each footfall disturbing the ground, each boot print revealing black-and-gray ashes beneath the white snow.

Buckle had his evidence. In his mind, he plotted his revenge. He would tear down the flimsy wall of canvas and cut a section of the iron cross free, roll the swath of fabric into a bole, and carry it home. Then he would unfurl it in front of Smelt for everyone to see in Pinyon Hall, in front of Balthazar, Horatio, and the ambassadors. It was damning evidence, unassailable proof that the Imperials had been the ones who had bombed Tehachapi and killed the innocents, killed his mother, Calypso, and either killed or kidnapped Elizabeth.

Buckle's blood boiled. His ears burned despite the freezing air.

Buckle would demand that Smelt admit his guilt. He would demand that Smelt release Elizabeth from captivity in some Imperial dungeon. And if Smelt refused, if he even hesitated one whit, Buckle would draw his sword and run the devil through. He would stand over Smelt as the man lay dying upon the skin of his own airship, his lifeblood seeping across the iron cross, and there he would promise the chancellor that his clan would be destroyed, his legacy ground to dust. When Smelt had choked out his last miserable breath, Buckle would ship him home on a tramp with a declaration of war pinned to his bloody shroud.

Buckle reached the base of the zeppelin's starboard side and halted, looking up at the towering curve of the envelope's flank. He clutched two handfuls of the loose canvas—it was stiff with ice, but its doping left it still pliable—and yanked downward with a furious twist of sinew and muscle, as if he were attempting to pull the sky itself down from the very heavens.

With a shuddering rip, high up on the curving girders, the whole of the skin fell in one massive wave. It came down hard and fast with the roar of snapping rope hooks, tearing fabric, and splitting ice. Buckle, hearing a muffled shout from Pinter and the startled shrieks of the horses, had to lunge backward, stumbling over broken wood and iron, lest he be buried alive under the avalanche of canvas.

The flank skin collapsed into a long pile at the base of the superstructure, sending up a wall of airborne snow and ashes that forced Buckle to duck and hold his breath. The wave of debris passed over him, and he lifted his head.

He gasped.

He blinked.

The envelope skin of the dead airship and its black iron cross had completely fallen away. But another skin remained, having been hidden beneath it.

And upon this age-yellowed, once-white skin towered a great silver phoenix.

–III–

SKELETONS WITHOUT HEADS

BUCKLE STARED AT THE GIGANTIC emblem of the phoenix. It rippled and rustled ever so slightly along its sweeping length—a hint of a breeze had come up, and the snowflakes fell with a hair more density.

"Well, ain't that a kick in the arse!" Pinter shouted, coughing in the cloud of ashes and snow that was quickly settling out of the air. "The Founders' bird, eh? I didn't see that one comin'!"

Buckle just stared. Katzenjammer Smelt had told the truth. It was not the Imperials who had attacked the Crankshaft stronghold at Tehachapi, but the Founders, who had disguised their airships as Imperial ones. In their treachery, the Founders had planned to set the Crankshafts and Imperials against one another, and it had worked. Buckle had taken the bait. Bitten down hard. Had he been left to his own devices, he would have declared war on the Imperials and bled both clans, making them easy prey.

And it meant that Elizabeth, if she truly was alive, was now in the hands of the Founders.

Curse the devils!

Buckle charged forward, clambering atop the mountainous heap of fallen canvas. He wanted one more piece of evidence. He wanted the airship's name.

"Where are you going, Cranker?" Pinter yelled with a sudden anger. "It is time to take our leave! Aye! It is time to go!"

Buckle halted atop the stack of canvas and glared back at Pinter, who was allowing his horse to make small, nervous circles, and jerked his head around on each turn to keep his eyes on him. Pinter was anxious, and he was making his horse anxious. "Stand fast like a good lad, Pinter," Buckle said. "I'll be just a moment."

Pinter pointed at the churning snow and ashes beneath his horse's hooves. "You see this, boy? You see it? With yer eyeballs? Look!"

From Buckle's elevated perch on the canvas wall, perhaps seven feet up, he could see exactly what was making both Pinter and the horse so agitated. On the ground in front of them lay a scattering of human skeletons, perhaps a dozen in total. Buckle's boot prints tracked right through the middle of the skeletons—he had not noticed the bones, so struck was he by the wreck—and the rib cages and femurs were badly cast about, still wrapped in bloody black tatters of clothes, and partially drifted under by blowing snow.

Buckle felt a pang of sympathy for the stranded survivors of the enemy crew—but only for a split second. Served them right. Fogsuckers. Murderers. "We figured that we would find some bodies, Pinter," Buckle said. "Looks like the ones who survived the crash did not make it. Serves them right."

"But look at them, boy!" Pinter snapped. "Look at them! You see any skulls? No, you don't see any skulls! Why? Because they ain't got no skulls! They ain't got no heads!"

Buckle scanned the macabre remains. He certainly did not see any skulls in the graveyard, no.

"They ain't got no skulls," Pinter said breathlessly, as his horse finally stopped spinning. "Because them beasties, the sabertooths, they take the head, you see? Bite it right off and crack it like a walnut to feast on the steamin' brains! Then they come back and gobble up the rest."

"The beasties are not here now," Buckle said. Pinter was crazy. Of course the beasties slunk in during the night and made a meal out of the vulnerable humans. That was what beasties did. Buckle had been raised in Tehachapi. He had even lived in the same mountains as a child. He was well familiar with the nature of the alien sabertooth, and its preference for human heads.

"We must go!" Pinter bellowed.

"The dead are no concern to us as long as we do not join them."

Pinter shook his head. "No, no, no, sir! You are no captain on this mountain, you hear me? Where is yer weather eye, lad? Look up! The sky grows dark. The wind is up. The snow comes thicker and thicker until the world becomes a murk! A twilight! That's when the beasties wake up. And we need to be off the mountain or in a cave by then."

Buckle looked up. Pinter was right. A colossal stretch of low black clouds was rolling in over the northern peaks like an ocean wave. The soft gusts of the wind were noticeably more blustery than a few moments before. And the atmosphere was growing darker by degrees; the torch in Buckle's hand seemed to burn a fraction brighter with each passing second.

"Just one minute, I said!" Buckle replied, plunging through a gap in the airship skin and emerging inside the ruin. He cursed himself for not having noticed the turn of the weather. A sky captain had no right to ever allow himself to be as blinkered as he had just been.

"One minute, boy! That's all!" Pinter yelled from outside, his voice already muted at the edges by a low whine of wind.

"But one moment longer and you'll find yerself alone here, brass buttons or no, damn your hide!"

Buckle ducked and wove his way through the guts of the foreign-built wreck. He peered through the labyrinth of collapsed girders, ropes, and wires—a crushed grappling cannon collapsed from the roof—all charred black and crusted with ice. There had to be a clue—there had to be—that might lead him to Elizabeth. Buckle stopped to dig at the jumble where the piloting gondola might lie beneath. Sharp metal tore his gloves and he cursed. His right forearm ached where the steampiper had cut him in battle three weeks before, and Buckle was certain he could feel the bandages becoming wet. If he had broken the stitches again, well, Surgeon Fogg could sew him up and chew him out yet another time.

But none of that meant anything to Buckle in that moment, especially the pain. He knew one minute was all Pinter was going to give him. He brushed aside snow and clawed at a loose catwalk grating. He found the shards of a chattertube hood and a tinderbox. No name. He found a wad of papers covered in handwriting: they were partially burned and brittle. He stuffed them inside his parka. He jammed his hands beneath a splintered wooden hatch—what looked like it could be an access to a flattened piloting gondola beneath—and heaved it aside.

Buckle had lifted the lid of a coffin. The mummified body of a man, withered and desiccated by a year of relentless cold, his skin gray and shriveled, his eyes sunken away beneath the closed lids, his face stern and horrible, teeth gritted and glimpsed behind shrunken lips, lay trapped in a tomb of crushed wood and metal. His sunset-reddish-orange hair and heavy sideburns apparently had not lost any color in death. His uniform was ridged with frost and ice, but it was black, Founders black, and judging from the amount of silver and red piping on the collar and cuffs, he was a high-ranking officer, perhaps even the captain.

Buckle gazed at the dead man for a moment, the face ghastly under the shadows cast by his torch. The fellow was somewhat lucky, entombed in the bowels of his airship as he was—at least the beasties had not had at him. But Romulus Buckle felt no natural kinship with this fellow airman—not for him, and not for the rest of his treacherous Founders breed.

Buckle grasped the frost-rimed silver phoenix pip on the dead officer's collar. The metal was cold, the collar cloth rough and stiff against the backs of his knuckles. He ripped the insignia loose, snapping it off its securing post, and jammed it into his pocket.

Buckle had his evidence.

-IV-

SABERTOOTH

"GET YER ARSE OUT HERE and on yer horse, sky dog—or you be leavin' me no choice but to abandon ye!" Pinter howled outside the ruins of the Founders zeppelin. The man's voice sounded oddly thin and far away. Then Buckle realized why. The wind had whipped up to a gusting snarl, howling and whistling though the fire-charred wreck, casting about waves of loose snow and ashes. Buckle turned and started back through the hedgerows of broken metal, reaching the skin gap and hurrying over the high raft of deceitful canvas beyond.

Buckle's first unobstructed glimpse of the sky shook his survival instinct by the scruff of the neck. The weather had turned more quickly than he had ever seen before: the clouds churned with an unkind, dark-fisted gray—what he could see of it through the snowfall that now descended in thick, waffling, wind-tossed waves—and the light was rapidly draining away to a preternatural murk.

Pinter's horse snorted, making tight circles again, and aboard her, Pinter, his bug eyes bright, clutched his musket with its oil rags unwound. "Run, boy!" Pinter screamed. "They come with the darkness! They be here! They be here!"

The sabertooths? Storm or no storm, the sabertooths only came at night. The old mountain man surely knew that. Terror had driven Pinter mad, which was probably as easy to do as it looked.

But Buckle's instinct, raising the hairs on the back of his neck, told him otherwise. He broke into a sprint, his boots throwing ash-laden snow as he covered the thirty yards between him and Cronos, who was wide-eyed and pulling at his tether. Buckle unhooked his coat as he ran, exposing the pistols in his belt.

"Beasties!" Pinter shrieked, and swung his musket around in Buckle's direction.

In the same instant, something came at Buckle from his right—a low, broad shadow inside the undulating snowfall—with such speed that it was upon him in a heartbeat. Buckle only had time to swing his torch into the path of his attacker.

Pinter's musket boomed, a muffled burp lost under the wind, the phosphorus-laden ball slicing away through the storm in a bright yellow streak.

The sabertooth beastie veered away from Buckle's fluttering torch, exploding past him in a pummeling of heavy footpads, claws slicing ribbons in the snow, insanely green eyes filled with hunger—four of them, two set on each side of the monstrous, tigerlike head—with the buffeting displacement of air only a hugely muscled creature at high speed could effect. Bright-blue blood splattered across Buckle's thighs as the sabertooth plunged into the snowstorm, uttering an agonized wail so piercing, so nerve jangling, and so foreign to the earth that it was all Buckle could do to resist clapping his hands to his ears.

Pinter's musket ball had grazed the beastie, severely pissing it off. The sabertooth that had just missed Buckle was an adolescent, half-grown, about as big as a large pork hog. The adults, the full-grown alpha males, were as big as draft horses, but far burlier, and damned near impossible to take down. The best way to kill one—for an expert marksman—was a head shot into the thinnest part of the skull, just behind the second eye socket.

Buckle gripped his torch tightly while his free hand jerked a pistol free of his belt. He charged toward Cronos, who was now little more than a shadow in the thickening snowstorm, though not more than fifteen yards distant. Both Cronos and Pinter's horse had gone half-mad at the appearance of the sabertooths: they bucked and kicked, whinnying with fright. Cronos was backing up, twisting his head from side to side with a great violence, desperate to free his reins from the girder where Buckle had wrapped them.

Buckle had faced sabertooths before: the beasties had attacked his family's cabin one night and nearly tore them and their home to pieces. He had been close, nose to nose, smelled their alien stink of rotten eggs, seen the bristling, matted, gore-encrusted fur, heard the click of the huge claws snapping out of their paws, and known the terror of seeing one's own reflection in their plasmatic green eyes. The sabertooths loved horseflesh. If it came down to a menu choice of men or horses, they often took the horses first. If a man faced by sabertooths was willing to sacrifice his mount on the mountain, it was said, he might make it home to tell the story.

Buckle heard a muffled thumping across the earth, horse hooves on snow, and spun his head to see Pinter galloping away, already a shadow in the murk. "Damn your hide!" Buckle screamed. "Abandon me here, will you?"

A large figure leapt through the air over Pinter's horse, and suddenly the shadow that was Pinter's head was gone. Pinter's torch dropped, whirling to the ground, a glowing witch's orb rather than a shadow. More shadows swarmed after the horse and it shrieked, a jabbering, high-pitched scream, and then everything vanished in sheets of falling snow.

Buckle reached Cronos. The horse stomped at the prospect of being free to run, bobbing his big head back and forth as if he might bite Buckle. Terror glittered in Cronos's big, dark eyes, mixing with the reflected blaze of Buckle's torch: if Buckle tried to mount the horse now, the crazed animal would throw him. Buckle hauled at the reins, but they did not slip free of the girder. He peered at the knotted mess of leather straps; the big horse, with all his terrified yanking, had somehow cinched the reins deep into a crevice in the twisted metal.

Buckle grabbed the handle of his sword but froze when Cronos suddenly stilled, motionless except for the back-and-forth switching of his ears, and blasts of hot vapor from his nostrils, his eyes soft brown pools of terror. Under the wind-battered light of the sputtering torch, Buckle could sense the horse's heart pounding, pounding so hard that he could feel its shockwaves through the wind.

The sabertooths were on them.

Buckle spun around, leading with his pistol and torch. The blizzard swirled in all directions at once, driving snow upward and downward in a churning murk. The sun was near utterly defeated, and the world was in a storm twilight. Buckle could see no more than fifteen feet in any direction, and most of that was undulating shadows. But the saber-tooths were close, circling, stalking him on their soft paws, readying to pounce.

A sudden shadow transformed into Pinter's horse, exploding out of the storm into Buckle's view, wild-eyed, teeth bared in terror, mouth slathered with foam gobbets, still carrying its headless rider. Buckle jumped aside, half-frozen finger still on his pistol's trigger, as the animal thundered past, its dead passenger flopping in the saddle, his fire horn still agleam. The mount and its ghastly rider disappeared into the murk again—one heartbeat after they had appeared—but a moment later, the horse screamed, a guttering shriek of agony, followed by a heavy thump that vibrated the earth, followed by the thrashing of legs.

The invisible sabertooths, perhaps a dozen of them, roared.

Silence followed, the deafening silence of the blizzard. Waves of snow, whipped into madness by the wind, flooded sideways, then shot straight up, blotting out the world three feet in front of Buckle's nose.

He was blind and deaf in a tiger cage.

Buckle could see them in his mind, though, the sabertooths, the green-eyed beasties slouched low, weaving back and forth as they returned to circle him, their long canines dripping with the blood of Pinter's horse. Buckle backed up against Cronos's muscled flank, and the horse stood still. His only hope was to run; cut the reins, climb on, and hold on for dear life—and even then, he figured his chances stunk.

Cronos shrieked. Another sabertooth was coming. Buckle felt the shake of the frozen earth under his boots as the heavy, agile claws of the beast bore down. But from which direction, it was impossible to tell. Cronos swung, stamping, to the left, his eyes locked in the opposite direction. Buckle flung out his pistol, aiming where the horse sensed the danger was.

Before Buckle sucked in another breath, the sabertooth was on them: launching airborne from the storm, its green eyes afire, terrible claws extended, the mouth wide open in rows of bone-yellow, dagger-bladed teeth streaming with saliva, sailing over Buckle's head.

The beastie was going for the horse.

Buckle fired the pistol up into the sabertooth's throat; steaming blue blood spewed as the creature instantly went slack, its limp body sailing away in the waves of snow, landing in a skidding crash at some point beyond.

Buckle cast the empty pistol aside and frantically dug inside his coat for the second. Sabertooths attacked in packs, like wolves. He was surprised another one had not hit them yet. Cronos—now bucking and shrieking—bumped into Buckle, nearly knocking him off his feet.

And then it was there. This sabertooth was bigger than the first, surging out of the snowstorm, a locomotive of flesh and fangs, the horrible mouth flung open. Buckle, aiming the wrong way and off balance, could do nothing but accept his doom.

~V~

THE BLACK ANGEL COMES

A MUSKET THUNDERED. IT SOUNDED muted, far off, but inside the maelstrom of wind and snow, it had to be close at hand to be heard at all. The crack of the musket coincided with a brutal jerk of the sabertooth's head to the right, a blow that split the massive skull open immediately behind the second eye and spun the beastie sideways in a burst of blood and brains. The creature was dead before it slammed into Buckle, but the weight of the blow knocked him down as if an oak tree had been felled across him.

For an instant, Buckle was smothered by beastie, the rolling weight upon his body threatening to crush his bones, his mouth and nose full of sabertooth fur, his nostrils thick with the pungent reek of carrion and the burned-hair stink of the alien mammal. Then the weight was gone.

The momentum of the dead sabertooth's body sent it somersaulting over Buckle's head, but he barely saw it go. He was flat on his back, his head spinning like the sky and the twirling torch descending within it, suffocating, his lungs abruptly clapped free of every molecule of air they had once contained.

Something materialized out of the blizzard above Buckle: the head of a black horse with frantic eyes, and above that, a black figure with fluttering, sweeping wings upon its shoulders.

A black angel. Buckle gurgled, trying to speak, trying to recover where his body was in relationship to his mind. His breath suddenly came to him in ravenous gasps, gasps painful due to the freezing air, an agony his oxygen-emptied lungs reveled in.

The air between Buckle and the black angel cleared, a momentary eddy in the gales, and he saw the figure above him, clad in a long, black bear-fur greatcoat and a swirling black cape with the breadth of wings. The figure cast a smoking musket aside. Buckle saw the long, graceful face, pale white adorned with ornate black stripes, a face dominated by a pair of goggles where the large black eyes within burned nebula orange.

What the devil? Max. It was Max. She had defied his orders to stay behind with the *Arabella*. She had defied his orders not to follow him on his fool's errand up the mountain. And now Max had saved him. Saved him again. He was glad to see her. And angered by the risk she had taken.

"Captain! Get up! You must get up now if you can!" Max shouted. She had pulled her horse aside and, leaning in her saddle, was clawing at Cronos's tethered reins, which she had yet to realize were hopelessly tangled.

Buckle rolled onto his side and then his stomach—spilling through a skeleton's rib cage as he did so, scattering the bones—and jumped to his feet, still gripping his pistol, and collecting his fallen torch as it sputtered in the snow.

"Aye! I am up!" Buckle shouted back. He tossed the torch to Max and quickly drew his saber as he advanced on Cronos. "He is caught! I will cut it!"

"Hurry, Captain!"

Buckle took a firm grip on the reins. The horse would bolt once it realized it was free. "You came alone?"

"Aye!"

"You are mad in the head!" Buckle shouted as he lifted his sword.

"That makes us a pair, then, sir!" Max replied, drawing a pistol.

The horses screamed. Max swung her pistol, but she never got the barrel around in time.

The first sabertooth tackled the head of Max's horse, wrapping its front paws around its neck, the claws sending out spurts of blood as the huge jaws clamped down on the poor creature's skull. The second sabertooth arrived a fraction of a second after the first, landing on Max's back before her dead horse had time to drop.

–VI–

THE BLACK ANGEL FALLS

MAX WENT DOWN IN A tangled mess of beasties, horse, and thrashing snow.

Buckle lunged forward. "Max!" he screamed. She lay facedown, her right leg pinned under the quivering mass of her dead horse, the gigantic sabertooth still upon her, its four green eyes afire, its claws punched into her back, its massive canines sunk into the cloak and greatcoat on her left shoulder. The beastie opened its mouth with a jerk, yanking free its incisors awash in Max's bright-red blood, and cocked its muscle-bound shoulders to land another bite—a killing bite—on Max's exposed white-and-black striped neck.

Buckle sprang forward, planted the muzzle of his pistol squarely behind the beastie's second eye, and pulled the trigger. The weapon burped in the storm current, its flash and black discharge instantly sucked way. The sabertooth thrust its head straight up with a smoking hole in its skull; it collapsed, stone dead.

Buckle dropped the spent pistol, snatching the last one from his belt as he strode up to the other sabertooth. It was crouched low, its fangs deep in the deceased horse's skull; its four green, split-pupilled eyes flashed as it snarled, a throaty, almost musical utterance, clamping its teeth tighter with a splitting crunch.

Aiming into the forebrain, Buckle fired, killing the beastie almost instantly—the sabertooth shuddered in its death throes, its fangs never releasing the horse's head.

Buckle jammed his last firearm in his belt as he leapt over the near-doused torch in the snow, scrambling to Max. She lay motionless on her stomach, twisted forward at the waist with her lower half still in the saddle, the mass of the horse across her right leg and the dead sabertooth slumped over her torso. When Buckle shoved the heavy bulk of the sabertooth's body away from Max, he discovered that the animal's claws were still buried in her back. He gripped the massive forepaw—with all the care he could, but the hooks were sunk deep—and drew each blood-soaked claw out of its fleshy bed beneath the heavy bearskin coat.

"Max!" Buckle shouted, tearing the ripped cloak away from her body. "Max! Can you hear me?"

Max raised her right hand but it dropped instantly, as if it had taken all her remaining strength just to lift it. Buckle felt both a great pang of relief and one of fright. Max was still alive, which was a miracle; by all rights, the sabertooth's pounce should have broken her spine. But he was shocked by how terribly injured she was. He scrambled around the horse, gently rolled Max more onto her side, and leaned close to Max's goggles, brushing back a sweep of black hair that had fallen across her face from beneath her pilot helmet.

"Max!" Buckle shouted again. "Stay still—you hear me?"

"Captain. Go," Max said with a faltering voice. "Leave me."

"To hell with that suggestion, Chief Engineer!" Buckle replied. He started badger-digging at the snow packed around Max's thigh, where it lay pinned under the saddle. More sabertooths roared in the wreathing vapors of the blizzard. Cronos whinnied nearby, less a frantic plea now than a sound of fore-boding, as if he had become resigned to his fate, tied to his own butcher block as he was.

Buckle's spine tingled as he clawed at the snow. The beas-ties, pack hunters, were closing in again. His back was utterly exposed. But surely the blood stink of the corpses of the dead beasties gave them pause. Of course. It must. To hell with them. Buckle continued digging.

"Captain," Max gasped.

"If you are trying to talk me into leaving you, I would sug-gest you save your breath," Buckle said. He scrabbled on his knees around to Max's head, shifted her onto her back, and placed his hands under her armpits. "I am going to pull you out."

"Aye, Captain."

Buckle eased Max back with half of his strength, hoping that her leg might easily slide free. It did not. Buckle hauled with more desperate force, near lifting Max's body out of the snow. Max's shoulders stiffened, but she made no sound. Martians rarely expressed pain, but her eyes betrayed her: inside the aqueous humor of her goggles, they glittered a swimming gold, the Martian color of agony.

"Damn it!" Buckle screamed. But he had to get her loose.

Swinging his body around to cradle Max's head in his lap, Buckle planted his boots on the withers and croup of the dead horse, bent at the knees, and clamped his hands under Max's armpits with a grim pressure.

"Out you go!" Buckle shouted. He yanked on Max with every ounce of strength he had. Max threw her head back, her face upside-down just below Buckle's. Her exposed white-and-black-striped throat quivered; her white teeth were clenched, the lips drawn back and rigid, stained by a stream of blood running from her left nostril. Her goggles, kept free of ice by the warm aqueous humor within, were covered in a smattering of melting snowflakes, each fantastic, crystalline pattern illuminated by the swirling, golden light from below.

Buckle pulled harder.

The leg suddenly jerked free, sliding out from beneath the horseflesh as smoothly as a sword from its scabbard. Buckle fell backward, still cradling Max's head in his lap, and as they landed, he heard her grunt and lie still.

"We've got it!" Buckle yelled. "You are out, Max!"

Buckle gently laid Max's head on the snow as he scrambled to his feet. She lay still, her goggles fading to darkness, into some chasm of shock. He saw that his left glove was soaked with warm, steaming blood, bright-crimson Martian blood, absolutely dripping with it. He realized that his legs and the front of his coat were wet with blood, too.

Buckle lifted Max in his arms, leveraging the slender, light mass of her body over his left shoulder. He knelt to snatch up the torch and paused, just for an instant. The light of the flames, playing upon the depression in the snow where Max had been trapped beneath the horse, revealed a large, ever-spreading stain of blood.

It was a horrific amount of blood for a lithe creature such as Max to lose. Her Martian heart, stout as it was, could barely still be beating.

Buckle ran.

-VII-

WHITEOUT

BUCKLE STUMBLED UP TO CRONOS and lifted Max onto his back, ramming his boot into the stirrup and swinging up into the saddle behind her. Cronos threw his head back and forth, scuffing his hooves.

Buckle drew his sword, slashed through the stretch of the reins between Cronos and the girder, and kicked the horse in the ribs. "Hah! On, boy! On!" Cronos, his shivering muscles firing, charged into the blizzard. Buckle leaned forward, gripping Max, letting the horse run. They were on the upslope, as far as he could tell, but he had no sense of direction now—he could see nothing. His whipping torch did no more than illuminate a wavering waterfall of snow that he could not see through.

Buckle clung to Max, who slumped forward like a rag doll, with little tension in her form, her head lolling with the rock of the horse's motion. Through the raging storm and the battering of the horse's muscles, through the clutch of his fingers against the blood-smeared coat, he sought to feel a movement from Max, a twitch, a heartbeat, to reassure him that she was still alive—but he could feel nothing.

Confound the disobedient Martian! Buckle thought. She shall not trade her life for mine. She shall not.

Cronos slowed a bit, beginning to tire, but Buckle let the animal run on. Buckle wanted to return to the ravine and hole up in one of the caves for the night—if only the wind would let up a moment, give him a view of the landscape about, he could surely point his mount in the right direction. He hoped that the horse, experienced on the mountain as he was, would instinctively head home along the ravine, seeking his stable and its hanging bag of feed.

A whiteout blinded Buckle for an instant. The memory it triggered came on so hard and fast it startled him, leaping from the darkness and bursting in the forepart of his brain. He was a boy again, in his parents' cabin on the mountain. He was terrified, perhaps no more than six years old, clutching a sword that was far too big for him. His mother had her arms clutched around him—and Elizabeth. His strongest impression was that of his mother's heart, a youthful organ, drumming hard against his back.

The sabertooths were attacking. Outside in the night, they roared. A horrible screaming came from the horses in the stable. The two cabin windows, both made of heavy, translucent glass, had been broken in by the beasties, and shards were scattered across the floor rugs in glittering bits. Fangs and claws had torn at the window frames, green-eyed nightmares had peered in, but the heavy timber of the cabin had defeated them.

Buckle was crying. Elizabeth was crying, tears streaming slick and glistening down her round cheeks. Buckle wanted to be brave for her, but he could not muster it. Their mother had snatched them from their beds with a pistol in her hand, and now they huddled in a corner wearing their nightclothes. The fire was low in the hearth, scarlet and orange embers, and the air felt cold.

Buckle remembered watching his father, Alpheus, striding back and forth across the room. He looked very big. His hair was mussed. He gripped both a sword and a pistol, and had a belt strapped around his waist with two more pistols stuck into it. The sabertooths, clever creatures, were slashing at the heavy oak door; its iron hinges, screws popping, threatened to burst.

Wood scraped across the floor, bunching the fur rugs with it, as another man shoved his parents' heavy oak bed toward the door. Alpheus was alongside the man immediately, throwing his weight into the push.

The other man? Buckle's mind grasped at a vapor in a fog. He had not remembered the other man being there that night—a detail almost lost to his memory—but Buckle was certain the other man had been there. He could see him now, shoulder to shoulder with his father, a long musket strapped across his back and a pistol at his waist, gripping a burning torch that filled the cabin with smoke. The man was taller than Alpheus, and wiry thin, clad in his day clothes, with knee-high leather boots lined with leather straps and buckles.

A beastie slammed the door with enough force to shake the world. Glittering dust streamed from the rafters. The fire threw sparks up the chimney. Alpheus and the other man froze for an instant.

"The door shall not stand much longer," Alpheus said. Buckle felt his mother stop sobbing and her spine stiffen. He clutched the handle of the cold sword his father had handed him, telling him to defend his mother and sister to the last, if it came to that, and that he was proud of him being so brave.

The other man clapped a reassuring hand on Alpheus's shoulder. "It most absolutely shall hold, Alpheus," he boomed. "I helped you build that door, and we built it to withstand exactly this, and despite your incompetence as a carpenter, I build damned fine doors!"

Alpheus smiled grimly at the man who was his friend. "And yet you cannot brew a decent cup of tea."

"No one has ever brewed a decent cup of tea. Vile stuff, it is," the other man replied heartily.

The cabin shuddered again. A sabertooth clawed furiously at the door, the vibrations of the strokes sounding as if the oak were being carved away at a terrifying rate of speed. The man sprang to the front window, a small portal fixed about five feet to the left of the door, drew his pistol, and stuck his arm outside with it. The pistol boomed, followed by a shriek and a roar from the beastie. The scratching stopped. The man yanked his arm back an instant before sabertooth fangs crunched on the pane in a burst of splinters.

The man punched the beastie's massive, splayed-nostril nose and it released, vanishing into the darkness beyond the window.

"Good way to lose an arm, Shadrack," Alpheus observed dryly.

"Tut, tut. No bother," Shadrack replied, turning to wink at Buckle. "I do have another one." Shadrack had a narrow, gaunt, but kindly face, bordered by a shock of long, dark hair, and a thick beard framed with gray.

***

Shadrack. The name roiled around Buckle's mind like a fox gone mad in a henhouse.

Shadrack! The same Shadrack whom he had seen locked in the prison of the City of the Founders, the skeletal madman, a moonchild who had beseeched him as a savior, with some crazy hint of recognition. There was no doubt it was the same man—Buckle was certain of it. Oh, what tales the madman might tell!

Buckle gasped, sucking in a huge slap of freezing air loaded with snow, making him cough. His plunge into memory had only lasted a second, yet it seemed as if he had been away from Max and the run of the horse in the blizzard for an eternity.

Who saves old Shadrack?

Buckle clutched Max's body closer to his chest. He was afraid that she might already be dead.

Something panicked the horse. Cronos neighed and bolted again, cutting left through the snowbound twilight. Buckle glimpsed the low shadow of a sabertooth loping alongside on the right, the glowing green of its eyes visible in the storm.

Cronos veered farther to the left. The roar of another sabertooth somewhere behind made him accelerate, foam spewing from his mouth, his head jerking from side to side as his eyes bugged in their sockets. Tree trunks exploded out of the murk, flying past on each side with high-pitched swishes.

"Easy, boy!" Buckle shouted. "Easy, lad!" But he knew his words could not crack the horse's terror. He could do no more than stay in the saddle and hold on to Max and the fluttering torch, and hope beyond all hope that the sabertooths did not bring Cronos down.

The loaded musket still lay across the front of the saddle, but Buckle could not reach it, not while holding on to the torch and Max at the same time. One musket shot was not going to save them, anyway. The trees they passed were denser now, whizzing by on either side at breakneck speed, but Cronos somehow avoided them.

Cronos was charging as fast as he could when he ran off the edge of the cliff.

In an instant they were in midair.

Buckle found himself in free fall, out of the saddle, plummeting through swirling whiteness, his arms locked around Max, with the kicking horse descending alongside.

A cliff? That simply wasn't fair.

–VIII–

THE CAVE

BUCKLE, MAX, AND CRONOS FELL into the white void, the yellow orb of the torch waffling weirdly as it dropped through the torrent alongside them. They glanced off a near-vertical wall of snow, and the impact spun their bodies. Buckle kept his arms secure around Max, his face buried in the thick bearskin on her back as they tumbled.

Then they were rolling, bouncing and rolling, down the steeply angled incline, each impact made soft by the snow, bringing down a small avalanche with them. What little Buckle could see of the world spun in rough, white bounces, and dark tufts of grass or splotches of stones.

They rolled to a stop, Buckle on his back, Max's limp form on top of him. Buckle gasped through the crust of snow coating his face and blinked. Even with the gale thundering in his ears, he heard Cronos stagger upright nearby, and then his frightened whinny trailing away along with the jangle of his tack as he set off running again.

No more musket. No more horse, for that matter.

Buckle carefully slid Max off his chest and leveraged himself to his knees. He should be running, but where? He could see nothing, but he guessed that the horse had dropped them in the ravine. His right forearm burned where the damned steampiper had cut him, and there were pains in his body, bruises and perhaps lacerations, but they were not injurious enough to slow him down. He leaned over Max, shielding her face from the storm, and yanked his hand from his glove to wipe a carapace of blood-streaked snow from her face and goggles.

Her nose and mouth emerged, striped pale white and black, but whether she breathed or not he had no way to tell. He jammed his hand back into his glove and gathered her body in his arms, cradling her against his chest as he stood. If they were in the ravine there were caves there, caves everywhere. He had to find shelter soon and tend to Max's wounds, or Max would most surely die.

If she is not dead already. A fear crept over Buckle that had nothing to do with the sabertooths.

Facing the incline they had just rolled down, Buckle turned right. He had no inkling why right was better than left. Given the choice, he preferred to turn right. The snow was deep and forced him to pump his legs high as he staggered forward, Max in his arms, advancing into the teeth of the raging blizzard.

Perhaps it would have been better to turn left.

The icy wind bit at Buckle's exposed neck—whatever skin his helmet, goggles, and beard did not protect. The goggles were damned near frozen over again, thickening up with even more ice from his frantic exertions. It did not matter much—he could not see anything, anyway. Buckle moved forward, ever forward, his legs slinging snow as they drove like pistons through the snowdrifts cast up against the cliff. He struggled through close-packed trees, his shoulders and Max's swinging boots shattering the ice encasing their branches.

The muscles in Buckle's thighs burned. He was stuck in slow motion, a fly stuck in molasses.

And the sabertooths, relentless predators, did not give up easily.

A shadow emerged from the murk on Buckle's left, and his hammering heart leapt. He veered straight at it, splintering through a thin, dead, frozen tree that blocked his way. It was a cave, the mouth of a cave, mostly blocked by a snowdrift, and overhung by rafts of snow and icicles, its maw as dark as night.

Buckle bounded through the deep snow between him and the cave in a matter of seconds. Once he'd plowed through the high snowdrift and stumbled in under the overhang, he found his snow-coated legs suddenly unencumbered, for the floor of the cavern was clear, the uneven granite gleaming under a layer of clear ice with a dusting of granular snow.

Buckle tossed his torch, the flames now burning much brighter, away from the wind, into the darkness. Through his iced-up goggles, he could see little of the interior of the cave, and he remained in a ducking crouch, unable to measure the height of the ceiling above him. He carried Max a few strides farther, as far as he dared, until he could see where he was going, and then knelt, gently laying her on the icy floor.

Buckle pulled his goggles up onto the brow of his helmet, knocking off the frosty crust that had accumulated there. The flickering torch lay about ten feet ahead, and in its ebbing light, he could see that the cavern was of a decent depth, perhaps thirty feet to the irregular back wall and wider on the sides, and the ceiling high enough for a man to stand. Small, secondary chambers honeycombed the rear and sides of the cavern, though how far into the mountain the subterranean intestines might reach, Buckle could not tell.

Buckle could build a fire here and tend to Max. He could make a stand against the sabertooths here. If he had the time.

Buckle removed his gloves and pressed his fingers against Max's neck, searching for the pulse of the jugular vein. At least, he assumed that Max had jugular veins. He had no idea. He knew very little about the anatomy of the humanlike alien creature who had saved his life so many times. They had stood together through many a happy hour and sad, and yet he hardly knew her.

The half-frozen skin of his fingertips managed to find the dull beat of her heart in the flesh, but it was weak and erratic. And the coldness of her body unsettled him.

"You are one tough bird, I'll give you that, Max," Buckle said, hoping Max could hear him.

Buckle lifted Max again. She sighed, not with an easy relaxation of air from the lungs, but with a shuddering tightness that suggested agony. Buckle carried her deeper into the cavern, closer to the back wall of the main chamber. He laid her on the ice-glazed floor and, after making sure she was as deeply folded into her warm clothes as he could arrange, reached into his ammunition pouch to reload the one pistol he had remaining in his belt.

He worked quickly in the weak torchlight, biting off the top of the paper cartridge and pouring the blackbang powder down the barrel, ramming it home with the wadding and the lead ball. His eardrums, for so long brutalized by the battering storm, now roared of their own accord, drowning out the wail of the wind behind him.

Removing his powder horn from his belt, Buckle poured fine-grained into the pan just under the flintlock. He grabbed the torch and stood up. "You hold fast, you hear me?" he said to the unconscious Max. "I shall be right back."

Buckle turned and strode toward the mouth of the cave, feeling oddly negligent for taking the torch with him, and leaving poor Max alone in the freezing dark. Max needed to be warmed up. He had to make a fire, and a fire required fuel. Beasties or no beasties, he had to go outside and gather wood.

–IX–

FIRE AND THE LITTLE PINK SCAR

LASHED BY THE STORM, BUCKLE thankfully did not have far to go in the unnatural twilight to collect the pieces of the dead tree he had snapped only moments before. He stuck his pistol in his belt—and felt insanely vulnerable, as he bent to pick up the loose wood. The spindly twigs and branches were good tinder. Enough to get things started. Big, living fir and pine swung in the roiling murk, promising a slow-burning, smoky fuel that might be wet enough to last through the night.

Once Buckle turned back toward the cave, his arms jammed full of twigs, his heart missed a beat when he could not see the entrance through the dense snowfall, even though he knew it was there. He stopped. He should procure a big chunk of wood now, or else he was going to have to come out and get one later: later, when night had fallen and the sabertooths would have had time to sniff them out again.

Buckle waded through waist-deep snow to reach the tall pines growing along the base of the cliff. Placing his tinder sticks in a pile, he shoved a raft of snowy branches aside to get ahold of a limb that he could snap away. As he rocked the branch back and forth, chunks of snow fell on him from the branches overhead, accompanied by the clatter of falling icicles.

44

The branch broke off with a satisfyingly loud snap, and Buckle ripped it out of its tangle with its brothers. He tucked the heavy limb under his arm, picked up his kindling sticks, and loped through the snowdrifts back to the cave. Max lay where he had left her, bundled deep in her coat, and the mournful wail of the wind made her plight seem even more grave, as if she lay in a tomb.

"Max! You stay with me, you hear?" Buckle whispered as he knelt beside her, expecting no response and getting none. Her eyes were shut inside her goggles, her lips slightly parted, the ashen paleness of her face startling in its nest of black fur. Buckle bashed each wooden stick on the floor to break away its casing of ice, and rushed to stack his kindling.

Max had lost what seemed like gallons of blood. The wounds had to be stanched. But to strip her down in subzero air invited death by hypothermia. To attempt to clean her wounds without boiled water invited death by infection. And infection was the biggest specter haunting the kind of wounds she had taken. If she survived the shock and blood loss, which Buckle believed—maybe desperately—she would, the sabertooth claws and teeth that had penetrated her body were infamously infective, rotten with death as they were, not to mention the bits of leather and bear fur they had driven deep into the flesh. If the wounds were not properly treated, if they were not flushed and cleaned before they closed, then even the expertise of the Crankshaft physicians might not prove enough against the fester and gangrene.

Buckle reached for the fire horn Pinter had given him—poor, unfortunate Pinter—and was surprised to find the horn warm to the touch, the flame still alive within it. There was a tinderbox inside the survival pouch on his belt, but the ready flame of the fire horn would be faster.

Max gasped, suffering a violent bout of shivers. Buckle unbuttoned the front of his parka—the wad of papers he had salvaged from the Founders' wreck spilled out onto the floor—and laid his fur on top of her. He still had on a sheepskin undercoat and his leather aviator coat beneath that, so the cold was of no concern to him now that they were out of the wind. "There you go, girl," Buckle whispered close to Max's face. He did not know why he felt the need to whisper, but he did. "We shall have you warm as toast in a few moments."

Max stopped shaking, but her sleeping face looked tense with pain.

Buckle removed his survival pouch from his belt and, unfolding the neatly squared oilskin they were packed in, arranged the contents on the floor: one tinderbox, a small box of sulfur-tipped matches, six paraffin candles, a foot of coiled kindling hemp, five squares of chocolate, one knife, one flare gun with three cartridges, one roll of gauze, one roll of heavy bandage, three vials of morphine, one steel-and-glass syringe, one tin of Dr. Fassbinder's Penicillin Paste, eight ounces of water in a cylindrical steel canteen, a small steel pot, and six firearm cartridges—three for a musket and three pistol shots.

"I think we lost the beasties, at least," Buckle said. "In a way, it is a bit unfortunate. I would have enjoyed chopping another one."

Buckle felt like he was running out of time. He cut off half a foot of the hemp and jammed it under his kindling tepee, tossing a half dozen of the matches under the stack as well. He lit one more match with the fire horn and tossed it in. The fire burst to life with harsh puffs of flame as the match heads ignited and set the hemp to burning. Thick gray smoke wafted up to the ceiling and pooled there, spilling away and upward into whatever depressions had the most elevation.

Buckle wanted to keep talking. To let Max hear his voice. He wanted to describe a shared memory they had from childhood. But, he realized, they had never shared anything pleasant as children. That had been his fault. "How shall we pass the time? I am awful at telling stories," he said, forcing lightness into his voice. "And I know you don't want me to sing."

Once the kindling, frozen, but dry as parchment, caught flame, Buckle tucked the steel pot against the wood and filled it with the eight ounces of water from the canteen. He carefully nudged the stem of the heavy tree branch into the opposite skirt of the fire, close enough to allow the flames to lick it, without smothering them with its cold weight and melting ice. The wood immediately began to smoke black, the bark splitting, and that was a good sign. Buckle placed the syringe near the fire so the cold glass would warm and not crack when he filled it with hot water.

"Look at that fire, eh? I make them good. Real rat cookers."

Buckle tucked back Max's hood and placed his fingers on her fur-lined flying helmet, squarely pressing the spring-loaded switch on the aqueous humor reservoir; the clear liquid evacuated from the interior of her goggles within a few seconds, and he lifted the goggles up onto the helmet.

"You have made quite a business out of saving my skin, Max," Buckle said as he slowly, carefully removed her leather helmet. "I would be most pleased if you would allow me to return the favor. If you care about my feelings one whit, you will kindly find a way not to die on me."

Max's eyes were closed, of course, but Buckle hoped that they might open. Once again, he pressed his fingers against the white flesh over her jugular vein, battling a lurking despair that she was going to die on him right there. Her neck muscles tightened against his cold fingers—she was still alive, if only barely, and the knot in Buckle's stomach eased a little.

"And when a captain gives an order, he expects it to be followed," Buckle said. "It appears that when I give an order, my own wicked officers only consider it a suggestion, as if I were asking them what they think of the Darwinists, or what, perhaps, might they like for dinner. I expressly forbade anyone to follow me up the mountain."

Max lay motionless under the heavy fur coats, her face now wreathed by her luxurious black hair. Her wide eyelids with their thick black lashes fluttered once as the flames of the fire rose and warmed her face, the yellow illumination pulsing across her white skin and the black, curving stripes that framed it. Her breath was coming and going, too quick and shallow for Buckle to feel good about it. On her forehead he noticed her little pink scar, thin and straight as a needle, which ran about two inches up from the end of her eyebrow to trail off into her hairline.

***

Buckle had been seven years of age, Max of an age unknown. Buckle and Elizabeth had recently arrived in Balthazar's house, the newest adopted orphans, and Buckle was confused, angry, and prey to night terrors after the violent deaths of his parents. Max and her brother, Tyro, were already there, well sequestered in the family, slender and striped, the stars of the classroom and imperturbable behind their liquid-sloshing goggles.

Buckle hated them. He hated them.

Dead-eyed freaks.

He remembered only fragments of the day that his parents had been attacked on the mountain. He mostly remembered running and pulling Elizabeth along. But he did remember that one of the attackers was a Martian.

He was always after them, both Max and Tyro, taunting, teasing, insulting, and when the opportunity presented itself, willing to inflict bodily harm. Such things were not an immediate part of Buckle's makeup—he had not been raised to entertain such impulses—but the rage within him drove him to it. It shocked him, but he could not control himself. It was as if the rage would take control of his body and mind, and he would be shoved back, a mere spectator to the mayhem, either unable or unwilling to referee his own actions.

Balthazar, Calypso, and the governess, Catherine Flick, always did their best to separate Buckle from the Martian children, but he was always looking for an opening to pull hair, splash ink, or trip up. His punishments had increased in intensity, from being sent to his room to shoveling the dung out of the mews, but it deterred him little.

He simply could not rein in his anger.

One day, Buckle caught Max alone in the corridor of the house, without the company of Tyro or an adult. They were both on their way to geometry class, Balthazar's leather-bound books tucked under their arms, and their paths from opposite ends of the house had somehow intersected.

Buckle immediately pounced. He swiped Max's books out of her hands, and they tumbled to the floor in heavy thuds. Her eyes flashed crimson in her goggles. He laughed, hating her, despising the slender, black-and-white striped hands that looked so out of place at the ends of her dress sleeves.

"Look at me, you black-eyed zebe!" Buckle snarled. He ripped off her goggles, the aqueous humor spewing as they came free. Face dripping, Max stared at him, her big black eyes brimming with defiance. Brimming with hurt.

"You look like a bug!" Buckle shouted, tossing the goggles aside. "Stinkbug!"

Max stepped forward in a way she never had before. Jammed in her left fist was a geometry compass, which she now swung, driving the sharp point into Buckle's right shoulder with surprising force, plunging it into the muscle deeply enough for the compass to remain stuck there even when she removed her hand.

Buckle froze. The Martians never fought back. The Martians had always endured his attacks stoically, covering themselves as best they could and waiting for an adult or an older child, like the eldest son, Ryder, to step in for them.

Not this time.

Max stared at him, her eyes calm, victorious, condescending, and aquamarine.

Buckle's shoulder suddenly hurt like hell. He jerked the compass out of his flesh and hurled it against the wall, where it left a little splotch of blood before dropping to the floor with a clunk.

Max turned and ran. Buckle sprinted after her.

He was going to kill her.

They ran and ran, down the long corridors of Balthazar's grand Tehachapi house. Max dashed like a gazelle, veering through doorways with elegant speed, her skirt fluttering about her legs, but Buckle, coming on with his greater size and speed, closed the gap; he grabbed one of her long black braids, lovingly threaded by Calypso, and yanked her head back.

Max lunged forward, jerking the braid out of Buckle's grasp. She stumbled and slammed headfirst into the oak jamb of the parlor door frame. Her forward motion suddenly arrested, Max dropped in a fluttering pile of skirt. She lay on her back, legs twitching, blood, bright red, crimson as cherry pigment, spilling from the gash in her forehead, trickling across both the white and black stripes.

Buckle could not take his eyes off her. Something strange worked inside him, a disconcerted, unspeakable, unfair remorse: something he had never felt before.

The sounds of boots on timber came pounding up behind him.

"Max!" Calypso shrieked.

Something powerful lifted Buckle from behind. He had been lifted up by the hair. He saw his feet kicking in the air.

Balthazar Crankshaft had never before raised his hand against one of his own children, and never would again. But that morning, as Max was carried bleeding to the infirmary by the weeping Calypso, Romulus Buckle had the tar beaten out of him by the grand old man of the Crankshafts.

And Buckle, his arse pink and his ears bruised, never cried. He deserved what he got. Part of him had wanted to be hated, had wanted to die.

***

Buckle took a deep breath and brushed Max's hair back from the scar on her forehead. The skin felt cold and clammy.

Max had expressly forgiven him—the very next morning over breakfast—but her graciousness, her concern for the offender's feelings, had done nothing but wound him to the quick. In later years, if the scar was noticed by a schoolmate, Max would claim that she barely even remembered the incident. But Buckle knew that Max remembered. And it pained him to think that she did.

Martians never lied, people said. Max said. But Max was only half Martian.

The water in the iron pot came to a boil, a thousand bubbles pinging against the metal. Buckle unsheathed the knife and stuck the blade into the rolling water.

Buckle was no surgeon, but he had a surgeon's work to do.

And Max's life depended on him doing it well.

–X–

THE APPRENTICE SURGEON

Buckle slid his heavy coat off Max and unhooked the latches of her bearskin. He tried to pull the fur lining from her left side, but found that the copious amounts of blood, now frozen in scarlet gobbets of ice, had stuck it to her woolen sweater beneath. He used his knife to cut the sweater away. The sweet, coppery smell of blood swamped his nostrils. As he worked the bearskin and the black woolen sweater out from under her light form, cradling her head against his thighs as he raised her upper body slightly, he found that the blouse beneath was in shreds, a white silk garment now utterly soaked the color of scarlet, heavy with slushy blood.

Buckle worked quickly, handling Max as he would a sleeping baby. He wondered if he should give her a shot of morphine. He decided against it. She was unconscious now. She would need the painkiller once she roused. There was not a lot of it.

Max started trembling. She was terribly weakened, susceptible to the cold. And the cave air did not feel much warmer, though the heat of the adolescent fire surged at his back. But it would have to do.

Applying the knife to Max's blouse, Buckle sliced it away, revealing the skin underneath: skin pale as cream where he wiped it, skin adorned with curving black stripes. Max's entire left side was awash in thick blood that looked black in the fire-light, down to where it had pooled over the belt at her waist. His heart sank, there was so much of it, steaming in places, dripping down the ribs. He pulled away the tattered remnants of the blouse, and she lay exposed from the waist up.

It would have surprised Buckle, if he had time to consider it, that Max's well-muscled stomach was all white. Buckle had never seen Max's body beyond her face, neck, and hands. She had always kept it hidden under sleeves and high collars. Hers was a beautiful form, very human in appearance, except for the black stripes upon it, tapering off along her rib cage and swirl-ing around her small, pink-nippled breasts, but Buckle was in no state of mind to register such things. Even though his inva-sion of her well-guarded privacy was necessary to save her life—he was her doctor now, after all—if anything, he experienced a sense of impropriety as he worked. And there arose another emotion, guilt, a despair at the violence of the wounds she had suffered in his defense, but he was too absorbed in his task to give such feelings any attention.

The sabertooth had sunk its fangs into Max's shoulder near the neck, plunging into the muscle just above her clavicle. The two puncture wounds were dark red, deep, as regular as drill holes, and still wide open, leaking both blood and clear fluid. They were awful wounds, to be sure, but the beastie had not locked down, or Max would most surely be dead. The saber-tooth's first bite was for capture; the second bite would have been for the kill.

More worrisome even than the bite wounds were the long claw slashes down Max's back. Buckle carefully shifted her onto her uninjured right side to investigate. There were four separate gashes, each one longer and deeper than the next, ripped down the flesh of her back from the top of the shoulder blade to the waist. The narrow, ragged wounds had bled badly, though he could not see that any had sunk deep enough to damage the bones or organs beneath.

Buckle decided to start with the bite wounds. He eased Max onto her back again, and then removed the pot from the fire, so the boiling water would not evaporate away. Taking the surgical knife from the pot, he cut away a section of the gauze roll, dipped it in the water, and began wiping the icy gouts of blood away from Max's neck. Blood oozed from the bite punctures, flooding the white skin immediately after he wiped it. He used a small handful of the bandages to continue cleaning, but the cloth was soon soaked completely through.

Buckle filled the syringe with hot water from the pot; he sank the point of the needle into the first bite wound and drove his thumb down on the plunger, expressing the near-boiling water with as much force as he could. He continued pressing the plunger until the water flooded out of the flesh clear and clean, and then repeated the procedure with the second wound. With the veins below freed from the debris and coagulate that had stifled them, new blood flowed from the bite punctures in rivers.

Buckle unscrewed the Fassbinder's Penicillin Paste tin and sank two fingers into the pale-green balm, then plugged the fingers into Max's wounds, stanching the blood flow. He placed a folded gauze bandage on Max's shoulder and pressed down on it. Max shifted, ever so slightly, uttering a small, plaintive sigh. The sound nearly broke Buckle's heart. She started shivering. He felt her quivering muscles tighten as if she might be coming around.

Buckle cautiously turned Max onto her stomach, allowing the weight of her body to maintain the pressure on her shoulder bandage, and immediately set to cleaning the claw wounds. Her thick black hair had become unbound from whatever device she had pinned it with, and he swept it aside. Her flesh continued to shiver, and he worked as fast as he could, a little more roughly than he would have liked, irrigating the length of the cuts with the syringe and wiping the excesses of blood away with the gauze. He used much of the rest of the penicillin paste to seal the wounds before laying strips of bandage along the length of each of them.

Buckle was going to have to wind the gauze around her body to fasten the bandages tight to the wounds. He leveraged her onto her right side again; the bandages, already half-soaked with blood, remained in place, stuck to the wounds by the combination of coagulate and Fassbinder's paste.

"Perhaps it would be best if I were to sit up for you to proceed with your wrappings," Max said in a hoarse whisper, startling Buckle. Her voice was even but quivering underneath, soaked with pain.

"Max," Buckle whispered, overjoyed at the sound of her voice, peering down at her face. "Stay still. I can manage. I am going to give you morphine."

Max opened her eyes, the big black orbs shimmering in the orange firelight. "Not yet, Captain. Finish your surgery first." Max planted her right hand on the floor and pushed with a feeble but determined heave, attempting to sit up.

"Stay still. Blue blazes!" Buckle cursed. "Damn it, Max. All right."

Careful not to disturb any bandaging, Buckle slipped his hands under Max's armpits and assisted her into a sitting position. She was shivering violently again, her teeth clamped against the convulsions, breathing hard through her nose. Her black eyes wavered gold in the deeper layers, the Martian color of pain.

Buckle began unwinding the gauze at Max's shoulder, looping it around her torso and under each arm, circling the back, and returning to cross the injured shoulder again. His face was often mere inches from hers as she waited him to finish his work, and if she was embarrassed by her nakedness, she never showed it, nor made any attempt to cover herself.

Buckle did not care one whit about her privacy right now. She was sitting up. She was speaking. She was very alive.

"You do not listen to me as your captain, but I will demand that you listen to me as your surgeon," Buckle said.

"Aye," Max whispered, with effort, followed by a rough swallow. She lifted her arms from her body slightly so that it would be easier for Buckle to loop the gauze. The motion must have caused her great discomfort, for she took a deep breath. Buckle tightened the bandages and tied off the ends. He laid Max down on the bearskin on her uninjured side, her frighteningly cold skin trembling under his warm fingers, and quickly covered her with his coat, tucking it up neatly under her chin. She was looking at him, looking at him with her big, bottomless black eyes, and he smiled at her.

"You will get through this all right, Lieutenant," Buckle said. "If you had not heard, I am one hell of a surgeon."

Max nodded. Martians were tough. A human being so torn up would have been dead by now, Buckle calculated. But her pain had to be immeasurable, no matter how she tried to hide it. He already had one of the glass morphine vials in his fingers. He worked his knife blade against the base of the nipple, weakening it enough that he could snap the cap away. He sank the syringe needle into the vial, drawing the golden liquid into the firelit glass.

Max exhaled in a way Buckle knew meant disapproval. Martians did not like morphine much, though it alleviated pain for them in the same manner it did for humans. Buckle lifted the coat and swung out Max's left arm. He searched for a vein inside her elbow, but the drained vessels refused to rise. He drove his thumb deep into the clammy flesh and finally found the flabby plumpness of a vein, and then he sank the needle home.

Buckle slowly depressed the syringe plunger until the chamber was empty, then drew the needle free and replaced it in the still-steaming iron pot. He placed a patch of fresh gauze over the hole, but it hardly bled—Max's body had little more to bleed with. Max released a sigh, a long, trembling signal of the onset of the morphine drowse, the release from the agony.

Max was fast asleep before Buckle had time to tuck her arm back under her covers.

-XI-

THE CHAMBER OF NUMBERS

THE FIRE BURNED WELL AND low, a gray husk packed with red embers, casting up bursts of sparks now and again, and Buckle hoped that the big chunk of wood he had procured would last them through the night. The blizzard still raged outside in the utter darkness where the weak illumination of the fire did not reach.

Buckle was exhausted, and he might have felt sleepy if he was not so worried about Max. She had not moved since he had drugged her with the morphine about an hour before. His attention had barely drifted away from her sleeping face since.

Her eyes moved back and forth beneath the lids, but he did not know if she was dreaming. He had heard that Martians did not dream in the same fashion as humans: rather than drifting into fanciful interludes that never escaped the confines of their skulls, like humans, they could somehow plug in to a massive Martian collective unconsciousness. Empowered in this mysterious way, some part of the mind could leave their sleeping bodies to travel, investigate, and interact with the conscious world.

Buckle wondered how far away Max was from him in that moment.

Would she remain that way forever? He was afraid that Max would die on him, and he knew the fear was justified.

Once, he had removed his pocket watch and edged its polished brass cover close to her lips, to reassure himself that she was still breathing, and was relieved to see traces of pulsing condensation on the cold metal.

Enough, Buckle thought to himself. He had been sitting there, his saber resting across his knees, the blade agleam with the firelight, long enough. He shoved the pile of bloody gauze and bandages—already frozen stiff—away from the fire, and filled the little flask with water from snow he had melted in the iron pot. As he screwed on the cap of the flask, the metal squeaking with each turn of the wrist, he appraised his remaining medical supplies: there were enough gauze and bandages left for one more dressing, plus enough penicillin paste to complete that job, but that was it. He could boil more snow for water. What worried him more were the two vials of morphine: enough to keep Max drowsing through the night and into the middle of the next day, but after that, her comfort would be her own.

He had to get her down the mountain in the morning, but how? She was far too injured to carry, or even place on a horse, if they still had one. He could not fathom leaving her alone in the cave to traverse down the mountain on foot: there would be no way, even on horseback, that he could make it back to her before nightfall. And at nightfall, the sabertooths would come again.

Buckle rose to his feet unsteadily. His knees felt stiff and cold. He stretched to get the blood circulating again, and looked around the cave. There was not much to the long, oval space and its shallow side chambers, but he noticed that the walls were streaked with a dark corruption. Buckle stepped to the wall and ran his fingers along the stone; sure enough, the tips came away black with soot. The cavern had been used for shelter before. It was coated with the greasy detritus of poorly ventilated cooking fires; judging from the thickness of the stains, it had been used for an extended period of time.

Drawing his pistol from his belt, Buckle walked to the mouth of the cavern. The outside snowdrift obscured what little view there was through the swirling snowfall, but the trail left by his last foray was nearly erased, and he was thankful for that. His vision, now that he was away from the fire, slowly adjusted to the darkness, and he noticed an irregularity at the right-hand side of the cave mouth—a thick black line. As he stepped toward it, his eyes widened. It was a pipe, a section of black stovepipe, partially sunk into the rock, and bolted to it, as well.

Buckle blinked. The outside end of the stovepipe was covered in a weather cap. The interior pipe ran into the cavern and turned a hard left to angle high along the front wall. Buckle followed the pipe inside, where it ran into the small adjoining chamber closest to the front of the cave, one he had not considered worth investigating. Buckle snatched up the torch and relit it in the fire, hurrying forward to the little chamber as he followed the stovepipe home.

He entered the small cave, which, deceptively shallow-looking from the main cavern, on the left turn opened into a space about as big as a cottage.

Buckle froze. Before him, in the wavering orange light of the torch, the stovepipe disappeared into a stone wall, and in the middle of the wall stood a heavy door, sheathed in iron plates and rivets, its surface running with rivers of rust. A horizontal slot had been cut into the face of the stone just to the right of the door, and Buckle peered into it with the torch. A metal handle gleamed, sunk deep in the recess. Without hesitation, Buckle reached in and yanked it.

The mechanism responded: somewhere inside the wall, a set of gears and cogs rolled into a distressed motion, slowly sliding the door open with a rumbling complaint of squeaking metal and grinding stone. Ten seconds later, the multitudinous noise stopped as the door came to rest inside the wall, leaving an open doorway leading into a darkness that reeked of musty old wood.

Buckle advanced with his torch. The chamber was a small, enclosed space, but spacious enough to house a handmade bed frame, dressing table, writing desk, and bookshelf. All the furniture was warped from the cold and damp, and laced with old cobwebs.

A large candle rested in a copper sconce on the table, its tubular form misshapen by the tendency of the wax to flow with gravity over time, the wick flopped over and splayed at the top, like a jester's hat. Buckle lowered the torch gently over the candle. The wick caught flame, sputtering, and added its small sphere of yellow light to the room.

The walls were covered in a riot of bizarre scribblings applied by sticks of charcoal. A black potbellied stove sat in one corner, home of the stovepipe that ran up to the ceiling and across, to exit through a hole cut just above the top of the doorway. Buckle noticed a large iron wheel protruding from the wall to the immediate left of the door, the device that would close the door and reload the mainspring. Beside the wheel, tucked in the corner, sat a stack of neatly cut wood, as dry as old brown bones. And there was an axe.

Someone, a long time before, had made this little chamber his home, a little home safe from the beasties. And now the little chamber would make humans—well, a human and a Martian—safe from the beasties once again.

Buckle heard a roar, a rough-throated, loud, echoing roar.

A sabertooth had discovered their hiding place. And he was calling the others.

Buckle spun on his heel, pistol and torch leading, and charged back into the main cave, suddenly fearful that the sabertooths might have slipped inside: inside where Max lay, helpless and inexcusably undefended. He found Max untouched and the chamber empty, but when he spun to the mouth of the cavern he saw a sabertooth, its massive black bulk atop the snowdrift in the churning darkness, pacing back and forth, its green eyes occasionally catching the glow of the fire and shining in a ghastly, jade-gold, ghoulish sort of way.

The shadow of another sabertooth appeared alongside the first, looking straight in.

Buckle needed to buy himself a few seconds—enough time to pick up Max and carry her into the little chamber—so he shouted the zeppelineer boarder's cry of "Hurrah!" and attacked. He booted the fire in an explosion of swarming red embers and sent the burning log rolling along the floor toward the entrance of the cave, followed by the clattering iron pot. The burning wood and iron sizzled as they slid to a stop on the ice.

The pacing sabertooth halted, glaring at the flaming log. Buckle rushed forward, swinging the torch, his pistol leveled. They saw the pistol, the damned clever beasties, lunging away into the storm just as he fired. The muzzle flash illuminated the cavern for one brilliant red instant, the contained *crack* of the shot walloping Buckle's eardrums.

Buckle jammed the pistol back into his belt, turning back from the hanging cloud of powder haze to leap the scattered remains of the fire and scramble to Max. Tossing the torch toward the side chamber, he gathered her in his arms, bundled her up in the parka and bear fur, and carried her into the secret chamber. Not trusting what was left of the heavy-timbered bedframe, he laid her down as gently as he could in the middle of the little floor, a floor that glimmered in the candlelight, as smooth as polished stone.

He needed the survival kit.

He needed the morphine.

Drawing his empty pistol as he leapt through the doorway and picking up the torch on his way, Buckle was aware there were things slinking into the main chamber, things that were not made of stone.

As Buckle skidded to a stop in the middle of the scattered remains of his fire, the icy floor studded with a thousand glowing orange embers, he swung around his sword and pistol to find one sabertooth, a massive brute coated with ice, its fangs at least a foot long from upper lip to tip, already creeping in under the overhang.

Buckle could hear more roars piercing the wind outside. The pack was coming, collecting, preparing for the final rush.

Buckle grabbed the survival pouch. The capped syringe, morphine vials, and Fassbinder's jar were loose, lying on a gauze strip, and he scooped them inside the pouch as he rose, pointing the pistol at the sabertooth's face. It paused, regarding him with its four malevolent green eyes, then slowly kept on coming.

The devil, Buckle thought. How the hell could the beastie know the pistol was not loaded? The ruse was over, and he jammed the pistol back into his belt. He reached into the pouch and grabbed one of the musket cartridges.

The sabertooth dashed forward. Buckle beat it back with a shove of the torch at its face. The hulking creature came so close he could smell the rotten-egg scent of its hot breath, shooting out of its nostrils in pumping columns of mist. The beastie scrambled back a few feet, snarling so vehemently that the walls of the room seemed to rattle.

Two more beasties appeared at the cave entrance, gliding in with an ease of anticipation that was unnerving. Buckle bit off the top of the paper musket cartridge and dumped out the ball, the lead sphere landing with a little pop on the ice and rolling away. Buckle sidled slowly to the right, back toward the inner chamber, and the sabertooth veered to cut him off.

Buckle lunged, and the big beastie lunged with him. Buckle swung the musket cartridge so that the blackbang powder spilled through the air in a wide arc between him and the sabertooth. He thrust the head of his torch into the black arch of gunpowder, which ignited with a loud, rippling flash.

The sabertooth roared, a furious baritone howl, as it jumped back, cowering under the unexpected wall of fire that had just exploded in its face.

Buckle dashed, biting the head off a second cartridge as he ran, tossing the ball and setting another crackling arc afire with a rearward swing of his torch, just as he ducked into the adjoining cave. He scrambled headlong into the chamber of numbers, and dove to the winding wheel. He yanked at the spokes, hauling the ancient iron device with its brass fittings around, hand over hand. The wheel creaked, rust spilling from the hole where its trunk pierced the wall; cogs creaked, thick and dull with mold and ice-locked oxidation, and the heavy iron door slid, closing the gap far too slowly, no matter that Buckle gave its course every ounce of strength his body could bear.

Out in the main cavern, the indignant sabertooths roared, a mass of foul voices.

Buckle snatched up the torch and tossed it out the doorway, hoping the fire would slow the beasties a bit. If he had enough time to crank the door shut, he could keep Max safe.

If only he had the time.

–XII–

THE ISLAND IN THE STREAM

MAX WALKED ALONG THE FOREST path. It was sunny, the sunlight beating down through the tall trees in pale gold-white columns framed by moving shadows as the branches swung in the light breeze. She felt warm and happy. The air was full of the rich, sweet smell of grass, pine, and heather.

It was quiet. Her boots swished along the dirt trail. She was skipping. She was very young.

She heard the low rush of a stream not far ahead, and the light tinkle of wind chimes.

She was dreaming. She knew she was dreaming.

And it was quite all right.

Max lifted her chin to the sun, its brilliant white orb slipping past above the trees, stinging her eyes. The sun unbound the world, glorious in its heat, unleashing such greenness and luxurious smells.

She was dying. She knew she was dying.

And it was quite all right.

She had saved Romulus Buckle. She had placed her body in between his body and death, and gladly accepted the result. Her life for his.

He had done the same for her, before.

It was sad, but quite all right.

She almost floated as she walked now, and she arrived at the banks of the wide, slow-moving stream, where the dark, clear water danced with the gleams of mineral stones beneath, and slipped under tree-lined banks, the trees forming a canopy of shadows and bursts of light overhead.

The wind chimes jingled, louder now. Max turned her head to see a small island in the center of the river, a sandy sanctuary where a small monastery sat, a white cross atop the dome. A set of silver wind chimes lolled languidly in the breeze as they hung above the front doors, both set wide open.

The sunlight warmed Max's face, and she stood still. She was alone. She was in no hurry.

A memory came to her as if bidden, spilling into her awareness with the surety of the current sweeping past the toes of her boots. She was a child, running, running down the halls of Balthazar's house in Tehachapi, running away from Buckle. There came the yank on her long hair, her head jerked back, and when she drove it forward, there was the low, sudden whack of the door frame against her skull, and a vague sensation of falling.

The vision drifted away as if carried along by the water of the stream, and Max was left alone with the whispering leaves in the trees and the answering whisper of the sunlight dancing on the water, and the music of the wind chimes.

Max heard the far-distant clop of horse's hooves thundering across rough ground, approaching. A seeping cold at her back made her shiver. Clouds suddenly blocked out the sun, making the world a shade darker.

The breeze died away and the wind chimes fell silent.

Max was in no hurry.

But the horsemen were.

–XIII–

THE GOOD LIEUTENANT

SABRINA SERAFIM STOOD ON THE weather deck of the *Pneumatic Zeppelin*'s launch, the two-hundred-foot *Arabella*, eyeing the mountains surrounding the town of Tehachapi. It was two o'clock in the morning and the cloud-bound moonlight was odd, having just reappeared after the snowstorm, casting the snowy peaks with a translucent purplish light.

Sabrina brushed a crust of snow off the rail in front of her. She liked the *Arabella*. The launch was light and highly maneuverable, but still robust enough to carry a four-pounder or two, if necessary. She rested easily on her mooring hawsers, alongside a pair of trader-guild tramps, ugly little merchant dirigibles.

The town of Tehachapi to the north was picturesque, its cottages, with their busy chimneys and their windows glowing with the orange of the hearth fires within, nestled in the shallow valley.

A dark pang crept into Sabrina's heart. To the northwest loomed the bombed-out ruins of the old Crankshaft stronghold, blown near to smithereens by the Imperial Blitz the year before. A large stone cairn stood on a bluff nearby, its stones chiseled with the names of the dead.

Including her adoptive mother, Calypso.

But these were old pains. As the first lieutenant and chief navigator aboard the *Pneumatic Zeppelin*, and currently the acting captain of the *Arabella*, she had far more pressing concerns to deal with. Captain Buckle, scheduled to return by midnight, was long overdue. And she had decided to go after him.

"Here, ma'am," Lieutenant Andrew Windermere said, bringing Sabrina a steaming cup of coffee. He was wrapped in his thick gray bearskin, his eyes glowing in the buglit darkness on the *Arabella*'s deck.

"Thank you, Mister Windermere," Sabrina said, accepting the metal mug; the aroma cut through the woody outside air and made her mouth water. By the time she lifted the coffee to her lips, it was unfortunately cold—the steam draining the liquid of its heat in the frigid air—leaving only a very bitter, lukewarm, hastily prepared soup brimming with hard, black grounds.

"It is lovely," she said.

"It is shite roasted on an open fire—beg your pardon, Lieutenant," Windermere replied, taking a big sip from his mug.

"Lovely shite, then," Sabrina said, and shivered inside her wolf-fur coat. It was inordinately cold on the partially exposed weather deck of the moored *Arabella*, and as she listened to the rattle of the anchor chains through their capstans, she could only imagine how uncomfortable the cold was for the crew members on the envelope ratlines above, as they prepared to launch the little airship.

"Envelope is swept," Windermere reported. The snowstorm had forced the crew to sweep the snow off the fragile skin and spars as it collected throughout the night. "And sentries are in."

The crew dashed past Sabrina and Windermere in the lantern-lit darkness, boots plumping across the deck boards, coiling ropes and valving the hydrogen cells. The crew knew that the captain had not returned from the mountain by nightfall, as was planned. And now Sabrina deeply regretted giving him a few extra hours to make it back.

"Mooring ropes are ready to be detached at your order, Lieutenant," Windermere said. "Boilers are about two minutes shy, and after that we are ready to be away."

"Well done, Mister Windermere," Sabrina replied, giving him a smile. Lieutenant Andrew Windermere, or Windy, as his crewmates called him, smiled back at her over his ruined coffee. His was a smile both stern and appealing, and he often used it. He was a tall, rail-thin man, twenty years of age, with a handsome, pleasant face, intelligent eyes, and a laugh like a donkey. His skin and eyes were a milk-chocolate brown, his hair short, black, and tightly curled—his family bloodline was heavy with something his mother described as Cajun. Nobody knew what Cajun was, but her dinner meats were dense with spices burned black.

It was then that Sabrina wondered where Max was—she would normally have been in the thick of it, with the engineers. "Tell me, have you perchance seen the chief engineer?" Sabrina asked.

Windermere shook his head. "No, ma'am, I have not."

"Very well. Prepare to cast off. I shall be on the bridge."

"Aye, Lieutenant," Windermere said, jumping to assist a crew woman as she heaved a rope through a ratchet block. He was an excellent junior officer, just transferred to the *Pneumatic Zeppelin*, and promoted by Buckle from ensign to lieutenant. He was the chief elevatorman, replacing the late Ignatius Dunn. Buckle had also made him the acting master of the launch. Buckle had given Windermere a big role to fill—difficult for a new crewman who was not yet familiar with the Imperial-designed *Pneumatic Zeppelin* and her boisterous launch—but Buckle liked to vet his new officers early, overloading them without pity.

Windermere did look a bit tired.

Sabrina looked out into the night. The *Arabella*'s weather deck was open to the freezing air at her flanks, through the rigging-laced gaps between the fabric arches of the envelope skin overhead. The air was clear, and the cloud cover blanketed the pristine white snow with moonlight, while the rock-strewn world slumbered its ancient sleep. It was the kind of night in which men and women might feel their insignificance, and painfully so.

Damn it, Romulus. Where are you?

Over Sabrina's head, the hydrogen cells rapidly inflated, hissing loudly through their wide-open supply valves, their tops pressing and creaking against the doped canvas skin, ribbing girders, and baggywrinkle-wrapped wires. The crew was hard at work at the winding wheels of the hawsers and anchors, planting their boots against the ballast tanks as they pushed. The airship bobbed, near imperceptibly, growing more buoyant. The buglight lanterns swung easily on their hooks, illuminating both sides of the deck at intervals of five yards.

Sabrina was glad she had kept the crew aboard. The launch carried a standard complement of nineteen loyal souls, to be sure, but they tended to get scattered in the night if allowed to patronize local taverns. Tehachapi's infamous watering hole, the Bloody Haunch, would have left them disoriented by song, fiddle, and rotgut—and impossible to collect quickly.

Sabrina breathed in through her nose, trying to smell the intentions of the weather. Somewhere a dog barked, the familiar sound instantly muted by the overwhelming presence of the surrounding wilderness.

Sabrina tossed the cold coffee over the side and strode down the wooden stairs of the companionway, the one known for wailing like a mad cat in heavy weather. She arrived in the long tubular main hold of the *Arabella*, her stern end a beehive of activity as the engine crew stoked the boilers, the open hatches flooding the hold with a furious red-orange glow.

Danny Faraday, the lead engineer, gave Sabrina a coal-stained salute. "We shall be all fired up in a jiffy, ma'am!" he shouted.

"Aye, Mister Faraday," Sabrina replied, and hurried forward to the bridge. There, the sprawling banks of instruments glowed green with bioluminescent boil, standing out brilliantly against the blackness of the night outside the glass nose dome, a darkness broken only by the swirling gleam of two buglight lanterns that rocked back and forth as their lines were hauled back up into their coil barrels under the envelope's bow pulpit.

Caspar Wong and Charles Mariner were already at their stations at the elevator and rudder wheels, and Alison Lawrence, the ballast officer, turned to Sabrina as she entered. "Cells at ninety percent, ma'am," she said.

"Flood to one hundred," Sabrina ordered, plunking the empty coffee mug on the chart table. "It is damnably cold."

"Aye, aye," Lawrence responded, turning her valve wheels.

"Has anyone seen Lieutenant Max?" Sabrina asked.

"No, ma'am," came the universal response.

Sabrina's sixth sense tingled. She suspected, perhaps even *knew*, that the newly unpredictable Martian female had popped off on her own and followed Buckle up the mountain. Sabrina had seen Max's eyes flash green and disturbed inside her goggles when Buckle made his decision—in his typical fashion—to climb the dangerous heights alone, with only the wild-eyed mountain scout to accompany him.

Sabrina heard footfalls moving quickly, coming toward the bridge from the main hold. She turned to find her assistant navigator, Ensign Wellington Bratt, dashing onto the bridge, near breathless, his face flushed, with Windermere and Lansa Lazlo, one of the riggers, close at his back. They were pulling a local man, dressed in thick sheepskins, with a leather slouch hat in his hand, along with them.

"Lieutenant!" Welly shouted. "We have word on the captain!"

"No need to shout, Mister Wellington," Sabrina said calmly, as she turned about to face them, but the frightened look on Welly and Lazlo's faces made her stomach grip hard.

"Old Caruthers here, he owns the stable," Welly said hurriedly. "He says that Captain Buckle's horse came back a few minutes ago, riderless."

Of course. Damn that reckless Romulus Buckle, Sabrina thought. "And there is no sign of the captain or his mountain man?"

"Nothing," Welly breathed.

Sabrina looked at Windermere, whose face was pale. The fear that she had anticipated had materialized. Captain Buckle was in trouble. "Damnable curses! Master of the Launch—screw in the hawsers and cast off on the double quick."

"Aye!" Windermere replied, striding forward onto the bridge, barking orders.

"What about me horses?" Caruthers snapped. He was a skinny stableman with a light brown beard, who reeked of manure, horse sweat, and hay, and when his breath hit Sabrina, it was vastly more vile than all the other stinks put together. "You sky dogs paid for only one! Yer captain only rented my black, and if he dies I want satisfaction!"

"The captain's horse," Welly said. "The horse named Cronos that the captain was riding, it was badly clawed across the haunches. Caruthers says it is a sabertooth wound, says beastie wounds often get infected and the animal dies."

Sabrina drew in another breath through her nose, the kind of inhalation that reached the bottom of the lungs and was not so cold as air drawn in through the mouth. But it was not the air that chilled her nerves. If Buckle had gotten into a scrap with some sabertooths and lost his horse in the melee, then he was lucky if he was not already eaten and digested by now.

"What does he mean, 'horses'?" Sabrina asked. "The captain only took one."

"Your weird-eyed Martian took me other, me good mare," Caruthers chomped. "But I ne'er trust no zebe, so I made her pay full price for her, and good thing, considerin' she's already in a beastie gut!"

Sabrina nodded internally. Max was up on the mountain— of course she was up on the mountain—and there was no telling what fix she might be in, either.

"We shall pay you for the animal—if it dies," Sabrina said, turning back to face the nose dome. "And now, Mister Lazlo, please escort Mister Caruthers off the ship. Toss him off, if you have to. We are about to depart."

Lazlo hurried Caruthers away.

The *Arabella*'s maneuvering propellers whirled up as Windermere brought her around into the wind. Caruthers was going to have to make a small jump to the ground, as it was. The main propellers thrust the lithe little airship forward, the surge of the engines rippling through her deck.

Peachy, Sabrina thought. Just peachy.

–XIV–

NIGHT WATCH

BUCKLE SAT IN THE OLD wooden chair in the chamber of numbers, watching Max as she slept. Her morphine-doused slumber was fitful; she often stirred, gulping air as if she found it difficult to breathe. The squarish room was full of soft firelight, orange from the candles and red from the wood burning in the potbellied stove. The now fire-warmed air was reassuringly comfortable, temperate enough for Buckle to remove his sheepskin underjacket and leather coat.

Buckle glanced at his pocket watch: two o'clock in the morning. They had been inside the chamber for roughly five hours now. He slipped his watch back into his pocket with a rattle of the fob, and resumed cleaning his four sabertooth claws, carving the seats of cartilage and sinew away from the wicked yellow bonecutters, which each measured about eight inches long.

It had been a near-run thing, closing that ancient portal. A sabertooth—probably the big alpha—had stuck a paw in, and Buckle had cut it off with the axe. The half-rotted handle split up the middle on impact, but the rust-encrusted blade had still managed to do the job. Victorious, Buckle was able to crank the door shut after that, his reward amounting to four twitching claws, a splash of blue blood, and a huge beastie screaming outside.

Buckle had had quite his fill of sabertooths for the time being.

Now Buckle allowed the stillness of the chamber to sink into him. All they could do was wait in the chamber of numbers until the dawn; by then, hopefully, the sabertooths would have returned to their lairs. His heartbeat was slow, bruised, and grateful for the respite, as if it had been hammering in his chest for days. His mouth was dry, his tongue resting, pulpy, in his mouth. He swallowed to wet it a bit; he was thirsty but did not want to drink the water in the canteen. Max would need that.

The morphine seemed to have done its work well: Max's face was serene, even if her sleep was restless. He felt thrilled as he watched her, thrilled that she was still alive. For an instant, he felt just a touch improper—he had never watched Max sleep before, not like this, and she was such a private soul that he could not escape the sense that he was in some way intruding, even though it was necessary. Part of him said he should at least not stare at her, but it was difficult to shift his eyes.

She was inordinately beautiful.

Buckle forced his gaze to the granite wall on his right, where, after a moment, he focused on the sea of numbers. Every inch of wall in the chamber was covered, floor to ceiling, in handwritten charcoaled numbers. The long, tortured mathematical musings and equations, hieroglyphic in the candlelight, far surpassed his own ability to understand what mystery the sequestered mathematician had been attempting to crack. Whatever the equation had been, it was complicated. The infinity symbol was prominent in the lines of numbers, but often it was half-erased, smudged, or furiously crossed out.

The potbellied stove in the corner pinged as its metal expanded against the fire within it. Buckle watched the red flames glow behind the grate. The thing was old, but just as usable as the day it had been forged, and the stovepipe had been ingeniously constructed, running up to the roof of the chamber, bending at an angle to be lengthened in sections and bolted into the stone with metal brackets, to run across the length of the ceiling and disappear into a hole drilled through the granite above the door.

Somebody had made a home of the place, but it had been a long time ago. The squat bed frame, a sturdy pine construction crossed with warping slats, had started to cave in, and the spiders had thrown up a community of webs within it. The table and writing desk were made of oak and had fared better, the edges of the wood paled and grayed by the constant cold. Buckle ran his fingers across the surface of the writing desk, where thousands of tiny strokes had been pressed into the wood by a pen furiously scribbling across paper atop it, jotted down hard by a man or woman trapped deep in the agony of the numbers that populated the walls, thousands of numbers crushing inward with a question they could not solve, nor apparently escape.

What mystery, what question, would have caused someone to come here to live the life of a hermit, at least for a time, every morning waking to the numbers that had accompanied them into their dreams the night before?

Buckle stood up to stretch his aching legs, holding his scabbard so it did not clank on the furniture. He unclasped the scabbard from its belt frogs and carefully laid it on the desk.

He stepped to the opposite wall, where a tiny fan, its mechanism set in motion by the heat of the stove, spun in its metal frame inside a tunnel in the front wall, a three-inch-diameter hole bored through six feet of solid granite and out the front of the cliff face, pulling in a small but steady stream of cool air to ventilate the room. Buckle would have really liked to know how the mathematician managed to make a hole like that.

Buckle watched the little fan as it spun in the sea of numbers, until time seemed to slip away.

Then came the bloodcurdling scream.

-XV-

DELIRIUM

MAX TWISTED, HER HEAVILY BANDAGED body sprawling out from beneath her furs, her spine arched so her head was thrown back, her hands clawing at the air. She convulsed horribly, her black eyes rolled up in her head to the white. But the thing that most frightened Buckle was how suddenly pale she was—even the black stripes had faded to a deathly gray.

"Max! Max!" Buckle shouted, fear a lightning bolt striking his heart. He dropped to straddle her as he grabbed at her flailing arms. Max was strong, even in her weakened state. Martians were damned strong. "Max! I am here! Max!"

The icy slap of Max's flesh under Buckle's palms shocked him. She was panting, rapid and shallow, her mouth flung open, the tongue and gums a sallow pink-gray around the teeth. Her skin was slick with sweat pumping out of the pores, flowing in trickles, her black hair flung out in a silken fan, shivering in the firelight. Her very skin seemed to be shivering independently of the shivering muscles beneath.

Max had already bled heavily through her bandages, drenching the white gauze with her bright-scarlet blood—bleeding to death.

"Max, it is me," Buckle said. "Hold on, girl, you hear me?"

Max jerked her head to the right, in the direction of Buckle's voice, and calmed. The thrashing subsided. Buckle pulled her coat-blankets up to her chin, but she still trembled with enough force that her teeth chattered and her breathing rattled—where her hip pressed against his thigh, the sensation was jarring.

"I am cold," Max said, her words whispered so weakly Buckle almost did not hear them.

"It is all right, Max," Buckle whispered. "It is all right. I shall warm you up." Buckle tore his shirt open—sending mother-of-pearl buttons skittering across the floor—and swung under the parka to press his bare chest against her freezing skin.

She was as cold as death.

It was like being shoved into a snowbank. Max's body was icy at every point, as if her biological engine could no longer generate its own heat; even her bandages were warmer against his skin than her flesh. Buckle pinned Max's legs under the crook of his knee, wrapped his arms around hers firmly but gently, so as to not unsettle her dressings, and tried to expose her skin to as much of his as he possibly could.

They were face-to-face, her breasts soft against his chest. Her breathing, cool against his chin, rose and fell in erratic chokes, a wheeze sounding in the depths of her chest cavity. A weird fear crept into Buckle; he had never considered a scenario where he might lose Max, and the idea was unsettling to a depth that startled him. She was his friend, yes, an adopted sister raised partially in the same house, but he had never been all that attached to her.

"Do not you fear, Max," Buckle whispered. "I shall warm you up. Sabrina says I never fail at warming up the girls."

Max stopped shivering. She held very still. Her heart struggled to beat, fluttering erratically.

"Max?" Buckle asked reflexively. He waited, watching her face, so close to his. The stove crackled with heat; a spark popped, flinging a wave of reddish light, illuminating the numbers haunting the shadows with an endless question Buckle did not understand.

But Buckle cared nothing for the numbers now. He smelled the warm sweetness of the burned wood and the carnivore mustiness of the bearskin, but he railed against their inability, and that of his own warm body, to impart any heat to Max. She still felt frozen against his chest, and he fought the urge to shiver. She was very still.

Death crept into the chamber of numbers, slouching over Max, investigating.

"Max," Buckle whispered. "Be a good girl, you hear me? You just hang on."

Buckle rubbed Max's back. He was slicked with cold dampness from her body, but beneath the dark blankets he could not tell whether it was sweat or blood.

Max bucked, the new fit of shaking so violent it knocked Buckle loose.

"Max! No!" Buckle shouted, snatching at her hands. He clambered atop her thrashing body, pinning her down with his weight.

Her eyes flung open, all black, unfocused, unhinged, alien. Buckle did not see himself in their reflection.

"There is a good girl," Buckle said, having a difficult time holding on to her arms. "Max...Max—try, try to lie still, girl. Try your best, aye?"

Max wrenched her arms and legs until her right arm twisted free, slamming into the table leg, breaking the old wood away in a spray of spinning splinters.

"Max! It is me, Romulus!"

Max's clawing right hand snatched up the broken end of the table leg, which had struck the wall and rolled back, and before Buckle saw it coming she had swiped it upward in an arc, striking him across the left side of the head.

Stars and chunks of soft wood exploded in Buckle's vision; he fell to his right, and as he dropped, he felt Max lurch under him, throwing him off, escaping his weight. His right cheek slapped the cool stone of the floor, the pain balanced against the ache in his left ear, and before he regained his senses, Max was on him, straddling him at the waist, shoving him onto his back, one hand gripping his throat, the other gripping what was left of the half-split table leg.

Buckle had a knife strapped against his boot, but in the instant he should have drawn it, he could not bring himself to do so.

Max lifted the wooden club, her sweat-slicked naked torso, swathed in loose bandages and blood, agleam in the firelight, her black hair swirling around her face where the black eyes now burned with surreal flashing prisms of colors, and poised her arm to strike.

"Max! It is Romulus!" Buckle shouted, raising his arms.

Max stiffened. The table leg dropped from her hand, hitting the stone floor with a dull *thunk* next to Buckle's ear. She released a long, shuddering sigh and fell forward, collapsing atop him, her hair cascading across his face.

Buckle held still. Max's heart hammered against his chest, surging through her cold skin, striving too frantically, too hard. He carefully pressed his arms around her, intending to gently roll her over onto her bedding again.

Max lifted her head above Buckle's and looked into his eyes. For a long moment she stared at him, stared at him from very far away, the blacks of her irises streaming with purple flickers.

Max leaned forward and, closing her eyes, brought her trembling lips to his.

Buckle, his ears still ringing, realized that she was kissing him, her lips cold but velvet, and tasting slightly of blood, a soft, tender lover's kiss.

Yet he responded, kissing her back, but what manner of moonlit mess was this? She was near dead, drained of blood, half mad and exhausted. And yet, as her kiss continued, her mouth moving on his, her body upon his, her weak heart suddenly pounding with a vitality he would have been certain was lost to her, he felt a deep-buried yearning rise in his soul.

Max was cooing in the way that contented Martians cooed. It was faint and small and deep in the recesses of her throat, but Buckle heard it.

Buckle needed to get her covered up again, back into bed—she was half frozen and so terribly wounded. Gently, oh so gently, he placed his fingers on Max's cheeks and lifted her head. The cooing stopped. The kiss stopped. Max jerked her head up. Her dark eyes looked deep into Buckle's, searching for something, groping blind, and then lost their coherence, the sparks vanishing away as if dropped into a bottomless well.

"Max..." Buckle whispered.

Max's eyes closed. She uttered a sigh and went limp, her head dropping on Buckle's shoulder, the length of her body quivering with a million tiny quakes. Buckle reached for the bearskin and pulled it on top of them, letting Max's light body remain atop the length of him, her face mere inches away, the eyelids fluttering as the eyeballs beneath. She was dreaming, perhaps. Good. If she was dreaming, a morphine-fueled lotus sleep, then she was far away from the pain and the cold. He would get her good and warmed up by the time she awakened.

And she would wake up. Romulus Buckle had cheated death many times before, and, taking Max under his wing, he would do it again.

Buckle could smell Max, her breath, her skin, and it was a pleasant, sunburned meadow sort of smell, detectable under the sickly-sweet stink of sweat and coppery-scented blood.

It was so strange to be so close to her.

He pressed her to him, close, for a long time, and slipped into a mild drowse.

-XVI-

THE BLACK CARRIAGE

MAX WAS RIDING IN A carriage; the interior was all black, velvet and leather, and the window curtains were open, the world outside passing in the dark-gray-and-purple blur of night. She heard horses racing, the carriage team, iron shoes pounding the earth, noses snorting breath. She was wearing black, she knew, a heavily stitched gown, but all she could see of it were her tight-fitting sleeves of embroidered satin that covered all but the fingers of her hands, the seams lined with black pearls.

She was there but she was not there.

But she was not cold anymore. She was not in pain.

She did not feel anything.

Her perspective shifted, and she was outside of herself now, a spectator perched high up on a stone wall studded by burning torches, overlooking the peaks and valleys of a mountain range. Fifty feet below, a trail emerged from the dense pines, winding its way up the throat of the rocky valley. A black carriage appeared, rumbling and rattling, drawn by four horses with gleaming hides the color of midnight, eyes wide but calm, straining against their harnesses. A coachman sat atop the carriage, cracking his whip, completely obscured by a heavy black robe and hood despite the two lanterns jiggling on hooks on both sides of him.

The coachman pulled back on the reins, and the black carriage creaked to a stop directly below. The carriage door swung open. Max saw herself step out. She wore an ornate black dress, glittering with black pearls and obsidian that formed fantastic patterns along the entire length of the bodice and skirt. The collar of the gown framed her head in a tall sweep of fulsome black feathers, each three feet in height, as if the tail of a peacock sprouted from the back of her neck. Her hair was bound up atop her head in a beautiful contortion pierced with lancets and glittering with dark jewels.

The patterns on the dress shifted and started streaming, rotating, becoming row after row of numbers, endless variations of numbers.

The Max at the carriage paused to look at the fluctuating surface of her gown and then looked up at her.

Max was suddenly below again, looking up. The towering stone edifice in front of her, cut out of the face of the mountain, was a monumental riot of alien stonework, its pillars curving, its statues a menagerie of inhuman figures both beautiful and grotesque, adorned with symbols similar to those now alive on the sleeves of her dress.

And somewhere not too high up squatted the thing that was watching her; she only glimpsed movement, for the dark figure slipped back into the shadows of some impenetrable recess, as if a gargoyle had just slipped out of view.

The horses behind Max shifted and tossed their heads, impatiently stamping the frozen earth. The coachman sat silent and motionless, a corpse inside a black hood.

Max smelled burning wood, smoke mixed with blood. She knew she was dreaming. But she was aware of a thousand other dreamers inhabiting the ethereal landscape with her, whispering in the silence, though their journeys did not seem to intersect with hers. She felt exiled, excluded—as if her half-Martian blood was enough to get her to the gates of heaven, but not enough to let her in. Was it no more than a dream? The light wind touching her face felt so real; the thick fabric of her long gown was abrasive, scratching her skin—a gown designed for the dead, not the living, with nerves that still felt such things.

She stepped forward, placing her black-sheathed shoe on the first of the wide, sweeping stairs that led up to the entrance of the towering alien cathedral. High above her, something big unfolded its wings, two sweeping white wings with gray-black stripes on the interiors, and leapt into the sky, swooping down toward her.

Max watched it.

The winged creature landed softly despite its weight, planting its black boots on the steps above Max. It was a full-blooded Martian male, like her but unlike her—it was of a different kind, a great, winged, long-headed species with almost translucent skin, its white flesh laced with the rampant coursing of blue veins beneath and only hints of gray stripes upon it. He wore ancient midnight-colored garments made of cloth and chain mail, draped loosely upon his frame.

The winged Martian folded his wings upon his back and gave Max a desultory look, a look made even more disdainful by the intensity of his large, brooding black eyes, which stood out under the high white forehead.

Max knew who he was. The Gravedigger.

The Gravedigger strode down the stairs to stop very close to her, ten inches taller than the crown of her head, his wings looming even higher. Max smelled him—it was an intense, unrecognizable scent that was still profoundly familiar.

"You do not belong here," the Gravedigger said in the language of the Martians, a language Max's father had taught her as a child. The creature's voice was deep but thin, the voice of a great being worn tired. He raised his right hand, the long fingers splayed.

Max plunged into a void. Then the pain came, a deep, stabbing, unspeakable pain. But worse than the pain was the fear. She screamed as she had never screamed before.

But in her ears she heard only a tiny whisper.

–XVII–

THE IMMORTALITY EQUATION

It was still and dark in the main cavern as Buckle stood over the place where he had bandaged Max the night before, looking at a large pool of brilliant red blood suspended in the clear ice at his feet. He massaged his brow—his brain still ached from the blow Max had landed on him. Lucky that table leg was rotted, or she might have cleaved his skull. Exhaustion blurred his eyes, and he rubbed his fingers against them, the rough, cold leather of his gloves biting the soft skin of the lids.

The cave was as hollow as a tomb, silent except for the sounds of dripping water at the mouth, where the stovepipe expelled its heat in small sizzles, the rock around it bare and trickling.

The storm had died away entirely, taking every trace of the wind with it. Outside, an ambient light leaked into the dark-blue sky, signaling the coming of the dawn. Buckle sniffed. The cave was rich with the fetid reek of sabertooth feces; the ice was scored by their pacing claws, and a frozen trail of green blood spilled in a series of tight circles in the middle of the floor. His torch lay in a corner, nearly snapped in half at the handle.

Buckle drew the flare gun and loaded a magnesium cartridge into the chamber, snapping it shut with a sharp *click* of metal.

Then he heard Max. He probably sensed her more than heard her, a scant whisper through her parched lips, but he *heard* her.

Romulus was the word, more the sigh of a ghost than a human sound.

Buckle hurried back into the chamber of numbers, where the fire still burned in the potbellied stove, consuming the last orange embers of its fuel in a bed of white ash, pouring illumination into the room that seemed quite bright after the near darkness of the main cavern. The grating cast wavering shadows on the floor, warm shadows and light that played across the number-covered walls and the roof, and over Max's white skin. The chamber seemed very small, and Max's form very close, bundled on the floor where Buckle had lain with her in his arms all night. Her body had warmed enough to make him feel better, though it seemed that his body had exchanged its heat with hers, and now he felt cold and was glad for it. She was still, her heart and breathing regular, and seemed to have fallen into a deep sleep. But now and again she tensed. The morphine must have been wearing off—but with Martians, you could never tell.

Buckle knelt beside Max, searching for a sign that she might be awake, that the sound he had heard had not been imagined. She looked small and fragile, her eyes closed, her black hair pillowed under her head, and though the fire and his body heat had warmed her, her black stripes remained a ghastly gray, her white skin featureless and slick as alabaster, her lips drained of color.

"Max?" Buckle breathed.

Max opened her eyes, blinking before she focused those deep, endless pools of violet blackness on him.

"Drink a little," Buckle said, collecting the canteen, full of cool meltwater, and carefully raising Max's head to bring the metal canister to her lips. She took a few swallows, forcing it down her throat with tortured gulps.

"Hello," Buckle said, laying her head back on her fur, trying to be lighthearted, unable to suppress a grin. "Are you warm?"

Max nodded. "Romulus," she whispered again.

Buckle placed his fingers on her cool lips. "No, just rest," he said. "Unless you are in pain. Tell me if you are in pain."

Max shook her head a little, and winced.

"Ah, do not move, girl," Buckle said hastily. "I am going to give you some medicine." He began unloading the syringe and morphine vials from the emergency pouch.

"I would prefer you hold back on the morphine, Captain," Max breathed, soft but clear.

"No arguing with the doctor," Buckle said, sawing off the nipple of the morphine vial and draining it into the syringe. He tapped the glass to free it of bubbles, then carefully drew Max's arm from beneath the cover and sank the needle into her artery.

"I submit a formal protest," Max whispered, her voice paper thin.

"Nice to have you back, Chief Engineer," Buckle said, retracting the empty syringe and pressing the hole with a small wad of gauze. "How was your journey through the land of the dead?"

"Dark, but not entirely unpleasant," Max said.

"Nice to hear it," Buckle replied. "Though I personally have no intention of ever visiting the place."

"Of course Captain Buckle shall live forever," Max breathed, then clamped her jaw, her body tensing.

"Sleep. You need it."

Max's eyes fluttered as the morphine swept through her, then refocused and scanned the walls of the cave. "Numbers," she muttered. "Immense calculations. The infinity symbol appears many times."

"So it does. Enough with the mathematics. Sleep."

Max looked at Buckle that way she sometimes looked at him, a sort of intense, curious scrutiny that he always found slightly amusing. She closed her eyes and took a deep breath. "The one who lived here before, he or she sought to live forever."

"What do you mean?"

"The numbers are a Martian mystery. The immortality equation. Find the answer, and you discover the secret to eternal life."

"So the former occupant was a Martian?" Buckle asked.

"Possibly. Either way, their efforts would have been in vain. The immortality equation is a dead end, a myth. It is unsolvable."

"Either way, it is of no concern to us," Buckle said. "Get some sleep." He dug around in the survival pouch for fresh bandages, but when he raised his eyes he saw that Max was already asleep, the coat lifting and falling evenly over her breast. He picked up the flare gun and quietly backed out of the chamber of numbers.

Buckle strode through the cavern with his heart bounding; the world, the painful, uncaring, merciless world, held a hopefulness once again. He kicked through a new, thin snowdrift at the mouth and stepped outside into the preternatural light. He paused, listening. The air was cold, motionless, heavy, expectant. Sparrows, cardinals, and chickadees sang in the trees, a chorus chattering for the coming of the day. The dark clouds above, still glistening silver with the last traces of moonlight, began to glow pink in the creases of their endless ripples. Buckle could see the sweep of the snowy ridge before him as it led to a cliff and dropped away into a sprawling vista of snowbound mountains and sky. Behind him, a steep slope loomed, the near-vertical incline he and Max and Cronos had tumbled down the evening before.

The snow in front of the cave entrance had been trampled by the pacing sabertooths. Ice droplets lay scattered about, frozen globs of saliva that had dripped from the bladed incisors.

Buckle had escaped the sabertooths again, as he had once before. The damned beasties were always trying to make a meal of him.

He strode forward, his boots swishing long troughs in the fresh snow, and made his way to the crest of the cliff. The air was cold in his lungs, sharp with the tang of pine. Not far below, though blocked from his view by a high ridge, lay the town of Tehachapi, where the *Arabella* was moored with her crew on the night watch. Sabrina would be concerned about him by now, for he and Pinter had been scheduled to return before midnight. He did not know whether Sabrina would yet be aware of Max's foray up the mountain as well, for the Martian must have slipped away without informing Sabrina, senior to her in rank, knowing she would not have permitted her to follow Buckle.

Buckle raised the flare gun. A well-placed shot would send the burning arc high over the intervening ridge, and the lookouts would most surely see it framed against the dark sky.

Buckle did not want the *Arabella* to come up this steep altitude, the small launch being vulnerable to the season's sudden, violent storms, like the one that had sprung up the day before. But Max needed immediate help. His red flare would signal an emergency. Sabrina would send a rescue team up on horseback.

Surely she would do that, for to try to bring the *Arabella* up to this height in the Bloodfreezer season would be far too risky a proposition, even for his gutsy chief navigator. Although he supposed that he would brazenly steam the *Arabella* up there if he were in her boots, but that was him—far too reckless. Surely the cool-headed, green-eyed Sabrina had better sense than he did, when it came to such choices.

In his heart, though, he half hoped and half feared that she night not.

Buckle aimed the flare gun and pulled the trigger. The pistol fired, kicking with its usual *tonk*, hurling the flare high into the sky. The cartridge burst, a bright-scarlet pop against the clouds, and arced on its little parachute, casting a haunting glow as it drifted over a wilderness still hidden in darkness.

The *Arabella's* lookouts would surely see that.

Buckle watched the flare fall away, its last sputters of magnesium burning off as it descended beyond the long ridge, now more white than red. The vast world suddenly fell silent—even the prattling birds hushed, clamping their tiny breaths in their heaving breasts. They waited. Buckle knew what was coming. When it was cold enough and the rising sun was angled just the right way above the cloud cover, it would happen.

The dawning bore.

A spectacular wash of pink and purple swept across the heavens, rippling through the clouds in a breathtaking pastel wave of color. The entire cloud roof of the world flooded in a tidal wave from gray to brightening reds and pinks, and in the instant it took for the sky to flip to morning, every bird on the mountain burst into furious, elated song.

The rare sight moved Romulus Buckle's heart. Max was going to live. And he was going to carry her home.

–XVIII–

THE MAGNESIUM FLARE

"Flare sighted, Lieutenant," Wellington shouted from his station in the nose of the *Arabella*'s cockpit. "Northeast. Two points high off the starboard bow."

The lookouts shouted into the chattertubes at the same instant, instantly followed by the ringing of the ship's bell on the weather deck.

"No need to shout, Mister Wellington," Sabrina said. "I am right behind you." She felt an indescribable joy at the sight of the flare, a surge of anticipation that made her throat constrict and her hands clamp tight on the wooden instrument panels. The mountain, with its sweeping cliffs of snow and ice, no longer appeared too vast, inscrutable.

"Aye, Lieutenant," Welly replied, glancing back at her, smiling, his eyes gleaming with excitement. "My apologies, ma'am."

Sabrina was smiling, too. After four hours of searching, they had found Captain Buckle, his guide, and, hopefully, the missing Max, as well. "Helm, bring us to bear on the base of the arc."

"Aye, Lieutenant," Charles Mariner replied, easing the rudder wheel over in his hands. Mariner, sallow-faced but husky, was the assistant helmsman aboard the *Pneumatic Zeppelin*.

Most of the crew assigned to the launch were the assistants and apprentices aboard the mother airship.

Sabrina leaned forward into the big glass nose bubble, with its arching cast-iron frames, brushing shoulders with Welly. She scanned the ridges and cliffs above, the snow glowing with the early blue illumination of the dawn. The *Arabella* was buzzing, alive with the sounds of crew members shouting back and forth and the rustle of bodies dashing up and down the companionways and ladders. She wanted to double up the lookouts, but she had already doubled them—if she tripled them, there would be no one left to drive the launch.

The *Arabella*'s nose dipped, forced down by one of the mild downdrafts they had been fighting all the way up the mountain. Sabrina sensed the airship rotating slightly on her axis, rolling a hair over to port.

"Downdraft, Lieutenant!" Mariner yelled, whirling the rudder wheel to starboard.

"Compensating forward pitch, three degrees up bubble!" Ensign Wong, the elevatorman, cried, cranking his wheel over with considerably more effort than Mariner had needed for his.

"I am getting tired of being shoved around," Sabrina grumbled. She clicked the chadburn handle forward, from all ahead standard to all ahead full. "All ahead full!" she shouted into the chattertube.

"All ahead full, aye!" came the reply from Danny Faraday in the engine room, the chadburn engineering dial clicking into place atop the piloting dial with an abrupt puff of steam.

The propellers roared up to a pleasant whirl.

The *Arabella*'s nose swung easily through the gulf of open air between her and the steep face of the mountain. Sabrina grinned to herself, both at the success of having located Buckle and at the elegant lightness of the *Arabella*, handling deft as a feather, despite the heaviness of the freezing air at altitude.

"Back on original bearing, ma'am," Mariner said.

"Static inertia good, zero bubble!" Wong reported.

"Very good, sky dogs," Sabrina said. "I shall deliver a glowing report about all of you to the captain if we live through this."

Suddenly, the dawning bore, a meteorological phenomenon causing the light of daybreak to flood across the sky all at once, ripped through the clouds, roofing the world with a ceiling of flower-colored pinks and oranges.

"The bore!" Welly gasped.

"Eyes on the ground, Navigator," Sabrina said. She had no time to regard the beauty of the rare atmospheric display; dangerous weather conditions caused such phenomena and, as her breath wreathed around her chin in dense issues of vapor, she was concerned about a precipitous drop in the temperature. She eyed the barometer glass—the quicksilver hung steady in its tube, but she was not convinced.

Looking out at the sky, she studied the undertones of the atmosphere, the scud and colors of the altocumulus mackerel layer. Already, the morning sunlight was flooding down upon the world, pinking the silvery sea of clouds, pinking the nose-dome glass, as the sun, long lost behind the permanent overcast, rose unseen once again. The snowbound peaks and valleys sparkled in the soft light, each ridge and crest rippled with ragged lines of ice-sheathed pine and fir. Sabrina could just make out the towering black column of the Sequoia Obelisk, barely visible far to the north off the port forward quarter.

She cleared her cold throat—it tasted of bitter coffee.

"Lieutenant!" Welly shouted, lowering his telescope and pointing straight ahead, across a valley toward a long, narrow cliff set in the face of the mountain beyond. "I see the captain! On the mountain. Dead ahead."

"I am standing right beside you, Welly," she said, wanting to screw her finger in her ear for effect. She raised her telescope and swept it along the cliff, quickly training it on the small black figure of a man standing in the snow, flashing a mirror at the airship. He fired another red flare, and Sabrina's heart happily leapt into her throat with it.

~XIX~

RESCUED, FOR NOW

SABRINA WAS SHOCKED BY MAX'S ghastly appearance—her face looked so awfully pale and gaunt, tucked deep inside her black bearskin hood—as the crew hurried her stretcher up the nose loading ramp of the *Arabella*. She was relieved that they had rescued Buckle and Max, but that emotion was warped under anxiety. Despite Max's wounds, Sabrina trusted enough in the famous Martian resilience to believe that her adopted sister would recover. But Romulus looked so stricken, so ashen-faced, his hands and coat crusted with dried blood, as he approached her.

"Damn you, Serafim," Buckle said, drawing his usual self up and out of a well of haggard exhaustion, sounding both angry and relieved as he strode alongside Max's litter. "This mountain is no place for a skinny little launch. Have you lost your mind?"

It was always impressive, Sabrina thought, that Buckle could chide her, while at the same time thanking her profusely with his bright, expressive blue eyes—eyes that were also deeply wounded. "How is Max?" she asked.

Buckle gripped Sabrina's arm at the wrist, clenching it tightly with his bloodstained fingers as he followed the stretcher bearers up the ramp. "Sabertooths got her. But she shall pull through." He leaned close to Sabrina's ear and whispered quickly,

"It was the Founders. The Founders raided us at Tehachapi—not the Imperials."

It was the Founders! Katzenjammer Smelt had been telling the truth. Sabrina slowed to a stop, as Buckle and the stretcher bearers carried Max up the gangway and into the *Arabella*'s hold. Buckle had given her a secret, another secret to store along with all the other things she kept hidden from the world.

"Mister Lazlo!" Sabrina shouted.

"Yes, Lieutenant?" Lazlo, a thin, small fellow with a pleasant smile, replied immediately. As the junior rigger, he was responsible for the *Arabella*'s field-mooring crew.

"Cast off lines and weigh sky anchor, on the quick!" Sabrina ordered, already marching up the ramp and striding into the *Arabella*. "We are getting the hell off this mountain."

"Aye, aye!" Lazlo replied.

Sabrina hurried up into the cockpit, where Windermere and the bridge crew were at their stations. It was a bit warmer in the small piloting cabin, and freezing air streamed off her long leather coat.

"Waiting on hawsers and anchor, Lieutenant," Windermere said. "Launch is at the ready, ma'am."

"Very good," Sabrina replied. Mariner, the helmsman, knew enough to step aside as Sabrina immediately took hold of the rudder wheel herself. She could hear the chains rattling under the deck as the steam-powered capstans hauled the sky anchor up against the cathead.

"If I may, Lieutenant," Windermere began, "inquire about the captain and the second mate?"

Every face shifted toward Sabrina.

"The second mate has been badly injured by beasties," Sabrina said. "The captain appears only to have suffered a few scratches." Sabrina was speaking of Buckle's body, not the pain she had seen in his eyes.

Windermere and the crew turned their faces forward, worried and grim.

"Lines away!" Lazlo's voice boomed up the chattertube. "Anchor secure!"

"About damned time," Sabrina muttered. "Up ship. Like a feather, Miss Lawrence. Ten percent hydro, ten feet altitude."

"Ten percent, ten feet, aye, ma'am," Alison Lawrence, the *Arabella*'s ballast officer, replied.

"No crosswind or downdrafts in the windsocks," Welly announced.

The *Arabella* rose with a soft creak and a sigh of canvas, floating ten feet into the air.

Sabrina slapped the chadburn handle back, dinging the bell and leaning through its puffing steam to the chattertube hood. "Engineering. Quarter reverse."

"Quarter reverse, aye!" Faraday answered on the speaking tube. The engineering pointer on the chadburn swung to match the first.

The propellers at the stern eased up into a whirl—with the odd, chopping sound they made when in reverse—and the *Arabella* backed away from the lip of the towering cliff where Sabrina had parked the nose.

"Coming around to port, one hundred and eighty degrees," Sabrina announced, as she carefully rotated the helm wheel, swinging the *Arabella* to the left. Ensign Wong cranked his wheel back and forth to keep the launch's keel level in the turn. Although they were now away from the cliff face, this was a tricky maneuver even in still air. Downdrafts were sudden and perilous this tight against a mountain.

"We are away, Lieutenant—clear of the cliff," Windermere said, steadying his tall form against the whirl of the airship by gripping a set of pipes overhead. "Twenty-two souls aboard. And a bang-up job of tucking the launch in, if I may say, Lieutenant."

It was a bang-up job. A damned excellent bang-up job. Sabrina had nudged the nose of the *Arabella* against the edge of the snowy cliff, a thing impossible to do if there was any wind at all. "Piece of cake, as the captain would say," she replied.

Windermere placed his hand on the binnacle, gently, in a new-fatherish but nonpossessive manner. "The *Arabella* is one spry eagle, aye."

"Aye, a fine little wart she is," Sabrina replied, leveraging her balance as the launch swung around on a gentle 180-degree curve, watching the passing mountain through the less-than-perfect nose glass.

Windermere grinned, his eyes glittering, then he turned them to the barometer. "We are fortunate that the weather has held as long as it has."

"I am not trusting that steady glass," Sabrina said. "The weather is unnatural."

"The lookouts are reporting sporadic refraction to the north," Windermere added.

Sabrina nodded. Refraction was a land mirage, a disruption of the lens of the air, caused by superfreezing air passing over the warmer earth; it often heralded an abrupt change in the weather. She clicked the chadburn to neutral and swung the wheel, zeroing out the turn so the *Arabella*'s nose pointed down the slopes toward Tehachapi. She eyed the water compass until the floating needle held secure over the *SW*. "Bearing due southwest."

"Due southwest, aye," Welly repeated.

Sabrina stepped back from the wheel. Mariner immediately moved forward to take the station. "I am going to check in on Lieutenant Max. The bridge is yours, Mister Windermere. Go to all ahead full and get us off this mountain as fast as you can."

"With pleasure, ma'am," Windermere replied. He gave Sabrina a crisp salute, which was unnecessary, but he always saluted anyway.

Tapping the brim of her bowler in response to Windermere, Sabrina exited the bridge, pulling off her mink-lined gloves and folding them into her belt. She emerged into the main hold, where Faraday urged on his engine crew with gruff curses, their shovels scraping the coal bunkers as red light swirled out of the open hatches of the fireboxes. Sabrina could feel the heat of the fires on her face, and she was seventy feet away.

Cornelius Valentine, one of the older boilermen and a crusty customer, had come forward to check the coal-bunker trim. He doffed his cap at Sabrina with his coal-stained fingers. "Ma'am," he said gruffly.

"Mister Valentine," Sabrina replied. She clambered up the companionway and turned into the narrow port-side passageway, which ran along the inner hull of the *Arabella*. On her left ran a series of hatchways, and on the right was the port bulwark, thick with bracings, sloping upward with the contours of the hull. Oil lanterns lit the gloom with pools of light; she passed through them as her boots creaked on the wooden deck. Sabrina shivered, feeling both strangely terrible and good. She was worried about Max and about Buckle, but relieved that they were both lucky enough to still be breathing, considering what kind of beasties they had run into. And Buckle's whispered words...

If he had proven the Founders responsible for the blitz on the Tehachapi stronghold, then the Founders had been attempting to set the major clans against one another, laying the groundwork for their invasion for at least a year. And, incalculably important to Buckle himself, the Founders were the ones who had kidnapped Elizabeth.

War was coming, and she would surely be provided the opportunity to cross swords with the Founders again.

Her heart drummed in her chest.

Sabrina passed Shelley Nightingale, the *Pneumatic Zeppelin*'s nurse assigned to the *Arabella*, in the passageway. She carried a metal tray with an empty vial of morphine, a stack of bloodstained bandages, a near-full bottle of rum, and brown-sugar cubes for a missing cup of tea.

"How is she doing, Shelley?" Sabrina asked.

"As well as can be expected, Lieutenant," Shelley replied, careful to balance her tray. Blood, bright, sparkling Martian blood, drained out of the bandages and pooled on the flat metal. "Martians are tougher than shoe leather, I must say."

Sabrina nodded as she passed Shelley and stepped into the low hatchway of the *Arabella*'s sick bay.

The tiny medical cabin was barely more than a closet lit by one lantern; two bunk beds hung against the forward bulkhead, and a large medicine cabinet left little extra space for the chair and table between. Buckle was sitting in the chair, holding Max's hand, which was startlingly white, in his; her bare right arm, black-striped and slender, draped across the brown blankets of the lower bunk, looked like the limb of a skeleton.

Sabrina stepped in, swaying her hip away from the reedy little table where a wet, empty rum glass sat alongside a cup of vapor-drifting tea and Buckle's scabbard. It smelled like a sick bay: the rotten apple and molasses aroma of morphine clung to the air, along with the eye-stinging waft of iodine, disinfectant, and Fassbinder's Penicillin Paste, all underpinning the sharp stink of the oil lantern. Sabrina peered at Max's face as she lay on the pillow, her black hair flung back in a dark halo about her head, her eyes still and shut.

"Hello, Navigator," Buckle whispered.

Sabrina swung her eyes to Buckle. He looked up at her with his gentle smile. His cerulean-blue eyes shone at her. But even with all his fortitude, she could see the tightness of the skin on his face, the dark tinges beneath his eyes.

"How is she?" Sabrina asked.

"Sorely sliced. Those beasties did a job on her, I am afraid. Once we get her back to Fogg and Lee, they shall patch her up properly. Fogg knows a little about Martian insides, or so he says."

"Fogg will zip her up tidily, aye," Sabrina whispered. She cleared her throat as quietly as she could. She found it difficult to speak without her voice rasping. She was worried about Max, yes—but it was the pain flowing from Buckle that haunted her, chewed her up. Sabrina had always been protective of Buckle, but now, since she had witnessed the intimate moment between him and Max in his quarters, when she had seen the hungry, enraptured glow in Max's eyes, she ached for something more. She wanted to snatch him up and swallow him in her arms, to press her mouth against his, to let him pour his agony into her body, to absorb his pain like a sponge.

But Sabrina could not act on this desire. She could never act on this desire. She cleared her throat again, softly.

Buckle lifted his free hand to Sabrina, and she took it. It was encrusted with dried blood, but she enjoyed the warmth of his skin and the strength of his fingers as they tightened around hers.

"She saved my life, Sabrina," Buckle whispered.

"I know," Sabrina answered. Something darkened the light between her and Buckle. Had the lantern with its restless flame shifted? "She has always been fond of you—in her way, of course—though for the life of me I cannot understand why." Fond—interesting choice of a word, Sabrina told herself. One thing about Buckle—he was quite the romancer, but blind and dumb as an earthworm when it came to the accelerated heart-throbs of the female species. Max was in love with him, and he had not the slightest inkling of it.

"All the damn time she is saving my hide," Buckle whispered, returning his gaze to Max. It hurt Sabrina to have him move his eyes from her; she was caught by a surprising twinge of jealousy toward Max—an illogical desire to trade places with her, despite her wounds.

Buckle released his hold on Sabrina's hand. Her fingers felt abandoned. He reached into his pocket, and when he opened his hand, Sabrina saw a silver Founders collar pip sitting in the middle of his bloodstained palm.

Her nerves tingled. "The evidence, eh?" she whispered. "The devils."

"Aye," Buckle replied, looking at the pip. "And they must have Elizabeth." He tucked the phoenix back into his pocket and returned his gaze to Max.

The lantern rocked lightly on its peg. The hull creaked with a low groan.

"The wind is up," Buckle said.

"I was certain we would get something, despite no sign of weather," Sabrina replied. "I do not like refraction sightings and air heavy as an obelisk. We are running fast, bearing southwest, descending southwest as fast as the topography will allow."

Buckle tucked Max's exposed arm back under the covers and checked the cinches on the leather straps securing her to the bunk. "I'll come to the bridge."

"Stay here. I'll go," Sabrina said.

Buckle stood up so quickly he startled Sabrina, so much taller he was than she, his shoulders blocking the light from the lantern.

"Romulus...," Sabrina continued. "You need not..."

Buckle's face was inches away from hers, his breath, pulsing easily between his slightly parted lips, warm from a recent shot of uncut grog. The lantern behind him imparted reddish tinges to the edges of his sandy beard, and along the sharp line of his jaw. His eyes were hidden in hollows of shadow, untouched by the light, but she knew he was looking at her—he was looking at *her*.

Buckle sighed—it was a soft, quaking, vulnerable sound—and then he sucked in a great breath of air. He wrapped his arms around her, drawing her body tight against his in a gentle hug. She stood stiff for a moment, struck with delighted surprise, and then gripped him fervently, her cheek pressed against the brass buttons on his chest. She closed her eyes, smelling cold leather and the sweet copper of Max's dried blood. Buckle's arms were strong, but she also felt a quiver in them, a shaking of the overstrained fibers.

She wanted the moment to go on forever.

Was she even breathing?

It was then that she heard the sharp creak of the deck and bulwarks as the propellers, suddenly rising to a higher pitch in their incessant drone, shoved the airship forward at a harsher rate, increasing the rip of the wind across the envelope and through the rigging.

Buckle and Sabrina disengaged and jumped toward the hatch, Buckle grabbing his saber from the table. In the same moment, the sound of the ship's bell clanged loudly in its belfry on the weather deck above, sounding the alarm.

Martin Robinson, the young assistant signals officer, jumped in through the hatch, the whites of his eyes wide against his dark-brown skin. "Storm approaching, Captain! Lookouts say she's a bad one!"

-XX-

THE TALE OF THE BAROMETER

BUCKLE FELT A TOUCH OF weightlessness and the downward tilt of the deck under his feet as he, Sabrina, and Robinson raced along the lantern-lit passageways leading back to the *Arabella*'s bridge. Windermere was on the fast descent: the first instinct of a zeppelineer pilot when faced with an oncoming storm was to try to fly under it. Buckle shook off a wave of lightheadedness—exhaustion. Between the sabertooths and Max's condition, sleep had been a rare commodity. What is this? he scolded himself, stowing his weaknesses away. Captains never tire. Never.

As they burst onto the bridge, Windermere spun to face them and threw a finger at the starboard sky. "Off the starboard beam, Captain! I have never seen anything like it!"

Buckle looked to his right to see a wall of black, a towering wave of dark, churning clouds, fast approaching, blocking out the horizon and the sky.

"Engines are all ahead flank, sir," Windermere reported. "We have battened down, and storm lanterns are lit. I initiated descent to one hundred, but she looks to be a ground hugger—I do not think we can get under this one."

Buckle glanced at the plummeting quicksilver in the barometer. Sabrina's worries about the weather had proven prophetic.

They were in a world of trouble now. "Level out and maintain altitude. Zero bubble."

"Aye, aye!" came the chorus of shouts from the bridge crew, driving wheels and ballast wheels spinning.

"You are correct, Mister Windermere," Buckle said as the deck swung up under their feet. "There is no getting under a blizzard." He felt his stomach tighten. He had been caught in a blizzard once before, when he had been the navigator aboard the Crankshaft trader *Bromhead*, and it had nearly been the end of both him and the entire crew.

"Altitude holding at two hundred seventy-five," Sabrina reported from the navigator's station. "Bearing, west-southwest."

"Out of the frying pan and into the fire," Buckle muttered, folding his hands behind his back and setting his feet. The *Arabella* was roaring down the mountain, pushed beyond her maximum steam, furnaces roaring, driving propellers throbbing—but it was not going to be enough. The storm was going to catch them. And the only way for a zeppelin crew to be certain of surviving a winter storm was...to not let it catch them.

Sabrina had rolled the dice, bringing the *Arabella* up the mountain to rescue Buckle and Max, and she had rolled snake eyes.

"Take us up; emergency ascent," Buckle said. "If we cannot fly under this devil, then we shall fly over it."

"Up ship! Emergency ascent!" Windermere howled, both to the bridge and into the chattertube, as Elevatorman Wong heaved his elevator wheel.

"Valving hydro to one hundred and five percent. Dumping blue ballast," Alison Lawrence shouted as she cranked the wheels on the ballast board. The *Arabella* surged upward, her decks trembling.

Buckle eyed the approaching storm, so much closer now that it startled him. They could not fly under the blizzard, and any attempt to ground or moor would only result in the *Arabella* being torn to pieces on the earth. Reaching for altitude was risky when he stood no chance of topping the storm clouds before they hit, but he needed the height; the superfreezing air was heavy, robbing an airship of buoyancy, not to mention the icing that would plague her. Engines and extra hydrogen valving could compensate to a point, but the vertical face of the blizzard was immense, the thunderheads perhaps a mile high. If the *Arabella* was to stand a chance, she needed all the altitude she could get.

"Four hundred feet, sir, and climbing," Sabrina reported.

"Clear the weather deck," Buckle ordered.

"Weather deck clear, Captain," Windermere said, having just taken the elevator wheel from Wong; he craned his neck back to catch glimpses of the storm as it approached from starboard.

"Eyes up, Mister Windermere," Buckle said calmly. "Watch the bubble, like a good gentleman."

Windermere snapped his face back to port and held it there. "Aye, Captain. My apologies, sir."

Buckle stared straight ahead, through the clear sky in front of the nose, at the jagged sweep of the mountain slopes as they zigzagged to the valley far below. He did not need to look to starboard to see the storm coming, perpendicular to the starboard beam, for its sweeping black mass was already advancing into his peripheral vision.

"Five hundred feet," Sabrina reported.

"Cells at one hundred and five percent capacity, sir," Lawrence said.

"Valve to one hundred and ten, Miss Lawrence," Buckle said. "And continue valving to maintain buoyancy." That kind of pressure risked blowing a bag, he knew, but to hell with it—he needed altitude.

"One hundred and ten. Aye, Captain!" Lawrence replied.

It was imperative that Buckle swing the *Arabella* hard a'starboard, leading with her nose to meet the teeth of the maelstrom, rather than being caught broadside, corkscrewed, and ripped apart. But every yard he purchased that brought him farther southwest off the mountain might prove precious at a critical moment. Buckle stood still, his hands clamped together behind his back, sensing a fast-rising tension gripping his crew.

"Stand fast, mates," Buckle said. "Hold your course." He could smell the storm coming now. He knew that smell, knew it from his years living on the mountain, that burned-metal, moist, churned-atmosphere, cold freshness that always preceded the most brutal blizzards.

"Looks bad, sir," the helmsman, Mariner, muttered.

Buckle whipped a glare at Mariner that made the young man physically shrink. "Watch your tongue, Mister Mariner! Do not look at it, damn your hide!" Buckle leaned forward, addressing the entire bridge. "Just a bit of a blow! Piece of cake! Am I not accurate, Navigator?"

"Crumbly pudding on a plate. Just peachy," Sabrina replied.

Buckle clenched his hands together behind his back so hard they hurt. He had gotten as far southwest as he was going to get. As the furious thundering of the storm washed over them, he gathered every church bell in his voice and bellowed. "Hard a'starboard! Heave to! Put your back into it and put our nose into it, Mister Mariner, you miserable sky dog!"

Mariner needed no prodding. He spun the rudder wheel to the right in a blur that threatened to break a poorly placed finger as he snatched at the passing spokes. "Hard a'starboard, aye!"

Buckle leaned on the binnacle for support as the airship swung nimbly, despite the heavy air. He had not flown in the *Arabella* for a while—he had forgotten how much more agile she was than the vastly larger *Pneumatic Zeppelin*.

"Coming around on new bearing, due northwest, aye! Six hundred and fifty feet!" Sabrina yelled.

As the *Arabella* straightened her course, her nose pointing northwest, she faced a churning wall of surging gray and black that blocked out the entire sky. The deafening roar of the maelstrom, drowning out all but the most strident shouts, set Buckle's ears to ringing. The deck vibrated, rattling with such violence that it blurred his vision—he had to keep blinking to clear it. He leaned into the chattertube hood. "All hands brace for impact!" he shouted. "Goggles on! All hands brace for impact!"

"Ten seconds!" Sabrina shouted. She glanced back at Buckle, her red curls swinging about her temples under her derby as her green eyes met his, her face shadowed and soft under the impending shade of the storm, and—for an instant that he would only recall later—Buckle was stunned by how beautiful she truly was.

She smiled and lowered her goggles over her eyes.

Buckle smiled back.

The bridge began to darken rapidly, as if night was falling at great speed.

"Eyes on your gyro, Mister Mariner," Buckle said. "You will not have a horizon in there."

"Aye!" Mariner replied, his voice rattling.

"Steel your spine, Helmsman!" Buckle shouted, planting his hand on Mariner's shoulder. "This is what you signed up for!" The madness was on Buckle, the exhilaration, the surging bravado he felt when faced with insurmountable odds; it was not a suicidal urge, nor a reckless one that might endanger his beloved crew, but a confidence born of necessity. If the captain surely believed things would shake out all right, then the crew could believe it as well.

"Leveling out!" Windermere shouted, winding the elevator wheel to neutral. "Leveling out at eight hundred!"

Eight hundred feet. Nowhere near the altitude the *Arabella* needed. "Equilibrium, drivers! Keep a tight grip on the wheel, Mister Windermere!" Buckle yelled. "This cold devil is going to try to shove the nose down!"

"Aye, Captain!" Windermere answered.

"Five seconds! Engage boil!" Sabrina shouted, though Buckle could barely hear her any more.

"Boil engaged!" Lawrence cried, flipping her agitator switches.

The *Arabella* began to rock back and forth, lanterns swinging and floorboards groaning. Buckle saw a rippling flash rip through the interior of the miasma and disappear.

Buckle's pounding heart missed a beat. Electricity. The myths of lightning were true.

The sprawling array of instruments crowding the dark bridge stations lit up with the gentle green glow of the bioluminescent boil, rapidly brightening as the agitators stirred up the algae soup.

The instant before the *Arabella*'s nose plunged into the churning maelstrom, Buckle realized that the snow and mists were hurtling upward—*upward*—at a breathtaking rate, as if the storm were upside-down.

The wood of the hull started seizing up, sounding off with loud, restless cracks. The nose dome suddenly clattered as a burst of silver-white frost erupted on the glass, rippling in long, crackling fingers across the panels, obscuring the view in jagged tributaries of ice.

This was no blizzard. It was far worse than that.

"Bloodfreezer," Buckle whispered to himself in utter, despairing awe. He then screamed "Bloodfreezer!" as he yanked his goggles down over his eyes. He shouted it again, though he could not tell if anyone could hear him over the cacophonous rush of the atmosphere.

And then the storm swallowed them whole.

–XXI–

BLOODFREEZER

IF A MAN WERE TO die and be cast into hell, he might not find himself in a place so uninviting, Buckle thought. Almost hurled to the deck as the airship shot upward like a crossbow bolt, his head was forced down in near-utter darkness as he clung to the binnacle, planks splintering at his knees, overhead pipes bursting with scalding steam, glass instruments splitting into shards and collapsing into glittering streams of fantastically bright-green boil, cuffed about the eardrums by the terrific roar, his lungs agonized as they fought to keep from freezing solid in sucking air unfathomably far below zero.

Buckle breathed shallowly, through gritted teeth, preventing the air from overwhelming his lungs. The moisture in his nose and eyes had immediately frozen, and it felt like a hundred tiny daggers stabbed his eyelids whenever he blinked. His goggle lenses were half iced over, but they were of the highest quality—Alchemist glass—and there were still enough clear spots for him to see. And what he saw was a nightmare: the figures of the crew were shadows in a black hole lit brilliantly green by the thousands of glass boil spheres, tubes, feeders, and liquid dials that were still intact on the bridge. But outside, outside the icebound glass nose, the darkness heaved and writhed in upward-driven torrents of snow and small, frightening flashes of light.

Flashes of light. An electrical storm. It was said that the Bloodfreezers generated charges of the mysterious force called *electricity* at altitude, within their bodies, but few had ever survived seeing such things to verify the tale. Electric charges loose in the clouds were not a good thing—such things surely blew up zeppelins.

Buckle fought to find his voice again. "Maintain equilibrium!" he tried to shout, but his cold-seized vocal cords failed him. It did not matter; the bridge crew clung to their stations, each knowing what most absolutely had to be done.

Buckle clawed his way up the binnacle and peered at the still-intact gyroscope in front of him, dipping around in its glowing green sphere, as were the bubbles in their inclinometer tubes alongside. The *Arabella* was still pointing northwest, but drifting to port, up at the nose by about five degrees, rocking with an odd sharpness, but they were upright and close to an even keel. The mere fact that the Imperial-built launch was still in one piece was impressive; she had bowed a bit on impact, yes, but she had taken the punch—her spine had held. The hull was good, but the brutal updraft might have torn the entire envelope away, for all Buckle knew.

Buckle wrenched his head toward the ballast board: the glowing boil in the hydrogen-pressure tubes read well, so his concern for the envelope was momentarily eased. Pushing up to his feet, Buckle heard his crew shouting reports through iced-up throats, but he could not make them out. He cleared his throat again and again, trying to heat up his voice box, and choked—the freezing air was thick with a vile, sulfurous, skin-itching smell, which he first feared was a shipboard fire, then knew to be the atmosphere itself, rife with sizzling energy.

"Helm!" Buckle croaked. "Hold your course! Helm!" Buckle turned to see Mariner on his knees, blood streaming from a cut above the hairline, his face contorted with effort as he battled the rudder wheel—and the wheel was slowly twisting him down. Buckle lurched aft to grab the opposite spokes of the wheel and, with an effort that threatened to snap his collarbones, helped Mariner inch the wheel back to starboard.

Windermere fought the same kind of war with the elevator wheel, both he and Wong gripping the shuddering instrument with all their might.

The *Arabella* took a sudden, stomach-lifting drop, nosing down; three seconds later, the updraft caught the launch again, and hurled the little *Arabella* upward into the storm.

"Captain! Captain!" Sabrina howled, her shout a bare hint under the thunder. "We are a'scudding, sir!"

"Aye, Navigator!" Buckle yelled back. His shout tore out through his throat, rough and loud, but he paid a price for it.

"Altitude one thousand, five hundred! Fifteen hundred and rising fast!" Sabrina yelled, her voice shrill. "Faster than the dials can spin, Captain!"

Buckle saw Sabrina's shadow in the nose dome, her goggles gleaming green in the light of the surviving boil spheres, a lightning flash illuminating her for an instant in silhouette. "Aye!" he replied. He straightened out his back and thighs, but now the ship was being shoved from port and starboard, threatening to roll, Windermere and Wong's efforts notwithstanding.

"Damage report!" Buckle shouted, hurting his throat.

Sabrina looked back at Buckle, shaking her head in an exaggerated fashion. "Cannot hear the voice tubes! Two thousand, five hundred feet and climbing!"

Buckle nodded, the underside of his chin scratching a line of ragged frost on his collar. Certainly the *Arabella* had taken shearing damage at various points, but her flight controls were responding, and that was all that mattered. If so—if the *Arabella* was truly intact and sound—then it was a miracle that the Bloodfreezer updraft had not ripped away the fragile cruciform fins and rudder.

"Hydrogen pressures all good!" Alison Lawrence shouted. "Buoyancy unknown!"

"Three thousand, nine hundred feet!" Sabrina bellowed.

"Hold her steady, mates!" Buckle commanded, his spine aching against the pummeling lift, somewhere in the back of his mind glad that he had not brought the ship's mascot, Kellie, along for the trip. "We'll let her spit us out, aye!" He rubbed at the glass surface of the water compass, which was now frosting over.

"Five thousand feet. Ice, Captain! Ice!" Sabrina shouted.

Ahhh, shite, Buckle thought. The insanely freezing, moisture-laden air of the Bloodfreezer—which would render the airship as heavy as a stone once it stopped lifting her—meant that every inch of the *Arabella* was coating up with ice. This added weight, immense when taken in its totality, would soon send the launch plummeting to earth, even with engines overdriven, ballast tanks empty, and hydrogen cells socked full.

Buckle leaned into the chattertube hood and yelled, doubting anyone aboard could hear him as he did so. "All axemen to the assembly station! I repeat, all axemen to the assembly station!" He took a staggering step toward Robinson at his aft signals station. "Mister Robinson! Axemen to stations! Pass the word!"

"Pass the word, aye!" Robinson answered, then turned and ran through the small passageway, veering to maintain his balance.

The big inclinometer above the helm, encased in ice, burst open, the glass splitting down the seams of its copper casing. Bright-green boil spewed forth, splattering Buckle and the deck with running splotches of glowing green liquid that vibrated and rolled with every punishment the superstructure took. Buckle smelled the boil—it had an ocean-water, fishy, seaweed stink.

"Seven thousand feet and rising, but I think rate of ascent is slowing!" Sabrina announced. "Seven thousand!"

Buckle tucked his top hat in a cubby and buttoned his leather coat up to the chin. "First Lieutenant! You have the bridge! I am going topside!"

Sabrina stumbled back toward Buckle in the darkness, her boots sliding in the greasy boil and shards of glass as Welly slid into the navigator's station behind her. "No, Captain!" Sabrina scolded. "Send Windermere or me on the roof! It is our job!"

"Aye!" Windermere affirmed.

"Captain stays on the bridge, sir!" Sabrina continued. "And you are already exhausted, sir!"

"I shall have none of it!" Buckle howled, annoyed. "The bridge is yours, Lieutenant—you have nothing better to do in this black hole as it is, Serafim, you bloody mutineer!"

–XXII–

AXES

ROMULUS BUCKLE CHARGED UP THE *Arabella*'s main companionway, pulling on a pith helmet and a topman's greatcoat,
a heavy tan coat with a high collar and a waist lined with
safety clamps, hastily securing its clasps. The companionway,
screaming like a cat in heat, as it always did in inclement
weather—some annoying effect of design—shuddered and
rocked. It was dark, the lantern curiously missing from its
hook, and crowded with crew members—mostly the hastily dressed engine rats, smelling of coal and fire. Signalman
Robinson carried a storm lantern; the black iron banister rail
gleamed evilly under its soft, weaving, orange light, glazed
with scant frostings of ice.

They burst up onto the weather deck and found it a howling
cavern, unnaturally dark, except for a few undamaged buglights
swinging wildly on their posts. Vertical rents thrashed about
the envelope's flanks, ripped along several of the frame girders
towering five stories above, the patching and needles hanging,
barely begun, abandoned by the skinners who had been called
away to the axe teams. The long fabric shell billowed in and
out in violent ripples and billows, surging with such force that
Buckle was amazed the envelope had not been ripped away. As
Buckle turned, he slipped and nearly fell, but managed to catch

himself on the frame of the belfry: the decking, already slick with a thin sheet of clear ice, gleamed treacherously as the airship bucked, and powerful gusts of wind tunneled in over the open gunwales.

Montgomery Muhammed Darcy led the six-member topside axe team, mostly riggers and skinners. Darcy was a barrel-chested, brawny-forearmed boilerman, with tawny skin and heavy-lidded eyes. He was bald as a billiard ball but furred with a dense brown beard he liked to chew on. He handed Buckle an ice axe. "Here, Cap'n," Darcy said. "Your weapon, sir."

Buckle hefted the axe; the long wooden haft was well weighted, the steel head forged into a sharp blade with a blunt pick on the back end, the pick the more effective implement when one was trying to bash ice away from the envelope. "Thank you, Mister Darcy," Buckle shouted.

"Aye, sir!" Darcy replied.

Buckle turned to face the group huddled around him on the heaving deck. The crew members resembled grotesque beetles in the wavering yellow buglight, snapping their leather breathing masks up under their topmen's goggles, completely shielding their faces, and shoving the small oxygen canisters into cloth pouches stitched into the greatcoat waists, taking care not to foul the rubber tubes. Lothian Blake, propulsion airman, passed out firefly lanterns. Carmen Steinway, skinner, was responsible for sounding the warning should the *Arabella* climb higher than breathable air, and had a bulky quicksilver altimeter strapped to her forearm, its long glass tubes lit up with bioluminescent boil.

"Iron up, lords and ladies," Buckle yelled. "How about we trim this beauty clean?"

"Aye, Cap'n!" came the response.

"Current altitude eight thousand, six hundred, sir!" Steinway screamed into Buckle's ear as Blake handed him a lantern.

"Eyes up for tanglers! Mind your safety lines!" Buckle shouted, looping the axe handle's leather strap around his wrist. "Hurrah!"

"Hurrah!" the shout returned.

Buckle clambered up the amidships ladder, his greatcoat and equipment making his boots and gloves heavy on the metal rungs; he ascended into the surging, roaring envelope cavern where the stressed superstructure rattled and the gasbags heaved, their whalelike backs appearing half-alive in the swaying buglights, glittering with the copper lacings of their stockings, grinding and squeaking against their backstays and securing wires.

The noise, the earsplitting rip of the storm, threatened to stun the mind. Buckle sensed that the *Arabella* was already getting heavy, weighted down, sluggish—icing up fast.

He caught the scent of blood, or rather, the memory of the smell of blood. It was not his blood, not even human blood, but rather the sharper, sweeter odor of Martian blood. It was only for a heartbeat, but for one instant he felt a fear for Max's life, as she lay helpless in her bunk below.

Buckle reached the observer's platform as the Bloodfreezer coursed above the glass of the nacelle bubble, its black churn lighting up with erratic, ominous flashes of blue-white. Buckle slammed the securing bolt aside. When he opened the hatch, it was nearly torn out of his hands.

"Let us dance, you surly devil!" Buckle shouted, knowing only he could hear his words, and plunged up into the maelstrom with his lantern at the fore.

-XXIII-

IN THE BELLY OF THE BEAST

BUCKLE EMERGED FROM THE HATCH of the amidships observer's nacelle into a gauntlet of whips, of lashing wind, ice particles, and snow. The maelstrom sucked at his goggles, trying to tear them off his head. It was difficult to see. The *Arabella*'s canvas roof rippled and billowed like a surging sea, every stitch straining at the seams; even the two grappling cannons seemed to be rocking. Visibility was no more than forty feet, and Buckle experienced a sensation of falling as the walls of churning snow swept upward over the flanks and into the churning obscurity above.

And everything was coated in ice, clear, thin, glassy ice.

Buckle moved aside in a crouch, hooking his iron safety-line clasp onto the heavy cable of the main jackline—smashing that section of its ice sheath—as Darcy crawled out of the hatch behind him. Their lanterns whipped about their hands, the fireflies scattering inside the glass as they were walloped about.

"Nasty weather, Cap'n!" Darcy howled, pulling the next crew person—the rigger, Lansa Lazlo—up onto the roof with a powerful tug. "Nasty!"

"And I neglected to bring my parasol!" Buckle shouted back; he did not snap his oxygen mask up to his face, although he already felt the frostbite sinking in—he needed to be able to shout and be heard. Darcy had not attached his face mask either.

Buckle waited, hunching as the severe cold bit through his clothes and buffeted the flat of his axe blade, until all the ice team had made it up onto the envelope and secured their safety lines. "Two and three forward with me!" Buckle shouted. "Mister Darcy, take the remainder to the stern! We shall meet amidships!"

"Aye, sir!" Darcy replied.

"Have at it, choppers! And mind your blades!" Buckle howled.

Darcy led his three ice cutters—skinner Hector Hudson, and riggers Ilsa Gallagher and Lansa Lazlo—along the envelope spine toward the stern, slipping and scrambling through the wind gusts. Buckle signaled for his two—skinner Carmen Steinway and the propulsion airman Blake—to accompany him forward to the bow. Buckle grabbed ahold of the stem of the forward grappling cannon, using it for support as he advanced, his boots skidding across layers of bumpy ice. It was a long scramble across the seventy-five feet of slick spine board and canvas to the crest of the nose, the wind exploding over and over again into their faces.

A flash of lightning, terrifyingly close, ripped through the murk off the port beam, its reflection flashing across the ice coating the length of the airship. A burned-metal smell stung Buckle's mouth and nostrils—electricity.

Buckle and his axe team reached the crow's-nest nacelle at the leading edge of the envelope, where the rounding of the nose fell away in a steep curve to the quivering bowsprit thirty feet below. "Top down! Top down!" Buckle shouted.

Steinway and Blake rappelled down the flanks of the bow, heads ducked against the beating blizzard. Buckle raised his axe against the maniac wind, bringing it down with a fine glancing stroke, despite the waffling of the axe head. The force of the blow exploded the immature, thin ice at the point of impact, the mirrorlike fragments sucked away into the storm, while sending long, shivering cracks through the surrounding carapace. Buckle struggled to keep his feet. Clearing the roof of the new ice was the easy part; trying to keep one's footing in the mess while swinging an axe was not.

Buckle fought to keep a good grip on the axe handle. There was already a slick slip to it, and it shifted in his grip as he swung—a problem when the angle of the blade was the only difference between chipping away ice and gashing a hole in the fabric beneath it.

Suddenly, the violent storm abated, the dark, churning surface of the blizzard falling away below as if the *Arabella* had just leapt up out of a stormy sea. The atmosphere was clear except for a gentle snowfall, the night sky above Buckle a high ceiling of lightning-shivered clouds that cast a ghastly, uneven illumination of silver and ultraviolet black. Buckle was nearly thrown from his feet as the *Arabella*, released from the clutches of the updraft, bounded forward, her engines and propellers roaring.

Buckle gasped; it was now easy to breathe the painfully cold air, without the wind trying to suck his collapsing lungs free of it. The *Arabella* had burst up into a higher altitude of the storm, a hidden, twilit world with an atmosphere dramatically different than the layer of clouds below it. Visibility was much better, despite the falling snow—and the snow was *falling,* for the updraft had vanished with the storm.

Buckle also felt the *Arabella*, despite her hydrogen bags filled beyond capacity, and her boilers on the red line, begin to founder.

Get us the hell out of here, Sabrina, Buckle thought, and slammed his axe down again, splitting streams of ice that seemed to be re-forming as quickly as he cut them away. A forked bolt of lightning tore downward past the starboard side of the bow, perilously close, making Buckle's skin itch and tingle.

"Twelve thousand, four hundred, Captain!" Steinway yelled from her perch on the starboard flank below.

Not high enough to require oxygen, but colder than hell.

Buckle glanced backward, hoping to gain a glimpse of Darcy and his aft team despite the obscuring drifts of the snowfall. It was then that Buckle, from the corner of his eye, glimpsed a great shadow rise behind the stern, a hulking presence of a deeper shade than the dark, silk-silver murk about it, a hovering monstrosity equal to the size of the *Arabella*, its beating bat wings wider in their sweep than the length of the airship on either side, the nightmare body alive with a writhing mass of tentacle arms.

Along with the shadow came a strange noise that instinctively made the stomach sour and the nerves ache, an ancient, nasty clicking.

Steinway had spun around on her line and, espying the looming monstrosity above the stern, she screamed. "Kraken! The monster of monsters is upon us, Captain! It be the kraken!"

~XXIV~

THE KRAKEN

THE KRAKEN DESCENDED, ITS HUGE wings beating, a flesh-and-blood nightmare shedding the unreality of myth, an alien beastie so ravenous that no aviator unfortunate enough to face one had ever come home alive. The fables described the kraken as a hunter of human sweetmeats, devouring entire crews in mere minutes, a pitiless crusher of airships.

For an instant, all Buckle could do was stare. The kraken resembled a giant squid, reddish yellow in color, though the head was almost blue, nestled amidst countless muscle-bound tentacles, the tubular body long and sheathed in an armored carapace, crowned with a horn-lined frill—a triceratopian head. The four sweeping wings, bat-like with their translucent, veined flesh and the protuberance of the skeletal structure beneath, beat slowly but powerfully, each one leaving massive vortexes in the snowstorm, each one as big as the *Arabella* itself. Blue-white arcs of electricity crackled back and forth across the kraken's skin.

And the eyes—the beasties always had such terrible, glowing eyes. The kraken had seven of them—one huge, multichambered orb in the center of the head, and three smaller eyes aligned on each side. They were hypnotic, drenched with malevolence, and frightful in their intelligence.

It had to be killed, and killed quickly. And all Romulus Buckle had in his hand as he hurled aside his safety line—a deadly hindrance now—and scrambled amidships with a heart firing like artillery...well, all he had was a blunt axe.

It would have to do.

"Lazlo! Raise the alarm!" Buckle screamed back at the rigger, who stood just ahead of the amidships nacelle, staring dumbfounded at the apparition ahead. "Alarm! And muskets!"

"Aye, sir!" Lazlo shouted back, sliding into the observer's nacelle to sound the emergency bell.

Buckle suddenly found himself catapulted forward, the deck dipping down in front of him. The kraken was latching on to the envelope roof, drawing the weight of its monstrous lobster body onto the canvas and heaving the *Arabella* down at the stern.

Buckle landed hard on his stomach, sliding a few feet on the treacherous ice before recovering his feet at the leading tips of the beastie's tentacles, dozens of them, writhing on the deck, the suckers clamping on the envelope skin.

He saw Darcy and Ilsa Gallagher trapped at the stern, chopping frantically at the sea of arms coiling back and forth around them. An overhead scream made Buckle snap his head up to the brilliantly lit sky of shimmering lightning and falling snow— Hector Hudson thrashed in midair as the tentacle that had just lifted him squeezed, then ripped him in half.

Something exploded in Buckle's brain.

Buckle hurdled over tentacles, moving beneath dozens more that lashed back and forth in the darkness overhead. "Have at the monster, mates!" Buckle shouted into the teeth of the wind, and slammed his axe down upon the joint of a thick tentacle arm. The blade sank deep into the jellyfish muscle beneath, sending up gouts of yellow blood. The arm yanked back reflexively, nearly tearing the axe out of Buckle's hands as it snapped away.

Buckle howled. A murderous ecstasy ripped through him at the feel of the chop. He wanted to rage at the killing of Hudson—the kraken had committed the unforgivable, attacking his airship and its crew—but the strategist inside Buckle had already taken over. To win, he had to prevent the kraken from clamping down. To win, he and his crew, gnats against a lion, had to kill the beastie in a matter of seconds. The eyes. Take out the eyes. And then the eviscerating could begin.

"The eyes!" Buckle screamed as he leapt over a lashing tentacle, battling toward Darcy and Ilsa at the stern. "Chop the bloody eyes!"

Darcy and Ilsa lay to, delivering vicious cuts to the kraken's squishy flesh, but the beastie seemed unperturbed—it brought the upper half of dead Hudson's torso to its mouth and jammed it into the fetid hole, a circle of overlapping hooked beaks, each snapping and grinding in its own motion, and slewed the remains of the poor fellow down its gullet.

Once finished with its mastication, the kraken slid its bloodstained beaks back and forth across one another with an ear-numbing *CLICK, CLICK, CLICK.*

Blake and Steinway were now at Buckle's side, axes whirling, and Lazlo joined the battle line a moment later. They swung their axes back and forth, fending off the growing number of tentacles snapping in from every angle in the flashing light, throwing up waves of yellow blood wherever the blades sunk and bit. Slowly they worked their way forward to Darcy and Ilsa until they were only a half-dozen yards away. The *Arabella* groaned and shuddered, still sinking at the stern—the kraken had secured itself upon the rear of the airship now, its slithering arms constricting around the envelope, the suckered append- ages pulling along its rippling length in great accordion-heaves of muscle, the great black wings, quivering overhead like death- ship sails, slowly folding down onto the long curve of its back.

The kraken intended to stay for a while.

Buckle broke through, hacking at an arm as thick as a tree trunk until ten feet of the end fell off and slithered away. He lunged toward Darcy and Ilsa. The canvas at his feet was awash in yellow blood, the jackline cable screwed in a jumble, its iron securing bolts having been separated from the superstructure girders beneath by the awesome force of the beastie's suckering arm when it had snatched Hudson from the deck.

An orange tentacle caught Ilsa by the boot and jerked, upending her; she lurched forward, hacking at the swaying appendage as it lifted her, carrying her to her doom.

Buckle lunged for Ilsa, but his gloved hand missed, his fin- gers brushing the end of her puggaree as it dangled from the upside-down pith helmet. Ilsa dropped her axe, folded her body up, and popped her foot out of the tentacle-wrapped boot; she dropped free, landing hard on her back amidst a nest of writh- ing kraken arms at Buckle's feet. He yanked the gasping, one- booted woman to her feet as Darcy parried a tentacle, its suckers festooned with an axe, alongside.

"Are you in one piece, aviator?" Buckle shouted at Ilsa.

"Yes! We won't let the beastie get away, Cap'n!" Ilsa shouted, drawing a knife from her belt.

"That's the spirit, Gallagher!" Buckle yelled back, sidestep- ping a tentacle as it curved toward him from the murk. "Go for the eyes! The damned eyes!"

The kraken suddenly withdrew a raft of tentacles and stacked them like lumber, one by one, down upon one another, forming a wall of beastie flesh as impenetrable as a portcullis between the zeppelineers and its face.

It was as if the beastie had heard Buckle, understood his intent—but that was impossible.

They needed muskets.

"Back up amidships!" Buckle screamed, swinging his axe left and right. "Stay tight! Stay tight!" The group retreated slowly, Darcy, Ilsa, Lazlo, and Steinway, their picket fence of axes slashing under the writhing archways of tentacles in a twilit world of lightning. Splatters of hot, yellow kraken blood slopped the deck and stank of wine vinegar, melting the ice in irregular, steaming valleys.

Suddenly a tentacle, a massive, snaking whip of sucker and quivering muscle, rolled in upon the little phalanx, knocking Buckle and Darcy to their knees, and nearly bashing Lazlo over the side, so great was the force of its collision; then the arm snapped away, and Steinway was gone.

"Carmen!" Ilsa shrieked, but the poor skinner was out of reach, the beastie whipping her body back and forth high overhead.

"You bloody devil!" Buckle bellowed, hewing at the writhing mass of tentacles in front of him as his crew did the same.

The kraken, ignoring the vicious blows inflicted upon its arms, stuffed the screaming Steinway into its beaks and ripped the unfortunate woman to shreds, the last flails of her arms punctuated by a sparkling burst of boil and quicksilver.

The kraken spit a blood-soaked boot onto the deck. The eyes, the seven iridescent bug eyes, peered down with cold calculation as it chomped and chewed. A flash of lightning lit the world white and blue, and the eyes reflected in hundreds of tiny prisms, in murderous rainbows.

Fury throttled Buckle, banging the blood his brain, pumping adrenaline into his muscles as he swung his weapon. "On me!" he screamed, waving his arms. "On me, you ill-looking brute! You've got a big brain, do you?"

The huge center eye swung to Buckle, watching him.

"Know this—you shall die this day!" Buckle howled, raising his blood-slicked axe high. "You have slithered into your grave and here I stand, your bloody executioner!"

Surprised by the theatricality of his words, Buckle felt like he was onstage in the devil's theater. He was going to split open the kraken's skull, chop the gooey brain out, and pickle it in a grog barrel for Doctor Fogg to inspect upon their return home.

"Captain!" Sabrina shouted, appearing at Buckle's flank with a blackbang pistol in each hand.

"Good lass!" Buckle said, grabbing Sabrina's offered pistol, whipping out his arm, and taking aim at the kraken's biggest eye. He fired.

The kraken, apparently well aware of a firearm's effect, slammed its pinkish, armored eyelids shut. The ball struck the lid and ricocheted away in a corkscrew of sparks.

Buckle hurled the spent pistol aside. "Down, Captain!" Sabrina shouted, yanking him, and shoving another pistol into his free hand. "Everyone, get down!"

Buckle dropped to one knee, turning to see six crew members advancing in a ragged rank along the roof, each one recognizable to Buckle despite their faces being buried inside goggles and the grasshopperish oxygen masks. It was Faraday's gondola ice team, along with the signalman Martin Robinson, the boilerman Cornelius Valentine, and the gunner's mate Samantha Frost, armed with axes and muskets with bayonets gleaming from beneath the muzzles.

"Aim!" Sabrina screamed into the wind, raising her pistol.

The firing squad lifted their weapons.

"The eyes! Target the eyes, musketeers!" Buckle yelled, ducking lower, yanking Ilsa and Darcy down by their collars on each side of him.

"Fire!" Sabrina screamed.

The six muskets and one pistol erupted in a ragged volley of booms, blackbang-powder clouds leaping from the flash of each barrel before streaming away in the darkness.

Buckle snapped his head around to see the musket balls, each loaded with burning white phosphorus, zip through the snowy air and pelt the face of the kraken. But the great beastie clamped its armored lids shut again, flinging them open once the balls ricocheted away. Annoyed, the beastie ground its beaks from side to side with their awful CLICK, CLICK, CLICK.

Guns were not going to do it.

"To hell with the peashooters!" Buckle shouted, jamming his pistol in his belt and waving his axe above his head. "Form up a wedge and have at the blade!" And with a battle cry, Buckle raised his steel and charged the kraken.

–XXV

TENTACLES

As BUCKLE WADED INTO THE forest of lashing tentacles, each swing of the blade slicing satisfyingly deep into yielding jellyfish flesh, he found Sabrina and her reinforcements on his flanks, bayonets and hatchets flashing.

"Who is driving the damned airship?" Buckle screamed at Sabrina.

"Windermere. He is more than capable, Captain," Sabrina answered, swinging her axe.

"Ah, splendid!" Buckle shouted as he lay about with his axe, fending off the beastie's slithering attempts to rope him and his mates as the wedge advanced.

A man screamed overhead. Buckle looked up to see Cornelius Valentine, who had accompanied Sabrina up onto the roof, being lashed back and forth by a tentacle wrapped around his right leg. A sickly snapping sound came as the bones broke apart, and Valentine's body flopped at a disturbing angle.

"Save that man!" Buckle shouted.

Darcy, the closest to Valentine, was on him in an instant, severing the beastie's arm with one massive swing of his axe.

Valentine dropped to the deck, writhing in utter agony.

Buckle heard a familiar *bang*, a large powder cartridge fired behind him, and a grappling hook whizzed over his head, a clawed projectile of spinning silver, trailing its rope behind. The kraken saw the flash of the grappling-cannon muzzle and instantly slammed its big eye shut; the grapnel slammed into the armored eyelid and spun away to port. The beastie tightened its grip on the envelope with a violent shudder of ripping canvas, snapping rigging, cracking ice, and the frightening groan of the bending girders beneath—while the six smaller eyes, remaining open, sought the source of the attack.

Buckle glanced back to see Martin Robinson manning the forward grappling cannon, its oilskin wrappings hastily ripped aside and flapping as they dangled about its post. Samantha Frost, gunner's mate, hunched close at Robinson's side, was rapidly clearing the anchor chamber of the rope so she could load a second shot.

A tree-size tentacle sailed through the air above Buckle, uncoiling in a whip of suckers and muscle, and the end of the huge arm snapped through the grappling cannon's stock and into Robinson's chest, launching him up and backward over the starboard side, and into oblivion. Frost stood motionless, in shock, her hands splayed over the twisted ruins of the grappling cannon, completely unscathed by the blow.

Buckle turned his head forward, opening his mouth to urge his crew forward. But suddenly he could not breathe. He was locked in a great squeeze about his upper chest and neck. He tried to twist, to inhale, but the air was crushed out of him. A tentacle had dropped upon him from above, wrapping snake-like about his torso, and he could do nothing for it now; he was lifted into the air, the upside-down world a whirl of lightning and falling snow, a fallen lantern flashing as it rolled across the roof. His ribs, bending into his organs, pinned them into stasis. His muscles went limp, his mouth gaping, his vision shuddering to black.

In the last moment of consciousness, a consciousness of what seemed to be the end of his life, Buckle felt the monster's suckers—somehow penetrating between his pith helmet and the collar of his greatcoat—latch on to the skin at the back of his neck and take hold.

Then the kraken dropped him.

Buckle, near blind and half-dead, was jolted back into coherence. The impact of the fall, soft with the give of the envelope skin, and hard with the slap of the ice and the unforgiving girder underneath, punched a shot of air into his chest. Sabrina was on him, her axe blade and goggles awash with yellow beastie blood, her bright red ringlets swinging around her head, her white teeth gritted.

"Romulus, damn you!" Sabrina shouted as she tore at the tentacle binding his body. "Stay with the wedge, sir, damn you, with all due respect, sir!"

Though his head swam, Buckle heard Sabrina's words; with his lieutenants constantly saving his life—Max and now Sabrina—perhaps he should be more careful.

Darcy was there, his mighty hands alongside Sabrina's as they pulled the tentacle loose. The sucker that had latched onto the back of Buckle's neck was torn free; he felt a disc of his skin rip away with it. Buckle wheezed, sucking in snow-filled air that near froze his lungs solid, but the pain reanimated him.

Buckle forced himself to his knees, gasping over the hacked remains of the beastie tentacle that had been one squeeze away from killing him. The rancid ammonia reek of the beastie blood cleared his senses. He lurched to his feet and picked up his axe—it came up with a sticky snap, the blood-slushy haft already half frozen to the deck—and found himself alongside his crew, battling the weaving net of tentacles surrounding them. The kraken hunched forward, foot by foot, and with each heave the *Arabella* shuddered under Buckle's feet.

Sabrina, standing right in front of Buckle, dropped hard on her back, losing her axe, and was jerked away toward the kraken. A tentacle had secured Sabrina's left leg from heel to thigh in loops, the reddish-purple muscles locked down despite her attempts to lurch forward and pry at them with her hands. The beastie had her.

"Lieutenant!" Darcy howled, grasping, but the curling brawn of a beastie arm knocked him back into Buckle as he lunged.

Sabrina's helmet bounced away, her red hair bursting loose of its pinnings, swirling about her head like fire in the twilight, and she vanished into the beastie's thicket of arms.

Sabrina Serafim, having just saved the life of her captain, now only had mere seconds to live herself.

CLICK, CLICK, CLICKETY-CLICK. The kraken sawed its beaks in anticipation.

Buckle scrambled to his feet and charged.

"Captain! Wait, sir!" Darcy howled as Buckle sprinted past him.

A mistake to wait, Mister Darcy, Buckle thought. A mistake to charge as well. Buckle chose the better mistake.

Swerving through tentacles, Buckle plunged into the forest of writhing whips and roots. He kept his axe tight against his body, ducking and weaving under the grasping suckers that sought to wrap him. He ran straight ahead—straight at the kraken. Buckle had attacked out of instinct—but he trusted his instinct to be right. The big-brained beastie would expect the zeppelineers to try to save their crewmate. The last thing the kraken might expect would be a sprint right down its gullet.

Before he was even ready for it, Buckle found himself springing along a main appendage, launching in a great leap up and over the beastie's wall of tentacles. He arrived, in midair, under the creature's cheek, face-to-face with snapping jaws slathered with an awful mix of human blood and alien saliva.

Buckle's small, mortal eyes met the huge center eye of the monster, with its thousands of glittering chambers. The kraken saw Buckle—it *saw* him—and Buckle was suddenly aware of an unfathomable weight of centuries, of endless light-years of distance in the far reaches of space, of the weariness of eternity; he was hypnotized in the split second between his leap, his body in the air, axe raised high over his head, and the delivery of his blow.

The middle eye slammed shut its massive, armored lid, but Buckle sailed past it, having launched his jump to the right. The three small eyes on the left side of the kraken's head were still open; Buckle hewed his axe blade through two of them in one swing, rupturing them in guttering gouts of clear fluid. The eye-lids slammed shut over the slashed orbs, but too late. The kraken recoiled, its tentacles wrenching the *Arabella*'s airframe, making girders shriek and bolts pop like gunshots. Buckle slammed into the side of the kraken's head, losing his grip on his axe as it stuck fast in an eye socket. He grabbed ahold of the beastie's bone-ridged brow, swinging over a nest of snaking arms.

A tentacle had him, prying him loose. As Buckle's hands tore free of the gelatinous flesh of the brow, he found himself suspended by a great anaconda coil of tentacle, wrapped around his waist. The kraken flung open its big eye as it dangled Buckle in front of it, the honeycombed lenses scrutinizing him, the beaks slewing back and forth below it.

CLACK, CLACK, CLICK, CLACK, CLACK.

The tentacle tightened about Buckle's body, slowly lowering him into the horrible sawmill of the mouth, as if the beastie intended not only to consume him but to enjoy the agonies of his slow death.

Buckle drew his pistol, jammed it into the center of the gigantic, multichambered eye, and pulled the trigger.

The blackbang pistol boomed; the great eye collapsed, imploding, the chambers flickering between light and darkness, the eyelid blinking madly, sloshing-over iridescent fluid pouring out of the bullet hole, followed by streams of yellow blood.

The kraken's beaks stopped grinding and flung open in a death splay. The beastie clenched up, gurgling as it made a last, vain effort to draw sense from its riven brainpan, and then fell limp. The wavering forest of tentacles all dropped to the deck at once. The arm binding Buckle released him—he fell onto the envelope, landing in a pool of blood and eye plasma. He nearly slipped through a hole, which would have been unfortunate, for he would have plummeted five stories down to the *Arabella*'s weather deck, below.

The beastie slid backward, slowly, but gaining speed, as the weight of the huge carapace dragged the corpse off the end of the stern.

No brain stuffing for this kraken, Buckle thought as he staggered to his feet, sidestepping the streams of dead tentacles as they slithered away with their dead master. He saw the beastie's face, the light in the center eye going black as its life was extinguished, a life he knew to be as old as the world.

"Romulus!" Sabrina shouted.

Buckle spun to see Sabrina, her leg still wrapped in the dead kraken's tentacle, being dragged with it over the side.

–XXVI–

SKIES OF GLASS

"COME INTO THE ATRIUM, MY dear Sabrina, please," Sabrina heard her mother, Chelsea, ask in her dulcet voice, which reminded her of warm tea, strawberry jam, toy dogs, and amateur but well-acted theatrical productions. "Isambard has powered up the cloudbuster—you can come in and take some sun with me."

***

It was strange to Sabrina that such a memory would come as the dead kraken carried her off stern of the *Arabella* and into oblivion in the Bloodfreezer. Such things that leap into the mind of the doomed!

Yet Sabrina had not given up. She still fought for life with all she had; having lost her axe, she hacked at the thick, rubbery tentacle with her knife. But she could only lean forward in lunges at the flesh that held her as it dragged her in a skittering slide across the roof, delivering jarring blows to her arse and spine at the hump of every girder.

Her vision was a blur of flashing sky and tentacles.

"Damned, wretched beastie!" she swore, barely aware that she was yelling. Her helmet had fallen away, taking her goggles with it. Her cheeks and ears were numb, and the wind cruelly whipped her scarlet hair about her face and eyes, half blinding her. She had slashed her shin several times as she stabbed at the tentacle, but that did not really matter.

She knew that her crewmates were running after her, shouting and slipping across the ice, but they had no chance of reaching her in time. A vision appeared to her of her frozen body forever suspended in the dismal storm, a dead navigator turned to ice, never to fall to earth again.

She was going over the side.

And she had not gotten her revenge.

But it was mostly all right. She had given her life to save Romulus Buckle.

***

"Sabrina, please come in the atrium, dearest," Chelsea asked again, her voice soft, deepened by a hint of annoyance. Chelsea was easily disappointed, a trait shared by many members of the Goethe family bloodline.

"I am coming, Mother," Sabrina replied, studying a yellow canary as she balanced the little bird on her finger. "I shall be in presently."

"We only get sun for four minutes, dear. I would suggest you should come in here now," Chelsea said.

Sabrina pursed her lips. She had been told that she was far too introspective for a seven-year-old girl, but she knew that her father loved how smart she was. And it was not a show: she liked to read the old books about all things—which thrilled her tutor, a stuffy crane with a gentle soul, named Edward Marter—fiction, mathematics, geography, and especially art, which was her father's favorite subject. Yesterday she had drawn him a rather brilliant portrait of his horse, a strawberry roan named Barbarossa, and he had pinned it to the window sash in his office, where the soft sunlight made it glow.

She peered at the canary, observing how it bobbed its head back and forth, feeling the sharp but comfortable clutch of its little talons as they played across her fingers. The massive crystal palace was full of thousands of canaries of every color and size, hopping to and fro in elaborate cast-iron birdhouses built for them long ago. The birds were necessary, her parents said, for the canaries were watched closely for any signs of distress, the birds being sensitive to trace amounts of the poison fog surrounding the city.

Sabrina jiggled her finger; the little canary chirped at her, then almost reluctantly fluttered away. It was a "little rogue," from one of the small colonies made up of canaries that had escaped their cages over the decades; they were allowed to live free inside the palace, sometimes splattering white guano on the nice table linens. But Sabrina liked the little rogues; she wondered if the birds in the cages envied them, or if they were even capable of it.

Sabrina stood up from the rim of the gurgling fountain, where she had been sitting with her fauna sketchbook. It was full of her bird drawings—quite good ones—and one drawing of a chubby rat she had seen in an alley, which amused her father and disturbed her mother. Chelsea had suggested that the vermin sketch be destroyed, but Sabrina had not obeyed her; it was a good drawing, and Sabrina quite liked it. She sniffed, flattening out her white wool dress with the palms of her hands, looking down past the ends of the blue ribbons in her pigtails, over the little hump of her tummy to the polished toes of her black shoes, below. The company of the canary had proven an effective antidote to the undercurrent of nervousness that had been running through her all morning. She had observed her father and others whispering furtively in the hallways, large, dark figures of family members and friends she had known all her life, who had suddenly and inexplicably taken on a hint of menace—not in their actions toward her, which were as kind as usual, but in the darting of their eyes, in the clamp of their jaws, and in the way they hunkered in the shadows.

The salty smell of the seawater splashing in the fountain was pungent in her nose, and she liked it—it was a nice accompaniment to the aroma of the roast beef being broiled by the cooks in the kitchens. Snorting air in and out of her nostrils, Sabrina tried to separate the scents of the seawater and roast beef, seeing if she could isolate which part of her nose detected salty and sweet. She caught a rancid whiff of bird guano, and it ruined her whole experiment.

"Sabrina!" her mother cried, exasperated. "The beautiful sun!"

Sabrina turned and took off at a skipping run. She was all alone in the grand gallery of the crystal palace, a small white dot in the midst of a sprawling architectural marvel. The palace was constructed of huge sheets of plate glass—the ceiling and walls all supported by frames and columns of black cast iron. The cast iron itself was ornate, fashioned to emulate vines, tree trunks, branches, hawks, owls, and gargoyles. Muted sunlight burst in through a few spots on the soot-covered glass roof, its pale yellows playing oddly in the blue-white illumination of the gas lamps, the beams gleaming on the pink-white marble floor. Five seawater fountains lined the middle of the hall, though three had fallen to mere dribbles—Sabrina liked to think there were little fish stuck in the pipes of the feeble ones.

Sabrina hurried toward the archway of the atrium entrance, which was rich with the yellow glow of sunlight. She wanted to visit the sun, to feel its tender and stinging heat on the skin of her face, and she suddenly felt a bit frantic—she was furious with herself. Why had she not listened to her mother? If she missed out on sunbathing this week, she would have no one but herself to blame. Oh, such a sorry state of affairs. It was never good to have only oneself to blame.

When Sabrina arrived in the atrium, she skidded to a stop right at the place where the shadow of the archway met the daylight pouring down on the floor from above. She loved stepping from shadow into light and back again, for such opposites of illumination rarely existed in a world of blue gas lamps and constant gray fog. She squinted; the overhead glass, washed clean by the servants, swam with liquid light. It was very bright sunshine.

When Sabrina saw her mother, Chelsea, she caught her breath. Chelsea was a woman blessed with a tremulous beauty, and she never looked more beautiful than when she chose to bask in the golden sun. She lay draped on a couch in the center of the atrium, toying with a gold and garnet locket about her slender neck. Chelsea Goethe was trim and proper, an elite lady of the first class, but when she found the sunlight, the precious few minutes she could have of it once every week, there emerged from within her a being much more hedonistic, even careless. The couch was Chelsea's favorite place to sun and therefore left empty by everyone else who visited the atrium, leaving her to lounge in its vast plunge of faded green velvet with red-striped pillows; and once sequestered there, warmed up, eyelids closed,

Sabrina had learned she made an easy mark for her children's requests.

Chelsea smiled when she saw Sabrina. "Hello, my darling bird child. Scoot yourself in here or you shall regret missing the sunbeams, like you always do."

Sabrina stepped into the sunlight with one great dramatic stride. She blinked in the light, instantly feeling the sun roast the top of her head, and the warmth reflected up from the floor. She smelled heated glass, iron, and dust.

"Come, sit with me," Chelsea said, patting the couch.

Sabrina stepped to her mother, a woman who was exactly what Sabrina wanted to be when she grew up. Chelsea was tall and graceful, the length of her body accentuated as she lay on her side, her shoes kicked off and her legs bared—she had pulled her skirt up to her thighs with her legs crossed, though the crossing did little to reduce the languidness of the effect. She propped herself up on one elbow as she looked at her daughter. Her shoulders, arms, and hands were small and fine, and her long blond hair was almost always pinned up at the base of the neck, though she liked to leave two small tendrils dangling in ringlets at the temples. Her eyes were dark blue and never missed a detail, though she often allowed small transgressions to pass, and her pale skin, unblemished as fresh goat's milk poured from the morning bucket, glowed in the precious light of the sun.

There were many people in the atrium that afternoon, but Sabrina only saw one, only remembered one.

Sabrina dashed to the couch and hopped on the spot at her mother's waist; they sat quietly, absorbing the sunlight together. Chelsea put her arm around Sabrina and closed her eyes. "Hmmm, this is the life, isn't it, my dear?" she asked.

"Hmmmm, yes," Sabrina replied. "I am a sunbeam now."

Sabrina felt her mother's chest shudder, the small breasts pressing against her back, as Chelsea quietly laughed.

"What is so funny, Mother?" Sabrina asked.

"Just you, little one," Chelsea said, sighing. "Just you."

"I wish Father was here," Sabrina said, and when she spoke, she felt that odd feeling of uneasiness creeping into her insides again.

"So do I. But there is an important meeting in the parliament today."

Sabrina nodded, kicking her feet a little, so they bounced off the padding of the couch. The top of her head was getting very hot. She loved the sun, but it always got the best of her in the end, leaving her toasted under her clothes. But the atrium days were special. Every Wednesday was a citizen holiday, when Isambard Fawkes had the cloudbuster machines part the fog and clouds above, allowing a spectacular column of sunlight to pour down upon the city. The miracle, the "pleasant four," only lasted about four minutes before the capacities of the big cloudbusters were exhausted, their great hums dying away. The fog and clouds would roll back again in, swaddling the world once more in endless gray.

A miniature locomotive train came chugging into the atrium along its elevated track, the tiny smokestack snorting little puffs of steam.

"Oh, picnic time in the sun!" Chelsea enthused, though she did not move. For such a thin woman, she was a great lover of food.

The small toy train, its flatbeds loaded down with decks of sliced roast beef, asparagus spears, Yorkshire pudding, strawberries, black toast, and butter, chugged up to a long banquet table and stopped there, its serving cars parked alongside waiting stacks of plates, utensils, lace napkins, and a bowl of sugary lemon punch. The atrium was full of tables, and the Wednesday sunlight picnic was a popular weekly event for the elites of the original Founders families in the palace.

"Where is your sister?" Chelsea asked. "She would not want to miss this."

"I do not know, Mother," Sabrina replied, her mouth watering. She wanted to eat all the strawberries.

Outside, the low hum of the cloudbuster stopped. The sunlight wavered overhead, lost its brightness, and faded away into the familiar soft grays of the clouds. Everyone in the atrium sighed, pausing to enjoy the last pulses of sunlight, only moving again when the shade had completely returned.

"Oh, well. That wasn't very long this time, was it?" Chelsea said, folding her skirt down her legs as she sat upright. "But lunch does look lovely, and fun!"

Sabrina glared at the miniature locomotive puffing on the rail, the shine of its polished brass and copper muted in the overcast light, and she felt angry with herself for having waited so long to come in and get some sun.

***

In the last second, Sabrina knew she was going to die. The dead kraken had slipped off into the void, and the great tentacle wrapped around her leg was dragging her over the precipice with it.

Suddenly, she jerked to a joint-popping stop, the heels of her boots dangling off the stern, the tentacle still coiled around her leg falling into a quivering heaviness of dead weight. Something bounced her calves, a pressure from below, and she knew that a gasbag had been pierced and was venting hydrogen, venting with a fury, for the bags had been overpressurized in the battle against the ice.

Sabrina looked up: Romulus Buckle stood over her, coated with ice and kraken blood, tall and handsome as ever, his blue eyes piercing behind his rimy goggles. He leaned into the wind with a yellow-splattered axe in his hand, having just severed the tentacle with one titanic blow, a blow that had also punctured the *Arabella*'s skin and the gasbag beneath it, and he gave her a victorious, white-toothed grin.

–XXVII–

THE UNBEARABLE
WEIGHT OF ICE

BUCKLE PULLED SABRINA BACK FROM the brink of the *Arabella's* envelope as the corpse of the kraken fell away into the swirling vortex of the Bloodfreezer, taking swathes of ratlines and rigging with it. It was a great relief to have ahold of her, rumpled as she was, gripping her knife, awash in both yellow and red blood. Their lives had just been hanging by threads—threads that the kraken had nearly cut—and they had saved each other.

For one instant—as Buckle dragged her back, the sudden softness of her breasts under layers of leather and fur against his arms, the dulcet swirl of her red hair in his nostrils—he was blindsided by an intense desire for the girl. Shocked, he shoved the feeling away. His blood was up and he was half-crazed. It was improper. Unmentionable. Insane.

Buckle grabbed Sabrina roughly by the collar, lifting her to her feet. He shoved his mouth close to her ear. "Are you still in one piece, Navigator?" he asked.

"Aye, Captain!" Sabrina yelled back, kicking the last suckers of the severed kraken tentacle loose from her bloodstained boot.

The world suddenly shifted from darkness to light, zapping Buckle's brain. The *Arabella* had breached the backside of the storm, escaping the lightning-fraught maelstrom and bursting out into the bright grayness of the daytime sky. His wide-open irises slammed shut, injured by the sudden brilliance even through his goggles' polarizing lenses, forcing him to squint. They hurtled high above an earth of endless snow-covered mountains, one pierced by the faraway purple tower of the Sequoia obelisk. He breathed easily, his tortured lungs no longer laboring against the brutal vacuum of the Bloodfreezer.

The zeppelineers on the roof of the *Arabella*, blinking in their ice-encrusted goggles, were thrown into weightlessness as the airship, heavy with jackets of ice and no longer suspended by updrafts, fell into a precarious drop.

As the crew of the *Arabella* battled for their lives against the kraken, the ice had collected voluminously on her gondola and flanks. Now it loomed in great, ghostly white humps on every surface—thick, deep, dense stuff, hard to crack, defiant of the axe. The weight was too much for the hydrogen-socked cells, too much for the engines and propellers, even as they churned up to screw-rattling whirls.

It was quite something, Buckle thought as he and Sabrina scrambled up onto the *Arabella*'s slick spine board. It was quite something to fight off a kraken, fly through a Bloodfreezer, and then go down to your doom, story untold, legend unforged, in an inglorious block of ice.

Buckle swung his axe, jagged cold bits biting into his face when the blade struck, as the rest of the crew continued whaling about the roof with axe, hatchet, and bayonet, left and right, the air around them exploding upward with glittering bursts of ice chips.

But Buckle knew no one could save the *Arabella* with the blade. "Reaper's breath, Mister Darcy!" Buckle shouted as the airship plunged. "We start amidships! Now!"

"Aye! Aye!" Darcy shouted, and took off toward the bow in a bent-low run, his broad body bearlike in his heavy greatcoat.

"But Captain," Sabrina shouted at Buckle's shoulder. "We have holes!"

"Get to the bridge, Lieutenant! Shut off the valves on the leakers and flush the pipes! Go! You have got one minute! Go!" Buckle shouted.

Aye!" Sabrina replied, and set off at a slippery run toward the observer's nacelle.

"Mister O'Brian, you are with me!" Buckle shouted. "And Mister Headford, you shall second Mister Darcy! Assist with the reaper lines!"

"Aye, Captain!" O'Brian and Headford, the hydroman, yelled back, hurrying forward. They were big men, and Buckle wanted big bodies anchoring the hoses.

"Mister Faraday!" Buckle howled.

"Aye, Cap'n!" Faraday answered, clutching an arm that looked to be broken against his chest.

"Get the rest of the hands below, you hear me? All hands below! Axemen work the keel and the gondola, but eyes up!" Buckle ordered.

"All hands below, aye!" Faraday replied. He spun and herded the rest of the crew forward with him. "If you ain't on the hoses, you are with me! Move! All hands below!"

Buckle peered toward the stern as the towering black wall of the Bloodfreezer fell away at considerable speed, though still blocking out everything to the southeast. He turned toward the bow, figuring the that the Arabella was now at twelve thousand feet altitude and dropping fast—they had a little time, but not much.

Darcy, O'Brian, and Headford, pink-faced and gasping, hauled two rubber reaper hoses out of the observer's nacelle, the ignition flames flickering restlessly in glass cases under the chins of the nozzles. Buckle took one hose as O'Brian jumped behind him. Buckle clamped his hand on the firing trigger—he did not want the hose going off before he was ready for it.

"Darcy," Buckle shouted. "We work out from here. You sweep aft. I'll take forward."

"Aye, Captain," Darcy yelled.

"The jackline is snapped! Attach your safety lines to the stanchions!" Buckle shouted over the wind. "And do not broil anyone by mistake."

Darcy waved at the mountains below, rising up with terrifying speed. "I'd much rather be toasted than cracked open like an egg, sir."

"Aye!" Buckle answered. Over the thunder of the rushing air, he heard a deep, metallic boom; glittering walls of water rushed upward past both flanks and disappeared. Sabrina had dumped the white-water ballast tanks. The *Arabella* bobbed, slowing her descent, but she was still in free fall.

Buckle clamped his safety hook to the rail of the observer's nacelle. He wrapped his gloved fingers around the heavy brass firing handle of the hose and aimed the nozzle at the wall of ice below, rippling in murky-white waves along the starboard flank, the weight of its mass already ripping the fabric loose of its stitchings. Reaper's breath—he had never been in a situation where he was required to use it before; it was the nastiest stuff imaginable for a zeppelineer, a pressurized mix of hydrogen, oxygen, and gelatin that, once fired through the ignition flame at the mouth of the nozzle, hurled a jet of liquid fire up to twenty-five feet in distance. Pure hydrogen was a safe commodity—near impossible to ignite—but hydrogen mixed with oxygen was as dangerous as any soup could be, an invisible phantom that could incinerate entire airships if given the opportunity.

Buckle hoped that Sabrina and Windermere had sealed off and flushed the leaking hydrogen cells and closed the valves; if not, once the reaper hoses engaged, they would all be launched into the afterlife in a blinding flash.

Buckle set his feet and slapped the copper firing handle back. The reaper hose thrashed, becoming violently alive in his hands as the nozzle erupted in a jet of fire. Leaning into the force of the recoil with O'Brian's husky weight at his back, he swept the geyser of flame across the roof and down the slope of the starboard flank. The ice splintered in resounding cracks, exploding in hissing sprays of water droplets, with big chunks of ice falling away under the steaming clouds. The envelope skin beneath, its fabric thickly doped with chemicals for strength and fire resistance, bubbled and curled and scorched black, sending up a stink like burned hair, but if one could maintain the angle of the jet at just the right height, one could destroy the ice and move away before the singed material actually caught fire.

It took three minutes for Buckle and Darcy, working both flanks, to clear the amidships envelope of ice—three minutes and five thousand feet of altitude. Buckle kept an eye on Darcy's progress aft, for too much clearance on one end would tip the *Arabella* precariously out of trim.

Buckle and O'Brian advanced on the bow, reattaching their safety lines to the forward grappling-cannon post. The axe team had done some good work on the roof here—the ice was hacked away in rough trenches—but when Buckle leaned over the port side and peered down, his stomach knotted: ahead, on the chin of the rounded envelope, where the canvas under the nose-hub window plunged down to the nose of the gondola, the ice had accumulated in a fantastic, grotesque riot, bulky and silvery white, deep as a man's arm.

Buckle signaled O'Brian and they rappelled down the wind-buffeted flank to the ratlines just above the gondola bulwarks. The airship fell at a dizzying speed, and the mountains, the bloody mountains, now looked huge, filling the horizon with sharply defined, snowbound peaks and valleys. They were now close enough for him to make out the black dots of individual trees.

There was no more than four thousand feet between the *Arabella*'s hull and the peaks. Her propellers could do her no more good, roaring beyond the limits of their manufacture, the port-side prop throwing bursts of smoke and making an unhealthy rattle.

Buckle slapped the reaper hose's firing trigger open, releasing the flame. He aimed low to counter the wind, and swung the blazing orange stream up and down the bow of the *Arabella*'s envelope. Wreathing waves of mist swept upward. Buckle worked his way topside, laying the column of fire as close to the skin as he dared, trusting O'Brian to support his back as the hose kicked at him. After a minute, the port side of the bow was relatively clear, a singed wall of smoking black. Buckle gave the top of the envelope a quick scrape of flames before he and O'Brian crossed the roof and rappelled down the starboard side.

The starboard side of the envelope was trapped under a massive iceberg, a curving wall of ice towering four stories high.

In his bones Buckle could feel the *Arabella* finding her wings, pulling out of her fall as her lift and propulsion escaped the terrible weight of the ice. But was it too late? Through his water-streaked goggles, Buckle saw the mountains heaving up over the airship on both flanks. Sabrina had turned the *Arabella* down the throat of a valley, buying them a few more seconds. Buckle could easily see the rocks in the ravines, the irregular patterns of the fir trees, the dotting of animal trails, the wide scars of countless avalanches scarring the slopes.

Three hundred feet left to fall, perhaps.

Buckle yanked the hose firing trigger and ripped the fire stream into the huge edifice of ice. The vortex of steam and water flooded back, battering him and O'Brian, now that the *Arabella* had gained forward momentum. Buckle raised and lowered the nozzle, seeking the seam between the canvas and frozen water.

The *Arabella* was almost level now, hurtling at a tremendous speed that bent the girders in the bow, but she was still slipping lower and lower. Their lives were now down to a matter of inches.

A long swath of pine trees, dark and green and dense, suddenly appeared under the bow nose. The prow of the gondola plowed into the treetops, instantly filling the air with the explosions of snapping branches, shearing rigging, popping tackle, and the sharp, sappy smell of pine.

It was as if the very world were coming apart right under Buckle's feet.

Buckle swung the river of fire against the envelope, separating the ice where it clung to the skin. Flame appeared in splotches across the blistering canvas, blinding Buckle with smoke, but the giant slab of ice shifted as it was separated from its perch. The frozen glass on the nose hub blew apart—a shivering belch of shards. The massive block of ice groaned, then dropped away from the airship in a long, canvas-tearing shiver, plunging into the trees in a hail of splintering wood and gunshot cracks.

The *Arabella* gradually lifted, found her stride, and swung up into the open sky.

Buckle shut off the reaper hose and hung still on his safety line, wafting in the slipstream of black water droplets and smoke, listening to the roar of the passing air and the sounds of the propellers and engines being throttled back a step. A surge of exhilaration dissolved into exhaustion as the sprawling earth fell away below the bow. He realized that both he and O'Brian were covered in ice and broken glass.

"Well done, Mister O'Brian," Buckle said, looking back at the stoker, whose left goggle was scarred black, the right one frosted white.

"Aye. And you as well, Cap'n," O'Brian said.

Buckle smiled, but he was suddenly worried about Max.

-XXVIII-

FORMULAE

Max was back in the Tehachapi Mountains, where the saber-tooths had bitten her, standing in the chamber of numbers, surrounded by the endless, charcoal-scribbled formulae. The cave overhead was roofless, open to a cloudless sky ablaze with stars. She knew she wasn't conscious but she was *there in the cave*, in mind, at least. Her body was lying on a hospital bed, far, far away.

Something was bubbling. Pinging. Boiling water in metal.

She had a lantern in her right hand, a lantern filled with golden morphine. Inside it, three wicks burned, three flames surging inside the liquid, casting gold-yellow light on the walls.

Everything was still. The fire in the potbellied stove was frozen in midflare, its pipe soaring straight up, disappearing into the sky.

Max peered at the numbers, but she could not see them well—they were blurred, distant, out of focus. Yet they drew her in, endless strings of questions ending in infinity symbols or furious slashes of charcoal. Everything, every number, was a quest to solve the immortality equation.

Furious charcoal scratches.

The immortality equation was a chimera, a dead end, an unsolvable wish.

Who were you? Who was the mathematician who locked himself or herself on a mountain for what must have been months, perhaps years, to struggle with a mystery he must have known he could not solve?

And yet, there was something there, something hiding under the streams of numbers that Max could sense but could not grasp, something that *did* suggest an answer. It was seductive, inviting obsession.

Immortality.

The bubbling grew louder.

A sharp metal *clang* echoed somewhere. Someone in the infirmary had dropped a bedpan, and it rang a wallowing note as it wobbled on the floor. The stink of disinfectant wafted past.

The numbers started moving, skimming slowly around the walls, positioning and repositioning themselves in never-ending columns, pausing at times, but never locking down.

Max stepped forward, lifting the lantern closer to the wall. Something bumped against the toe of her boot.

Max looked down. A small metal pot sat on the floor, shoved into the middle of a roaring campfire. The pot was full of boiling water, the surge of bubbles rising so violently that they rattled against the iron. A knife rested in the pot, the blade gleaming in the superheated roil.

The water was red. The pot was not full of water. It was full of blood.

Not matter how she tried, Max could not stop moving forward. Her boot struck the pot again, and this time it tumbled over. The blood spilled into the fire, sizzling, flashing, burning. Boiling blood flooded across the frozen floor, melting jagged channels in the ice as it coursed across it.

The floor was awash in blood. Her boots were sloshing in it.

Far away but coming closer, the sabertooths were roaring.

–XXIX–

OLD FRIENDS

MARTIANS LOOKED IMPLACABLE WHEN THEY slept, perhaps due to the expansive sweep of the white eyelids over the large eyes, Buckle thought. He sat alongside Max in the *Arabella*'s sick bay, his arms crossed on the back of the chair, his chin tucked on his left forearm, where the sleeve smelled of the rum he had just spilled across it. He felt the urge to close his eyes, to rest, but he did not shut them.

Max was far, far away. She lay buried under the launch's rough wool blankets, her breathing deep and slow under the morphine drowse. Her skin had lost a fraction of its paleness; her parted lips provided a glimpse of a reassuringly pink tongue nestled behind.

The stillness of the cabin, with the buglight motionless on its hook, encased Buckle in its warm cocoon, and he allowed himself to be lost in it. His body ached, he realized—the muscles racked by effort against ice and beastie, the ribs bruised, the back of his neck a blood-encrusted, stinging mess. He had been leading the *Arabella*'s repair teams for hours, as the crew stitched holes and hammered props up against deformed girders. But the noise of battle fell away from him now; there was only a zeppelineer's quiet in his ears, the cruising-airship lullaby of throbbing propellers, coursing wind, and creaking decking, matched by the low, soft beat of his heart.

Buckle was, for a moment, cloistered in ease, a man leading a different kind of life.

The man on the upper bunk moaned, and Buckle glanced up. It was Cornelius Valentine, the boilerman, heavily sedated, his right leg splinted and wrapped. Valentine was an old salt of the saltiest variety, older than much of the crew at the age of thirty-one, and a bit of a brawler and a barracks-room lawyer. Valentine had always been standoffish, always instinctively suspicious of officers. Buckle did not know him particularly well. The surgeons would most likely have to amputate the mangled leg, and Valentine was the kind of man whose life *was* his zeppelin—it would ruin him to be retired from the air corps.

The sick bay door sounded with a gentle rap, followed by the squeak of hinges. Sabrina slipped in, easing the hatch shut behind her.

"How is she, Romulus?" Sabrina asked.

"Reported to be resting well," Buckle whispered. "Nightingale says she is holding her own, despite the terrific bloodletting."

Sabrina gazed at Max. "Aye," she said under her breath. "Sabertooths—now there's a nasty beastie to meet up with in the dark."

Max was still secured in her bunk—it was a necessary precaution in winter weather, but the leather straps suddenly bothered Buckle. He considered removing them, but thought better of it. "How are things on deck?" he asked.

"We are running at five hundred," Sabrina answered. "Heading southeast as the crow flies. The damaged stern girder sections are jacketed, propped, and holding. Patches to skin and bags are holding."

"Very good," Buckle replied. His voice sounded distant to him, as if somebody else had spoken.

"Considering we just had tea with a Bloodfreezer and a kraken, I would say the launch got off lightly."

"Casualties?"

"Four lost—all missing," Sabrina said softly. "Martin Robinson, signalman; Hector Hudson, skinner; Carmen Steinway, skinner; and Henry Stuart, mechanic. Leaves us with eighteen souls aboard."

Buckle nodded. He had not seen what happened to Stuart. Good people. He knew the names. He knew them all. Zeppelineering was not for the faint of heart.

"Aye," Sabrina whispered, then carried on. "Injuries are a range of scrapes and bruises. The worst are Valentine, with his leg, and Faraday—a badly twisted left arm, though not broken. He lambasted Nightingale when she tried to sling it. Refuses to leave his post either way."

Buckle turned back to Max, resting his chin on his forearms again. He heard the fabric on Sabrina's arms rustle, felt her hands touch the collar of his shirt and pull the blood-crusted linen back.

"Oh, Romulus..." Sabrina sighed, both sympathetic and annoyed. "Why didn't you have Nightingale take care of this?"

"Forgot about it, really," Buckle said.

"Bollocks," Sabrina grunted through pursed lips. She turned to the washing basin and poured water into it from the decanter. Buckle heard the soft wind of a gauze roll unwrapped, the gravelly squeak of an iodine bottle unscrewed. "A kraken sucker latches on to the back of your neck, tears away a pancake of your hide, and it doesn't hurt like the blue blazes?" she huffed.

Buckle actually *had* forgotten about the wound, or at least, he had decided to ignore it. But *now* it hurt, hurt like hell, hurt like double hell. And Sabrina was about to dump iodine all over it.

Sabrina tugged the back of his shirt collar. "Unbutton the top of your shirt," she said. Buckle unbuttoned. She tugged again. He heard her huff again. "Sit up straight and put down your arms, will you?"

"Look, Sabrina—"

"Either lower your arms or I'll cut the shirt off you, Captain," Sabrina said.

Buckle sat up straight. Sabrina drew the loose collar back and dabbed the wad of wet gauze around the wound.

"The blood is frozen and dried," Sabrina said. "I lack nurse Nightingale's tenderness, but you'll get what you get."

Buckle winced as Sabrina wiped harder, the gauze feeling like sandpaper. He heard the clink of the iodine bottle and the gurgle of the liquid as she upended it against a bandage. His nostrils caught the brassy bite of the iodine.

"Here we go," Sabrina said. "Don't make a fuss."

Sabrina planted the iodine-soaked bandage on the wound. It felt as if it was covered in burning oil. Buckle refused to tighten up, refused to wince or shrug, but he did smile, it stung so badly.

"Mercy me, that has got to hurt," Sabrina mused. "This is one pretty rip. And a perfect circle, mind you."

"If I did not know you better, my dear erstwhile navigator," Buckle said, "I might suspect that you are somewhat enjoying my discomfort."

"Hold still, sir, please," Sabrina said as she scissored tape and secured the bandage into place.

"Of course, Doctor," Buckle said.

"I would like to say, sir, thank you for saving my skin out there on the roof today. I was certain I would be going over the side with the kraken."

"Mister Darcy informed me that you were the one who cut me down from the tentacle gallows I was in, so I would say were are quite even—in saving one another's skins, that is."

"Perhaps," Sabrina said.

Sabrina tucked Buckle's collar up over the bandage. He heard the deck board creak as she stepped back. "You should let Surgeon Fogg look at that when we get home. Either way, it is going to be one odd, round scar."

Buckle stood up, turning to face Sabrina in the cramped space of the cabin. "Thank you," Buckle said, buttoning up the top of his shirt. "I appreciate your concern, Doctor Serafim."

Sabrina nodded with a little smile. It was difficult to tell under her red ringlets, but Buckle thought her cheeks had taken on a hint of a blush. She had looked good up on the roof, swinging the axe and pistol, her fiery red hair loose around her pith helmet and goggles. "You should really just throw that shirt away," Sabrina whispered. "It being ruined with blood and kraken offal and whatnot."

"That I shall do."

"I have been told that there is a new bottle of Irish Standard's left alone in the captain's cabin, sir," Sabrina noted with a wry smile.

"And who told you that, Lieutenant?"

"Why, a little bird, Captain," Sabrina replied, grinning, her green eyes bluish in the yellow lantern light, and sparkling.

–XXX–

NEW FRIENDS

BLISTERS WERE RISING ON BUCKLE'S hands, the result of frantically wielding an axe into ice and kraken for nearly an hour. He peered at the raised red-and-white bubbles on his palms and fingers as he strode along the main passageway of the *Arabella*, scrutinizing the painful marks with the stoicism of a man who had just escaped death and now felt vaguely surprised at having suffered a hurt so small.

Ducking under a buglight on a thick wooden peg, Buckle shoved open the captain's door and stepped into a cabin barely a hair greater in length and width than the mole's den of a sick bay he had just left behind. There was just enough room for a bunk, a logbook desk, and a small table and chair. A fat, green glass bottle with the red-and-black label of Standard's Irish Rum rested on the table, along with half a dozen glass tumblers. The crew had already received a double ration of rum after the kraken fight, drained from Orkney barrels neat, not watered down, as usual.

The cabin smelled of lacquer—something had been recently varnished, and the gleaming logbook desk was the culprit. Buckle took hold of the desk, scraping its feet across the wood planking and using it to prop the door open to let the chamber air out. He collected the rum bottle and laid out the six glass tumblers in a line, then twisted the cork. The blisters on his fingers stung. His neck burned. His forearm ached. The three-week-old steampiper sword cut on his forearm still grumbled with pain. Blue blazes, he was well thumped. The cork, squeaking in the neck of the bottle, popped free.

The ponderous, sugary fragrance of the rum birthed a memory, a terrible memory descending from nowhere, unannounced, and he was unprepared for it. He saw his best friend, Sebastian Mitty, looking at him from the burning deck of the *Zanzibar*, the armed trader's decks collapsing, the hydrogen cells about to explode—a dead man looking out at him from the soft-edged realm of memory.

Buckle shoved the vision away. He did not wish to see the *Zanzibar* incinerate again, as she had done only once in the world, but a thousand times in his mind thereafter. The Imperial raid had been successful. The *Pneumatic Zeppelin* had been taken as a Crankshaft prize—as Buckle's prize. And Sebastian Mitty had lost his life. Such had been the deal that Lady Fortune cut. Such had been the price.

Pouring the honey-colored rum into the first tumbler, Buckle let it rise until it hugged the brim. When he raised the glass, the lukewarm alcohol sloshed out over his fingers. To Sebastian Mitty. He drained the glass and poured another. To the dead. He drained the glass and poured another. To the living. He drained the glass.

Buckle lowered the tumbler to the table with a deliberate movement, placing the glass between two wet rings of slopped rum, and filled it to overflowing again. He took a deep breath, still annoyed by the stink of the lacquer, despite the harsh reek of burning coal seeping in from the passageway.

A fist rapped on the door. Buckle turned to see the Windermere leaning in. "I have the updated damage reports,

Captain," Windermere said with a smile. "And I believe you have the good rum."

"Ah, so I do. Come in, come in, Master of the Launch. These are your quarters, after all."

Windermere ducked under the lintel and stepped to the table. "Not when you are aboard, sir. But I must admit to a desperately bruised ego regarding the matter—a stiff whack of Standard's would go a long way to speeding my recovery, sir."

"Here you are, wounded duck," Buckle said, passing the overflowing tumbler to Windermere.

"Thank you, Captain," Windermere said, holding the glass between thumb and forefinger to avoid letting the rum dribble from his fingers to the sleeve. In comparison, Buckle noticed, his own cuff was soaked with rum.

"How are we doing?" Buckle asked.

"Well, much better than we probably could ever have hoped, considering what we have been through."

"All so not very specific, Lieutenant," Buckle said with a false gruffness, the alcohol making him playful.

"No, sir. My apologies, sir. Ah, propulsion, engine, and flight systems are all good. The upper rudder fin is bent—the freaking kraken sat on it—but helm can handle it. The stern superstructure had to be triple propped, but the fixes are holding even at best speed. The increased drag is limping us a bit, but we should make it home by midafternoon, barring any further encounters with Bloodfreezers and krakens."

"Very good," Buckle said, raising his glass. "You handled the airship artfully in the storm, Mister Windermere. Well done."

Windermere shot his glass up quickly enough to splatter the deck with rum, an excited motion, then paused and tapped the lip of his glass against Buckle's. "Thank you, sir. I shall pass your compliments on to the crew."

"To the crew, living and dead," Buckle toasted.

"To the crew, living and dead, aye," Windermere repeated.

Buckle swallowed the rum—it was going down quite easily now, and when it started getting too easy he usually chose to stop.

"Ah, Standard's Irish," Windermere enthused, holding his glass up to the light to admire a trickle of the honey-brown alcohol pooling in the base. "Lovely."

Buckle slid the bottle to Windermere. "Help yourself to more of the 'lovely,' Lieutenant."

Windermere nodded as he plunked his glass down beside the bottle. "Perhaps in a moment. Thank you, Captain. I am not much of a drinker, I am afraid. Lightweight."

"Aye, a good predicament, however. The grog is nothing but a troublemaker," Buckle said, grabbing the bottle to pour another glass, which he threw back.

"How is First Officer Max doing? I have not yet had time to look in on her, I am afraid."

"Tough as Martians are, I am not so sure," Buckle replied. "Honestly, I think if it were either you or I who had absorbed such ravages, we would be sewn up in canvas sacks with pennies on our eyes by now. I think she shall make it."

"I would not bet against her, sir."

"Nor I," Buckle replied. He did not know Windermere well. Though of similar age, Andrew Windermere had been a sickly child, often excused from school and outdoor events, so Buckle had not grown up with him, as he had so many of the others. Later in life, when Windermere had recovered his hale-ness, they had always been posted to different training classes and airships. But upon Windermere's recent transfer to the *Pneumatic Zeppelin*, Buckle had immediately liked the lieutenant—liked his warmth, his genuineness and above all else, his ability.

Buckle took the silver phoenix emblem from his pocket and laid it on the table, right in the middle of a puddle of rum.

Windermere squinted at the insignia. He picked it up and rotated it back and forth between his fingers. "A Founders phoenix, sir?"

"A uniform pip. Freshly ripped from the collar of a dead zeppelin officer, frozen solid on the mountain."

"I see," Windermere said, looking Buckle in the eye. "So you found the mystery airship."

"It would appear so."

"And it was the Founders."

"Aye, though well disguised as Imperial."

Windermere placed the phoenix on the table, positioning it clear of the gleaming grog pools. "Shall this set us to war?"

"I would say we were already at war, whether we knew it or not."

Windermere nodded slowly.

"We all know that Balthazar and the council have been hearing rumors, reports that the Founders are on the move, gearing up for something big," Buckle said.

Sabrina entered, rapping her knuckles across the wood as she strode in. "How posh, gentlemen," she said, with a gleam in her green eyes. "I see you found the Standard's."

"Well on our way to knocking it off, Lieutenant," Windermere replied, tapping the brim of his hat to Sabrina.

"Well, while you are at it, please pour me a snort," Sabrina said.

Windermere slid a new glass forward and poured.

"We have news." Sabrina unrolled a hastily scribbled note and handed it to Buckle. "The lamp station at the Pondecherry outpost relayed this signal from home. The clan ambassadors are already arriving at the Punchbowl. Balthazar requests the *Arabella* return home at best speed."

Buckle nodded, refolding the cold paper and handing it back to Sabrina.

"He wants you to be there, sir," Sabrina said.

"He wants all of us there," Buckle replied.

"One more for each of us," Buckle said as Windermere handed Sabrina a nicely topped glass. Windermere quickly swamped the two already sticky tumblers and handed one to Buckle.

"If I may, Lieutenants, let us raise a glass to the Crankshaft clan and a new alliance," Buckle said.

"To the Crankshaft clan and a new alliance," Sabrina and Windermere answered.

All three shots of rum were swallowed, and the glasses thumped on the table. Buckle cleared his throat and stuck the Founders phoenix back in his pocket. "Keep us at best speed. Bang-up job, mates. I shall be on the bridge presently."

"Aye, Captain!" Sabrina and Windermere replied in unison and strode out, Sabrina in the lead. They passed Ilsa Gallagher, whom Buckle realized had been waiting patiently with a handful of papers out in the corridor, wearing mismatched boots because the kraken had stolen one.

"Ah, Miss Gallagher. Come in," Buckle said.

Ilsa stepped into the cabin. She wore her dense but tight-fitting leather skinner's jacket, resplendent with hooks, pockets, and strappings, her hair loose about her shoulders. The skin on her face was flushed, her eyelids heavy, her lips slightly parted, and she eyed him with the soft certainty of a hawk.

"You have the cordage numbers, I see," Buckle said. He suspected what was coming and, though he was exhausted, he was of no mind to prevent it. Ilsa occupied a soft spot in Buckle's heart; she was a good salt, an excellent rigger, tough, pleasant, fearless, extra pretty because she did not fuss about her appearance, and she had shared his bed with him occasionally over the stretch of the previous year. Theirs was a friendly, playful association, but not a romantic one: after their first night together, Ilsa had gently informed him that she could never love an airship captain, and Buckle had easily accepted her caveat, loose and unencumbering as it was.

Ilsa stepped closer, tossing the papers on the rum-splotched table and grabbing the bottle to take a long swig.

"Would you like a drink?" Buckle asked.

Ilsa kicked the hatch shut with a backward thrust of her boot. "The ratlines are fine, Captain," she whispered, snapping open a button at the throat of her collar, exposing a tiny patch of lily-white skin. "But I need tending to."

PART TWO:

COUNCILS OF LOVE AND WAR

~XXXI~

THE DEVIL'S PUNCHBOWL

SABRINA LIFTED HER HEAD FROM the eyepiece of the *Arabella*'s navigator's telescope and scanned the wide, snowy plain of the Antelope Valley as it led them southeast toward the Devil's Punchbowl, a Crankshaft stronghold. Formerly a pirate's den, it was built into a sprawling formation of massive sandstone rocks that erupted from the slope lands just below the San Gabriel Mountains. The flat stomach of the valley was beginning to undulate with gentle rises and shallows, the whiteness of its snows streaked by the dirty lines of the wagon roads that followed the cracked asphalt of the old highways underneath. Ragged black bunches of frozen Joshua trees and junipers passed thicker and thicker.

Sabrina resumed looking through the telescope eyepiece, ratcheting the viewfinder dial, rolling it around to its longest focal length, and the world sprang forward in a tight tunnel with the Punchbowl magnified in the middle. She could see the sentry towers with their red-and-white flags.

Her stomach warmed. She loved coming home. "Watchtowers in sight," Sabrina announced. "Altitude five hundred feet and descending. Airspeed, thirty-one knots. Light crosswind from the south."

"Helm compensating for crosswind, aye," Charles Mariner responded; the rudder wheel tocked once as he nudged it.

"Splendid," Buckle replied from his station behind Sabrina. "All ahead half."

Alison Lawrence cranked the chadburn dial. "All ahead half. Aye."

"All ahead half," cried Faraday on the chattertube, the chadburn engineering dial dinging the bell as it clicked into position.

Sabrina felt the *Arabella* begin to slow as she watched the brass dials of her airspeed mechanism and her altimeter winding down. "Airspeed slowing...twenty-five knots. Four hundred feet."

Something caught her eye over the mountains—a long, cigar-shaped shadow over the San Gabriel peaks, its outline silhouetted against the bright late-afternoon clouds. Sabrina flicked her magnifier lens into her scope and trained it on the hulking, familiar zeppelin. "*Khartoum* is on patrol, due south, high off the starboard bow."

"Very well, Navigator," Buckle replied.

Balthazar had invited all the clan ambassadors—with the exception of the Founders, of course—to his negotiating table in an emergency parley. But such an invitation was always a risk, as the debacle of the Palisades-Truce kidnappings had recently proved, and the big Crankshaft war zeppelins—the *Khartoum*, the *Waterloo*, and the pocket zeppelin *Constantinople*—were surely deployed at altitude in case an invitee tried to make a raid.

The bridge had gone momentarily quiet under the drone of the propellers. Even the chattertube, its hood usually amplifying a constant prattle, was still. The brass-and-copper daughter-compass casing at Sabrina's station rattled distractingly. "We shall need to apply a screwdriver to that, Welly," she said.

"Aye, Miss Serafim. Will do," Welly answered.

Sabrina glanced back at Buckle. He stood in the center of the *Arabella*'s crowded little bridge, his arms folded comfortably behind his back, Windermere and Wong hunched at the elevator station on his left hand, Mariner at the helm wheel at his back, and Alison Lawrence at the combined ballast and engineering station on his right.

Buckle gave Sabrina one of his wry, handsome grins, and she smiled back. She wanted to ask him how his neck was feeling, but she knew he did not like to discuss any of his own physical ailments in front of the crew. "If you live long enough to die a grizzled old bear in your bed, Romulus," Sabrina sometimes told him, "you will have no skin left but scars."

She turned to her altimeter, and the pain in her backside made her take a deep breath; her arse had taken a considerable beating when the kraken had dragged her across the roof.

Sabrina suddenly felt even more uncomfortable. She had seen Ilsa Gallagher standing in the passageway of the *Arabella*, waiting for the officer's meeting to end, waiting for them to leave, waiting to be alone with Buckle. Sabrina was well aware of the relationship Ilsa carried on with Buckle—the pretty, petite skinner could have the much-adored captain, strings free, apparently at her whim.

Bollocks. Sour grapes and dirty rotten apples.

Why did Buckle's much-noticed romantic entanglements, which were relentless, suddenly bother her so?

"Miss Frost," Buckle said. "Send a message: 'Two crew members critically injured. Request physician at the dock.' Use the lamp."

"Aye, Captain," Samantha Frost said. She was the *Arabella*'s gunnery officer, but now she was the acting signals crew person after the death of Martin Robinson. She moved from her hydrogen boards to the multihandled lamp and mirror controls of the signals station.

"And tell them that one of the wounded is the Martian, Miss Frost," Buckle added, stepping forward alongside Sabrina to snap out his telescope and raise it to his eye.

"Three hundred feet altitude, Captain," Sabrina said. "Twenty knots."

"Aye, Navigator," Buckle replied, the sandy-brown whiskers of his scruffy beard glowing with reds and yellows in the dull sunlight.

They were close enough now for Sabrina to see the flag signalman on the airfield tower, swinging his blue and red flags as he guided the *Arabella* in to her mooring hub.

"Harbormaster signaling mooring tower five," Sabrina announced.

"Mooring tower five. Aye," Buckle repeated under his breath.

The northern outskirts of the Devil's Punchbowl passed slowly under the *Arabella*'s port side—a bustling town of seven thousand people, with busy streets winding around the great rock outcroppings and guard gates, the air streaked by hundreds of drifting lines of forge and chimney smoke in every shade of black, gray, and white. Sabrina could make out the glimmering roofs of the greenhouses, their glass swept clean of coal dust, the long timbered tops of the merchant warehouses, and the squat brick octagons of the smithies. To the west, separated from the main town by a low ridge, stood the massive rubber factories, their rooftops lined with dozens of chimneys, all flooding every imaginable shade of black smoke into the sky, over gabled doorways glowing deep red with the heat of vulcanizing fires.

The city walls still lay another half mile southward, anchored deeper within the jumble of stone bastions that had provided an excellent defensive position for the pirate clans who had built the original fortress, and for the Crankshaft clan who had taken it as their own.

"One hundred feet altitude," Sabrina said. "Fifteen knots."

"Maintain one hundred," Buckle ordered.

"Maintain one hundred. Aye," Windermere repeated.

At the heart of the rock formation loomed the citadel, a stone-and-timber complex ringed by high crenellated walls, from which the endless town roofs with coal-blackened shingles radiated outward along dozens of narrow, crooked streets. Atop the highest tower of the citadel flew the Crankshaft clan banner, with the scarlet lion rampant on a white field. The elders always said the lion was stained the color of Crankshaft blood.

"Home, sweet home," Sabrina said.

–XXXII–

UNDER THE DEVIL'S CHAIR

THE CRANKSHAFT AIRFIELD LAY CRADLED in the wide space between the southern reaches of the town and the mountain foothills, forming its own city of mooring towers and monstrous hangars, with a busy population of ground crew. Watchtowers with mounted cannons stood at each corner of the airfield, connected by a high earthen wall crested with a palisade.

Buckle felt an excitement surging inside him at the sight of the airfield—the *Pneumatic Zeppelin* was there, so close he could *feel* her. But he could not see her—not yet. A row of moored airships largely blocked the view of her at her repair dock. Hands held behind his back, the impatient Buckle looked out the starboard side of the nose dome at the dull gleam of a large brass cannon barrel, a twenty-four-pounder, its black mouth traversing with his airship as it passed. The cannon was perched on the Devil's Chair, a high spur of rock overlooking the airfield, the watch crew cranking its revolving turret, tasked with keeping a bead on all new arrivals, regardless of what ensign they flew.

The Tehachapi Blitz had made the Crankshafts an untrusting bunch.

"Mooring tower five dead ahead, Captain," Sabrina reported. "Crosswinds still negligible. Airspeed at ten knots."

"Aye, Navigator," Buckle replied. The *Arabella* passed down the center of the airfield now, through canyons of mooring towers and docked zeppelins, all of them cranked down so hard on their hawser lines that their gondolas nearly touched the earth. Buckle turned to Windermere. "Descend to fifty feet."

"Fifty feet. Aye!" Windermere repeated.

"Five knots," Buckle said.

"Five knots. Aye!" Lawrence repeated, swinging the chadburn to quarter full.

The *Arabella* slipped down to fifty feet like a feather. Maneuvering the launch, even bent and dented, was a dream compared to the heaving and nudging required of a big sky vessel like the *Pneumatic Zeppelin*.

"Take her in, Master of the Launch," Buckle said to Windermere. "The bridge is yours."

Windermere strode forward. "Aye, Captain."

Buckle turned back to the nose window. Three thousand feet overhead, visible in the upper frames of the glass, he espied the sharklike silhouette of the great Crankshaft flagship, the *Khartoum*, steaming overhead, her bronze-cased propellers whirring slowly at half full, her three copper gondolas gleaming in the sunlight. The *Khartoum* was Admiral Balthazar's airship, though Buckle was certain that Balthazar was not aboard her right now—her captain, Pandora Malebari, most likely commanding—for Balthazar would be in the thick of things on the ground.

Buckle craned his neck, but he still could not get a decent look at the *Pneumatic Zeppelin*. He mollified himself by scanning the airships looming at each flank; most of them were clan tramps, but the fast Crankshaft clipper, the *Ladybird*, was also there, along with two of the long-distance armed traders, *Peregrine* and *Avalon*.

Then, as the *Arabella* cleared the *Ladybird*, the massive, beautiful, cigar-shaped dun envelope of his own airship, the *Pneumatic Zeppelin*, came into view, moored to the repair dock where Buckle had left her three days before. Buckle's heart drummed. She looked good, floating easy on her hawsers, her gasbags plumped to carry loaded shot lockers, brimming coal bunkers, and full water-ballast tanks. It looked as if the repairs to her main envelope were complete—he could see only one skinner on the roof, bent over a canvas seam. Though he could not make out his face, he guessed from the shape of him that it was probably Rudyard Tuck.

There was still plenty of activity in the work stands of the repair dock under the *Pneumatic Zeppelin*; handfuls of ground crew were active in the shadows a few feet below her gondolas; victualing wagons and repair pallets crowded the access road of the refitting wharf, beneath. Buckle grimaced. Three weeks in repair dock, and they were still provisioning and banging his airship back into shape? He was itching to get his zeppelin airborne again.

"Imperial ambassador's rig to port, Captain," Sabrina said. "The *Briar Rose*."

Buckle eyed the small Imperial airship with great interest—she was a corvette not much larger than the *Arabella*, the black iron cross adorning her gray envelope. Her design bore a striking resemblance to that of the *Pneumatic Zeppelin*, though with a sleeker envelope, a single teardrop gondola, and six driving propellers: she was built for speed. With the polished copper gleam of her gondola, and its fine glass windows, the *Briar Rose* was a stately craft. While most clan warships and traders were somewhat hodgepodge affairs, their gondolas and belly armor bolted together from whatever metals could be had in quantity at the time, the ambassadorial airships were usually uniform in materials—built to impress.

Alongside the *Briar Rose* hulked the much rounder and less aerodynamic form of the Alchemists' ambassadorial ship, the *Pollux.* Buckle had never seen an Alchemist airship before. The Alchemists were groundlings—one of the nonaviator clans— and they usually paid neutral clans for use of airships when they needed them. Buckle had heard of their ambassadorial ship, an oddity because it was one of the few sky vessels the Alchemists had made for themselves. The fact that it looked more like a geometric cluster of balloons than a zeppelin reflected the Alchemist desire to proceed slowly through the air, an element they distrusted.

The *Pollux*'s round gondola glittered with layered metal cogs interlinked together like sheets of chain mail. It was a windowless, unendearing beast—the opposite of the *Briar Rose.* Dozens of sooty black chimney tubes protruded from the center of the roof, their heads angled away from the gold-painted balloons above, releasing small dribbles of white smoke as the crate grumbled on her hawsers.

"Airship approaching!" the lookout's voice rang down the chattertube from the observer's nacelle. "Twelve o'clock high!"

Buckle stepped alongside Welly and peered out the nose, scanning the sky with his bare eyes and finding the dark dot against the southern clouds before swinging up his telescope. The magnifying lens caught the zeppelin's head-on oval silhouette; it was a long way off, perhaps fifteen miles, but from the looks of her smoke trail, she was coming hell-bent for leather, and she looked big.

Buckle lowered his telescope and snapped it shut. "I cannot make out who it is, but they are late," he muttered. Something about the size of the airship bothered him. Who was bringing a pistol to a tea party?

"So are we," Sabrina said, never taking her eyes off her altimeter.

"But we are fashionably late," Buckle replied, a little too jauntily for his own taste, he decided. His eye caught the gleam of the brass cannon on the Devil's Chair, now a good distance behind their stern, being cranked upward—the new arrival had caught the eye of the watchdogs as well. Good.

Tucked in against the much larger flank of the *Pneumatic Zeppelin* a tiny but familiar sky vessel floated, a Brineboilers yawl, the *Beryllium*, the copper sheathings of its gondola turned a dozen streaming shades of dark and light creamy green by the sea air of the western coast. The Brineboilers were more a chemists' guild than a clan, the distillers of the bioluminescent boil, among other expensive concoctions. Their livelihood depended upon commerce, and their small green-oxidized airships, with their tapering white envelopes, were a common sight in the skies over the Snow World.

A short distance beyond the *Pneumatic Zeppelin*, on the opposite side of the docking row, tight on its hawsers, floated the *Cork*, the ambassadorial corvette of the Gallowglasses, the most powerful inland clan, and secretive masters of many of the trade routes into the vast, mysterious American continent beyond the Eastern Pale. The aggressive, brawling personality of the Gallowglasses, who called themselves the Irish, was reflected in the appearance of the *Cork*; unkempt and strong, a big corvette constructed not for looks, but rather with a love of muscle and battle scars. Her once snow-white envelope, with its emerald-colored harp symbol, was mottled, stained, and dense with shot-hole patches. Of her two gondolas, both armored, pied in more types of metal than Buckle could count, the forward hull carried four cannon ports—that many cannons was unusual aboard such a small airship—while the rear engineering gondola, soot-stained and blackened, bulged with vents and chimneys that hinted at boilers far larger than a sky vessel that size would need. Even the propellers appeared outsize.

Decorating the bow of the *Cork*'s lead gondola loomed a battered and worn but wonderfully carved figurehead—a fierce-looking woman with voluminous bare breasts, glaring at all enemies forward.

"The nipples are too small," Sabrina grumbled. "On a woman endowed in such a fashion—the nipples are far too small."

"My dear Lieutenant," Buckle said. "On a woman endowed like that, who would care?"

Windermere laughed out loud, but a glare from Sabrina caused him to cut it off abruptly.

Buckle glanced back and forth across the airships and hangars. Key players were missing. The ambassadors of the Tinskins and Spartak were glaringly absent—they were two huge clans, rich both in airships and armaments—and their partnership could easily tip the balance of the impending war. The Tinskins were notoriously slippery. But the Russians of Spartak, difficult to negotiate with, were said to be forthright in their associations. Balthazar would have to find a way to bring Spartak into the alliance.

"Fifty feet to mooring tower five, on the nose, Mister Windermere," Sabrina announced. "Approaching at four knots."

"All stop," Windermere said, cranking the chadburn dial. "Prepare to dock and down ship."

"All stop, aye!" came the engineering response down the chattertube, the bell dinging on the chadburn.

The *Arabella* responded nicely, her maneuvering propellers a lazy, chopping whirl as she hedged forward.

Soon they would be on the ground with Balthazar and the ambassadors, in the midst of their diplomatic maneuvering and distrust. In a way, Buckle did not want to land.

-XXXIII-

HORATIO CRANKSHAFT

Buckle and Sabrina accompanied Nurse Nightingale and four stretcher bearers as they carried Max and Valentine's litters down the *Arabella*'s loading ramp. Buckle could still taste Ilsa's rum-warmed tongue in his mouth. He remembered Max's cold lips trembling against his in the cave and felt vaguely guilty. The pleasant atmosphere was quickly erased by the acrid slap of the town air—laden with the smoke of wood and coal fires—and the relentless smell of Burbage tar, cordage, envelope canvas, and the chemical-garlic stench of fabric-stiffening dope permeating everything around the airship docks.

Above them, the *Arabella* floated, the winched-down anchor lines securing her keel to the wooden structure of the repair dock; she was a battered sight, with her stern partially caved in, roof tangled with rigging debris, and the envelope flanks ripped and singed black by reaper's breath. Repair crews were already clambering up onto the dock platforms, attaching their rope ladders and unloading fabric boles and belts loaded with tools. Mooring dock five, one of the three repair docks, was hemmed in on three sides by docked zeppelins, but if Buckle looked north, straight ahead, he could just see the tops of the citadel's watchtowers over the boulders between the airfield and the town.

Doctor Fogg, waiting at the bottom of the gangway with his ambulance wagon and its horse team, rushed forward to the litter. "What have we got?" Fogg asked. The stretcher bearers halted as Fogg lifted Valentine's blanket and peered at his heavily bandaged leg.

"Boilerman Cornelius Valentine. Femur and knee joint are shattered, Doctor," Nightingale said. "Kraken got hold of him."

"Kraken?" Fogg muttered with a detached surprise. He pressed the back of his hand against Max's forehead. She lay nestled under heavy blankets and a thick wool infirmary cap, looking content, asleep under her morphine, the definition between her stark-white skin and the gray stripes looking more ghastly out in the overcast sunlight. Buckle could not escape how much blood he had seen pour from her body.

"Sabertooth attack," Nightingale said. "A single penetrating bite just above the left clavicle. Severe claw lacerations down the back."

Fogg nodded in his reassuring fashion, as he always did, even when he dealt with the mortally wounded. He pressed his fingers against Max's jugular, lowering his head as he concentrated on the pulse.

"When did this happen?"

"Yesterday evening," Buckle said.

Fogg lifted Max's eyelids, scrutinizing the jerk of each black iris. "She lost a lot of blood, did she?"

Nightingale nodded. "Yes. Severe exsanguination."

"I am worried more about infection than the blood loss," Fogg said, more to himself than anyone else. He motioned for the stretcher bearers to follow him to the cart.

Buckle strode down the gangplank alongside Fogg. "It took a while for me to get to her. I cleaned the wounds as best

I could and slathered them with Fassbinder's before I bandaged her up."

"And I changed her dressings when we got her aboard this morning," Nightingale added. "No sign of infection, Doctor."

"And she's been on morphine the entire time?" Fogg asked.

"Yes," Buckle answered. As they reached the end of the ramp, his boots sank into the churned slush of the access lane, a brown mix of half-frozen snow, horse manure, coal dust, and mud. Buckle followed Fogg to the front of the wagon, while Nightingale led the stretcher bearers to two orderlies in white coats waiting at the rear.

"What is your appraisal of their conditions, Doctor?" Buckle asked Fogg.

"It looks like Valentine will lose the leg. As far as the lieutenant—she is a Martian. What do I know about Martians? Bloody upside-down anatomy," Fogg said, climbing up into the front seat of the wagon and collecting the reins. A chubby stray dog—the airfield crew must have been feeding him—yipped at the horses before tucking its tail between its legs and scuttling away. "But if I were a gambling man, which I am not, I would not bet against that extraordinary Martian constitution."

"Nor would I," Buckle said.

Fogg snapped the reins with a shout of "Ha!"

Buckle watched the four buckskins stamp, lurching forward and settling into a good pace down the lane as the ambulance wagon lumbered behind.

"They will both come out all right, Captain," Sabrina said at Buckle's shoulder. "I am sure of it."

Buckle smiled at Sabrina. She always had the ability to soothe him, even in the worst predicaments. But her red hair—the two red ringlets curling from beneath the sides of her derby—angered him somehow, in an obscure yet intense way, a dagger behind a curtain. If she had once been a member of the Founders clan, she must know some of their secrets, so she was choosing to keep those secrets from him.

"Your transport is arriving, Captain!" Windermere shouted from the weather deck of the *Arabella*, leaning out under the arch of the envelope skin, pointing to the access road.

"Very good, Mister Windermere," Buckle said, then turned to Sabrina. "Go over to the *Pneumatic Zeppelin* and double-check the repairs with Ivan. I want her ready to go."

"Aye, aye," Sabrina said, striding away toward the repair dock.

A tall man riding on a black horse clopped up, leading another mount by the reins; unlike his heavyset brother, Horatio Crankshaft was long and lean and straight as a yardarm, with the pointy-chinned face of a heron. He wore a long gray riding cloak over his dress uniform, with white gloves. His hair and beard were cropped short, and white as snow. Horatio was a field officer to the bone: where his brother Balthazar was diplomatic and resolute, Horatio was brutally honest and daring—not an accomplished tongue biter—and while he was rarely invited to the negotiating table, much to his relief, his inborn aggression made him the best warship captain in the fleet.

Buckle bore great affection for Horatio, whose temperament more closely matched his than Balthazar's. In the early years, the uncle had proved a far more rambunctious playmate than Balthazar tended to be. Horatio was a tester, a teaser, always challenging his nieces and nephews, not to mention raising five refined but headstrong daughters of his own. And while Balthazar had always kept tight purse strings with his children, thriftiness being a cardinal virtue he admired, Horatio was the uncle who showed up with coins jingling in his pocket that were not there when he left.

"Mount up, nephew," Horatio said. "Negotiations are about to begin."

"And you gallop off on escort duty, sir?" Buckle asked, grinning, planting his boot in the second horse's stirrup and swinging up into the saddle.

"Balthazar wants you there and not I, thank the milk goat's tits. I am merely the messenger boy," Horatio said. It was vintage Horatio. "Who is in the ambulance?"

"One of my boilermen. And Max."

Horatio's eyes widened a bit. He was quite fond of Max. "Is it bad?"

Buckle nodded. "Sabertooth."

"Bah!" Horatio grinned, the teeth-gritted kind of grin he got when action was imminent. "If she is still alive, she shall make it. Martian blood courses with particles of steel, do not forget. Now, you need to get inside and get washed up. You look like you've been dragged through dung."

"And kraken dung, at that," Buckle said with a wink.

Horatio raised an eyebrow at Buckle. "Now, there is a tale I'll want to hear when I've got some rum in me. But now, let us go. Ha!" Horatio dug his spurs into the flanks of his favorite horse, a gray-speckled gelding named Bourbon, and the big animal took off down the access road. Buckle's horse, a brown mare, spun and followed at a gallop, without Buckle having to do much encouraging at all. It was exhilarating to be on the horse's back, its unruly mane whipping back and forth under his face, the jangling bridle, the points of his weight in the stirrups, and for a moment Buckle was able to forget his exhaustion, his multitudinous worries.

But nothing could make him forget Elizabeth.

–XXXIV–

PINYON HALL

BUCKLE STRAIGHTENED HIS SPINE, NOT wanting his nerves to get the best of him as he strode across the courtyard of the citadel. He looked at his pocket watch, turning the winder, and walked quickly. It had taken him and Horatio over twenty minutes to ride through town to the citadel, and another half hour to get washed and dressed. He feared he would be late, although no one seemed to have any idea of what time the proceedings might begin. A light breeze whirled in through the high gate, fluttering the scarlet-and-white banners festooned across its stone face. The courtyard was bustling—the whole place was buzzing—at the arrival of the ambassadors. Buckle dodged past rushing servants, milling surreys, and soldiers on horses whose hooves clattered on the courtyard flagstones.

This was the first time Balthazar had invited Buckle to attend a negotiation session with an outside clan, and Buckle feared that he had no aptitude for the subtleties and nuances of such a strained parley. At least he looked presentable—he knew that—with his white pith helmet tucked under his right arm and his left hand on the scabbard of his saber. He felt rather proper and pinched inside his crimson dress uniform, with tight gold buttons that made him feel propped up. The high collar choked him—if he took the time to notice it—and the pressure of the cloth against the bandage on the back of his neck scraped like a branding iron. Damned kraken. He much preferred his airman togs—the leathers and wool fit loosely, and let a man breathe.

Buckle's head felt tight, his longish hair combed back and held in place in the stiff clamp of Cottington's Gentleman's Cream, and he was scrubbed, scrubbed pink, at least about the face and hands. The twins Jasmine and Jericho, the youngest of Balthazar's adopted imps, had helped the servants lay out Buckle's uniform in his chamber, pestering him with wide eyes for the story of the kraken as he stripped and dressed. Burgess Sibley, the family butler, had ushered the youngsters out, but not before he had trimmed Buckle's beard with scissors; picking up a straight razor from his barber's kit, he had vainly argued that he be allowed to shave off Buckle's "bird's nest of a beard."

Buckle charged up the broad front steps of Pinyon Hall, a sprawling stone-and-log structure and the heart of the Crankshaft government.

"Tin-headed bastards! Too fast!" the captain of the guard shouted from atop the gate, pointing upward.

Buckle glanced behind him. A gigantic oblong shadow passed overhead, like an eclipse blocking out the sky. It was a huge airship, flying very low, the keels of her four gondolas no more than seventy-five feet above the tops of the watchtowers— a Tinskin war zeppelin, emblazoned with old Spanish coats-of-arms, Aztec hieroglyphs, and snake heads, her gun ports bristling with cannons. The sky vessel's mass appeared so great from Buckle's position under its shadow, it seemed that if it were to drop, it might crush the entire stronghold under its immensity.

The Tinskin airship was coming into the airfield. Her exhaust pipes sizzled, the engines having just been shut down, leaving her momentum to carry her the last half mile; the strangely quiet airship split the air with the windy *hiss* of her canvas, her six titanic bronze props turning languidly. Tinskin airmen, dressed in overalls gleaming with armor plates and square-lensed goggles strapped over morion helmets, peered stoically down at Buckle as they perched at their docking stations amidst the rigging, mooring ropes at the ready in their hands.

The zeppelin *Khartoum*, wheeling above, obviously unhappy with the appearance of a first-rate warship, had fired up her boilers with great blasts of white steam from her exhausts, and had dropped to four hundred feet to shadow the Tinskin behemoth.

Buckle stumbled on the steps. It was difficult to take his eyes off the Tinskin zeppelin as it swept off to the south, the great length of its underbelly ending in a bank of gleaming propellers and revealing the bright sky behind its rudder. Buckle studied the black emblem of an eagle clutching a snake looming on its straw-yellow flank and experienced a mixture of awe and anger. He had never seen a Tinskin airship up close before—it was an awesome construction—but he was also infuriated by the clan's lack of decorum; it was brutally indecent to dispatch a warship on an ambassadorial mission.

Buckle did not know a great deal about the Tinskins, but Balthazar had once told him that intimidation, veiled thinly if veiled at all, was the primary grease of their negotiating tactics. The Tinskins were a military clan, operating dozens of well-outfitted zeppelins in the skies to the far south, and their suzerainty over those lands made them haughty, overbearing, and aggressive. "Bring a Tinskin to the negotiating table," Balthazar would say, laughing but with a serious blue coldness behind his gray eyes, "and treat him as a poisonous snake whose venom you need for an antidote."

But the Crankshafts needed the Tinskins, especially if the Spartak clan remained aloof from the proceedings. And the Tinskins would be well aware of it.

Within the towering pine doors of Pinyon Hall, the great public chamber of the citadel, servants dashed about with decanters and chair cushions. The ambassadors were still sequestered, making their own last-minute preparations. Buckle marched alongside the huge pine table that dominated the center of the rectangular chamber, thirty chairs on each side. Narrow glass windows in cast-iron frames soared up three stories on each flank, all the way to the heavy timber crossbeams of the roof, allowing sunlight to flood the hall. It was the best lit room in the citadel, and there was no need for lanterns or candles during daylight hours.

Balthazar's ready chamber was located behind a small door at the head of the hall. Four Gallowglass attendants—three men and one woman, none of them peacocked enough to be the ambassador—emerged from an adjoining corridor and stopped, eyeing Buckle with a muted hostility. They wore light-green tricornered hats and fine dark-green cloaks clamped at the throat with gold frogs, but despite their finery, their faces seemed tavern lit, bull eyed, quick to take offense, oozing a street-hardened brawn.

Buckle offered the Irish nary a sideways glance, walking straight on to Balthazar's door, where he delivered a rap of his knuckles to the wood. The eyes of the Gallowglasses bored into his back, and he felt a touch of relief when Balthazar's voice boomed from within.

"Enter!"

He stepped into the chamber, a medium-size compartment with a low timber roof. A crackling fire burned in the stone hearth on the left wall, its yellow glow lost in the gray light flooding in through the large window at the front; a seven-foot-tall grandfather clock hugged the wall opposite the fireplace, the tight click of its pendulum mechanism beating behind the quiet. The large desk had a lantern on it, the oil wick lit—strange for that time of day, but not if it had been brought in by someone emerging from one of the pitch-black secret passages that abounded in the stronghold. The pirates who had built the place had been overly fond of secret chambers and passageways—even after thirty years of occupation, the Crankshafts would stumble across new ones now and again.

Balthazar stood behind the desk, leaning on his hands, his black evening coat bunched about his armpits, peering down at a set of papers. To his left stood Ryder, his only natural-born child and the eldest (not counting the unknown ages of the half-Martians), who had inherited the short, burly form of his father, though he was well squared in his dress cavalry reds.

Balthazar's hoary head jerked up. "Romulus. Good of you to make it."

"Hello, Father," Buckle said, shutting the door behind him.

"Hello, brother," Ryder said.

"Good to see you, Ryder," Buckle answered. Although his relationship with Ryder had always been a cool one, he did feel a healthy connection to his brother. There had been a surly competitiveness between them as boys, but once they had outgrown the eye-spitting and fistfights, with maturity, they found common ground. Buckle had shown an early affinity for daring and zeppelins, but Ryder had eschewed such wild pursuits, preferring rather to develop himself into a cavalry officer, and one of

Balthazar's most capable diplomats. Buckle had won his captaincy early—by taking the *Pneumatic Zeppelin* as a prize—and Buckle knew that it irked Ryder to watch his more flamboyant brother achieve such glories.

Ryder's right arm was in a sling; he was still recovering from the wound he had received—a sword thrust to the ribs while defending a doorway—attempting to shield his father the night he was abducted by the Founders at the Palisades Truce. It had pained Ryder greatly to be left behind, unable to participate in the raid to rescue Balthazar from the City of the Founders.

"It was Max in the ambulance wagon, was it?" Balthazar asked, his face tight.

"Yes, Father," Buckle said. Seeing the worry in Balthazar's eyes for his daughter almost hurt Buckle more than when he held her, bloody and near death, in his arms.

"Are her wounds grave?" Balthazar asked. Buckle noticed Balthazar's left hand twitching—not in a convulsive, uncontrollable way, but a rapid rubbing of the fingers.

"Aye. Sabertooths. She lost a great deal of blood."

Balthazar nodded, his gaze angled toward the floor. He pulled at his white silk tie with a thick finger—Buckle knew he hated it. "Well, she is in Doctor Lee's capable hands now."

"And Surgeon Fogg is with her as well," Buckle added.

"I shall check in on her immediately after the proceedings," Balthazar said. He drew his ornate pipe out of his pocket and clamped it between his teeth, making no attempt to light it. It was something he did when he was upset.

"Martians are resilient, Father," Ryder offered.

"She is only half-Martian," Balthazar said softly, turning to look out the window with its murky glass that overlooked the back of the citadel, the town, and the snowy foothills beyond.

The daylight was softening, preparing for its long fade into night. He cleared his throat. "That I relented—that I let you go on that damn fool mission up into the mountains..."

"I found what I was looking for," Buckle said. He reached into his pocket and placed the silver Founders phoenix collar pip on the oak table with a solid little *click*.

The sound made Balthazar turn around; both he and Ryder stared at the pin. Ryder made a low, barely audible whistle and picked it up, scrutinizing it in a shaft of sunlight.

"Ripped from the collar of a frozen corpse, an officer, trapped in the ruins of a Founders zeppelin—the one we shot down over Tehachapi—a zeppelin disguised as an Imperial war machine," Buckle said.

Balthazar looked at Buckle and then to Ryder. "So it was the Founders who attacked us at Tehachapi."

"I owe Katzenjammer Smelt an apology," Buckle said, even though he could not believe that *he* was saying it. It actually pained him to say it. "He was telling the truth, after all."

"I still would not trust him," Ryder said.

"Have I taught you nothing, Ryder? One can trust one's ally without exposing one's back," Balthazar said. "We were fools," he growled. "Falling for the Founders' deceptions, lock, stock, and barrel. They bomb us and we raid the Imperials in return. The cutthroat dogs!"

"And we did a fairly good job of it, did we not?" Ryder added. "We limped over to New Berlin and tore the Imperials up nicely."

The three men stood in silence, the profound *ticktock* of the grandfather clock suddenly loud in Buckle's ears. Balthazar switched his cold pipe back and forth between his teeth a few times, stopped, and looked at Buckle. "Anything else?"

"Just this," Romulus said, pulling the Founders papers he had liberated from the wreck out of his pocket and laying them on the table. The thin parchments, yellowed and brittle from frost, were covered in handwritten notes. "I found these in the wreck, but they are nothing more than provision and navigation records."

"Have Silas look them over," Balthazar said to Ryder.

"Yes, Father," Ryder answered, carefully folding the papers into his uniform pocket.

Balthazar set his jaw. "Our only hope against the Founders is a grand alliance, an alliance we must forge this very day. We have near a full house: Alchemists, Imperials, Brineboilers—even the Gallowglasses. And the Tinskins have just arrived."

"I saw their war zeppelin on the way in, aye," Buckle said softly, picking up the Founders pip and tucking it back in his coat pocket.

"Infamous buggers," Ryder grumbled.

"It looks as if Spartak has not responded to our invitation, however," Balthazar said.

Buckle felt a knot rise in his throat. "We need Spartak with us. We are better off without the Tinskins. We can manage without them."

"Not if they join the Founders, we cannot," Balthazar replied sharply, then softened his tone. "Both Andromeda Pollux and Katzenjammer Smelt are here in person, at my request; their presence adds a great weight to the proceedings. Together, we should be able to manage the Tinskins."

"Lady Andromeda has a calming effect," Ryder added. "And that is no small advantage, considering who is out there. This whole thing could quickly get out of hand."

Balthazar sat at the desk and rubbed his eyes. It surprised Buckle that Balthazar took the seat—he never sat down in times of crisis. He was still his old self—the lion—but he looked tired, frailer than Buckle remembered. He looked smaller.

"Obviously we cannot trust the Tinskins much," Balthazar said. "The Imperials possess excellent warships, but they are few in number, decimated as they are, as are we. The Alchemist machines are capital, but they are groundlings. The Gallowglasses have many airships, but they vary immensely in quality, mostly on the lower end, and their discipline is poor. The Brineboilers are militarily insignificant, but to deny the Founders their chemicals would be no small thing. It is also vital that we win the support of the All Blacks with their coal. But we need Spartak's Grand Fleet to stand any chance at all. We need Spartak."

The grandfather clock bonged, counting its way toward five o'clock.

Balthazar collected his official papers on the desk and thrust the stack to Ryder, who tucked them in a leather valise. "Well, boys, time to take tea with the vipers," Balthazar said.

–XXXV–

VALKYRIE SMELT

BACK IN THE MAIN CHAMBER of Pinyon Hall alongside Balthazar and Ryder, Buckle felt oppressed. The lofty ceiling and airy space of the towering chamber made no difference. Politics involved endless talking, a polite chat with hidden daggers. A spider's game. He would rather be fighting the kraken—at least it was an honest foe.

"Fellow ambassadors and friends, you honor me with your presence here today," Balthazar said, throwing his arms open in a sweeping gesture. He looked big again. "Please be seated. I am afraid we have things both heavy and fearful to discuss!"

The ambassadors and their small retinues, clustered uneasily in separate groups of vastly different fashions and colors, moved to the table. The three other members of the Crankshaft clan's contingent stood waiting alongside Balthazar's chair: Rutherford Washington, the clan's hoary old chief ambassador, in an expensive black suit and tails; Orlando Churchill, pirate king turned respectable—and fabulously wealthy—merchant and mayor; and Silas Greenbriar, fingers stained with ink, the clan historian.

"I am sure that most of us are well acquainted, but please allow me a moment to make some brief introductions," Balthazar said. "I am most honored to welcome Andromeda Pollux and the Alchemist clan to our parley table."

Lady Andromeda was on the immediate left of Buckle. She sat comfortably in an ornate brass-and-iron wheelchair powered by a small steam engine. Buckle thought she looked weak, her cheeks and forehead crow's-footed with pink marks from the shrapnel that had cut her during her rescue from the Founders' prison, but her dark violet-black eyes were clear and resolute. Caliban Kepler was at Lady Andromeda's back, big as an ox in his double-breasted white riding coat. General Scorpius was also there, the copper astrolabe on his breastplate agleam in the sunlight.

Andromeda nodded graciously to Balthazar, and then looked at Buckle; he saw both kindness and sadness in her glance as she smiled at him. She was so genuine that it seemed she could never lie—a powerful attribute. Buckle received a strong sense that Andromeda had something to say to him, but this was neither the time nor the place for it.

"We are also honored to welcome Mace Mardigan and the diplomats of the Gallowglass clan," Balthazar said.

Buckle followed Scorpius's glare across the table to the Gallowglass ambassador.

Mace Mardigan, a portly, hound-faced fellow in forest-green tails, slapped his tricornered hat with its white cockade on the table. Mardigan seemed to have absorbed the looks of both a buccaneer and a purser: his thin hay-colored hair, laced with a white ribbon at the back of his neck in piratical fashion, and his beefy, scarred knuckles spoke of a life of action—but his thick spectacles and overbearing cinnamon cologne, an excess of lace in his clothes, and a gold pocket watch tucked above his white cummerbund spoke of a fop. The four Gallowglass aides framed him, each clutching a bulky leather document case. Mardigan turned his eyes to Balthazar and removed his glasses with a theatrical flourish. "Pleased to be here, I am sure," he boomed.

Balthazar turned to the Brineboilers. "To Thaddeus Aleppo and the Brineboilers, who covered many leagues in order to be with us here today, a hearty and humble welcome to you."

"Thank you, Admiral Balthazar," answered Aleppo. He and his assistant had stationed themselves far down the table, physically separating themselves from the others. Both were thin men of average height, light-brown hair, and tepid personalities, unremarkable in every way. "It is, of course, an honor to be invited." Aleppo and the other man wore black suits with translucent buttons that glowed with a faint green bioluminescence when they moved.

"Harrumph!" Mardigan cleared his throat loudly, disdainfully turning his shoulder to the Brineboilers. "If this be a council of war, as described, I do not see any need for salt cookers to be here. They have no warships, no infantry—just potential to be a liability."

Aleppo's eyes swung contemptuously to Mardigan, but he said nothing.

"May I remind the ever-so-gracious Gallowglass ambassador," Andromeda said, "that the Brineboilers may be a small clan, yes, unwarlike, yes, but if they were to deny an aggressive clan the fruits of their chemical and biological productions, they could quite hamper their efforts."

Mardigan huffed and shook his head.

Buckle eyed Mardigan. He was a good soldier, a solid tactician. His buffoonery was nothing more than a well-calculated ruse designed to make his opponents underestimate him—which would be a serious mistake, for he was actually sharp-witted and dangerous.

And Aleppo was buying the sham.

"I agree with the Alchemist, Lady Pollux," echoed the low voice of Katzenjammer Smelt as he strode into the hall with four officers, all smartly dressed in Imperial powder blues, and pickelhaubes with gleaming silver spikes. "If we decide to resist the Founders' dreadnaughts and armored trains, we should be most grateful to any and all brave souls who might choose to stand with us."

"May I introduce Chancellor Katzenjammer Smelt and the Imperial contingent," Balthazar said.

Smelt arrived at the table, alongside the Brineboilers. "The Imperials are honored to be here," he said, removing his pickelhaube and tucking it under his arm in one quick, smooth motion; the four officers tucked their helmets as well.

The Imperial leader's four aides-de-camp were all blond, but there was one, the only female, whose hair was the color Buckle thought pure sunlight would be. Smelt placed his bony-fingered hand on her shoulder.

"May I introduce my daughter, Princess Valkyrie. Consider yourselves warned," Smelt said with a poorly concealed pride.

Buckle scrutinized Smelt, the old stork, straight as a fence-post in his monocle and medal-draped blue uniform, glowing with paternal satisfaction. And there was plenty to be proud about. Valkyrie was tall, a swan-like creature, her lithe frame buttoned up and shoehorned into her stiff Imperial uniform, but it was her face, inescapable and relentless in its beauty, long in the cheeks like her father's, but sensually feminine in its proportions, haughty in its perfection, pristine and untouchable as a fresco on the dome of a cathedral, that irresistibly drew every gaze toward her. Her eyes, clear and pale blue as new ocean ice, light-lidded under thin, straw-colored brows, took possession of all things.

A spoiled Prussian brat. Everything handed to her on a silver platter, Buckle concluded instantly.

"Good day, ambassadors," Valkyrie said coldly, placing her spiked helmet on the table, where it sat like a gleaming silver turtle. Her hair was drawn up against the back of her head so severely that Buckle could clearly make out the flattering curves of her skull; her long neck plunged down into the high collar of her powder-blue tunic, which was embroidered on each side with rich red borders and a gold iron cross. Her uniform fit her perfectly, tailored to the curves of her female form, the buttons polished to a gleam, the epaulettes thick with gold and red lace.

Valkyrie turned her eyes to Buckle, eyes hostile and cold as blue glass.

Buckle returned her glance with a smile.

–XXXVI–

TINSKINS AND AMBASSADORS

THE MEETING HAD ONLY BEEN running for five minutes, and already Buckle was desperate to escape. He appreciated the fact that Balthazar had wanted him to be there, as well as the opportunity to steal long looks at Valkyrie, but his heart simply wasn't in it. He was worried about Max and his zeppelin, and he wanted to immediately attend to both.

"Before we begin the proceedings," Balthazar said, "I must first offer our sincerest and most heartfelt apologies to Chancellor Katzenjammer Smelt and the people of the Imperial clan. We Crankshafts were tragically deceived into believing that our Tehachapi stronghold was bombed by Imperial zeppelins, only to discover now that the attack was carried out by Founders warships disguised as Imperial hawks. Our retaliation, mistaken as it was, was swift and deadly, and there are no words which can take back the damages we inflicted upon the Imperials and their city. It was never our intention to make an enemy of the Imperial clan without just cause. It is my hope that now, in this desperate hour, we can both see through the veil of machinations and recognize our mutual enemy, and know that it is he, through agents of both dishonor and trickery, it is the Founders who have spilled both Crankshaft and Imperial blood."

Buckle watched Smelt, who in his turn was peering at Balthazar through his monocle, clearly taken aback by the unexpected revelation and its attendant apology. Then Smelt's jaw tightened and he nodded to Balthazar. "If you tell the truth, Balthazar—and I do believe you do, then we are both victims of the Founders. I denounce all oaths of vengeance taken against you. The Founders I shall damn until the last breath I take." Smelt turned his gaze on Buckle. Buckle stared back, feeling the animosity between him and Smelt draining away. Buckle also felt a surge of relief. He had worried that Smelt might demand the return of the *Pneumatic Zeppelin*—an Imperial airship taken as a prize in an ill-begotten war—but Smelt did not.

"Their little shell game worked, though, did it not?" Mardigan said. "You two tore yourselves to pieces, reducing your fleets. You are easy meat for the dreadnaughts now, unless all of us rush to your rescue, hmmm?"

Andromeda patted her hand on the table. "We are *all* easy meat, Ambassador Mardigan," she said. "None of us is strong enough to resist the Founders armada alone."

"You have no idea how strong we Gallowglasses are, my lady," Mardigan huffed.

"So you believe that you can stand alone against the Founders?" Andromeda asked.

Mardigan said nothing. He sniffed and looked at his watch.

"I have brought you all here to propose a grand alliance, a pact of mutual defense, which the Crankshafts and Alchemists have already agreed to sign," Balthazar said. "A united front against Founders aggression is our best hope to avoid an all-out war."

"Or to assure the destruction of each and every one of us," Aleppo said. "Can the five clans gathered here today muster the might to resist the Founders' onslaught? Perhaps the only road to survival is to accept their domination."

Buckle disliked Aleppo for reasons he could not quite articulate—the man had disinterested, unreadable eyes—but despite Buckle's confidence in his clan's ability to fight, he understood the Brineboiler's suggestion. Without Spartak or the Tinskins in the ranks, the proposed Grand Alliance was small potatoes.

Buckle tensed for the reaction he knew was coming.

"Coward!" Mardigan snapped at the Brineboiler.

Aleppo faced Mardigan, his eyes burning. "You! You brutes! It is easy for you to rattle your swords in defiance, swarming in numbers and so far away—but we Brineboilers are a small guild clan, defenseless under the shadow of the Founders' city. We learned, over the years, that neutrality was our only salvation."

"Be a slave, then, salt cooker," Mardigan growled.

Mardigan was not putting on an act now, Buckle thought—he truly despised the Brineboilers.

Aleppo opened his mouth to fire back, thought better of it, and clamped his lips together.

"The Brineboilers are in the most difficult position of us all, Mardigan—surely you can see that," Andromeda said.

"And what if we all sign this pact, this commitment to mutual defense?" Mardigan asked. "Does that mean that if the Brineboilers, a tiny, insignificant, ragtag clan, are invaded by the Founders—who will most surely do so—we are all bound to toss aside the logics of tactics and strategy and deploy to protect them, to sail into the basin and confront the Founders on ground of their own choosing? I am no fool. It has disaster written all over it."

"We have not asked anyone to die for us," Aleppo said softly. "Nor shall we."

Buckle suddenly liked Aleppo a little better. The man had at least a bit of steel in him.

"The Brineboilers are vulnerable to occupation, of course," Balthazar said. "Their contribution to the alliance would be to transfer their boil and chemical devices into our control, and thus deny those resources to the Founders. But our immediate concern is that we pool our armaments, gather a fleet and face down the Founders before they can destroy our clans piecemeal, as is surely their intention."

Mardigan narrowed his eyes at Balthazar. "And how do you know the Founders' intentions?"

"We have all heard the rumors of the Founders shipyards gearing up for war," Balthazar replied. "And none of you would have come here today, in secret, if you did not fear the worst."

The ambassadors held an uneasy silence.

Buckle prevented himself from grinning. Balthazar had them. Nothing more to do than wait for the ink to dry on the parchment.

"We have suspicions," Mardigan said quietly, brushing at something unseen on the table with his hand, "that the destruction of our pocket zeppelin, the *Erin*, over the Boneyard five weeks ago, at nighttime, was not an accident. Some of you sent illegal expeditions to salvage her hydrogen." He gave Balthazar a nasty glare as he said that. "But we got there first—we even beat the filthy yellowfingers to it—and despite the charred wreckage, one could see that her hull had been severely holed. Big cannonballs. Big cannons. Pirates and privateers do not carry ship smashers like that. Only we do, and a few of the major clans. And the Founders carry guns like that."

The assembly nodded in silence.

"There are still not enough of us yet," Smelt said. "To stand a chance in open battle against the Founders, we shall need the well-shipped Russians."

"Yes," Mardigan added. "We need Spartak."

"The Spartak clan is notoriously neutral," Aleppo said.

"Not this time," Mardigan blustered. "Each clan will find itself on one side or the other before this mess is over, and this fledgling alliance will be finished if Spartak joins the Founders."

"Spartak declined our invitation today, but I shall see to the matter personally," Balthazar said.

"And the Steamweavers," Aleppo asked. "Where are they?"

"To hell with the Steamweavers," Mardigan groused.

"And where are the Tinskins?" Aleppo continued. "The Tinskins are reported to be here. Where are they?"

"Fear not, my friend, for the Tinskins have arrived," came a woman's strident shout from the hall entranceway.

Buckle turned to see the Tinskin ambassador, a woman agleam in a coat and long skirt beautifully stitched with gleaming scales of bronze, striding in with the captain of the guard, Garnet Cantrell.

"Take heart, fellow conspirators! The conquistadores are here!" the Tinskin female boomed as she strode up to the table.

-XXXVII-

THE GRAND ALLIANCE

"THE TINSKIN REPRESENTATIVE, ALHAMBRA CORTEZ, has arrived, Admiral," Cantrell, the captain of the guard, declared, looking a bit harried by the new guest.

"Admiral Balthazar Crankshaft!" Cortez said. "How grand of you to invite us to your little parley here in your castle of boulders! We are most honored to be included, of course, we humble children of the south."

Cortez was a graceful, silver-tongued woman with brown-black hair and a baritone voice clear and polished as a vespers bell. Her armored clothes glittered about her, and a high-combed morion helmet with cheek-guards rested in the crook of her arm, its tall peacock feather framing the left side of her head. Her skin was sand colored, her eyes deep brown and expressive, her face both pleasant and belligerent.

Buckle studied Cortez—she was young, perhaps only a few years older than him, but he sensed there was precious little youth left in her. He knew next to nothing about the Tinskins, but their ambassadors were reputed to be arrogant snakes— arrogant snakes with a lot of cannons behind them.

"We are most pleased you could attend upon such short notice, Ambassador Cortez," Balthazar said. "Welcome to the Devil's Punchbowl."

"I would not have missed it, of course," Cortez said with a wave of her white-gloved hand. She perched at the center of the table and with one sweep of her eyes, it seemed to Buckle, gathered all the details about the participants she might ever need to know.

Cortez placed her helmet on the table. "I offer my profuse apologies regarding my late arrival to the party. The captain of my airship has been suitably reprimanded, I assure you. So have we yet formulated any battle plans regarding the destruction of the Founders?"

"We do not seek their destruction, Madame Cortez," Andromeda said. "We are organizing a mutual defense in the face of an expected invasion."

"Ah, yes," Cortez said thoughtfully. "The *invasion*."

"We must move quickly," Balthazar said as he folded his hands behind his back. "As soon as is physically possible. The Founders are on the move. Freight trains are crowding at their railheads, stocking supply depots. Their airfields are also experiencing heavy activity—provisioning, bunkering, arming—and the steampiper corps has activated its reserves."

Cortez smacked her lips and narrowed her eyes at Balthazar. "If I may ask, Admiral—how did you obtain such detailed intelligence?"

"These things are well-known."

"No, they are not well-known," said Cortez.

"We have sources," Balthazar replied cautiously.

"So do we," Cortez said. "Excellent spies. In the port. But never has one ever been able to infiltrate the city proper."

"Who says that our informant is inside the city?"

Buckle's spine tingled. Balthazar was talking about Aphrodite.

"Oh, please, my dear Balthazar," Cortez huffed. "Please do not play me for a fool. Of course you have an operative inside the city. How else could the Crankshaft and Alchemist rescue mission have ambled in and out under the very noses of the Founders themselves?"

"For a clan with few well-placed spies, you know quite a few things," Balthazar said.

Buckle watched as a tense silence filled the hall, emanating from the stare between Balthazar and Cortez. The south-facing windowpanes rattled, thumped by a gust of wind rolling down from the mountains.

Cortez smiled, but there was nothing but suspicion in it. "How trustworthy is this spy of yours, this traitor to his own people, Admiral? There are numerous conspiracies of fanatics inside the city—anarchists and rebels—zealots who care nothing about our alliance, and who are determined to bring an apocalypse down upon the city."

"Such is a risk I am willing to take," Balthazar said evenly.

"Fine," Cortez replied. "Considering the circumstances, it appears the rest of us have no choice but to trust your spy as well."

Buckle got a sense of Cortez—she was a narcissist and a charmer, but also a realistic midwife to the aspirations of her clan. Conquest and plunder were what interested the Tinskins the most.

"We respectfully request that you join us," Balthazar said. "I am certain you realize that none of us, not even the Tinskin fleet, can withstand the Founders alone."

"Perhaps," Cortez replied slowly, splaying her fingers, stretching them, glancing at each ambassador in turn with obvious deliberateness. "But is this motley crew all you have?

Please forgive me, but the Brineboilers possess no weapons, the Alchemists possess no warships, and the Gallowglasses are about as dependable as a cracksman in a jewelry shop."

"Damn you, Tinskin!" Mardigan yelled, slamming his fist on the table. "A Gallowglass lives or dies by his word! Not like you, you slippery, nasty, carbuncled Aztec blood drinkers!"

"Oh, my," Cortez said evenly, an amused smile rising on her lips. "Perhaps we should leave you to die on your own, then, should we?"

"Charlatans!" Aleppo snapped.

Buckle almost laughed out loud. Hate her if you wish, but Cortez was antagonizing the ambassadors with aplomb. He wished he had a glass of rum to accompany the show.

"Please!" Smelt blurted. "Enough. We must avoid fighting amongst ourselves."

Cortez's dark eyes slipped back to Balthazar. "You have the right idea, Admiral—but in my calculation, even with the addition of our mighty fleet to the combined arms of your five, I would predict that still we would not be able to field enough men and machines to resist the Founders. The dreadnaughts would still prove too much for us."

"I assure you that we shall soon count Spartak as one of us," Balthazar said. "And I have high hopes to bring in the Steamweavers."

Cortez raised an eyebrow. "Spartak? Really, yes? If you could bring in the Russians, then your Grand Alliance would live up to its name, and our strength would be sufficient to win the war." She straightened her back, the metal plates on her coat glittering. "I can help you with the reluctant Steamweavers—we have a relationship with them. But with Spartak, those wretched, penny-grubbing Cossacks, I am afraid we are not on speaking terms."

"Your help?" Aleppo blurted. "So may we assume you are in, then?

Cortez looked at Aleppo as she might regard a cockroach. "In? Of course I am in. The Tinskins are in, you fool. Just by steaming here to your little 'secret' parley, we have cast the die. Do you really think that the Founders spies have not been watching, do not know exactly what we are up to? Your secret alliance—even if the Founders had not been planning an invasion before, we may well have triggered one. In the eyes of the Founders, just being here has made all of us their mortal enemy. Oh, yes, we are in. We are all utterly, perilously, irrevocably in."

In the heavy silence that followed the Tinskin ambassador's words, Buckle realized he was tense, sitting at the edge of his chair. Cortez was right. They were all in the stewpot now.

But he would rather risk a kraken as his ally than a Tinskin.

Where the hell is a bottle of rum?

-XXXVIII-

WHISPERS IN THE CORRIDOR

"THE TINSKINS?" SABRINA SPLUTTERED. "RYDER is hitching a ride with the Tinskins?"

"Quiet, Sabrina," Buckle whispered, glancing through the doorway and into the infirmary where Balthazar sat between Max's bed and Tyro's iron lung. Buckle did not want Balthazar to hear their heated discussion. The decisions had been made and war seemed inevitable—there was no point in him knowing that his children might disapprove. "It is a diplomatic mission."

"It's a bloody farce," Ivan grumbled. "Ryder is as good as dead, I tell you."

"I do not think so," Buckle replied, taking a firm hold of his adopted brother and sister by the shoulders. Balthazar had called—demanded, really—that they come in from the airfield and attend that evening's Seasonal ball. And it was something of a feat to keep Buckle, Sabrina, and Ivan away from the *Pneumatic Zeppelin*.

"You trust the Tinskins now, brother?" Ivan asked. The light from the corridor lamp gleamed on the copper plate covering half of his face—he was something of a contraption now, if only a temporary one. The injuries he had sustained to the left side of his body from the steampiper bomb three weeks prior had been brutal. His left arm had been shattered by shrapnel; amputation had loomed as a real possibility until Fogg and Doctor Lee found a way to get the circulation flowing properly through the flesh again. He been back on his feet for a week now. The left side of his face was covered by a brass-and-copper faceplate crawling with cogs and gears, dominated by a brass-ribbed medical half goggle over the left eye. Brass rods ran down Ivan's neck into a large shoulder piece, which supported a mechanical assist encasing the length of the injured arm, a clockwork exoskeleton creaking with turning springs and hinges that ended in a knight's gauntlet of metal fingers.

Ivan would have to wear the mechanical arm until the muscles and skin beneath had been given enough time to recover. He hated it. Being an inventor himself, he constantly criticized and cursed the clan inventors' effort of design. The screws on the shoulder were too loose, the neck support too restrictive, the goggle reservoir too wet, and the fingers too tight, ready to crush anything fragile he held in his hand. The "bloody nutcracker," he called it.

"Ryder's presence among the Tinskins will show the Steamweavers that the Grand Alliance is real," Buckle said. For some strange reason, he trusted that Cortez would take care of Ryder. She had guaranteed his safety, of course—mere words— but Buckle believed she would safeguard him, if only to secure Crankshaft loyalty.

"Who is in charge of this Grand Alliance?" Sabrina asked, looking unconvinced and worried, ever the skeptic.

"Balthazar," Buckle replied. "It took two hours of arguing— mostly between Cortez and Mardigan—but Balthazar will become supreme commander of the combined fleet, with the exception of the Tinskins, who would only accept a condition of joint command. Once the city falls and Fawkes is dead, we shall embrace the citizens as brothers and sisters. No plundering."

"Once the city *falls*," Sabrina whispered. "As if that will be easy."

Once the city falls. Buckle felt a shiver run up his spine. Here, in the quiet whisperings in the darkness, the reality of the situation suddenly grabbed him with sharp, ice-cold fingers. War.

"When does it begin?" Ivan asked.

"The fleets are to rendezvous over New Berlin two weeks from today," Buckle said. "But before that we must engage Spartak and the Steamweavers with all haste, to garner their loyalty before the Founders can coerce them into their own ranks."

"Who is sending an envoy to Spartak?" Sabrina asked.

"The Imperials," Buckle replied.

"The Imperials?" Ivan huffed. "They have been in a skirmish war with Spartak forever. The Russians are not going to warm to them fast enough."

Buckle nodded. "They know that. So Balthazar is sending them one of our airships, to carry the Imperial ambassador to Muscovy. Once again, presenting a united front for the Grand Alliance."

Sabrina and Ivan stood silent, considering the new information, mired in helpless disapproval.

Buckle heard the flame crackle in the overhead lantern. War made for uncomfortable bedfellows. "What is done is done," he said softly.

"And Balthazar is going ahead with the Seasonal ball?" Ivan muttered. "Is that appropriate?"

"I agree with his decision," Buckle replied. "It looks like we are in the last few days of peace, Ivan. We should raise a glass of beer and celebrate this moment, for I fear much blood and pain awaits us on the morrow."

–XXXIX–

THE MARTIAN IN THE IRON LUNG

IVAN AND SABRINA DEPARTED, AND Buckle strode into the citadel infirmary, where Balthazar huddled close to his wounded daughter.

The quiet hospital was Doctor Edison Lee's little healing kingdom, a long chamber, bright with double-paned windows, and every surface scrubbed with disinfectant. It was a place of white walls, a white ceiling, and white-painted floor timbers, of black iron bedframes, of light-gray blankets, gray pillowcases, and gray infirmary gowns. The soft daylight easing in through the windows—all the heavy white curtains were drawn back—glowed sweetly as it illuminated rainbows of color inside the medicine bottles lining the shelves. Even the whale oil in the glass reservoirs of the night lanterns glimmered, in a lugubrious way.

But the quiet was relative; two fireplaces at each end of the chamber crackled with wood burned to translucent red honey-combs sunk in drifts of gray-white ash. And there was the steady, mechanical beat of Tyro's iron lung, a long cylindrical copper apparatus enclosing his bed. The pipes screwed in to its base ran up to the ceiling and through holes in the wall to the adjacent room, where a small boiler and pneumatic bellows were maintained.

The man inside the iron lung—or, more accurately, the Martian inside it—was Tyro, Max's brother, lying in a coma since he'd been severely wounded during the Imperial raid. His head was the only part of him visible outside the apparatus, propped on a pillow, with a thick rubber seal around his neck; inside the iron lung, the rise and fall of air pressure induced normal breathing movements in his lungs.

Tyro had been a quiet young man, a capable engineer, though not as exceptional as his sister Max, whom he staunchly defended at every turn. He bore a great resemblance to his sister, though he was considerably more robust. His fine Martian nose bore the slight irregularity of having been broken at some point, though not flattened, and his hair was striped, black and white, the streaks matching the skin beneath. In this respect, his genetics differed from Max, whose mane was entirely black.

When the *Pneumatic Zeppelin* was home and Max was off duty, she could be found in the hospital, sitting beside Tyro. Nurses had confided to Buckle that Max would often read to her brother well into the night, and occasionally—if the rest of the infirmary was empty—she would sleep in the empty bunk beside his. There had always been an intense connection between Max and Tyro, Buckle knew, for the Martians possessed some sort of collective mind as well as an individual one, and he often felt sorry for Max, left alone without her brother, the only other Martian in the clan.

Buckle felt sorry for both of them. Now, as they lay close together, the hissing pulsations of Tyro's machine sounded reassuring, or at least soothing. This was a good thing, for Buckle, a man who would never allow fear a stage inside his system, knew that a despair did lie deep inside him, out of sight in the darkness, but present nonetheless, that Max might die.

Balthazar sat beside Max's bed, leaning his bulk close to her, his big hands cradling her long white fingers; he was listening to her steady intake of air as well.

Buckle stopped beside Balthazar, placing his hand on his father's shoulder.

"She looks so very troubled, my little girl," Balthazar said softly.

Buckle looked at Max. She slept, unconscious within a lotus fog of morphine. Under the pale-gray blanket she appeared small, like a child. She was breathing easily, to a constant beat, and that encouraged Buckle.

It was hard to forget Max, pressed against him in the cave, her cold, naked torso against his, the quaking shivers of her stomach making the fight for her life all too real, a broken baby bird clutched against his breast. He had not wanted to lose her. In the very depths of his soul he had not wanted to lose her. And the *kiss*. Buckle's brain still could not even begin to compute the ramifications. But his heart was certain—and silently asking for more.

When hell freezes over.

"I think she appears rather relaxed, Father," Buckle said, peering at Max's face in search of troubles and not finding any. A memory of Max being snatched by the sabertooth struck Buckle, and he suppressed a shiver.

"Hmmmm," Balthazar replied. After a long pause he spoke again. "I have decided to dispatch you and the *Pneumatic Zeppelin* to Spartak for the negotiations."

Buckle blinked. "Yes, Father."

"With my sons and daughter aboard—you, Sabrina, and Ivan—along with the Imperial contingent, that should give the Russians ample evidence of my resolve," Balthazar said.

"I am honored that you would ask this of my ship and my crew."

"I am also sending Ambassador Washington along with you."

"All right, sir," Buckle replied, with a deflated nod. Rutherford Washington was a bit of a stick-in-the-mud, and Buckle would have preferred that his father trust him enough to stand for the clan at the negotiating table, but he also knew that was too much to ask.

"Take it easy on him," Balthazar said, reading Buckle's mind. "Yes, Rutherford is difficult, but I trust him."

"Yes," Buckle replied.

"How is our patient doing?" Doctor Edison Lee asked, appearing from a doorway, rubbing his hands with a white towel in front of his crisp light-blue smock. Lee was the clan's chief physician and a man of considerable intellectual and professional prowess—verging on arrogance, Buckle felt—but while clinical, he was always kind.

"I cannot convince myself of her condition either way," Balthazar said plaintively. "I do not seem able to separate what I sense of her health and what I wish it to be."

Lee stopped at the foot of the bed and studied Max with an expert air. He was of medium height and slight build, his straight black hair and narrow, serious eyes strongly suggesting the Asian blood of his father. "Well, Doctor Fogg did have to assist me with an emergency transfusion from her brother as soon as he brought her in. It was good of Doctor Fogg to stay—I am not the expert on Martian physiology he is—but her vitals are holding and there is no sign of infection, which is a very good thing."

"She is doing well, then?" Balthazar asked.

Lee nodded. "She is holding her own, though it is a battle to keep her hydrated. Her recovery will be slow, perhaps three weeks to a month before she can return to duty, barring any complications. But one never knows what to expect with the superb Martian recuperative arc."

Balthazar kissed Max gently on the cheek and stood up. For a moment he looked unsteady, then he recovered. "All very good news, Doctor." Balthazar smiled his strong, reassuring grin. "Now, my son, when shall the *Pneumatic Zeppelin* be ready to depart?"

"We should be airborne before dawn, Father," Buckle said. "Once the *Arabella* is taken care of."

"Splendid. Proceed at your best speed; you must reach Spartak as quickly as possible. The Imperials may depart tonight, but they shall wait for you to catch up with them at New Berlin."

"Understood, Father."

"Gentlemen," Balthazar said, slapping Buckle on the shoulder as he stepped into the aisle. "And take care of my daughter, Doctor Lee," he added as he strode out of the room.

"Where is my other crewman, Doctor? Name of Valentine?" Buckle asked.

"He is being prepared for surgery. He is going to lose the leg," Lee replied with clinical propriety.

Buckle looked at Max, but he was thinking of Valentine. Old salts like Valentine—zeppelineering being his life—usually did not fare well when injuries forced them out of the air corps. They often became sad, pension-financed drunks in the local taverns, eventually discovered frozen in a back alley one morning, clutching an empty bottle.

"Captain Buckle, if I may have a moment," Lee said.

"Of course."

Lee glanced back, as if to make certain Balthazar had departed, then motioned for Buckle to follow him ten paces beyond the iron lung, down the aisle from Max's bed, as if he somehow also feared that she might overhear what he had to say. "I have some serious matters to discuss with you regarding the health of your father."

"Yes?" Buckle asked, dread creeping up his spine.

"I must ask you some questions, questions you may find intrusive—but I claim physician's prerogative in the asking. Of course, respond as you see fit."

"All right."

"Has your father told you anything of what happened to him while he was in the hands of the Founders? I have asked him, but he refuses to provide any details."

"He says they handled him reasonably well," Buckle replied, but his original suspicion, that Balthazar's story of his pleasant three-day imprisonment by the Founders was not the complete truth, surged back to haunt him.

"Yes," Lee said, trailing off, completely dissatisfied. "That is all he had said to me as well, and I have pressed him rather uncomfortably over it."

"Perhaps he is telling the truth," Buckle offered, though for some reason he only half believed his own argument. "Perhaps they were only holding him for an ultimatum, as a bargaining chip."

"And how do you explain his worsening condition?"

"The stress, perhaps."

"If stress has inflicted damage upon your father's health, then he is suddenly a different man than the one I have known, lo this last twenty-odd years," Lee grumbled.

"I have noticed more tremors, more pronounced," Buckle said.

"What you are seeing is a result, not a precursor," Lee said. "He experienced a terrible attack of convulsions last night while you were gone. The most unsettling episode I have seen thus far."

The dread flooded into Buckle's abdomen, making his gut clench. "He spoke nothing of it to me."

Lee nodded. "No. But I am gravely concerned. I have done all that I can do for him, and I believe that whatever happened to him in the City of the Founders has severely aggravated his condition."

"Who knows about the event last night?"

"Only your brother Ryder and your lead servant—Sibley, I believe his name is. They called me to Balthazar's chamber at three twenty-two this morning."

"Three twenty-two? This seizure was violent enough to awaken both Ryder and Sibley in their rooms down the hall?"

Lee shifted his weight uncomfortably. "Ah, no. There was someone with your father, in his bedchamber with him."

Buckle paused. Of course his father had taken a lover, though he had known nothing, suspected nothing, of it. Calypso had been dead for over a year now, and Balthazar was a man, a man finished with his mourning, a man of a physically ravenous nature. But this understanding did little to blunt the profound, if unreasonable, sense of betrayal Buckle felt in that instant. "Then there were three who witnessed his infirmity. Who was the third?"

"I am afraid I cannot disclose her identity," Lee answered with a whisper. "I am sure you understand—I must protect all confidentialities not directly concerning your father's health. Rest assured, she is a respectable lady."

"Of course I understand." Buckle nodded. He appreciated his father's right to privacy. But he would find out. Ryder and Sibley would know who this woman was.

─XL─

TYRO AND THE IMPERIAL RAID

WHISPERS. MAX HEARD VOICES IN the chamber of numbers. Many whispers. But she could not make out the words. There were many people in the little room with her, but she could not see them. Even Buckle was gone.

There was music as well, faint and distant, waltzing music.

She peered at the walls but the numbers remained blurry, as if protected behind foggy glass. She rubbed at them, but the charcoal smeared, leaving her fingers black.

A fluttering buzz arrived at Max's left ear. She turned to see a hummingbird hovering there, a pretty little fellow of emerald green with a ruby-red throat. He stared at her with his tiny black eyes, and the throbbing of his wings grew louder and louder, rising from a papery flutter to a heaving *huff* of machinery bellows that assaulted her ears.

Max was not awake. But she was semiaware of that. She flowed, swimming in a morphine current under the surface of her consciousness, dragged down by the rhythmic lullaby of the iron lung as it breathed for Tyro...

***

"We have taken hits!" Max shouted over the thunder of the propellers, quickly wrenching hydrogen-feed handles and shutting valve switches, taking in the readings of a hundred dials and gauge pointers all at once. "Hydrogen pressure critical! Compensating!"

"Aye!" Captain Halifax shouted back. "Keep the *Cleopatra* out of the dirt, Engineer!"

A fistful of grapeshot skidded past the gondola, a screaming swarm of phosphorus in the night.

Tyro was at Max's side, his eyes glittering orange in his goggles, tufts of his white-and-black hair poking out from beneath his flying helmet as he manhandled the ballast wheels.

Reflections arced like prisms across Max's goggles. She fought the urge to tear them off.

The light inside the bridge was bright green with bioluminescent boil, while outside the sky was afire, a riot of Imperial flares spewing magnesium white past the windows. The thunder of Imperial cannons rolled through her ears.

"There be the *Pneumatic Zeppelin!*" shouted Captain Halifax, cranking the chadburn dial back. "Half full! Hard a'port!"

"Hard to port. Aye," replied Lieutenant Romulus Buckle, the helmsman.

The chadburn dinged as the engineers slowed the propellers of the small, quick *Cleopatra*.

Halifax leaned closer in to the chattertube hood; he was a man of slight stature, but his bearing was that of a giant. "Gunnery, I want the guns double-shotted! Prepare to run a broadside through the target!"

"Gunnery ready, Captain! Aye!" came the response from the gun deck.

A massive explosion close to starboard lit up the world. A geyser of yellow flame and smoke erupted upward into the sky, blinding Max for an instant. An Imperial war zeppelin, caught defenseless at her moorings, had exploded in a mountainous ball of burning hydrogen.

"Take that, you spiker bastards!" the assistant navigator, Sabrina, her red hair lit up by the flames, yelled from her station in the nose bubble.

A strange stillness followed the titanic blast as the glowing red superstructure of the Imperial zeppelin crumpled to the earth. The Imperials were reloading their cannons. Consumed flares dropped, weak trickles of sparks plummeting from the sky.

"Captain Halifax," Buckle shouted from the helm. "The Imperials are stunned, sir. Let us take the *Pneumatic Zeppelin* as a prize!"

"Steady as she goes, helm," Halifax said before grimacing at Buckle; he was not fond of the young man's overaggressive tendencies. "We are not here to risk boarding attempts, Lieutenant. We are here to blast them—blast them to hell!"

The bridge shook with an ear-piercing *crack*, the air suddenly alive with spinning splinters of wood and shards of brass, copper, and glass. They were hit through a window.

"Grapeshot! Hold fast!" Halifax yelled, blood seeping from a deep gash in his forehead; he reached above Buckle to crank shut the flow valve of a severed pipe spilling boil on the helm wheel.

"The rudder is jammed!" Buckle shouted, straining at the wheel spokes. "I cannot budge her!"

Max saw a red-hot grapeshot ball lodged in the gap between the rudder wheel and its housing post, making the wood around it smolder and blacken. Tyro was already there, sliding to his knees as he worked to pry the ball loose with his knife.

That was when the world exploded.

Max, blown backward against the engineering panels, dropped to the deck, bruised, bleeding, and stunned, disoriented in a haze of smoke and fire, the air thick with dust scented of wood and blackbang, haunted by the moans of a dying woman. An enemy cannonball had struck the gondola low amidships on the beam, ripping a wide trough through the deck, and taking sections of the port and starboard bulkheads with it.

Max crawled forward through the ghastly murk toward the wreck of the helm wheel, over pieces of burning timber and pieces of Captain Halifax. She glimpsed Buckle in the rapidly clearing air, lying on his back against the signals-cabin bulkhead, head raised, blinking over a gaping, sucking hole in the deck, where the snow-covered Imperial airfield swept by forty feet below.

Max reached the blood-spattered planks at the edge of the hole, grasping at shorn copper tubes for support. She looked down just in time to see Tyro's body hit the ground—he must have managed to hold on to the keel of the gondola for a few seconds—his mass slamming into the frozen airfield in a burst of snow and dirt clods. Tyro's body lay motionless and broken, a black, crumpled figure on the white snow as the wounded *Cleopatra*, now heeling to starboard, passed over him and left him behind.

***

A young woman with a bright-blue scarf waved at Max. She was chubby, with a pleasant but common face, standing on the snow-striped Tehachapi airfield—it did not look like Tehachapi, but Max knew that was what it was—peering up at the departing airship. She looked anxious, sad, and proud.

Max watched the young woman as the zeppelin lifted away. The young woman waved until she became so small that she vanished.

Max fell, swept back and forth in the confused currents of her mind, and succumbed to darkness.

–XLI–

HOLLY CHURCHILL

SABRINA LOOKED AT HERSELF IN the mirror of her room, half-dressed for the ball as she was, and not with an uncritical eye—with her best friend Holly Churchill at her side and being so encouraging, it was difficult to get a good read on her ensemble. As a woman in a rough profession, Sabrina rarely had time to preen. Yes, she was adamant about the feminine character of the aviator clothes she loved, with the soft leathers, cuffs, and fleurs-de-lis, but she was normally unmindful of her looks, pulling her hair up tightly under her bowler with pins, and applying no cosmetics beyond splashing her face with cold water. She did comb her hair before turning in after her watch on the *Pneumatic Zeppelin*, yes, but she usually did that by feel, often in near darkness, and rarely looked into the small cabin mirror over her washbasin.

Still, her face in general pleased her, though she did not care for how suddenly her lips thinned out at the edges, making her mouth too serious. Of course, she had a love-hate relationship with the freckles on her nose and under her eyes, for though she considered them blemishes, they always seemed to be one of the characteristics that men loved about her appearance. She also thought that her elfish ears were awkwardly small, insufficient to hold back the locks tucked behind them.

Sabrina peered harder at her reflection, backlit by the warm, dying light of the day pouring in through the window. She knew she was looking at herself differently this evening, for she wanted to look as elegant as she could possibly manage. Holly, also partially dressed, exuberant under her characteristic seriousness, was helping with the complicated, frilly undergarments, garters, bustle, and gown. Holly was a milliner, a ladies' hatmaker—she had handcrafted Sabrina's beautiful derby for her—and she had a superb eye for the fashionable.

"Here we go," Holly announced, pulling two earrings out of the carved jewelry box she had brought from her house. Sabrina's jewelry collection was an utter failure, though Holly would never say so. Holly held the earrings in front of Sabrina's earlobes, letting two teardrops of pale-green jade, inlaid with gold, dangle under her fingers. "What do you think? Do they not set off your eyes?"

The earrings did look nice set against Sabrina's red hair, a characteristic that Holly openly envied, her own hair being luxurious, but a rather common shade of sparrow brown. "Lovely," Sabrina said.

"Lovely?" Holly sighed, shaking her head. "*Delightful* is the proper word. Very posh." Holly attached the jewels, each with a little jingle of the golden clasp playing in Sabrina's ears.

"You smell like marzipan," Sabrina said, catching the aroma of the almond-sugar candy.

"There is an entire box of it here that my mother made for us," Holly replied. "And I know you do not like sweets, but I shall demand that you have some before we are finished."

"Yes. I do like your mother's marzipan," Sabrina said, though she hated marzipan. Holly knew that she hated marzipan. But Holly's mother was the self-proclaimed marzipan mistress of the clan, and as such, no one could turn her confection down, pretentiously wrapped as it was in wax paper, and loaded into a little brass box.

"Perfection," Holly enthused, looking over Sabrina's shoulder in the mirror. "With the dress it shall be perfection."

Holly grabbed a boar-hair brush and attacked Sabrina's hair with long strokes; in her excitement, she was brushing far too vigorously, and Sabrina waited for the encounter with a tangle that would yank her head back. Sabrina was not used to someone else combing her hair, nor the feeling of her locks untethered at the back of her neck, the bountiful, silken, cascading slide of them against her skin. "Meagan is so excited about shipping with you," Holly said. "And I must say I am rather thrilled by the prospect, as well."

Meagan was Holly's younger sister, freshly graduated from the Crankshaft academy and assigned to the *Pneumatic Zeppelin* as an assistant signals officer to replace Martin Robinson, who had been lost to the kraken. "It is exciting for all of us," Sabrina said.

"It is quite an honor, is it not?" Holly enthused. "One's first assignment being a first-rate airship, rather than a tramp or a scout. But she did graduate at the top of her class. She will be superb for you, I am certain of it."

"Of that I have no doubt," Sabrina replied, oddly unhappy with any talk of zeppelins at the moment. Holly was not an aviator and Sabrina liked that, for it allowed their conversations to travel in any direction. If she could go one day without talking about navigation formulae...

"Of course, I do not have to request that you look out for her," Holly added.

Sabrina would have nodded if Holly did not have her hair tightly grasped, raking her brush through a knot. She felt her stomach tighten—in a time of war no one was safe aboard a zeppelin, and Holly knew it. "We shall all watch out for her, dearest. Please do not worry about that."

"What an adventure." Holly sighed, releasing Sabrina's hair. Sabrina's scalp ached from all the tugging. "Brushing is done. Now on to the dastardly corsets." Holly, normally reserved, lost her mind for parties; she nearly fainted three times at her first Seasonal. The daughter of the clan mayor and possessor of a smoldering look, she regularly fended off collections of suitors. She certainly had no problem with corsets herself, for the voluptuousness of her pirate forebears had found full expression in her form; she was buxom, with an hourglass figure.

How the serious and practical Holly might have come to accept the unkempt wooing of Ivan, Sabrina did not know. Sabrina loved Ivan, her adopted brother, but he did not seem to be anywhere near Holly's type.

Holly picked up a corset and folded it around Sabrina's torso from behind. The bone ribbing jabbed at a thousand points and Sabrina chewed the inside of her cheek. She was so used to her zeppelineer togs, well buttoned but loose-fitting as they were, that the miserable suffocation of the cinching corset seemed a torture unworthy of the result. Holly brought the back of the corset together and yanked on the bottom strings, tightening them enough to pinch the kidneys.

"Have your eye upon anyone special tonight?" Holly asked.

"No, no one in particular," Sabrina sighed, uttering both a truth and a lie. She did believe that she had no romantic inclinations toward anyone, but in her heart she knew that she wanted to look good, as good as she could possibly look, and for one man and one man only.

"Really?" Holly replied slowly. Obviously Holly did not believe her either.

"Things are far too complicated for a girl to embark on such shenanigans," Sabrina said, wincing at another jerk on the corset strings. "Fifteen-year-old debutantes have time for such dalliances, but I do not."

"Then why show up at all?"

"Free alcohol."

Holy laughed, flashing her brilliant smile. "And what about young Wellington?" Now Holly was teasing. "He is so smitten with you, and he tells everyone how much so constantly." Sabrina glared at Holly in the mirror. Holly was smart enough to know when to change the subject, but sometimes too stubborn to obey. She smiled, suddenly wistful. "Oh, sabertooth, you are so beautiful—there must be someone. There is always someone."

"Were you aware that the female sabertooth beastie only mates once, for life, and only after disemboweling all of her competitors?" Sabrina said.

Holly rolled her eyes.

"And of you, my darling?" Sabrina asked, wanting to avoid more scrutiny by her perceptive friend. "Have you a suitor whom you favor among your many beaus?"

Sabrina expected Holly to laugh, so when her face shifted into melancholy, it surprised her. "I was waiting for one in particular—we had a date scheduled, but his zeppelin crashed and he stood me up—but then he never came to apologize and renew his efforts, to which I would have been receptive."

"He was in hospital for a while," Sabrina said. Sometimes the importance of such details escaped Holly when it came to love affairs.

"Yes—I have marzipan in my hair. Oh, dear," Holly grumbled, snatching up the brush and jerking it in and out of a lock of her hair. "But I went to see Ivan—I called on him three times—every Monday, and he refused to see me. I was, I am, still desperately vexed by his behavior."

"Have...have you seen Ivan since his wounding?" Sabrina asked gently.

"At a near distance, of course, once he was released from Doctor Lee's care," Holly replied, returning to the corset strings. "I attempted to approach him and he avoided me like the carbuncle plague."

"And his injuries have not caused you to pause?"

"Oh, dear, do you really think so little of me? No, quite the contrary—his bumps have endeared him to me even more."

"It was an unkind question, forgive me," Sabrina said. "Ivan's medical clockworkings are only temporary, but he is self-conscious about them. I think he fears that this new shyness has made him appear to you to be an uncaring lout, which is the opposite of his true feelings."

"Does he not know that I understand? I wish everyone would think more highly of me."

Sabrina watched Holly's reflection as she pulled tightly on the drawstrings of her corset. The tugging moved higher, above her stomach. Sabrina coughed under the squeeze, the tops of her breasts plumping upward with each cinch. She eyed the freckles under the hollow of her throat, leading down into her cleavage in a pitter-patter pattern; the ones on her nose could be considered cute, but she disliked the freckles there.

"Though, of course, you barely know him," Sabrina said.

"That is true, but one can have a sense about a man in the beginning—one must, must one not? Or why would we ever even deign to go on with the entire procedure?"

Sabrina nodded. She did not doubt Holly's true feelings, but when it came to Ivan, she felt protective. "He is a bit of an odd bird, though," Sabrina said.

"Crazy Ivan, yes, but he is darling. And I have a soft spot for inventors—they fascinate me. And he is, or was, exceptionally persistent. I find persistence to be an underrated quality in a man."

"You do make something of an odd pairing, though."

"In what way?"

"Well, I mean to say, he is of the odd, antisocial engineering sort, and you are a much sought-after town beauty. It is obviously an offbeat pairing."

"Oh...beauty and the beast, is it?" Holly laughed when she said the words, but Sabrina caught the tone of indignity playing under it. "And a mangled beast at that? Oh, who could love such an ugly brute, even if he was a daring sky dog?"

Sabrina gulped—a difficult task inside the corset—and shook her head. "No, I simply mean that you are an odd pairing. But such matches often work out for the best, do they not?"

"I do not require a swashbuckler, dear friend, nor even a man lacking scars," Holly said, smiling. "And I do admire your protectiveness concerning your brother. But he has a good heart. I am enamored most by a good heart. The other details are unexplainable, except by love. I fully intend to adore him, if he lets me."

With the last word, Holly drew the top drawstrings of Sabrina's corset with a powerful yank, making Sabrina grunt as her rib cage threatened to crack.

"Yes," Sabrina replied, her voice a tight squeak.

They both laughed.

—XLII

YOUNG MEN, SQUARE-RIGGED

"YES, IVAN, YES—YOU ARE GOING to talk to her," Buckle said to Ivan, mildly annoyed, as Burgess Sibley, leaning in under Buckle's chin, attempted for the third time to properly tie his white silk cravat.

"Please stop moving around, Mister Buckle," Sibley moaned.

"I'm not moving, Sibley," Buckle answered, realizing that he had turned his neck as he was speaking.

Ivan was at the other end of Buckle's bedchamber, pacing back and forth in front of an amused Ryder, who was leaning against the wall, wearing his finest traveling clothes, his steamer trunk at the door.

"You cannot escape Holly Churchill, you know, brother," Ryder chuckled.

Flustered, Ivan stopped and repeatedly tried to light a pipe. He was mostly dressed, except for his waistcoat and frock. His hair, his unruly hair, stuck out in spikes from beneath his old, singed ushanka, which he refused to take off. His metal arm and goggle gleamed in the last of the afternoon light coming through the window, and when he turned, they reflected the amber glow of the wall lantern. Ivan had talked profusely for the last few days, unusual for him, about his latest experiment, a chemical analysis of women's tears—though his progress had been hampered by his inability to get women to cry for him. Buckle knew that Ivan was worried, not about his injuries but about what Holly Churchill might think once she saw him, maimed and patched up with clockwork devices. Ivan had avoided Holly for the near month since their return to the stronghold, even refusing her requests to visit him in the hospital. And once Lee released him, he had dashed into the depths of the *Pneumatic Zeppelin* in her repair dock, and had barely poked his ghastly head out since then.

But tonight Ivan was required to attend the ball, and Holly was going to see him, and he had screwed it all up anyway. He was quite nervous about it.

"I cannot engage with her," Ivan muttered, still poking a lit match unsuccessfully in his pipe bowl. "I really cannot."

"Why not?" Buckle grumbled, giving Ivan a sharp look as his cravat collapsed in Sibley's hands. Sibley sighed and started over. Buckle shrugged his shoulders a hair—his clothes fit nicely, the trousers tailored to a proper length over his leather shoes, but the starched shirt chafed under the waistcoat. His red cummerbund flashed its color about his slender waist, the gold chain of his pocket watch looped just so, and his black dress frock hung on a peg at his shoulder, a dark crimson cloudflower tucked into the buttonhole.

"Obviously, she is furious with me," Ivan said, jamming the unlit pipe into his shirt pocket and extinguishing the match with a sharp wave of his arm.

"That is not what I have heard," Ryder said.

"It is the truth. It is," Ivan muttered. "And let us just leave it at that."

Buckle laughed. "Holly is no wallflower, lad—she is going to march across that dance floor and claim you as her prize, despite your boorishness."

Ryder laughed. Ivan snorted. Sibley quickly finished Buckle's cravat knot, patting it once with both hands, and backed up to give it a satisfied glance. "Well done, sir," Sibley said.

"Very good. Thank you, Sibley," Buckle replied, turning to Ivan. "Look here—I am all gussied up. And now we need to get you ready."

Ivan held up his hands. "What? Polish up my head? It's no use, brother."

Sibley flung his finger at Ivan's breast pocket, where the pipe tobacco had stained a brown splotch through the white linen. "What is that, sir?" Sibley groaned.

"Do not worry, Sibley, it shall be obscured," Buckle said, picking up Ivan's black waistcoat and holding it open. "Turn around, Ivan. Give me your left arm first."

"I said it is pointless," Ivan grumped.

"Stop being such a wart!" Ryder said, jumping forward and easing Ivan around. Ivan sighed dutifully as Buckle, Ryder, and Sibley worked the armhole over the bulk of the clockwork machinery and into position on his shoulder.

"There—not so terrible. Other arm, if you please," Buckle said.

"I am sorry to miss the party," Ryder lamented as he tugged at the cloth. "It is a bit of a lemon if you ask me, with all the hungry young ladies about and me unattached, as I am."

"More for the rest of us, then," Buckle said.

Ivan, grunting, was able to ram his good arm through the right waistcoat armhole. Buckle yanked the front waistcoat flaps toward each other, but they would not come close enough together to be buttoned.

"Oh, well," Buckle said, leaving the waistcoat unbuttoned and patting it smooth on Ivan's chest. "You are going to look jaunty."

"As long as it hides the stain, sir," Sibley muttered.

"Does it really matter so much, Sibley?" Ryder asked, returning to his rum. "He will have four more stains on him in the first fifteen minutes—you know he will."

Ivan shook his head, despair shimmering in his good eye. "It is no matter. I am a fine mess as it is. The only reason I am attending at all is because Father has ordered me to."

"Stop fobbing on about it, Gorky!" Ryder blurted. "Do you forget that we have heard you moon on and on about the girl, over and over? All of your bruises are going to heal. I demand that you ask her to dance tonight and refrain from breaking her heart any further. She is beautiful. For the Oracle's sake, boy, wake up." Ryder handed Ivan a glass of rum. "Right, Sibley?"

There was an easy, rum-stilled pause as Sibley brushed the shoulders of Buckle's jacket. Buckle could hear the gentle whir of Ivan's machinery; it should have been soothing to him, but it wasn't. Inside, he was anxious. Lieutenant Windermere had yet to arrive, and he was bringing the latest status report from the *Pneumatic Zeppelin* with him. Buckle eyed Sibley and Ryder, and his unease was suddenly injected with a shot of anger. If they knew—if they knew of the woman whom their father was keeping. "Doctor Lee informed me that Father was stricken last night," he said.

Ryder's eyes widened a bit. "Yes. It was a difficult episode. But he has recovered as he always does. Must we raise such an unpleasant topic in the midst of these pleasant proceedings?"

"What episode?" Ivan asked.

"Father experienced a series of convulsions late last night," Ryder said. "We had to rouse Doctor Lee to look in on him."

"He looks fine now," Ivan muttered, sipping his rum.

"Yes, he does," Ryder replied. His eyes stayed on Buckle, warning him not to pursue the matter any further.

Buckle pursued the matter.

"Who was with him?" Buckle asked. Ryder did not flinch, but Sibley, the weaker of the two, glanced furtively at Ryder.

"Who was with him?" Ryder repeated, a barely perceptible surliness in his tone. Buckle knew he was stalling, figuring out his answer. "We were all with him." Sibley's jaw quivered.

"A woman was in his bedchamber with him last night," Buckle pressed. "Was there not?"

Ryder's eyes flashed. "Yes."

"What?" Ivan gasped, smiling. "The old fox is back in the saddle? Good for him."

"Who is this woman?" Buckle asked. He felt like punching Ivan.

"That is Father's private affair," Ryder replied.

"You will not tell me?" Buckle asked. His response was a silent glare from Ryder. Buckle was suddenly certain that the woman in question was the governess, Catherine Flick, a young-looking woman of forty-six, with dirty-blond hair pinned back under a white kerchief and the ampleness of bosom expected of her trade. She was pretty, in a domestic sort of way, and it would be easy for her to find her way into Balthazar's bed.

"Who cares, the old fox," Ivan laughed, draining his rum glass.

Buckle wanted to toss Ivan out the window. He turned to Sibley, who looked like a dog knowing it was about to be hit. "Sibley, old fellow, name the woman."

"Sir, I would rather not say, please," Sibley replied, his tone a hair more defiant than Buckle would have expected. "It is a privacy matter, sir."

Anger surged through Buckle and he allowed it to pass. "I am his son. Is it Catherine?"

Knuckles rapped on the open door, bludgeoning the tension aside. Sedgwick Watts, a young diplomatic aide-de-camp, peered in at Ryder. "Ambassador Crankshaft, the Tinskins are ready to depart."

It was time for Ryder to go.

"One moment," Buckle said, grabbing the rum bottle. "One snort before your journey, then."

"Of course," Ryder said.

Buckle quickly poured five glasses full, handing them around to Ivan, Ryder, Sedgwick, and Sibley, who did not seem to know what to do with his. Buckle raised his shot. "To Ryder. He shall do our clan proud." Buckle swallowed his rum with the others, but it was a tad bitter going down for some reason.

"I shall win the Steamweavers to our side," Ryder said. "I shall follow Father's advice. Offer no concessions. Impress upon them the advantages of a mutual defense."

Buckle grinned. "You are one of the young lions, my brother. Our future is secure with you."

Ryder plunked his glass on the windowsill. "I shall see you soon. And good luck with Spartak, brother," he said to Buckle with a wink.

"And do not dally with Alhambra Cortez," Buckle said. Ryder could never resist a pretty face, Tinskin or not, and the woman surely had wiles.

"Worry not," Ryder said as he strode toward the door. "Old Sedgwick here will keep me out of trouble. Right, Sedgwick?"

"Yes, sir. Is this all you have as far as traps, sir?" Sedgwick asked, grunting as he lifted the heavy steamer trunk in the doorway.

"That's the lot," Ryder chuckled. "We travel light!"

Ryder and Sedgwick strode out into the corridor, followed by Sibley. Buckle felt sorry for Sibley. As much as he wanted answers regarding his father's new mistress, he would not press the loyal old servant—for now.

Another worry assailed Buckle. He had sensed some honor in Alhambra Cortez, but as a whole he did not trust the Tinskins at all. Then he noticed that Sedgwick had left his rum glass sitting on the bedside table; though Sedgwick had raised it in the toast, he had left the alcohol untouched, and it annoyed Buckle in some obscure way.

"I do not trust a man who won't drink his rum," Ivan grumbled. "It's bad luck."

A tall figure appeared in the doorway. "Lieutenant Windermere reporting as ordered, Captain," he announced with a handsome grin.

"Ah, grand, Windermere!" Buckle said, jumping forward to shake his hand. "Please come in. Help me cheer up sourpuss Ivan here."

"With gusto, aye! I am most honored to be invited," Windermere replied. His dark-gray coat and tails hung from his tall frame with the perfect drape of a tailor's mannequin, and his milk-and-coffee-colored skin set off his white smile and green eyes. His black top hat, resplendent with a red feather planted in the band, was tucked under his arm.

"Windy is far too cheery a soul for me," Ivan groused, drawing his pipe out of his pocket again in a tumble of loose tobacco.

"I have the most current report, Captain," Windermere offered. "All goes well. We are on schedule, and we should be under way just after dawn."

Dawn. The word raised a fount of sadness in Buckle's heart. At dawn he would oversee the funerals of his lost crew in the citadel courtyard, with the empty pyres lit and burning, the mothers' faces streaming with tears. *Snap out of it.* Buckle forced his cares away. The funerals were at dawn. He could not be aboard his airship until after the Seasonal ball. He determined that he would enjoy himself at the dance despite it all.

Buckle winked at Windermere. "Now, my dear Windermere, please help me get that rat-chewed Russian beaver off the top of our chief mechanic's head."

"I swear by the ass hairs of the very devil himself," Ivan howled, backing up as Buckle and Windermere advanced upon him, "I shall geld the first blaggart who dares touch my topper!"

-XLIII-

THE SEASONAL

BUCKLE STOOD ON THE UPPER balcony of the great timber-and-stone ballroom, between two scarlet banners draped over the porticoes, and the swell of music rising up from the dance floor seemed to want to lift him off his feet. Eight massive chandeliers hung in spiraling wheels of metal and paraffin candles above the dance floor, along with sixteen smaller oil-lantern chandeliers, stacked squares, dispersed lower and between, while rows of buglights lined the walls—a nod to the airship tradition of the Crankshaft clan—their pulsing light imparting a living glow to the borders of the chamber.

On the western wall loomed a gigantic clock, its face the centerpiece of the room, above the gigantic stone fireplace, where cords of wood burned in multileveled andirons behind a chain-link screen. The clock was a complicated construction of mahogany, brass, copper, whale ivory, and porcelain, with quicksilver Roman numerals and two brass hands that swung quite visibly when the minutes and hours clicked. The frontispiece was illuminated with white boil—the glass tubes smoked with a chemical that made the emerald bioluminescence appear white—and the clock glowed with an unearthly, streaming light.

On the dance floor below, their paired forms illuminated in ebbing turns by chandelier, lantern, fire, and firefly, near one hundred couples waltzed, looking like the pied cogs of a fantastical machine from above, turning in unison, every man dressed in black, brown, or gray, every woman a splash of jeweled earrings, feathers, and bright, swirling-skirted color. The faces of the waltzers, glimpsed as they spun, were smiling, eyes bright in the ecstasies of dance and expectation. The bedchambers would be busy tonight. It was widely reported by the midwives that there was a flurry of births exactly nine months after the Seasonal gala.

The music of the waltz surged from the seventy-two valves of the pipe organ built into the northern wall of the room, its towering fan of polished brass pipes sweeping up to the ceiling. The organist, Percival Boyd, his hands pounding the ivory keys and pressure wheels, refused to sit as he played, his big back partially obscured by the jets of steam issuing from his behemoth instrument; the thirty-piece orchestra played with gusto from their podiums on the flanks, sawing the rosin off their bows.

The Crankshaft clan notables and their guest ambassadors, all glorious in their finery, collected at the fringes of the dance floor below, nursing glasses of gin. Horatio and his wife, Miranda, were there, accompanied by four of their daughters, including their youngest, Elektra, one of the debutantes. Horatio was the official chaperone of all the year's new ladies—Elektra and a dozen more fifteen-year-old females dressed up like glittering faeries—and the young men had to obtain his permission before they could scribble their names on one of the girls' dance cards.

Rutherford Washington and Orlando Churchill were both in attendance, along with the sprawling branches of their families, and so was Swordmistress Gweneviere Gray—her whiplike figure dressed in gray, of course, laced with white ermine and brilliant-green silk.

"The pastries are damned capital!" Ivan yelled at Buckle's shoulder, jamming a napkin-wrapped lemon tart into Buckle's hand. Ivan, as usual, had charged straight to the food. The banquet tables, buried under warming pans and steaming kettles, were a glorious confusion of pies, scones with clotted cream, fastmilk in ice, blood pudding, kidney pies, sliced roast beef and cuts of pork, endless boiled, roasted, peppered, and cheesed potatoes, punch bowls, beer kegs, coffee urns and teapots, black bread, soft butter, and, most exotically of all, cold tins of sliced greenhouse apples, oranges, whole cherries, and chilled asparagus.

"Thank you, Ivan," Buckle said. He already had a cold mug of beer in his hand—the dark ale, the first-rate stuff, the yeasty flavor of it bright on his tongue—and he placed the tart on the balcony rail.

"One must make it to the pastries early, you see—before the bounders snap them all up!" Ivan said, jamming a tart into his mouth. Despite his efforts to the contrary, Ivan looked good. Buckle and Windermere had managed to replace his ratty ushanka with the top hat now sitting at a rakish angle atop his head, and his open jacket allowed his red ascot and cummerbund to draw attention away from the machinery visible on his face, neck, and hand, which did not stick out in the crowd as much as Buckle might have guessed, for most of the Crankshaft women incorporated metal elements into their fur-trimmed wardrobes.

Ivan stopped chewing, crumbs cascading from his chin. "Awwww, criminy!" he muttered.

Buckle followed Ivan's stare. Gliding toward them through the crowd came the beaming Sabrina and Holly, each girl holding on to an arm of a grinning Balthazar.

The two young women were a sight to behold in their finery, appearing to float just above the surface of the earth as the bottoms of their dresses swept effortlessly across the waxed floorboards. Holly, her light brown tresses curled about her face and held up with a small white bird's-nest hat accented with cardinal fathers, wore a scarlet gown with elbow-length silk gloves. The tops of her breasts plumped up roundly above her bodice. At her neck, the stiff collar, brocaded with white lace, framed a choker cameo with a white whale-ivory silhouette set in relief over a garnet stone.

Sabrina wore an emerald-green dress edged in black fur, and her crimson hair, unfurled and sweeping about her shoulders, rippled brightly under the oranges and yellows of the lanterns and candles. The open tunic collar of her dress jacket sported a double row of black buttons edged with black lace, running along the length of the tapering coat as it plunged down to her waist. She wore short black gloves, for the sleeves of her dress jacket were long and snug, ending in cuffs at her wrists with swirls of black fur.

Buckle took a short breath. Holly looked gorgeous, but Sabrina was nothing less than a vision.

Ivan spewed an unintelligible excuse through his mouthful of lemon tart and started to bolt. Buckle snatched him by the scruff of his collar.

"Stand fast, damn you!" Buckle whispered loudly at Ivan. "Stand fast!"

-XLIV-

PECCADILLOES AND PETTICOATS

"WIPE YOUR FACE, QUICKLY!" BUCKLE yelled into Ivan's ear.

Ivan rubbed his mouth with his sleeve, downing a gob of tart in one swallow, nearly choking on it.

Balthazar released Holly and Sabrina as they arrived. "Gentlemen," he said. "I have delivered the young ladies into your care. Now, regretfully, I must return to our guests."

"Thank you so much, Admiral," Holly said, offering Balthazar a deep curtsy.

"Thank you, Papa," Sabrina said, kissing Balthazar on the cheek, bouncing a little on her feet.

"I demand that you all enjoy yourselves immensely," Balthazar shouted as he hurried away.

Buckle watched Balthazar depart. He felt strangely remote from his father at that moment, shouldered away by Balthazar's unwillingness to disclose the secrets of his love life to at least one of his sons, though feeling such a way made him aware of being petty.

"You see, I told you!" Sabrina laughed to Holly, her cheeks powdered but still pink and shining. "Romulus always comes up here and hides."

"I am not hiding," Buckle said. "Just getting oiled up for the party."

"That is a shame and a waste," Holly said, her eyes darting toward Ivan and then back to Buckle. "For a man widely considered one of the finest waltzers in the clan."

Buckle grinned. "High praise, though grossly misplaced. And yet I would be most delighted if you allowed me the honor of a slot on your dance cards."

Holly handed Buckle her card, but her gaze was on Ivan, who looked like he was about to be shoved into an iron maiden. "My younger sister, Meagan, has been assigned to the *Pneumatic Zeppelin* as the assistant signals officer, as I am sure you are aware, Captain."

"Of course," Buckle replied. Ivan was quaking at his shoulder.

"Meagan is beyond excited," Holly continued. "She reported to the *Pneumatic Zeppelin* an hour after she received her posting, and she is still aboard now, I am sure, her nose buried in a signals compendium. I have no doubt that you and Sabrina shall look after her."

"She is already under my wing," Buckle said with a smile. "Now, I am certain you are familiar with my brother, Ivan."

"Good evening, Ivan," Holly said as she curtsied.

"Good evening." Ivan coughed, bowing—and then he saluted.

Buckle laughed inwardly as he signed Holly's card. His first instinct was to try to save Ivan, to jump in and salvage whatever shred of a chance he might still have with the girl, but even Buckle knew—from the way Holly's eyes shone when she looked at Ivan—that Ivan's awkwardness was not going to deter the pretty girl who was enamored with the strange Russian-blooded mechanic.

The lovely Holly came to Ivan's rescue, anyway.

"I hate to trample all appearances of etiquette," Holly said, taking a step up to Ivan, who was pinned against the balcony rail. "But I do desperately wish to be dancing. Ivan, would you be so kind as to sign my card for the next waltz?"

Holly thrust her dance card at Ivan, who accepted it with a trembling hand. Ivan would readily stick his face into the guts of an exploding boiler, but here he was transfixed, confounded, utterly helpless—he was absolutely, spectacularly, deliciously doomed.

"I, I would find that to be most acceptable," Ivan mumbled, scratching his name on Holly's card and handing it back to her.

Holly paused, waiting. She raised an eyebrow.

Buckle slapped Ivan on the back. "Bow and offer the lady your arm, good gentleman," Buckle said. "And escort her to the dance floor."

Ivan bowed and jerkily offered Holly his undamaged arm. "Please, may I have this dance?"

"Most absolutely!" Holly said, snatching Ivan's sleeve with a grip so tight that it startled him. "Let us go then, shall we?"

Ivan carefully led Holly away through the crowd.

"Poor Ivan." Buckle laughed, turning to find Sabrina's jade eyes sparkling at him.

"Lucky Ivan," Sabrina said.

"Yes, you are right," Buckle said, tipping a swig of beer into his mouth. He did not really want the drink at that particular moment, but he needed to break eye contact with Sabrina. Her presence was as warm and familiar as always—so why was he feeling so unsettled about her?

"Oh, I so wish Max could have attended. She would have enjoyed the party."

"Do you think so?" Buckle asked. "She hates parties. She sulks when she has to put on a corset."

Sabrina smiled. "Yes, she *acts* like she hates it. But I know better."

She took hold of Buckle's arm, her gloved hand resting on the fine fabric of his sleeve, the weight of the fingers as if a bird had lit there—but the touch ignited an awareness in Buckle, an intense awareness of *her*.

"If I may be so bold as to steal a scene from Holly's last act," Sabrina said, offering her dance card, "may I also be so inappropriate and brazen as to ask you to sign my dance card, and the last dance of the evening at that?"

"Of course," Buckle answered playfully, though every nerve ending in his hands was tingling. He drew his pencil from his jacket and signed his name in the last slot—the most sought-after station on any lady's dance card.

"After all," Sabrina said, removing her hand from Buckle's arm as he handed the card back to her. "We are not here, either of us, with anyone special. So I say I shall take advantage and enjoy the last waltz with the finest dancer in the hall."

"I am sure you have just crushed the hopes of many young beaus," Buckle said. And this was true. Sabrina was a popular Crankshaft female. But she rarely entertained the hopes of potential suitors. Her passions always seemed to be distracted by other, more mysterious things.

"I am sure I shall not escape Wellington," Sabrina sighed. "Poor Welly. As soon as he finds me—and I am shocked that he has not popped up yet—he will most diligently attempt to fill five slots on my card."

Buckle laughed at Sabrina's discomfort. Four dances in one evening were all that a lady was permitted to accept from a single man and still maintain her propriety. "Shall I get you something to eat?" Buckle asked. "A scone, perhaps. I saw blueberry on one of the tables."

"That would be lovely," Sabrina replied. "Thank you."

"And a glass of beer?" Buckle continued. Sabrina liked beer. Especially ale.

Sabrina frowned. "No—I do not want beer."

Buckle looked at her, confused. "Uh, no?"

"I am a proper lady at a proper ball," Sabrina said, with an odd trace of hurt in her eyes. "As such, beer is improper refreshment. I would like a glass of punch. With an orange slice in it. Please."

Buckle nodded, but he did not understand. Why would Sabrina be upset with his assumption that she would want a glass of beer, even though she always liked to have a glass of beer at a party? "I shall be right back," he said, tugging off his white kid gloves.

Sabrina looked away over the balcony as if she were angry. Buckle hurried over to the table with the blueberry scones, loading one onto a plate with a scoop of clotted cream. Sabrina was just being catty, for some reason. But when she had turned her eyes from him, with the line of her jaw set against the lantern light, she had looked like Athena, a redheaded goddess gazing down upon the world, and the loss of her gaze had hurt him, hurt him in some new way that he did not understand.

–XLV–

THE APPRENTICE NAVIGATOR

CREWMAN DARIUS BANERJI, SEVENTEEN YEARS old and the *Pneumatic Zeppelin's* apprentice navigator, hated the night watch. It was a cold, dark, lantern-lit bore, especially in safe harbor, and even more so at the Punchbowl airfield. He wasn't upper-crusty enough to attend the Seasonal, but he could have been spending the evening at home with his family. Banerji loved zeppelineering—it was in his bones—but it also took him away from his loved ones for long periods of time. He wanted to see his parents, his brother, his sister, and the dog.

The iron grating of the keel deck occasionally creaked as Banerji walked it, moving at an easy pace, glancing through the compartment gaps at the girders and envelope walls beyond. At night, the inside of the zeppelin seemed like the inside of the moon—too big to truly comprehend, and filled with endless things, both inanimate and alive, that made endless little noises.

He did not make any sound to add to the quiet cacophony—he was a soft treader, he was. He made it a point to let the gratings creak as little as possible when he walked them.

Banerji paused at the top of the circular stairwell that led down into the piloting gondola and leaned on the rail. He wanted to smoke his pipe, but it was not allowed on board. But he was just a few steps from the galley. He liked to raid the pantry at night, much to the annoyance of Perriman Salisbury, the ship's cook.

Sweetmeats tasted brilliant when one was tired, hungry, and cold.

He turned to stroll into the galley.

A sound stopped him.

Banerji froze. He listened. He knew every one of the thousand sounds the *Pneumatic Zeppelin* made in her moorings at night—and that was not one of them.

The single soft sound of a compartment panel creaking open down in the piloting gondola had come and gone in an instant, but for Banerji, it had been clear as a bell.

He slipped his hand to the butt of the pistol at his belt as he peered down into the dark companionway. It was difficult to see—the boil was not lit on the bridge, and the only illumination was coming from the buglight lanterns hanging on the hawsers outside.

Another sound—the scuff of a boot on the deck. Banerji crouched. The person below could be another of the six-member night watch, but Banerji knew it wasn't. He was the only one patrolling the forward keel, and if someone had needed to visit the piloting gondola, they would have taken a lantern with them, or activated the boil.

Banerji wrapped his fingers around his pistol, wincing when the iron barrel squeaked against leather as he drew it. If he crept down, the intruder might see him first. He decided to descend quickly, treading lightly, and gain a view of the bridge before the intruder had time to react.

Heart pounding, Banerji rushed down into the darkness of the companionway.

He caught a glimpse of someone there—a squatting man wearing a black coat, leaning inside the access panel under the elevator wheel. But the man had heard him. He had not trodden softly enough.

A brilliant flash blinded Banerji, accompanied by the deafening boom of a pistol and an explosion of sparks against the iron railing in front of him. Banerji missed the next step and pitched forward, a lucky grab of the rail the only thing saving him from a headfirst tumble. He almost swung his pistol wildly and fired—his finger tight on the trigger—but he did not want to waste the shot.

By the time Banerji blinked, the man had jumped out over the port-side gunwale.

Banerji leapt to the deck, charged the gunwale, and launched out after him.

Cold air slapped Banerji, his ears ringing, as he dropped the eight feet from the gondola port to the repair dock. His boots hit hard and he rolled—and then he was up and running. He saw a dark figure duck down into the machinist's trench under the wharf. "Alarm!" he screamed. "Alarm!"

Banerji's shout was not necessary. The gunshot had brought every soul on the airfield running in the darkness, calling out, and the rest of the night watch was peering down from above.

He jumped down into the machinist's trench—a long corridor the length of an airship lined with machinery and lit by huge glass tanks of glowing green boil, where the machinists could work metal without worrying about sparks—and saw the saboteur darting ahead. Banerji took off after him, dodging a handful of surprised mechanics as they raised their goggles over their machines.

In a few strides Banerji was out of the dry trench and under the massive sweep of the *Pneumatic Zeppelin*'s envelope nose, his boots crunching in the dry snow.

The saboteur was about thirty feet ahead, snatching the reins of a guardsman's tethered horse and swinging up into the saddle. All around them, the shouts of Crankshaft guards and airmen closed in.

"Stop!" Banerji howled, aiming his pistol as he ran. "I have you! Stop!"

The saboteur did not glance back. Leaning forward in the saddle, he kicked the horse's ribs. The animal bolted.

Banerji, twenty feet away now, fired his pistol at the man's back. He plunged through the muzzle's flash and burst of black smoke to see the horse and rider galloping out onto the main road, picking up speed as they weaved around wagons and bowsers with copper-sheathed wheels and water tanks, all drawn by stamping draft horses, their nostrils pumping steam into the cold air.

Banerji stopped, eyes swimming with sparkles, ears ringing, breathing hard, his pistol muzzle smoking. It was impossible that he had missed the man with his pistol shot. Impossible.

The mounted saboteur disappeared into the darkness just as shouting people appeared from every direction: musket-carrying guards, wrench-wielding mechanics, big-gloved supply men, and other members of the *Pneumatic Zeppelin*'s night watch.

Lieutenant De Quincey, the helmsman and officer of the night watch, was suddenly at Banerji's shoulder. "What happened, lad?" De Quincey asked.

"Saboteur. In the airship. He escaped toward town on a horse," Banerji breathed. He wanted to say more, to explain what had happened, but he could not form any more words. "Saboteur," Banerji said again.

–XLVI–

SWEETHEARTING

SABRINA CLUNG TO THE EDGE of the dance floor, watching the sea of waltzing partners whirl about in smooth undulations of dark frock coats and rainbows of fluttering gowns; she was leaning forward, almost on tiptoe, and the stretch of the muscle made her shin ache where she had slashed it in her battle with the kraken's tentacle. Andrew Windermere and his wife, Julia, swept past, two people absorbed in one another, absorbed in happiness.

Suddenly, Sabrina hated not being in the game.

She caught sight of Buckle. He was out on the dance floor, and her pleasure was immediately stymied when Ilsa came into view, swinging in his arms, her antelope-brown hair drawn up in blue ribbons, her bosomy body resplendent in a dark-blue chiffon dress, her sensual face lit up in a smile, the smile of a woman who was content with her lovely fragment of Romulus Buckle. With her waist cradled in his arm, she seemed to be the princess of the hall.

Sabrina brought her glass to her lips and took a genteel sip—the sweet rum punch, further sugared by cherry and apple juice, nearly made her sick. She greatly desired a sip of beer—and instantly felt unladylike for it. She so yearned to be a lady this evening, an elegant, soft, beautiful lady—not a rough-edged, leather-clad, powder-blackened zeppelineer. She wanted to hate Ilsa, all of a sudden, because she was somehow jealous of her being with Buckle.

Sabrina smoothed out the silken backs of her black gloves. She was not willing to pursue Romulus. But then why did she envy Ilsa so?

Suddenly the assistant navigator, Welly, was at her side, smiling in his ever open and expectant way, his eyes full of her reflection. "Good evening, Miss Serafim," Welly said, bowing his lanky and awkward body deeply, then flashing his white smile. "I hope you are enjoying the ball. May I request the honor of a dance?"

Oh, Welly, Sabrina thought—not the schoolboy crush. Not now.

"You may have a total of three," Sabrina said, handing him her dance card. "For my sisterly affections for you know no bounds, my dear Welly. But I cannot keep you from the other girls—such a thing would be terribly unfair to them."

Wellington smiled shyly, quickly filling four spaces with his name. "I shall be at your beck and call, Lady Serafim," Welly said, bowing under her distracted smile before he doffed his top hat and strode away.

Holly appeared at Sabrina's shoulder, huffing and slightly pink in the cheeks from dancing. Sabrina wanted to *dance.* "Is poor Welly still so terribly enamored with you?" Holly asked. "The poor child."

"Actually, he has never asked me for anything more than a dance, Holly," Sabrina said.

"Just moons over you all day and night, then," Holly laughed, eyeing Sabrina's punch glass. "No beer tonight?"

Sabrina winced. How could such a harmless, and truthful, question sting her so? "I was trying," she said slowly, "to be a little more of a lady this evening."

Holly's eyes widened. "Well, I am flabbergasted. Have you not seen yourself in the mirror, young lady? You are the jewel in the crown this evening. You could guzzle beer all night long and still you would not lose one whit of your luster."

Sabrina could not help but laugh. "My dear friend, you are a wonderful liar."

"I have not uttered one falsehood, and you know it," Holly answered, tasting her punch and shuddering. "And personally I would prefer a nice lager to this sap; it is so sweet it closes the throat."

Sabrina handed her glass to Holly. "Would you mind, please?" When the music stopped, she was going to slip out onto the dance floor and commandeer Buckle for herself.

"Of course, my love," Holly replied. "Have you a dance on your card?"

"No. I am going to save Romulus from Ilsa Gallagher," Sabrina replied, committing to a visceral course of action she felt like her brain had not even considered.

"He does not look like he needs saving to me. They share a great deal of affection," Holly said.

Sabrina shook her head. The affair between Romulus and Isla was not a secret, nor did it need to be. Holly, she believed even with her considerable perceptiveness, had not sensed Sabrina's new attraction to her captain, thank the Oracle. But she needed an excuse. "He tires of her quickly."

"He told you that?" Holly asked, mildly surprised.

"Aye, he told me," Sabrina replied, lying again, a shocked spectator to the silver flipping of her tongue. *Stop it.* "And where is Ivan?"

Holly smiled happily. "Oh, he excused himself to get me more of this syrupy punch—he thinks I like it."

"You are frightening the poor lad," Sabrina said with a grin.

Holly gave a wry smile. "I told him he was a wonderful dancer, even though he kept stepping on my toes."

Sabrina smiled. She was inordinately happy for Ivan that her dear friend was smitten with him. "He is a bit raw, but my Russian-bred brother, as you plainly know, is a good egg."

"You see!" Holly enthused. "That is what I see in him, dear friend. Goodness pours out of every inch of his unusual, perplexing soul, and when I am near him I feel light, joyous, adored, and amused. And people do not understand how I could be smitten with such a fellow. Pah!"

Sabrina laughed. She moved forward as the music wound down to its ending flourish. Her eyes scanned for Buckle, found him, and latched on. She struck out across the dance floor before the folds of the women's dresses stopped swaying.

When Sabrina arrived at Buckle's place on the floor, she found him giving Ilsa a little bow, and Ilsa leaning forward on her tiptoes to whisper something amusing into his ear.

Their sweethearting made Sabrina sick. She stopped beside them, waiting for Buckle to notice her.

Buckle flashed his grand smile. "Hello, Sabrina."

"My apologies for the intrusion, Ilsa, but Romulus, could you assist me with one quick dance? Wellington is being pesky, and I am in need of sanctuary."

"Of course," Ilsa said, not in the least bit threatened. "He is all yours, Chief Navigator."

Sabrina stepped up to Buckle as Ilsa floated away and the orchestra wound up again, the opening strings of the waltz.

"Shall we, my dear?" Buckle said, taking Sabrina's left hand in his right, and encircling her waist with his long left arm, drawing her closer to him.

Sabrina felt a pure joy as they swung into the flow of the music, her waist cradled in the powerful loop of his arm, her right hand resting on the soft cloth of his coat shoulder, her left hand clasped in the strong, warm fingers of his right. She saw nothing but the tower of his chest and the amber and gold whiskers on his chin, and found herself in a trance of motion, a hypnotic state of bliss, a place where every sense hummed vibrantly, but only in the bubble that contained her and Buckle. Everything beyond was a muffled blur of colors and music that propelled them around and around.

It was so unfair that the moments one wanted to last in life always passed more quickly than one would expect.

~XLVII~

THE WARRIOR AND THE WALTZ

ONCE THE MUSIC ENDED, BUCKLE released his hold on Sabrina and stepped back to bow. "Thank you for the honor of the dance, Miss Serafim," he said.

"You are most welcome, Romulus," Sabrina replied with a curtsy, laughing at their formality. The laugh had a nervous trill to it, though.

Buckle felt off balance; Ilsa was a beautiful girl, a doe-eyed lover voluptuous both in face and form, but she held not a candle to Sabrina, standing before him in a vision of crimson hair and emerald silk, her freckled, elfin face turned up to him with a smile tinged with a promise of something he had never seen there before.

But she was Sabrina—adopted from an unknown blood-line, yes, but she was his sister, if in name only. She had been a latecomer to Balthazar's brood, adopted at the age of thirteen, and while she had always been fanatically loyal—a brawler when it came to the dignity of her family—she had always been a mystery to Buckle, a sibling without a history, and she had never once mentioned what had happened in her life "before," an earlier life now cast into darkness by its enigmatic links to the Founders, and the infamously red hair of Isambard Fawkes.

But Sabrina was his shipmate, his chief navigator and first mate. Buckle had a rule never to engage in dalliances with members of his own crew. This rule was maintained *most* of the time, Ilsa being his most current transgression, but he rarely saw Ilsa aboard the *Pneumatic Zeppelin*. With Sabrina, he was rubbing shoulders for an entire watch.

"I would love another dance, if you are available," Sabrina said. "I have an empty slot on my card, and it sounds like the band is warming up for a quadrille."

Buckle swallowed, tasting beer on the back of his tongue. He desperately wished to pull Sabrina into the crux of his arm again, to smell her perfume, to feel the slender rise of her hip against his fingers, the muscles taut beneath the cloth. No. He could not think clearly. He had to quickly extricate himself. Confusion was a condition foreign to his mind.

Balthazar's arrival rescued Buckle.

"Ah, my children!" Balthazar enthused, looking hearty and hale. Diplomacy always got his heart pumping, and he looked much better for it, strutting in his felt top hat and swallowtail jacket. Sibley, his black hair slicked rakishly against his head, followed at Balthazar's heels, the much-trusted old hen ready to whisk him away if his apoplexy started up again. It worried Buckle that the two strongest personalities in the Grand Alliance, the glue holding together the whole flimsy construction, were Andromeda and Balthazar, and both of them were badly damaged.

"Hello, Father," Sabrina said. "We are having such a grand time!"

"Then it pains me to drag Romulus away, but I must," Balthazar said, thumping his beefy hand on Buckle's shoulder. "Come with me, son."

Buckle followed Balthazar through the stream of dancers positioning for the quadrille.

"Katzenjammer Smelt has just arrived—fashionably late," Balthazar said, his breath smelling of his pipe. "And he has brought his daughter with him, dressed to the nines. I want you to dance with her."

"Of course, Father," Buckle answered. He did not want to dance with an Imperial girl, especially Valkyrie, beautiful as sparkling ice and just as cold, but he understood why Balthazar wanted his son to dance with Smelt's daughter. Ilsa's voice echoed in Buckle's head, words that she had spoken to him as they danced.

"Have you seen the Imperial princess yet?" Ilsa had asked. "Valkyrie?"

"Yes. She attended the negotiations with her father," Buckle had replied.

Ilsa had given Buckle her all-knowing look. "She is stunning, my dear captain—frankly, I cannot imagine how you might keep your hands off her."

Buckle had winced. "She is an Imperial princess, Ilsa. She is a Smelt, for crying out loud."

"If I may be so bold as to point out, sir, you have cracked far tougher nuts before. Myself not included."

"Horsefeathers," Buckle had countered. "And I must say I find it humiliating that you are so flip over the prospect of me wooing another."

"It is the only way a girl can have you, Captain," Ilsa had said, and laughed.

Buckle and Balthazar crossed the dance floor and arrived before Katzenjammer Smelt, his chest a wall of brilliantly ribboned medals. The Imperial officers in his entourage were dressed in their impeccable sky-blue uniforms with scarlet and gold piping, their boots and pickelhaubes all spit-and-polish.

When Buckle saw Valkyrie, he shivered. Her powder-blue gown, trimmed with red lace and white fur, the front of the bodice gleaming with a double row of gold buttons, was a masterpiece upon her slender body. Her face was a sculptor's dream, pale pink and perfect in proportion, framed by her lustrous yellow hair woven into a French braid that ran down the center of her back.

Valkyrie was looking away, and she had not yet noticed the approach of Buckle and Balthazar. Buckle knew that every man in the hall was looking at her, either out of the corners of their eyes or through the backs of their heads, and he was equally certain that she noticed none of them.

"Be nice," Balthazar whispered harshly into Buckle's ear just before they stopped in front of the Imperial contingent.

"Admiral Balthazar," Smelt blurted, his crane face forcing a less than genuine smile. "I commend you upon such a grand party. Many thanks for your kind invitation."

Balthazar opened his arms. "Thank you, Chancellor. The Crankshafts are honored that you chose to attend."

Smelt regarded Buckle, his glance standoffish and difficult to read. "And good evening to you, Captain Buckle," Smelt said coldly.

"Chancellor," Buckle replied with a nod of his head.

"My son has a request to make of you, Chancellor," Balthazar said.

Damn, that was quick, Buckle thought. Oh, well. "Yes, Chancellor," he said, clearing his throat. "I request the honor of a dance with the princess."

Smelt raised the eyebrow behind the glittering monocle. The request was no surprise—it was proper etiquette for the son of the host to dance with all eligible daughters of prominent guests—but he most certainly disliked the idea of Buckle touching his *own* daughter.

Valkyrie turned her inscrutable, ice-cold gaze to Buckle. He saw nothing in her eyes but disdain.

"Of course you have my permission," Smelt said with a forced pleasantry. "But my daughter makes her own choices."

Valkyrie stepped forward. She was almost as tall as Buckle, but as she scrutinized him down her strong, blue-blooded nose, she seemed taller.

"Princess Valkyrie," Buckle said with a bow, mustering his finest charm. "I would be most grateful—the entire Crankshaft clan would be grateful—if you would bestow upon me the honor of the next dance."

Valkyrie did not smile. "I, too, would be honored, Captain. Of course." Her voice was gentle, her tone dismissive.

Buckle offered Valkyrie his hand, and she slipped her white-gloved fingers into his, moving with him out onto the dance floor. The quadrille had just ended, and another waltz was about to begin. Buckle stopped, and she slipped into position under his hands. In the moment before the music began, he found her cool, confident, and bored eyes gazing into his.

The strings of violin and cello rose in the air; Buckle and Valkyrie set into the same motion as the seventy other pairs on the floor. Valkyrie's graceful body responded to Buckle's lead like the wing of a swan, but she was a touch slow in her steps and anticipation, a sign that she had been well schooled in ballroom dancing, but had not actually danced much. Buckle noticed a small brown mole on her throat, just above the lip of her high scarlet braided collar, and when he looked up, he found her eyes hard upon him.

"May I say, you look lovely tonight, Princess," Buckle offered, resisting the urge to say something witty, but settling on something safe.

"You are very kind, Captain," Valkyrie replied, her chin high. "But you need not feel compelled to compliment me overmuch."

"It is not duty but your beauty that fuels my compulsion," Buckle replied. That was a damned good line. Damned good.

"Please, reserve your treacle for the little girls, sir," Valkyrie said. "I am dancing with you as a diplomatic gesture."

"And yet," Buckle continued, undeterred, actually enjoying her disapproval of him, "would not my compliment on your loveliness also be considered a diplomatic gesture?"

"In that case, I am compelled to compliment you as well, sir."

"On my loveliness? Well, I do manage to clean up on occasion."

"You could do with a shave, in my opinion—if you are serious about cleaning up."

"Lose the whiskers?" Buckle replied. "I have been told they impart to my countenance a grand aeronautical air."

"They would, if there were more of them," Valkyrie said.

"Ah, my wounded manhood. I would be tempted to retort with a criticism of your appearance, but then again, you seem to be perfect."

"Perhaps all of my flaws are internal, as opposed to yours," Valkyrie said.

"I think I have just been insulted. A diplomatic incident may ensue."

Valkyrie's jaw remained set, but Buckle saw a spark of warmth flash in her glacial eyes. "I do love a good party," she said.

~XLVIII~

DISTURBING NEWS

BUCKLE FOUND HIMSELF ALONE ON the ballroom balcony, and it pleased him in some small, abstract way. The last vestiges of daylight had ebbed out of the high overcast, to be replaced by the brilliant, silvery issue of the moon. It was too early in the evening for the lovers to seek out the freezing privacy of the balcony to cling to one another behind the pillars, or for the smokers to seek an open space to light their pipes. The outdoor fireplace roared, two freshly oiled logs finding their full expression of flames, the last cinders of the kindling falling away at their haunches, spent and combusted. The two gargoyles guarding each end of the balcony rail seemed alive in the waving light, staring at the world with marble eyes, waiting, knowing that even they, one day, would dissolve away to dust. Festive double rows of oil lanterns hung from the battlement hooks, their tangerine light taking on a liquid, lavalike quality in the places where the frost had taken hold of the rock.

Buckle folded his arms across his chest to ward off the cold. He glanced back at the high ballroom doors with their rippled, murky glass and the beating pulse of light, color, and music within, and he was glad to be outside. He always preferred to be outside. Perhaps his early years in the wilderness were to blame.

It was not that Buckle did not like parties. He loved parties, when the mood was right. But he needed the quiet to clear his head. The two women inside the glass, Sabrina and Valkyrie, stirred him up in a witch's pot of lizard tongues and rose petals—his newfound attraction to Sabrina, subtle, strong, and unwanted and the undeniable fascination he had with the haughty Valkyrie almost infuriated him. He had a bloody serious job coming up. Negotiating with the wily Russians of Spartak required an unmuddled mind.

Buckle stepped to the balcony rail, overlooking the citadel's lantern-dotted courtyard and main gates. The portcullis was still raised, and dozens of coachmen and footmen milled about, muttering to one another over their pipes, offhandedly peering at an odd stack of chicken cages piled against the bailey wall, the birds within quiet at the fall of night. High overhead, the *Khartoum* patrolled, running at too great an altitude for Buckle to be able to hear her engines, an ellipsoidal shadow against the clouds, her gondolas twinkling with interior light.

The sight of the *Pneumatic Zeppelin* on the airfield, her elephantine back looming over the smaller airships hugging the earth at their mooring towers, her hawsers lined with cheerful rows of buglights, made Buckle's heart race. He so wanted to leave the party, hurry aboard, run the rudder wheel in his hands, boilers pounding in her guts, propellers awhirl, and drive her into the sky. To have air under his boots again! But, alas, his mighty airship was not quite ready to go. Dozens of buglights clustered under her belly, some in motion, as the ground crews, the copper-sheathed wheels of their mule carts gleaming dully in the lantern light, manned the derricks and swung the *Arabella*—the emergency repair crews still finishing their work aboard her—back into her berth inside the *Pneumatic Zeppelin*'s launch bay.

Buckle unfolded his arms and leaned on the balcony rail. Late arrivals to the party approached in clattering, lantern-bouncing carriages, coming along the main road as it meandered up from the packed houses and boulders of the town. In the courtyard, a guardsman strode with an oil lantern, two blackbang pistols gleaming at his belt; it was quiet enough for Buckle to hear the sounds of his footsteps, the leather soles of his boots padding across the flagstones. Buckle was used to the noisy quiet of a zeppelin running at night: the steady drone of the propellers, the hum of the machinery. He was not so familiar with the sounds of the city at night: the distant clang of the ironsmith, the slow rattle of the market carts with their braying donkeys, the random barking of dogs, and the faraway cries of the sweepers and streetlarks, the little boys who collected horse dung from the avenues and ran errands for halfpennies and farthings.

The back of his neck stung where the kraken had ripped him. A memory drifted into Buckle's mind, a memory of himself as a boy, running with a dragonfire lantern clutched in his small hand, many years ago...

Buckle heard footsteps behind him, soldiers' boots on stone, and he turned.

It was Balthazar, leading Katzenjammer Smelt apace. Both men smoked their pipes, and the gray tobacco smoke bearded them as they strode, the bowls glowing like red-hot bird's nests whenever one of them took a pull.

"Ah, Romulus, here you are," Balthazar said. "We must talk."

"I suppose we must," Buckle said, looking at Smelt as the firelight reflected in his monocle.

Then Smelt smiled. It was not much of a smile as such things went, a sort of tight grimace with positive intent, but it was a smile.

"Chancellor Smelt has made a kind effort to assist us," Balthazar said. "He has most graciously offered that his daughter, Valkyrie, join the *Pneumatic Zeppelin*'s crew as acting chief engineer. She is of course familiar with the airship design, and she shall hold this position for the duration of the mission to Spartak, and until Max recovers."

Buckle looked hard at Smelt. If Valkyrie was an effective engineer, then it was not a bad proposal—on the surface. But was Buckle to have a stranger, a foreign officer, acting as his second mate, his third-in-command? One well-placed Founders cannonball could easily make the Imperial princess the acting captain of the *Pneumatic Zeppelin*. And could Smelt be inveigling his daughter aboard in order to improve his claim if he was still planning to demand the airship's return to Imperial possession?

"Thank you, Chancellor. I would be honored to have her aboard," Buckle said. What else could he say? This was Balthazar's decision, made without consulting him.

Smelt nodded, clamping his pipe between his teeth. "She is highly experienced. She will prove herself the excellent officer that she is."

"Good," Balthazar continued. "Romulus, you shall dock briefly in New Berlin and take aboard the Imperial diplomatic team, which shall accompany you to Muscovy."

"Very well," Buckle nodded. He was trapped like a rat in a hole.

Someone came running up the staircase behind, out of breath and gasping. Buckle, Balthazar, and Smelt spun around.

It was Jacob Fitzroy, the *Pneumatic Zeppelin*'s young signals midshipman, and one of the officers of the night watch. His mouth was wide open, sucking air, his sweat-slicked face gleaming in the lamplight.

Buckle's entire body tensed. Something had happened on the airship. And it was bad.

"Captain! Here you are, sir!" Fitzroy coughed as he stumbled up the last step.

"Out with it, man!" Buckle snapped.

"There was a saboteur, Captain—aboard the airship!" Fitzroy gasped.

"What?" Balthazar shouted.

Buckle's heart lunged into his mouth. "Where? What was done?"

"He was caught in the piloting gondola, but Mister De Quincey thinks he had not had time to do anything yet. We can't find anything out of order, sir," Fitzroy continued.

"We may count ourselves lucky, then," Balthazar muttered, grinding his teeth on his pipe.

"Curse me straight to hell!" Buckle roared, though he actually felt a touch better, felt a touch calmed. But now the specter of well-hidden sabotage could be added to his mountain of worries. "And where is this saboteur now?"

"He escaped, sir," Fitzroy replied. "Toward town. The guard and the constabulary have been informed and are searching for him."

Damn it. More cursed bad luck. It would have been a capital revenge to get to interrogate the brute. "Who discovered him?" Buckle asked.

"Mister Banerji, sir."

"I must get back to the ship," Buckle said, heading for the stairs as Fitzroy fell in beside him. He cursed his decision to join the party. He should have been on the *Pneumatic Zeppelin* all along.

"Dispatch rider approaching, on the fly!" shouted a guardsman from the main gate below. "Make way! Clear the road!"

Buckle turned back and joined Balthazar and Smelt at the balcony rail. More shouts rang out in the courtyard as the guards hustled the lagging coachmen and footmen away from the gate. Buckle heard the horse approach up the road, its hooves thumping the tightly packed earth at a gallop.

"Who goes there?" the master of the watch howled.

The rider and horse burst in under the portcullis, the animal hitting the flagstones with a clatter of iron horseshoes.

"Quentin Heath, rider from outpost Bengal!" the horseman shouted, out of breath, fighting his mount as it tried to wheel. The horse was exhausted, its body steaming in the torchlight, mouth and flanks streaming with foam, tongue dangling out of the side of its mouth. "I carry an urgent message for the council!"

Buckle recognized Heath, though he would not have been able to recall his name—a small fellow, whose bandolier links glittered under the open flaps of his long duster riding coat, his face a shadow under the brim of a brown leather Akubra hat. Sending a dispatch rider rather than coded lantern signals— the pigeons did not fly at night—meant that the officer at the Bengal outpost considered the news a secret.

"Ho, there, Quentin Heath!" Balthazar shouted down into the courtyard. "I am Balthazar! What news have you to report?"

"Admiral, sir!" Heath saluted. "It is reported that the Brineboiler clan is under attack, sir!"

Buckle's heart jumped into his throat again. "Under attack from whom?" Balthazar asked.

"The Founders, sir!" Heath shouted, reining in his laboring horse as it spun around in a slew of foam, its hooves scraping loud on the flagstones. "The Founders have attacked the Brineboilers!"

Balthazar turned away from the balcony, his shoulders heaving as he struck his fist into the palm of his hand. "We are caught unprepared! Damn us to hell! While we sat here dancing, the Founders invasion has begun!"

‒XLIX‒

A MARTIAN NEVER LIES

Max heard Doctor Lee's voice, low, speaking in the kindly way doctors do, and she realized she was in the citadel infirmary. She was aware of Buckle's presence. He had not spoken, but she *knew* that Buckle was there—the one whom Lee was speaking to.

"She is slowly coming around," Lee said. "You may speak with her if you like, though I do not know if she will be able to respond."

"I only have a moment, Doctor," Buckle said.

Max fought to open her eyes; the lids fluttered, and her wide-open pupils stung at the soft flashes of pumpkin-colored lantern light. It was night. How long had she been unconscious? Her mind slipped away, wanting to drop off a cliff, but she clawed her way back. Sounds rushed in on her, loud in her ears: rustles of clothing, the scrape of a chair leg across the wooden floor, the hiss of the oil lanterns, the steady, metallic wheeze of her brother's iron lung beside her. Her body, tight with drug-blunted pain, warned her that her wounds were extensive. She could still feel the awful punch of the sabertooth fangs in her flesh, the rip of the claws. She shuddered. She was cold despite the heavy wool hospital blankets on her. And she was thirsty.

There was someone else in the room, Max sensed. A badly injured person, unconscious. She did not know who it was.

A wooden chair creaked at Max's bedside. She felt a hand, Buckle's hand, slip around her cold fingers, gently bundling them in his warm flesh.

"Hello, young lady," Buckle whispered in her ear, so close that she could hear the moistness of his tongue in his mouth. "The sawbones tells me you are recovering nicely."

Buckle was troubled. Max could sense it in his voice, even if he was trying to hide it by being soothing. Something was very wrong. Her heart pounded inside the distant, faraway cavern of her body. She tried to force herself awake. Her eyes would not open again, but she felt her body twisting.

"Whoa, take it easy, Max," Buckle said, his hand squeezing hers. "Take it easy. It is all right. Everything is all right."

"She is still in shock," Lee's voice echoed from across the room. "You may not get anything coherent from her quite yet. And it is time for her next dose of morphine."

Max heard the zip of the knife against the frail glass of the vial, the quick snap as the nipple broke off. She did not want the morphine. She wanted to be awake, no matter how much her wounds hurt her. She wanted to be awake long enough to see Buckle, to talk to him.

"Max, can you hear me? I have to go," Buckle said, releasing her hand. "I will check in on you as soon as I return. I brought you some presents." She heard his clothing rustle as he stood, the soft clatter of small things on the bedside table. "I took the liberty of bringing a few items from your cabin, a hummingbird nest and a chrysalis—is this from Sequoia? I don't know how you ever find the time to collect these things. They can help keep you occupied—you can study them while you convalesce. And there is a little gift from me as well. I made it myself."

Buckle was being calm, but he was in a terrible hurry.

Max lifted her eyelids and held them open. For a moment, all she could make out were shadows and shapes in the nebulous orange haze of lantern light. To her left loomed the bolted hump of Tyro's iron lung. Then the seams of the white-painted roof above her emerged into a set of soft vertical lines. She could not turn her head yet, but in the periphery of her vision she could see Buckle standing on her right. At the moment, his head was turned away toward Lee, and he had yet to notice that her eyes were open. He was dressed in his zeppelineer togs: his knee-high boots, the black trousers with the red stripe, his long leather coat with its double row of buttons, drawn in hard at the waist by his leather belt. He held his top hat, with its array of gears and gauges glittering in the lamplight, in his hand.

"Captain," Max whispered, her voice as weak and rough as if she had not spoken for a thousand years.

Buckle knelt down beside her. "Max—you are awake! Can you hear me?"

"What is happening?" she rasped. "Tell me." She wanted to say more, but she could not organize it, nor move her concrete tongue again so soon.

"Don't talk, Max," Buckle said gently. "Everything is fine."

Max felt Buckle grasp her hands. There was a nervousness in his touch. "Tell me the truth, Captain. You know Martians do not lie, and we can sense the lies of others. Tell me."

Buckle nodded. "The Founders have invaded Brineboiler territory. Balthazar has formed an alliance of clans against the Founders: us, the Alchemists, Imperials, Brineboilers, Gallowglasses, and, just barely, the Tinskins."

Max felt the stinging prick of a needle in the bend of her elbow, the heaviness of a morphine-filled vein. She realized that Doctor Lee was seated at her other side, and he was now withdrawing an empty syringe from her arm.

Max's eyes slammed shut and she fought them open again after two quivering blinks. "We need Spartak...the Steamweavers."

"I am on my way to Spartak. Ryder is off to negotiate with the Steamweavers."

Max wanted to be angry at herself but she could not muster it. Things were bad and here she lay useless in the infirmary, when the *Pneumatic Zeppelin* needed her most. She was only partially conscious now, being dragged away by the rhythmic lullaby of Tyro's iron lung.

"Get better. We need you," Buckle said. "I have to go now."

"What happened to me?" Max asked.

"You do not remember?" Buckle replied, sounding surprised.

"I remember the sabertooth on my back," Max said. "But no more."

"And nothing after that?" Buckle said. Max detected a hint of both relief and disappointment in his voice.

"I do not remember," Max whispered. She sensed the morphine torpor coming for her, and she allowed her eyelids to slip shut, surrendering to the void. She had lied. She remembered Buckle's naked torso pressed to hers, his chest a hot boiler against her frozen skin. She remembered her trembling lips finding his and the surge of life that kiss had poured into her ravaged body.

She remembered him *kissing her back*.

She remembered everything.

~L~

LADY ANDROMEDA'S CARRIAGE

CURSING IMPATIENTLY UNDER HIS BREATH, Buckle shared a concerned glance with Sabrina beside him as their dark carriage rattled and bumped up the rough-hewn access road of the airfield. It seemed like it was taking forever to get to the *Pneumatic Zeppelin*. He felt trapped in the lightless compartment, rocking back and forth, assailed by the noise of creaking axles and copper-sheathed wheels, the coachman's whip and pounding horse hooves. Fitzroy, Ivan, and Windermere crowded on the opposite bench, the latter two hastily dressed in their aviator togs, their faces pained by lovers' farewells.

The courtyard of the citadel had been a scene of controlled chaos: soldiers and servants shouting in the night as they dashed about in a near panic of swinging lanterns and torches, ambassadors and their aides shouting as they searched for the proper carriages in the lines, and their coachmen shouting out their passengers' titles as they fought to control spooking horses. Buckle had seen Thaddeus Aleppo and his fellow Brineboiler rush past. Aleppo's ruddy face was frantic, cold-slicked with tears; there was no knowing what they might find when they arrived home.

Buckle's gaze focused on Fitzroy. "You say the saboteur had no identifying markings, Mister Fitzroy? Are you sure?" Buckle had asked Fitzroy the same question four different ways since they had piled into the carriage, but he could not stop himself from asking it again.

"No, Captain," Fitzroy shouted back over the din. "But he was dressed pretty much all in black, according to Mister Banerji's account. Mister De Quincey sent me off to find you on the spot, sir. Perhaps they found something later, sir."

Buckle nodded, noticing that Ivan held Holly's whale-ivory-and-garnet cameo in his hands. "A grand token from your lady, Ivan?"

"Yes," Ivan replied.

"It is quite a lovely gesture of affection," Sabrina added.

Ivan smiled a little. "Yes, it is, is it not? Holly even offered to provide me with a teardrop for my chemical experiment, but I will be damned if I had anything in which to collect it."

"I am sure you will make her cry quite often," Sabrina said lightly. "You are far too difficult, after all."

Ivan nodded without protestation. He pulled the little wooden cardinal he had carved out of his pocket. "I forgot to give her my present. In the rush, I forgot to give it to her."

"It shall be a fine gift for her when you get back," Sabrina said.

The carriage hit a rough patch and groaned to a stop. Windermere hopped to the door and leapt out, holding it open. "There appears to be someone here waiting to see you, Captain," he called back in.

Collecting his sword, dismayed at the prospect of further delays, Buckle glared at Windermere as he stood outside the carriage door, backlit by falling snow and orange lantern light. "Someone? For the love of—Windy, be specific!"

"It is an Alchemist general, Captain," Windermere offered quietly.

"Lady Andromeda must be here," Sabrina whispered.

"Aye," Buckle replied, leveraging himself out onto the carriage steps and looking back at Sabrina. "Have Banerji show you exactly where the saboteur was when he found him. And see to the final preparations. I want to cast off before dawn."

"Aye," Sabrina said.

Buckle jumped to the ground. The air of the freshly fallen night met him with its harsh chill and coal fog, his boots crunching in a churned mess of ice, stiffening dope, soil, barrel dust, and mule manure—the perfume of every docked zeppelin. The repair dock in front of him was a lumber berth built twenty feet high, with the derricks and the huge mass of the *Pneumatic Zeppelin*'s flank looming like a mountain above that. Swirling yellow buglights hung on every rope, while the machinist trench under the dock, busy with the mumbles and clatterings of the ground crews, glowed green from its massive glass boil tanks.

"Captain Buckle, sir!" a man shouted, not far on Buckle's left. Buckle turned to see Sergeant Salgado and four marines, their scarlet jackets and red-puggareed pith helmets dusted with snow, marching up the access road with their duffel bags. They were newly assigned to the *Pneumatic Zeppelin* by Balthazar. Buckle knew Salgado; he was a good man.

"Sergeant Salgado!" Buckle shouted. "Good to have the marines aboard!"

"Glad to be here, sir!" Salgado shouted back with another salute.

Buckle immediately turned to his right and strode toward a waiting carriage, where General Scorpius stood beside the door, his plumed helmet tucked under his arm, his ornate breastplate gleaming with the flicker of a hundred lanterns.

"Greetings, Captain Buckle," Scorpius said with a salute. "It seems we only meet under harsh circumstances."

"Aye, General Scorpius," Buckle replied, tipping his hat. "I see they have promoted you to footman. Good show."

Scorpius did not crack a smile, nor had Buckle expected him to. He swung the carriage door open. "Please, Captain."

Buckle removed his top hat and ducked into the carriage. The interior was lit only by one small whale-oil lamp, whose small pool of light was abandoned in a sea of darkness after Scorpius slammed the door shut, nearly hammering Buckle in the arse with it.

"Please, Captain Buckle, have a seat." Andromeda's hauntingly melodic voice came from the blackness behind the lantern. She was very close, due to the cramped confines of the compartment, but she was beyond the limited reach of the lamplight. "I am honored that you might give me a moment when things are so hectic."

Buckle swung onto the opposite bench, gripping his scabbard to keep it clear of his legs. The seat was luxuriously posh, made of velvet and silk, and the wood panels glittered with gold etchings and tortoise wax. Andromeda was riding in one of the princely carriages reserved for visiting dignitaries.

"I am sure your matters are equally pressing," Buckle said. "It is not a good time to be far from home."

"No," Andromeda replied. She slid closer to the candle and Buckle could now see her fairly well, her elegant face with the appealing, gentle smile, the light hair, the still-healing scars from the prison-cell blast jagged but healing on her forehead, the hypnotist's violet-black eyes, now made even more powerful in the delicate half-light of the lantern flame. "As such, though it is a pleasure to see you again, please forgive me for being blunt."

"Of course."

"Do you know who you truly are? And who your sister is?" Andromeda asked. "From the time before Balthazar adopted you?"

Buckle blinked. He had not expected *that* question. "We are the offspring of Alpheus and Diana Buckle."

"Yes," Andromeda said, but she shook her head. "I do not mean to insult you, dear Captain, but that cannot be the entire story."

"What do you mean?"

"There is a reason why the Founders took Elizabeth, and we must find out why. It is imperative. Yes, your mission to Spartak is essential. But you must find a way to rescue Elizabeth, and rescue her quickly."

"Of course," Buckle said. "I would welcome any opportunity to rescue her. And I shall."

"And you must. I do not know very much, but I know that Elizabeth is the key to winning this war, the key to all of our futures. She must be rescued at all costs."

"Elizabeth is the key to everything?" Buckle asked. "How?"

"I do not know how, or why—but she *is*."

"Does Balthazar also believe this?"

"He has not confided such knowledge to me," Andromeda said. "What I am to recommend to you here and now, to ask you, is if you get the opportunity, no matter how risky, you must make every effort, even abandon your duties to the Alliance, to reclaim your sister from Isambard Kingdom Fawkes."

"Abandon my duties," Buckle repeated, as if the words needle-pricked his tongue. He was confused by Andromeda now, especially the certain feeling in his gut that she was telling him the truth.

Andromeda leaned forward and took his hand firmly in the grasp of her long, white, smooth-skinned fingers. "And, dear Captain, if you get to Elizabeth but she cannot be freed, you cannot leave her to the Founders. You must kill her rather than leave her to them—it will be a far more merciful fate than the one awaiting her as their prisoner." Andromeda leaned even closer, her voice preternaturally present in his ears, her fingers tightening around his bigger hands. "Romulus, there exists an ancient wickedness, the nature of which is unknown to me, but some terrible, awful evil has risen—and the Founders have made this horror their master. They need Elizabeth to achieve their goals, and if she cannot be rescued, then she must be destroyed, or all else, including all of us, will be ruin."

Buckle paused, staring into Andromeda's pleading eyes, eyes that promised that they understood. He heard himself breathing, heard the little crackle of the candle inside the lamp and the snorting of the horses outside. For a moment, he could sense the massive weight of the zeppelins looming around them in the night, the colossal void of the sky; he felt as if her hands were the only thing anchoring him on the brink of a bottomless pit of eternity. "I shall, Lady Andromeda," Buckle said, "profoundly consider what you have said to me here."

Andromeda sighed. It was as if she had used up much of her strength delivering her argument. She released her hold on Buckle's hand and leaned back into the shadows. Now Buckle could more hear her voice than he could see her.

"I can ask nothing more of you, Captain Romulus Buckle," Andromeda whispered. "I can only tell you what I believe, and promise every support from the Alchemist clan. It is up to you to choose your own course of action."

Buckle nodded.

"Look deep into your own heart, Romulus," Andromeda said. "You will find the answers to your questions only there."

"I shall, Lady Andromeda. But now I must go," Buckle said, standing, but still bent enough to avoid bumping his head on the low ceiling.

"Of course. I pray the fortune of the Oracle shall be with you."

"Thank you, Lady Andromeda," Buckle said, kissing her cool hand, which bore a lovely, unrecognizable perfume. "Farewell." He pressed the carriage handle down, swung the door open, and stepped outside where General Scorpius stood waiting in the lantern-lit snowfall.

The deep cold that had refreshed Buckle only moments before was now an icy slap in the face.

–LI–

CAPTAIN ROMULUS BUCKLE
AND HIS ZEPPELIN

Romulus Buckle was near infuriated. The *Pneumatic Zeppelin* was ready, lock, stock, and barrel, the *Arabella* launch secure in her berth, and now they had to wait.

The Crankshaft ambassador, Rutherford Washington, had yet to arrive aboard.

Buckle strode along the Hydro catwalk as it plunged through the mountainous heart of the airship, a massive elliptical cavern of canvas fourteen stories high, housing the huge gas cells and their spidery stockings, blast shields, ladders, catwalks, girder rings, pipes, valves, and wires sheathed in baggywrinkle, all creaking and hissing with their own gigantic life.

Kellie pranced at Buckle's heels, her bat ears pricked up through her leather flight helmet and goggles, following so close she bumped his calves. She was needy; she smelled the blood on the back of his neck, perhaps even the lingering scent of the kraken on him, and it worried her, but he could not carry her all the way through the inspection.

Buckle saw the newly promoted chief hydroman, Douglas Headford, hurrying along the Castle deck catwalk, high overhead. The airship was in good order—her hydrogen tanks at maximum pressure, her ammunition stocked, and her coal bunkers full—but Buckle could not escape an undercurrent of dread. It was odd—once he set foot on his zeppelin, he always felt free. But the saboteur, what the saboteur might have done, had left Buckle feeling heavy. Even though repeated investigations had found no evidence of tampering, the security of the sky vessel had been violated, putting everyone at risk.

And having an Imperial officer aboard did not lift his spirits, either.

Buckle drew out his pocket watch: five fifteen in the morning. Where the hell was Washington?

Buckle reached the forward staircase and headed down, his boots clumping on the metal steps. His second inspection in a row was complete. He decided to go to his quarters and fill in the logbook, and perhaps take some hot tea.

When Buckle reached his quarters and pushed the door open, Kellie dashed in and yipped happily at someone.

"Hello, you flea-bitten mongrel," Ivan said good-naturedly.

Buckle strode in to find Ivan sitting in a chair with his boots up on the Lion's Table, drinking Buckle's rum from a large glass. It appeared that Ivan had buried his sadness and replaced it with his usual obnoxious self.

"Now, witness the truly inappropriate, eh?" Buckle grumped.

Ivan slammed his boots on the floor, his ushanka cocked on his head, goggle lens gleaming, machine-encased arm lifting the rum glass, and saluted with his good hand. "Captain, sir!" he announced. The glass in his machine hand shattered in his metal-plated grip, falling to the deck in a tinkling of shards and a splat of liquid. "Blast it!" Ivan huffed.

"You are certainly full of piss and vinegar," Buckle said, stepping past the ruins of the glass to face out the towering nose window, folding his hands behind his back. The *Pneumatic Zeppelin's* bow was pointed at the mountains, their masses darker than the predawn sky above. The two nose mooring ropes, attached to docking hooks on the bow pulpit overhead and lined with buglights, ran down to their anchors in the airfield earth, where the ground crews and provisioners were loading tool kits and empty barrels into their carts, preparing to roll away.

The other zeppelins on the airfield rested easy on their mooring lines, sleeping behemoths skirted with firefly lanterns, dwarfing all things on the earth beneath them. The Imperial and Brineboiler airships had already departed. The Gallowglass corvette, the *Cork*, was in the process of lifting off, her gondola hulls seventy feet above the ground, her docking lines jerking as they were winched aboard, her portholes dimly aglow with the reflection of bioluminescent boil. For an instant Buckle envied them, for they were in the air again and he was not.

Buckle heard the gurgle of rum being poured into glass. "Have a shot of grog with me, shall you, Romulus?" Ivan asked.

"It is a bit too early in the morning for me, thank you."

"Early? It is late," Ivan said.

Buckle stepped down from the platform and took a glass from Ivan. Buckle wanted tea—Howard Hampton was supposed to be arriving with a fresh pot, along with sugar cubes and fastmilk—but he knew how happy Ivan was. Holly Churchill happy. It was rare to see his taciturn, socially awkward brother in such fine fettle—after he had gotten over leaving her behind.

"To the sweet ladies!" Ivan proclaimed, raising a new glass in his good hand.

"To Holly Churchill," Buckle said.

"Aye!" Ivan said.

Buckle and Ivan drank, and set their glasses on the table. The rum bit Buckle's esophagus all the way down to his stomach.

A rap sounded at the door.

"Enter!" Buckle said.

Sabrina and Windermere strode in, their hats tucked under their arms. Sabrina had been outside—snowflakes flecked her long black coat with the fleurs-de-lis on the collar and sleeves. Buckle was glad to see her at the rough and ready. But he was almost disappointed that he could not view her one more time in her brilliant-emerald ball gown.

"Captain, may we have a word?" Sabrina asked. The way Sabrina made certain that the door shut securely behind her signaled that something was up.

"Not unless you are bringing tea," Buckle replied, feeling grumpy. "And look out for the mess," he said, pointing to Ivan's broken glass on the deck. "Gorky has been wild this morning." Sabrina stepped to the Lion's Table. "Mister Windermere, where is the Imperial princess now?"

"On the bridge," Windermere replied.

Sabrina nodded, then turned to Buckle. "Captain, we know that we are acting on behalf of the Grand Alliance, and in that capacity the Imperials are our allies. And while, as such, we must trust them, we must also not leave ourselves completely exposed to acts of treachery."

"Imperial treachery?" Buckle said, both startled and exasperated. "Really? Do you have evidence of this?"

"No," Sabrina replied. "But—"

"Captain—" Windermere stepped in. "The *Pneumatic Zeppelin* is an Imperial airship, designed by them, built by them, and her extreme value, especially in a time of war, might warrant trickery in order to get her back."

"And lose us as allies in the process?" Buckle asked. "Such an act would seem self-destructive."

"Not if they took the airship and sided with the Founders," Ivan countered.

"I tend to think that the Imperials are with us," Buckle said. "Especially with no evidence to the contrary."

"I simply wish to be careful," Sabrina said. "After all, we took this zeppelin as a prize by force, in a night raid that turned out to be a mistake. And now we are going to sail her, big, fat, and happy, right back into their harbor?"

"I think you two are too suspicious by a foot and a hair," Buckle said. "But I understand your concern. We have to land at New Berlin to embark the Imperial ambassador. In the unlikely case they do attack, they will not destroy their own airship, but would try to take her back by boarding."

"Agreed," Sabrina said.

"We cannot risk insulting the princess," Buckle continued. "As we make our landing approach I want you, Ivan, and Mister Windermere to quietly assemble an antiboarding team on the Axial deck. Arm them with muskets and swords from the forward weapons lockers."

"Yes, Captain," Ivan said, suddenly quite somber. Pushkin the wugglebat poked his furry little head out of Ivan's pocket and chirped a little. "One cannot trust the damned Imperial lobster tails, sir."

Buckle looked at Ivan. "If we are attacked, we cut the hawsers, blast away the anchors, and get the *Pneumatic Zeppelin* back up in the air immediately." There was a pause, and Buckle slapped his hands together. "Good. I wager such precautions shall not prove necessary, but I agree one must watch one's back in times such as these. Now, where is that damned tea?"

A loud rap rattled the door.

"Ah, there Hampton is! About time!" Buckle said. He really wanted some tea, especially to settle his squeezing stomach. "Enter, Howard, and save me!"

The door swung open, hard on the hinges, and in strode Valkyrie Smelt. She was dressed in her stiff powder-blue Imperial uniform, her face and body all straight lines except for the swell of her hips and breasts. Her blond hair was pulled back severely and she was bareheaded, her pickelhaube jammed under her left arm, spike gleaming, the *Pneumatic Zeppelin*'s engineering logbook tucked under her right. She was long legged, her height amplified by the black leather jackboots that rose to her knees, and her double-breasted uniform jacket gleamed with gold lace and buttons. At her waist she wore a thick black leather belt lined with instrument pouches. Her cuffs and collar were heavily embroidered with red and gold braid, and her high cheekbones emphasized the disapproval burning in her cold blue eyes.

"Princess. Welcome," Buckle said, but his words sounded hollow to him. It could be of no comfort to Valkyrie, acting chief engineer, and therefore one of the airship's most senior officers, to find the Crankshaft bridge crew huddled in a meeting from which she had been excluded.

Valkyrie halted, eyeing everyone in the way a prison guard might scrutinize a cell full of prisoners where the sounds of digging had been heard. She cleared her throat. "Captain, may I have a word?"

"Of course, Chief Engineer," Buckle replied.

"In private, Captain," Valkyrie said flatly.

-LII-

A PICKELHAUBE AND TEA

ONCE THE DOOR SHUT AND Valkyrie and Buckle were alone, Buckle wondered if the Imperial princess might prove more dangerous to him than the missing saboteur.

Valkyrie placed the logbook and her helmet on the Lion's Table with a heavy metal *thump*, as if she owned it. Her pickelhaube's silver spike, rubbed with oilskin to a brilliant gleam, loomed over the front plate with its iron cross. "I do not appreciate being excluded from officer meetings," Valkyrie said, bristling, and turned to glare at Buckle, the edges of her hair glowing orange in the illumination from the lanterns outside the nose window. "Unless, of course, they are nothing more than insider whisperings, Crankshaft machinations meant to be hidden from me."

"You must expect," Buckle said evenly, disliking his words even as he spoke them, "that the Crankshaft clan carries out business that the Imperials are not privy to."

Kellie hopped off the bed and trotted up to Valkyrie's knees, tail wagging. Valkyrie looked down her nose at the dog. Kellie hopped up on her back legs, stretching her paws up onto Valkyrie's thighs.

"As long as your cloak-and-dagger conferences do not impede the efficient running of this sky vessel, then I shall ignore the insult implied by my exclusion," Valkyrie said. She knelt and rubbed the dog's ears roughly, in the way a person who is familiar with dogs knows how to rub them.

Valkyrie's unguarded, kind reaction to the animal surprised Buckle. The silly dog had broken the ice.

"You have an affection for dogs, I see," Buckle said. He considered people who disliked dogs to be lacking in fundamental humanity.

Valkyrie patted Kellie on the head and stood up in one smooth motion. "A dog would run into a burning building to save you. A horse would run itself until its heart bursts for you. One can rarely expect such loyalty from another human being."

"There is truth in that," Buckle said. "And what do you expect from me?"

Valkyrie's eyes flashed with both challenge and humor. "I see in your eyes the same thing you see in mine, Captain—distrust."

"Not a good condition between a Captain and his second," Buckle said. He did like Valkyrie's straightforward style, even if it was somewhat off-putting.

"No," Valkyrie answered slowly.

Buckle smiled. He could tell that his grin caught Valkyrie off guard, just a touch, by the slight rise in her yellow eyebrows. "It is as it must be, then, is it not? At least, for starters."

"Yes."

"I have faith in you regarding your care of my airship," Buckle said. "Just resist any urge to tinker with it."

"I do live my life to tinker," Valkyrie replied.

"As for the rest of it, well, my faithful dog is an excellent judge of character—and you seem to have made a smashing impression on her."

"I see," Valkyrie replied, narrowing her eyes. "I do feel it is important to inform you that I do not agree with my father's decision to allow you to keep possession of the *Pneumatic Zeppelin*, Captain. However, that said, I am your most humble junior officer and I shall act in perfect accordance with my duties."

Like her father, she considers me a pirate and a thief, Buckle thought. Well, he allowed himself some empathy regarding their position. Had somebody taken the *Pneumatic Zeppelin* from him—in a raid that would later turn out to be unprovoked and misguided—he supposed that he would be rather prickly about it as well. "I understand your position, Princess, and I would expect nothing less," Buckle replied. "May I offer you a drink?"

Valkyrie looked at the open rum bottle. "I think not, Captain. Thank you." She pointed the toe of her polished boot and nudged the glass shards on the floor. "I am not one for rum in the morning."

"Yes," Buckle said. "I am supposed to have tea coming, and I am getting grumpy about it."

Valkyrie planted her fingers on the logbook. "May I deliver my engineering report?"

"Deliver away."

"All systems at the ready. We are fixed to depart as soon as your ambassador arrives. There was a considerable amount of repair work done to the superstructure and piloting gondola. Your injured chief engineer—Max, I believe her name is—had installed an ambitious refitting schedule. I have inspected the ship, and I must say, you Crankshafts have very competent repair crews, Captain."

Buckle nodded.

A rap sounded at the door.

"That had better be my bloody tea," Buckle grumbled. "Enter!"

The door opened, propelled by the back of the blond-haired Howard Hampton as he balanced in his hands a silver tray holding a teapot, five china cups and saucers, a bowl of sugar cubes, a decanter of fastmilk cream, napkins, and five silver spoons.

"Ah!" Buckle said, hurrying forward to take the tray from Howard. "Good work, Howard, lugging all this all of the way up here!"

"Thank you, sir. No need, but thank you, sir." Howard beamed.

"Princess Valkyrie, this is Howard Hampton, cabin boy and gunner's mate."

"My lady," Howard said, dramatically bowing to Valkyrie.

"Thank you, Howard Hampton, cabin boy and gunner's mate," Valkyrie said kindly. "But you need not bow to me aboard a warship."

"Yes, yes," Howard muttered, almost bowing again, nervous. "Do you need anything more, Captain?" he asked.

"No thank you, Howard," Buckle replied, glancing at the clock on the bulkhead. "This is quite sufficient. Go on."

"Sir," Howard said, and he bowed to Valkyrie. "Thank you, Princess."

"Thank you, Howard Hampton," Valkyrie replied as the cabin boy scurried out the door.

Buckle placed the rattling tray on the table. "Would you join me in a cup of tea, Princess?" Buckle asked. "It will be almond, if we have any left, that is."

"Tea most certainly, Captain," Valkyrie responded.

"Please, allow me," Buckle said, placing two cups in their saucers on the table and lifting the teakettle by its carved wooden handle from its crocheted trivet, feeling the heat rising from the metal along the back of his hand.

"And if you please, Captain. You need not address me as Princess aboard a warship. "My acting rank here is lieutenant, and that will be quite sufficient as long as I am aboard."

"Of course, Lieutenant," Buckle said, pouring the steaming brown tea into two cups. "Do you take milk or sugar?"

"A dollop of milk. Never sugar."

"Sweet enough, are we?" Buckle said. It was a standard Crankshaft response to a woman who refused sugar in her tea, but in the instant it passed through his lips, he knew it was the wrong thing to say—far too familiar. "My apologies," he followed up quickly, offering her the cup and saucer with a folded napkin and spoon. "Less than appropriate, considering the present company."

Valkyrie took the teacup in her long fingers. "You need not walk on eggshells around me, Captain. We are shipmates, if only temporarily, and I do not wish for my crewmates to feel as if they must act differently around me. That would be distracting and impede efficiency, do you not agree?"

"Absolutely," Buckle replied, dumping milk and sugar into his tea.

"Pardon me, Captain," Valkyrie said. "But you have forgotten my milk."

"Forgive me, Lieutenant," Buckle said, leaning forward to pour fastmilk cream into her cup, where it swirled, turning the black liquid a milky chocolate brown.

Buckle reached for his cup, his mouth watering. Hot tea in the early morning was one of his favorite things.

A rap hit the door, a loud bang rather than a knuckle tap, and Windermere was on his way in just as the bosun's whistle rang out somewhere amidships.

"Captain!" Windermere announced. "Ambassador Washington is aboard. We are ready to cast off."

Valkyrie traded her tea for her pickelhaube.

Buckle set his cup down. No time for tea now. "Prepare to up ship," he ordered.

–LIII–

FUNERAL PYRES AT DAWN

"Bring her around, due west," Buckle ordered on the bridge of the *Pneumatic Zeppelin* as he rose into the soft blue-purple clouds of the predawn sky.

"Due west, aye," Helmsman De Quincey answered, turning the rudder wheel hand over hand.

The huge sky vessel groaned comfortably, finally free from a month in the repair dock, her hydrogen cells engorged, the airfield a sweep of orange lantern dots beneath her. Buckle felt the smooth tremble of the propellers as they wound up, felt the forward surge of their energy through the deck, and heard the rising rumble of the steam engines far behind. The *Pneumatic Zeppelin* smoothly gained speed as she passed over the Devil's Punchbowl; Buckle looked ahead through the slightly distorted glass panes of the nose dome, watching the wide, white sweep of the Mojave Valley plain as it unfolded far away toward the western horizon. The dusky peaks of the San Gabriel Mountains encircled them to the fore and flanks, brightening against the cloudy sky as the sun awoke behind them in the east, somewhere directly behind the stern.

Buckle could still see an airfield windsock hanging limp on its docking tower. Casting off before daybreak was good because the world almost always lay motionless then. It was still dark, but the atmosphere was lighting up fast, rapidly shifting into shades of lighter and lighter gray blue. There was no need for lanterns anymore.

Howard Hampton appeared at Buckle's side, between Kellie and the chart table, with a silver tray and a steaming teapot. "I thought you might still wish a cup, Captain."

Buckle beamed, taking the cup and pouring the bubbling black liquid out of the pot. "I declare you are a lifesaver, Hampton. Thank you, kind sir."

Howard Hampton beamed so widely Buckle feared his lips might crack.

Buckle dumped two lumps of brown sugar into the tea—he was too busy to bother with the cream—and his nod sent Hampton marching happily away. Buckle sipped the brew; it was almond, sugar bitter, and lip-scaldingly hot, and it tasted like peace and quiet.

Of course, such tranquillity could not last. When was he ever given a moment's peace aboard his own ship?

A few seconds later, Meagan Churchill shouted from the aft corridor. "We have been sent a flag message, Captain."

Here it comes. Buckle tensed, tea ruined, ready for bad news.

"It is Admiral Balthazar, wishing us all the best of luck, Captain!" Meagan reported.

Buckle relaxed again. It seemed he was to be spared for once. "Aye! Thank you, Miss Churchill." Meagan Churchill, the lovely fawn, was at her new station alongside Jacob Fitzroy in the signals cabin. Long hours, spent huddled together, two attractive kids—Buckle figured human nature would run its course and the two would be sharing a bunk before the month was out. He did not want to have to explain that one to Holly. He would let Sabrina do that.

Buckle peered down at the citadel through the floor observation window, which was partially blocked by Kellie's tail: the heavy stone walls, built in a hexagon into the natural ridges of the boulders, looked geometric compared to the sprawling, low, brownish town around it, where the irregular streets were interrupted by the India-rubber factories, and the cottages on the fringes expanded in all directions, though mostly west onto the plain.

It was then that Buckle saw the smoke, unmistakable gray-black columns of wood smoke, rising from the citadel courtyard, and the meaning of it struck him in the heart. The torches had lit the pyres of the dead—his four dead, his crew members lost to the kraken—in the center of the courtyard. Balthazar was overseeing the ceremonies in Buckle's place, comforting the mourners and the bereaved families—a role Buckle was already too familiar with—accepting the sobbing hugs of the mothers, the brave handshakes of the fathers, the grim, wet eyes of husbands and wives, and the blank stares of uncertain children.

The names would be read: Henry Stuart, mechanic; Martin Robinson, signals; Hector Hudson, skinner; and Carmen Steinway, skinner.

Right on cue, the ballast officer, Nero Coulton, the ship's resident awful poet, recited a verse from Elkhorn's *Dead Mates* and thankfully not one of his own barely rhyming disasters.

> A zeppelineer mourns those who fell
> With a sadness sharp and deep;
> He spits at hell and bids farewell
> And lets the dear departed sleep.

"Up ship, three thousand feet," Buckle ordered, swallowing his sadness, taking the poem to heart. They needed altitude to clear the San Gabriels.

"Currently at one thousand feet, Captain," Sabrina announced. Her voice was distant, bodiless.

"Up ship," Windermere said, nudging the elevator wheel.

"Up ship, aye," Nero repeated, hands on his hydrogen and ballast wheels.

Buckle barely heard his crew. He was lost in a memory, standing in the courtyard of the Tehachapi stronghold, his head wrought to putty by despair, his mouth bitter with the stink of the smoking ruins all around him, vainly searching for his sister, Elizabeth, whose body had disappeared under the rain of bombs the night before.

Elizabeth had loved Elkhorn.

***

"You cannot shout and caterwaul around in the council chamber," Elizabeth said, holding open the heavy timber door Buckle had just stormed out of. "Getting all riled up like that is counterproductive."

Buckle, his boots crunching in the snow, his eyes glazing momentarily as they adjusted to the night and the sputtering flames of the Tehachapi stronghold's street lanterns, spun around to face her. "They are fools!" Buckle shouted. "Damned fools!"

Elizabeth smiled empathetically with her perfect teeth; she laughed at Buckle and his passionate outbursts often, but always managed to mollify rather than anger him with her amusement. Elizabeth had a stately face, one harboring beauty, strength, and kindness. Her eyes, light brown and quick, were framed by the auburn hair resting lightly on her shoulders, the red tints afire with the oranges emanating from a lamp overhead. She was ever-so-slightly plump, and it made her buxom, but also imparted to her face a softness that might make one forget how relentless a negotiator she was—but only for a moment.

"I do not think that Balthazar shares your thirst for exploration, dear brother." Elizabeth sighed.

"And so we purchase another penny-pinching, fat-hulled tramp steamer?" Buckle asked, exasperated, though he felt his anger ebbing away. He released his hand from a death grip on his scabbard, stretching his knotted fingers. "We need to push the frontiers, to range out, Elizabeth. If we do not crack new trading routes into the borderlands, into the Eastern Pale and beyond the Offing, somebody else will crack them first. And you cannot explore new territory with tramps. We need fast traders and clippers."

"You are calming down, yes?" Elizabeth said, stepping out into the street and letting the door groan shut behind her. The door was decorated with a big pair of elk antlers—everything in Tehachapi was decorated with antlers. Elizabeth had a far cooler head on her shoulders than Buckle, which was why Balthazar had enlisted her into his diplomatic corps along with Ryder. "How about we stroll back into Pinyon Hall and you can apologize to the grand old men for your outburst, shall we? They are not too insulted anyway, so used are they to your strenuous protestations from time to time, son of Balthazar."

"Not yet," Buckle said. "I am not so proper nor astute as you. I am going to take a walk. You get inside—you are not dressed to be out here."

Elizabeth took hold of Buckle's arm and, leaning up on her tiptoes, for she was not as tall as he, planted a warm kiss on his cheek.

Then she released him and stepped back, crossing her arms. "Despite your serious shortcomings, I do so love you, dear brother of mine."

"And I love you, too, sister."

"Leave it to me to smooth things over in your absence, as usual," Elizabeth said with an exaggerated sigh. "I shall collect some of Mother's cakes from the pantry. Cherry pastries and coffee tend to soften the old fellows up a bit."

"And tell them we need a clipper!" Buckle howled over his shoulder, already striding away, street slush squishing under his boots.

"Oh, my dear, poor Romulus," Elizabeth shouted after him. "Always, always a little too brash."

"Good night, Sister," Buckle said. He glanced back and saw her watching after him, her face gentle and beautiful as it always was, warmed by her bemused smile. She lifted her hand and waved. He waved back. She was everything to Buckle, his confidant, loyal friend, and sympathetic ear, and he could never, no matter how delicate she might appear from time to time, ever shake the feeling that she was destined for something big.

Buckle walked away. Of course he did not know it, but that would be the last time he would see Elizabeth alive.

***

"Heading due west, Captain," Sabrina said. "Three thousand feet."

Buckle blinked. West. He stepped to the chadburn and grabbed the handle, slamming it back and forward, ringing the bell as he planted the needle on all ahead full.

"All ahead full," Buckle shouted.

Elizabeth was somewhere to the west.

~LIV~

NEW BERLIN

BUCKLE SCANNED A METEOROLOGICAL MAP on the small chart table on the bridge, the lines and numbers stained yellow by stinkum and blotted with what looked like spilled coffee stains, half-studying the now near-useless old wind patterns of the mountainous region where New Berlin, the main Imperial stronghold, was located on the western cliffs of a valley known as the Ojai. Buckle had flown over this terrain once before, but it had been on a moonless night, the night the Crankshafts raided New Berlin, and the night he took the *Pneumatic Zeppelin* as a prize.

The piloting gondola was relatively quiet despite the number of crew stationed within it; the wind streamed past against the hull and overhead envelope with a constant rustle, the propellers and engines humming loudly from behind, the pigeons cooing gently in the signals room. Buckle peered out the round porthole over the chart table. The gray sky was particularly bright on this first day of February, and the rough ridges of the tree-furred mountains stood out in a stark relief of harsh greens, whites, and browns. With the engines at maximum and no headwind, the *Pneumatic Zeppelin* was making seventy knots. New Berlin would be coming into view at any moment.

The apprentice navigator, Darius Banerji, walked past, on his way to the nose to assist Wellington.

"Mister Banerji, a word, if you please, sir," Buckle said.

Banerji spun on his heel and turned to face Buckle. He stood ramrod straight, frightened. He was of average height, quite thin, with dark-brown skin and a narrow face, and he was extremely intelligent. The young midshipman was a zeppelineer to the bone, bookish but also athletic, and he proudly wore the red kerchief around his neck, the privileged mark of a gun crew member. Somewhere in the back of Buckle's mind he had already tagged Banerji for accelerated advancement into the officer ranks. "Yes, Captain," he said.

"You have had a little time," Buckle said. "Do you remember any more details regarding our saboteur?"

"No, sir, I am afraid not," Banerji replied apologetically. "Other than that he was quite nimble, a true runner."

"Very well," Buckle said. He had not expected anything more—the poor apprentice navigator had already told his story several times to Sabrina, Valkyrie, and a host of junior investigating officers. "Take your post."

Banerji hesitated, then said, "Captain, I am deeply sorry that I allowed the saboteur to escape, sir. I accept full responsibility. I failed, sir, but I would have sworn I potted him, Captain. I was sure I potted him."

Buckle shook his head. "Do not consider your actions a failure. Do not give it another thought. A man fires a pistol in your face in the middle of the night, well, you have a right to be a bit punchy. You chased him off the ship. You acted well."

"Thank you, sir," Banerji replied, looking relieved, his eyes shining.

"Back to your post with you then, airman," Buckle said.

"Aye, Captain," Banerji said with a quick salute, and hurried forward.

Buckle had just enough time to return to his map when two pairs of boots came clomping down the circular staircase. Buckle looked past the marine now stationed at the landing to see Ivan and Valkyrie, both bringing the smell of machine oil and boiler heat with them, swinging down. Ivan's face was pinched; Valkyrie looked as calm as ever.

"A word, Captain?" Ivan asked.

Buckle glanced at Ivan and groaned internally. Ivan had pulled his magnifying goggles on over both his good eye and the medical goggle covering his left eye, which produced a bug-eyed, off-kilter effect.

"Take the blasted goggles off first, Gorky," Buckle said. "You look like a deformed dung fly."

"The temporary chief engineer has only been aboard half a day, and already she is messing with the boilers, Captain," Ivan muttered, lowering his goggles. "And I have taken exception. She is only temporary, sir."

Buckle lowered his head. The skin stretching across the kraken wound was painful. "What do you mean, *messing with the boilers?*"

"Ah, she got ahold of Faraday and had him screw down the exhaust valves so they were tighter, then lowered the radiator scoops two degrees. She claimed it would improve our fuel burning efficiency."

"Did you do this, Chief Engineer?" Buckle asked.

"Yes, I did," Valkyrie replied. She saw Pushkin poke his furry head out of Ivan's breast pocket, his eyes glistening. She gave Ivan a disapproving look.

"I suppose the boilers might explode when we ram the throttle, now," Ivan whined. He had taken on the habit of clicking his metal fingers against each other when he was annoyed.

"Did her alteration improve efficiency?" Buckle asked.

Ivan's eyes widened. "Perhaps, just a hair. Who knows? But it was not necessary."

"Yes, it did improve burning efficiency," Valkyrie offered. "I do know the best way to operate Imperial-built engine systems, Captain."

"Our chief engineer Max would be hurt if you were known to be more wizardly with her engines than she is," Buckle said, rolling up the chart and plunking it home in its leather case with a hollow *thunk*.

"She has done an excellent job with her systems, Captain, but there is always room for improvement," Valkyrie said.

"Yes," Buckle mused. "You are the chief engineer, of course, but perhaps it is best to leave things as they are, do you not agree?"

Valkyrie nodded, her blue eyes looking through him, not appearing in the least bit ruffled. Buckle wondered if she had any intention of obeying him at all.

"Captain Buckle!" Sabrina shouted. "New Berlin in sight, one point off the starboard bow, sir!"

Drawing his telescope from his hat, Buckle hurried up into the nose alongside Sabrina.

"New Berlin, dead ahead!" the lookout's voice rattled down the chattertube from the crow's nest.

Buckle felt a pang of annoyance as he looked forward, catching the distant patch of light gray against the greens, browns, and whites of the mountains before he lifted his glass to his eye. The barrelman—the forward lookout—should have seen the city before Sabrina did. Through the telescope lens, the dot of New Berlin leapt closer, a light-colored, sprawling mass of buildings built into the side of a mountain and resting atop a cliff. It was a grand, well-designed city, a proud Founders-built colony long ago, before the Founders' empire had fallen apart.

"Half full," Buckle ordered.

"Half full. Aye, Captain," Valkyrie repeated, cranking the chadburn and dinging the bell.

The propellers lowered their throaty roar, and Buckle felt the *Pneumatic Zeppelin* slow down as he glanced back at the helm. "We shall swing around the city to the north, Mister De Quincey. The airfield is on the north side."

"Aye, aye," De Quincey replied.

"Ambassador on the bridge!" the marine, a far-too-earnest corporal named Nyland, announced unnecessarily. Buckle glanced back to see the elderly Rutherford Washington exit the stairs onto the deck, wearing his fine white suit with its red ambassadorial sash and cummerbund.

"We are approaching New Berlin, Ambassador," Buckle said warmly, covering up his lack of enthusiasm at having another idler on his deck.

Washington nodded with his usual gravity and sidestepped to the observer's chair at the rear of the gondola. At least the old lion had sense enough to stay out of the way.

"Captain," Sabrina said, and the odd tone of her voice made Buckle whip around. She had just lowered her telescope a hair beneath her green eyes, which were now beset with a quizzical, worried look as they mirrored the sunlight reflecting off the mountains of ice, and then jerked the glass back up again.

"What is it, Navigator?" Buckle asked.

"Captain," Sabrina replied, her voice low and serious, "the Founders are here."

"What?"

"An airship moored at the airfield. The closest one to the city. The silver phoenix, sir," Sabrina whispered.

Buckle raised his telescope. There was no doubting Sabrina's sharp eyes, but he had to see it for himself. He caught sight of the Founders phoenix on the flank of a pocket zeppelin moored among the Imperial airships on their terraced airfield.

"It surely is," Buckle muttered. The Founders in New Berlin? Buckle had never heard of a Founders airship appearing outside their own city for the last fifty years—except, of course, to bomb Tehachapi and crash on a sabertooth-infested mountain. "Do you count more than one?"

"No," Sabrina said, scanning the airfield with her telescope. "Only the one, as far as I can tell."

"Damned unsettling," Buckle muttered.

"What do you make of it?" Sabrina asked in a whisper. Welly had his telescope up beside her, uttering a soft whistle.

"The Imperials are negotiating with the Founders at the same time they are making alliances with us, it appears," Buckle said.

Suddenly Washington was tight on Buckle's shoulder, smelling of pipe smoke and the pine needles his suit had been packed in, peering hard through the window, snorting through his nostrils.

"You say the Founders are in New Berlin?" Washington asked.

"Aye, Ambassador," Buckle replied. He glanced back at Valkyrie; she stood at the engineering station, looking forward with her usual calmness. He could not tell if she was yet aware of the Founders sighting or not.

"Unprecedented," Washington grumbled. "Inconceivable. Unsettling."

"Founders airship sighted!" the lookout cried down the chattertube, late again. "Founders airship sighted in the New Berlin docks!" Buckle closed his eyes for a moment and grimaced. He would bawl out the two weak-eyed barrelmen later.

"What are the fogsuckers doing here?" Welly stammered.

"Either they have been here all along or they have beat us to it," Sabrina said.

"Where does that bloody well leave us, then?" Welly asked.

"Do not jump to conclusions," Washington warned.

Buckle zipped his telescope shut and tucked it back into his top hat. "We stay the course."

"Just peachy," Sabrina muttered.

"Chief Engineer," Buckle ordered. "Come forward."

Leaving Geneva Bolling on station, Valkyrie strode up to the nose through a harsh silence. She stopped beside Buckle and Washington; Washington peered down his huge nose at her, his cataract-fogged eyes attentive but not necessarily suspicious—unlike Wellington's and Sabrina's eyes.

"Your people have visitors," Buckle said.

"A Founders airship. Aye. I heard," Valkyrie replied, calm as ever.

"How often does New Berlin entertain the Founders?" Washington asked.

Valkyrie cocked her head ever so slightly at the ambassador. "Never," she replied.

"Take a look," Buckle said, stepping aside in what little space he had to allow Valkyrie to slip forward into the nose bubble. Valkyrie drew a pair of bronze binoculars from her belt and raised them to her eyes.

"One mile to the airfield, Captain," Sabrina said, having turned back to her station.

Buckle looked ahead. The *Pneumatic Zeppelin* was still approaching the Imperial city at considerable speed; the airfield and the ramparts of the town were now plainly visible in detail.

"Quarter full," Buckle ordered. "Bring us down to fifteen knots."

"Quarter full, aye!" Bolling repeated, ringing the chadburn bell.

New Berlin was a large urban center that, despite hugging the uneven face of a mountain, displayed the regular lines and streets of a highly planned city with ring roads. The buildings were built mostly of gray stone, unlike the timber structures that prevailed at the Devil's Punchbowl, and their roofs were shingled with some kind of metal. The inner fortress loomed on the mountain crest, its ramparts in the shape of a giant cog, its walls sheathed in what looked like gunmetal iron.

Buckle recognized the topography of the town; he had seen it on the night of the reprisal raid, its outline accentuated by lines of torches and lanterns. The first sight of the giant orange-lit, cog-shaped stronghold against the black mountain was one of his strongest memories of the night. The city looked to be in good shape—if any of the bomb strikes inflicted on that night the year before had been profound, there was now no sign of damage.

Buckle turned his eyes to the airfield, with the famous dockyard and its massive construction hangars looming beyond, where a half-dozen small Imperial airships hovered at their docking towers. The stair-stepped terraces of the airfield, great swaths of dirty brown snow crisscrossed with wagon and bowser tracks, splotched with piss-yellow pools of dumped, stiffening dope and lacquer, dotted with discarded buckets, and horse and mule dung, was the place where Sebastian Mitty and Captain Halifax had died, where Tyro had fallen to a fate worse than death.

Valkyrie replaced her binoculars in their belt pouch and turned to face Buckle. "The Founders are here to deliver an ultimatum, I would presume."

"And we are supposed to take you at your word for that?" Ivan asked.

Valkyrie pointed to the fortress. "Do you see the brace of flags beneath our Imperial banner, Captain?"

Buckle looked at the fortress tower, where the large Imperial standard, a black iron cross set against a white background, flapped lazily atop its pole. Beneath it, on the circular balcony, hung a line of small, multicolored signal flags. "Yes," Buckle replied.

"The signals are for us. The green flag stands for a foreign ambassador of high rank. The blue flag with the vertical black stripe means they were not invited," Valkyrie said.

"And yet you still welcome them with open arms, eh, spiker?" Ivan sniped.

Valkyrie turned to face Ivan, who had crept up behind, further crowding the nose. "My clan would have received a Founders ambassador with extreme trepidation. We trust the Founders no more than you do. We fear them no less than you do. But to turn an ambassador away could only make matters worse."

"But your alliance is with us—or is it?" Ivan grumbled, looking as if he might take a menacing step toward Valkyrie, who somehow seemed to Buckle as if she might welcome such a move.

"That is enough, Ivan," Buckle said. "One must always avoid confusion when the hounds of war are afoot."

"The Imperial harbormaster is signaling the airfield approach, Captain," Sabrina said.

"Aye, Navigator," Buckle answered, eyeing the Founders phoenix below. "The hounds of war," he whispered to himself.

–LV–

AMBASSADOR BISMARCK

ROMULUS BUCKLE HAD NEVER RIDDEN in a steam-powered carriage before, though he had heard of them. The awkward, ponderous, vapor-wreathed contraptions were rare in the outland type of strongholds in which the Crankshafts existed, because there were no paved streets, nor mechanics trained to fix them, and they were constantly breaking down.

The armor-plated Imperial steam carriage was big, seating six in the dark passenger compartment, plus the driver and an armed coachman at the fore. A huge steam engine strapped on the back end drove the iron wheels of the impossibly heavy conveyance forward with a piston-banging power that made the whole thing shake and rattle and puff contemptuously along the cobblestoned streets of New Berlin. Buckle could just barely hear the clatter of the horse-drawn carriages both in front and behind, and the rumble of the cavalry escort alongside.

The interior of the compartment was lined with dark-blue velvet, which seemed to absorb the light from two gurgling boil lamps overhead, but could not obscure the gigantic bolts and rivets securing the iron sheets around them. Ambassador Washington was located on Buckle's immediate left, while Sabrina sat on the other side of Washington.

Buckle glanced at the three Imperials seated on the bench across from them. Valkyrie was directly in front of him, their knees almost touching, with her brother, Bismarck Smelt, on her right. Bismarck was the lead Imperial ambassador, and apparently made of the same genetic materials as she; he was tall, intelligent-eyed, narrow at the waist, and broad at the shoulders. A sandy mustache gave his boyish face a much-needed punch of manhood. His uniform was different from the other soldiers'; his collar tabs and cuffs were all white, and he wore a soft field cap, rather than the omnipresent pickelhaube. His chest was bedecked with medals, ribbons, and a wide white sash.

Just from the way Valkyrie and Bismarck sat together, hip to hip, Buckle could tell they were close, and a formidable team.

On the other side of Bismarck sat Colonel Rainer, the Imperial air-fleet commander, an unattractive middle-aged woman with a gold-spiked pickelhaube in her lap; her uniform, heavily laced with gold and crimson, gripped a body as thickset as a tree trunk. Her face was undeniably hard and gecko-featured, her long, hay-colored hair thatched into braids, and her leathery skin, bronzed by snow-reflected sunlight, presented deep wrinkles that made her look older than she was.

The six of them had been riding in the armored motorcar for only two minutes, and already the conversation had trailed off into an uncomfortable silence. Buckle had felt anxious about the whole thing even as he and Sabrina strode down the *Pneumatic Zeppelin*'s gangplank behind Valkyrie and the ambassador, their boots landing on the mushy airfield permafrost in the artificial chasm formed by the soaring envelopes of the moored zeppelins all around them.

Buckle could see the Founders pocket zeppelin docked nearby, its silver phoenix emblem gleaming like quicksilver in the daylight. He remembered the same silver phoenix emblem on the flank of the great sky vessel wreck on the Tehachapi Mountains. He had ordered Ivan to double the mooring guard.

Valkyrie and Ambassador Washington were met by a numerous and well-armed Imperial welcoming committee, backed by the armored motorcar with large black iron crosses on its doors, and two military carriages carrying soldiers, drawn by teams of six shaggy-legged draft horses apiece. A full detachment of cavalrymen in iron cuirasses, with white horsehair plumes flaring atop their pickelhaube spikes, was on hand as well.

Five Imperial officers had greeted them, all dressed in their powder blues, including Bismarck and Colonel Rainer; their faces had looked dead serious, their eyes darting, lids wide. Something was scaring them.

Buckle and the *Pneumatic Zeppelin* were supposed to simply take on the Imperial ambassador and be on their way to Spartak, but with the appearance of the Founders, everything had changed. The Founders' representative—somehow knowing that the Crankshafts were on their way to New Berlin—had demanded an audience with both the Imperial and Crankshaft ambassadors, and the Imperials had complied.

"Your presence here at this difficult time honors us, Ambassador Washington," Bismarck said loudly over the pounding steam engine behind. "Having you accompany our delegation to Spartak should impress the Russians with both the urgency and the imperative of our mission."

"And what of your other friends?" Buckle asked. He should have kept his mouth shut, but he could not.

Bismarck nodded with a bitter smile as he turned his blue-eyed gaze to Buckle, who saw suspicion there, but surprisingly little hate. "The fly in the ointment, so to speak," he replied.

"But the presence of the Founders in no way lessens my father's commitment to the Grand Alliance."

"It seems you are already at war, so numerous are the soldiers about us," Washington shouted over the rumble of the iron chassis. They were heading up a steep incline now.

"I apologize for the heavy escort," Bismarck said. "But there are assassins in the city, and we prefer to take no chances."

"Assassins?" Valkyrie asked, with genuine surprise in her voice.

Bismarck nodded gravely at his sister. "There were three attempts on three separate officials last night, mere hours before the Founders airship arrived. Magistrate Klopp, Colonel Von Camp, and Dorian Jacobsen. Only one of the murder attempts proved successful," he added.

"Who?" Valkyrie asked.

Bismarck gave Valkyrie a sad, tender glance. "Dorian."

Valkyrie's jaw went stiff. "I see," she whispered.

"I am sorry, my sister," Bismarck said, taking Valkyrie's hand. "I know you were fond of him. We were all fond of him." Bismarck turned his gaze to Buckle. "Jacobsen was the head of our diplomatic corps," Bismarck said. "A skillful man and a mentor to us."

Fury rippled through Rainer's eyes. "Stabbed to death on the very steps of his home," she said. "But we caught the bastard who did it. They are skinning him alive in the castle right now. But he refuses to speak. Not a word, the capital bastard. He is the monster spawn of the Founders, though—I guarantee you that. All mind-twisted. He is young, but his hair is all white. They were going to pack him into the iron maiden when I was leaving."

Buckle realized that he liked Rainer. There was no nonsense in her.

"I do express my most heartfelt condolences on your loss," Washington said.

"The arrival of assassins in your city at such a time does not bode well," Buckle added. "We just had a run-in with an airship saboteur last night."

"It is the habit of the Founders to cripple their victims before the attack," Rainer offered. "As we all learned, much to our own destruction, in the skirmishes that damaged our respective air fleets so profoundly last year."

Buckle nodded. He noticed that Bismarck was shooting furtive glances at Sabrina—at the red hair brushing her cheeks from under her derby. That scarlet hair. It intrigued, even galled, everyone Sabrina came across. Yet she made no effort to conceal it.

The clatter of the metal-sheathed motorcar wheels suddenly fell into a muted, smoother rhythm—the vehicle had moved from cobblestones to flagstones.

"My father told us of your discovery of the Founders zeppelin disguised as one of ours, and your apology for your reprisal raid," Bismarck said. "But I cannot say I blame you for what you did at the time. It hurt us both. I blame no one but Fawkes himself."

"Aye," Valkyrie said.

"The Founders airship arrived early this morning, unannounced, just before dawn," Bismarck said. "A biretta-hatted lackey disembarked—a noxious little prattler named Wallach—and told us to prepare for the arrival of their ambassador at nine o'clock this morning."

Buckle took out his pocket watch and held it under the green glow of one of the boil lamps: it was 8:27 in the morning.

"The Founders ambassador did not come on the airship?" Washington asked.

"Oddly, no," Bismarck replied. "He is arriving by locomotive."

"Locomotive?" Valkyrie asked, stunned. "No locomotive has rolled into New Berlin for fifty years."

"Fifty years, exactly. But the tracks are still there, more or less," Bismarck said. "And the Founders ambassador is coming by train."

–LVI–

THE RAILWAY STATION

THE ARMORED MOTORCAR CAME TO an abrupt, steam-wheezing, creaking halt. The armor-plated door was heaved open, and Buckle emerged into a day of cloudy brightness, eyes blinking. The windy bluster of the open air was a fresh wake-up, quite welcome, and under the monumental vault of the sky, he felt more at home. In front of him, behind the Imperial cavalrymen, a double set of railway tracks ran along the edge of the cliff twenty paces beyond.

Buckle turned around to peer up at the Imperial railway station, an architectural marvel that had been dazzlingly hewn out of the very face of the mountain cliff itself. Overlooking the castle-like facade of ramparts and turrets was a gigantic iron eagle, wings spread, perched atop an iron cross on the highest gable. The exterior metals suffered from severe corrosion, their bolts and undersides running with waterfalls of rust, while the stones showed the omnipresent fissures caused by expanding ice and other signs of erosion.

Sabrina and Washington were soon at Buckle's side, followed by Valkyrie, Bismarck, and Rainer. The household cavalrymen surrounded them, forming a cordon of cuirasses and steel helmets.

A cavalry captain politely ushered the group forward. "Please, Princess, Ambassador, ladies and gentlemen," the captain urged. "Let us get inside, shall we?"

"I must say, Captain Albard," Bismarck said. "Well done."

"Thank you, Prince Smelt," Albard replied, his olive eyes serious between his prodigious brown mustache and the polished brim of his pickelhaube. "It is not safe for you out here," he said, stepping forward to lead the way. "Quickly, if you please."

The cavalrymen escorted Buckle and the others through the towering glass-and-bronze front doors of the railway station, guarded by two magnificently rendered marble statues of warhorses, with armor plates on their skulls and swords on their saddles.

The towering grandeur and wide-open space of the Imperial railway terminal stunned Buckle's senses. The walls of the rectangular edifice soared up six stories to a roof constructed almost entirely of glass, the panes coated with a mix of snow and coal debris that imparted a glowing, liquid softness to the sunlight illuminating the room.

Sabrina elbowed Buckle, blinking and grinning as she looked up alongside him, taking off her derby. "Grand as they get, aye!" she whispered.

The station was surely nothing short of an architectural and engineering masterpiece, far finer than anything Buckle had ever seen. Arched doorways led away at every cardinal point, set in walls carved in glorious stone reliefs with ornately curved iron crosses. Old, discolored flags hung from marble facades, their folds thick with dust, framed by sculptures of hunting eagles and condors. The huge bronze-and-glass doors dominated the front of the building, opening onto the railway platform and the endless gray sky past the edge of the cliff beyond.

Light drifts of stone powder, chunky with marble fragments, sloshed around Buckle's boots as he walked, impregnating the air with dust. The grand Imperial station had been transformed into a sculptors' work studio: the original wooden benches were stacked high against the back wall to make room for a crowd of haphazardly arranged tables crowding the floor, some covered in small, rough-hewn statues, unfinished, emerging from the marble blocks that held them, others piled under hundreds of stone-cutting implements, buckets for chemical plasters, and smocks.

At the center of the room stood a huge, mostly completed statue of a pawing stallion, perhaps twenty feet high at the shoulder, nostrils flaring, tongue loose, eyes wide, saddled but riderless, a snapped spear gushing blood from its right flank, every muscle poised to initiate the final, defiant charge, to break free from the fortress of wooden scaffolding penning it in.

Chancellor Smelt, dressed in his usual military grandeur, stood in the middle of the room with four Imperial household cavalrymen near at hand. "Ambassador Washington, Captain Buckle, and the dauntless Lieutenant Serafim," Smelt said, without his usual venom. "Welcome to New Berlin."

"Thank you, Chancellor," Washington replied. "I wish our visit came under more auspicious circumstances."

"I profoundly apologize for the tight security. I am afraid the day has come that the avenues of New Berlin have become unsafe for the Smelts," Smelt said ruefully.

As they approached Chancellor Smelt, Buckle could see that the man was agitated—no, incensed—and his eyes sought out his children.

"What is it, Father?" Valkyrie asked, also having sensed Smelt's dismay, a hint of unguarded worry in her voice.

"There has just been an attempt on your mother's life," Smelt said.

"What?" Rainer gasped. "Where was the guard?"

Valkyrie and Bismarck stopped before their father; they were well trained, stoic, but their eyes flickered—Buckle knew that their hearts were pounding.

"What is Mother's condition?" Bismarck asked calmly.

Smelt placed his hands on his children's shoulders. "Fear not, my dear offspring. She is unhurt beyond suffering a shock, and she has Briar Rose and her chambermaids to comfort her now. The assassin was killed in her bedchamber, in the very heart of our manor, just a few moments ago."

"Thank the grace of the Oracle," Bismarck muttered.

"Thank the household cavalry," Smelt said, and looked to Albard. "Your brave man, Lieutenant Murat, gutted the fiend on the spot."

"The Founders dogs," Albard snarled under his breath. "The curs!"

"I am overjoyed that the queen escaped unscathed, Chancellor," Washington said. "Where is the Founders ambassador?"

"The man here now, the one that came on the airship—the name of Wallach—is not the ambassador," Smelt answered. "Just a foul-tongued herald, an envoy. I stalled him, then sent him the long way, in one of my royal carriages, hoping that one of his own assassins might blow him up by mistake. He will probably arrive without incident, unfortunately." Smelt turned to Valkyrie and Bismarck, his gaunt frame taut with anger. "The snakes are loose, children. Watch yourselves, in everything that you do. In every move that you make."

"We shall be vigilant, Father," Valkyrie replied softly.

"The cat is out of the bag, Ambassador," Smelt said, turning to face Washington. "If it ever was in it, which I doubt. I have sent a fast clipper to the Devil's Punchbowl with a warning for your clan. I cannot imagine but that the Founders have also dispatched assassins to your stronghold as well."

"Thank you, Chancellor. You have done us all a great service," Washington said.

"I assure you that you are safe here," Smelt said. "We are sneaking about like cellar mice, but I keep no secrets from the household cavalry."

A burly Imperial cavalryman strode in through one of the tall doors. "The Founders envoy has arrived, chancellor."

"Thank you, Sergeant Krupp," Smelt said, then turned to Buckle. "I was hoping the infamous brute wouldn't make it here alive."

-LVII-

THE ENVOY

THE FOUNDERS ENVOY, WALLACH, SLITHERED into the grand Imperial railway station holding a large pewter pocket watch, flanked on each side by two Imperial cavalrymen with their hands on their scabbards. Wallach was a small, slight man, dark eyed, clean shaven, and unsettlingly pale skinned, draped in a long black-hooded cloak with red facings. His four-cornered red biretta stood out oddly against his short-cropped orange hair. Wallach glared at Smelt. "Traveling in armored buggies, are we, Chancellor? Such things do not become you."

Buckle saw Wallach immediately notice Sabrina's red hair, readily visible now that she had tucked her derby under her arm.

"Our means of conveyance is of no concern to you, sir," Valkyrie replied dismissively.

"You are mistaken, Princess," Wallach snapped. "Since you are a Founders family—bred by us, fathered by us—your well-being is of every concern to me."

This is fascinating, Buckle thought. If Wallach represented the attitudes of the Founders—and there was no reason to believe that he did not—then the Founders still believed that they ruled the colonies they had lost a hundred years before.

"Watch your tone, sir," Albard said, his voice dripping with menace.

Smelt stepped in front of the much shorter Wallach. "It takes all of my self-control, sir," Smelt said, "to keep from drawing my sword and piercing your heart right here and now. My wife and nobles have been attacked. I demand you call off your assassins!"

"You vent your spleen upon an innocent, Chancellor," Wallach replied, scratching his neck in a detached fashion. "I am nothing more than a lowly envoy, a messenger who knows nothing of what you speak."

"I have warned you," Smelt growled.

Washington was silent, but he very deliberately stepped up alongside Smelt.

Buckle decided not to be silent. "If you think that any of us shall stand aside while you Founders try to conquer the world, you are sorely mistaken, sir."

If Wallach was perturbed he did not show it, barely glancing at Buckle; he held up his pocket watch, a bizarre timepiece with a red face and black hands. "It is eight fifty-six. Let us assemble on the platform and welcome the ambassador back to his loyal colony, shall we?"

"We have not been your *colony* for a very long time," Smelt snapped.

"I shall allow the ambassador to resolve that little misunderstanding," Wallach said. "Shall we?"

Smelt raised his hand. Two cavalrymen hurried forward to the front doors, slipping aside the bronze latches and swinging one of the great portals open. A whistling burst of mountain air swept in, raising whirlwinds of white stone powder. Wallach led the group out onto the platform, followed closely by Smelt, Washington, Rainer, and Albard.

It was like following a hangman, Buckle thought.

Passing out the doors and under the high archways of the train platform overlooking the high cliff, Buckle felt like he was facing the edge of the world.

"Here it comes," Albard said, his binoculars pressed to his eyes, looking southwest.

Buckle drew his telescope from his hat and stepped alongside Albard, finding the train in the lens as it came around a bend in the cliff. Two identical locomotives surged at the head of the train, metal monstrosities, hulking masses of iron plates and riveted window bubbles—the cars were likely sealed for transit through the noxious mustard—their driving wheels issuing rivers of vapor into the freezing air, their double smokestacks wreathed in clouds of black smoke.

The first locomotive pushed a big armored pod with a cantilevered plow that glowed red hot at the blade edges, melting the ice in great waves of hissing steam as it scraped the rails clear of decades of accumulated debris. Two massive iron arms, affixed to the armored pod, gripped the tracks behind the plow with iron claws, designed to straighten the rails before the locomotive wheels reached them.

A steam whistle blew. The locomotives slowed to a halt. The hatchways of the armored pod flung open, and men began to pour out of the hatches.

Buckle flipped his magnifier lens down from his hat and focused on the brawny bodies spilling out of the lead pod. They were work teams—a lot of them—leather-jacketed hammer men following a shift leader to a warped track. As the huge clamp arms, the steam valves at their joints pumping furiously, bent the rail back into shape with a wrenching squeal of bending metal, the hammer men laid newly oiled timbers and pounded spikes into place, their pickaxes sending up bursts of shattered permafrost.

After only a minute, the work teams hustled back into the armored pod, disappearing into the hatches. The steam whistle blew, its echo rebounding off the cliff, and the wheels of the train started rolling again, boilers thundering as the armored beast lurched up the mountain toward New Berlin.

~LVIII~

LEOPOLD GOETHE

THE ARMORED TRAIN ARRIVED THREE minutes late—though the wretched Wallach announced it was perfectly on time—coming to a halt alongside the station, its smokestacks belching banks of ashy black smoke. The iron-sheathed cars creaked under their own weight, their driving wheels sending up showers of sparks, every valve gushing waves of steam that eddied around Buckle and the others on the platform.

The train had seven cars: the boxy utility carrier pod at the very front, three locomotives, two in the lead and one at the rear, and two passenger cars in between, with a gunnery car behind. The gunnery car, even more heavily armored than the rest, had two revolving pillbox turrets, where cannon muzzles poked ominously out of the open gun ports. Buckle guessed they were thirty-two-pounders, judging from the diameter of their mouths.

Buckle saw Valkyrie's left hand drift down to the pommel of her sword and grip it reflexively.

"The duke is here!" Wallach shouted imperiously. "Prepare to receive Colonel Leopold Goethe!"

The hatches of the forward car banged open, iron on iron, and the hammer men emerged, barrel-chested apes, their long leather coats, and their faces and hands, stained black with tar and oil, their bodies humped from endless hours of backbreaking work, shouldering the tools of their trade—pickaxe, shovel, and hammer—with their cold-gnarled fists. They clambered one after another out of the steam-blurred hatches, forming a line on the tracks.

Buckle peered at the hammer men. There had to be at least fifty of them.

The doors of the two passenger cars clanged open as one. A soldier appeared, tall and straight, a sword and pistol at his belt. The sight of the finely fitted uniform gave Buckle a start. The man was not wearing the steam pack or the helmet, but there was no mistaking a steampiper. Nineteen more steampipers marched out, perfect tin soldiers in their silver-piped black coats and caps, their silver cuirasses emblazoned with the phoenix.

Buckle scrutinized the steampipers, scanning the strong-featured faces, the light-orange and strawberry hair. There were four females in the company, but the redheaded twin of Sabrina he had seen aboard the *Pneumatic Zeppelin* during the battle over Catalina was not with them.

"Is this an ambassadorial visit or an invasion?" Albard snarled.

The ambassador, Leopold Goethe, appeared; he was a man of medium height, gripping his gold-handled sword at his hip so the scabbard did not bang on the hatchway. With the steam swirling around him, Goethe looked every bit the conqueror, clad in a white uniform with silver buttons and draped with a crimson cloak that swirled to the heels of his black jackboots. His long, well-combed hair fell to his shoulders, blond and thick, and his beard, closely trimmed but full, was the same color.

Buckle sensed immediately—from the fashion in which Goethe strode, casting his glance in the way a slave owner might look upon property—that the duke was already counting New Berlin as Founders territory.

And there was something about Goethe, something about him…it was slight, but unnervingly familiar. Buckle could not put his finger on it.

"It is my proud duty to present to you," Wallach said with a flourish of his arm, "the honorable duke of industry and prime ambassador of the Founders clan, Colonel Leopold Goethe!"

Goethe stopped in front of Katzenjammer Smelt to bow and offer his hand. "Chancellor Smelt, I presume?" Goethe said in a solid, well-trained baritone voice.

"Colonel Goethe," Smelt replied with far less enthusiasm, shaking Goethe's hand, if almost reluctantly, his monocle gleaming in the swirling mist and harshening wind.

"It is a great honor to be here in New Berlin, to meet with you face-to-face to discuss the most pressing and urgent matters of our times, Chancellor," Goethe said.

Goethe glanced at Sabrina, at her brilliant-red hair, and Buckle saw a flash of dismayed recognition in his blue eyes. Goethe jerked his attention back to Smelt.

Damn it, Sabrina Serafim—who are you? Buckle thought.

"Most certainly," Smelt replied. "Shall we step inside to talk?"

"Very good, sir," Goethe said. "Please, after you."

Albard and the Imperial cavalrymen, their pickelhaubes glittering with half-crystallized condensation from the loco-motive steam, rushed forward to push open the glass doors as Smelt, Goethe, and the rest followed behind.

The twenty steampipers swung into single file and marched in after them.

~LIX~

ULTIMATUM

LEOPOLD GOETHE HAD BARELY TUGGED his white gloves free of his hands before Smelt launched into him. "I must say, Ambassador," Smelt announced, "I find your methods of negotiating unacceptable."

Goethe smiled, looking up at the roof. "I must say, the sketches I have seen of this edifice simply do not do it justice. Our Founders architects may have done their best work right here." He then looked over at Smelt, almost as if he had forgotten the man was there, and said, "But we have yet to even begin negotiating, my dear Chancellor."

"Do not play the fool's game with me!" Smelt snapped. "There are assassins loose in my city, killing my officials and threatening the lives of my family. You have attacked the Brineboilers without provocation. And now you show up on my doorstep, *uninvited*, with a trainload of armed soldiers."

"Please, Chancellor," Goethe answered calmly, a hint of condescending amusement in his face. "We Founders do not endorse assassins. Our conflict with the Brineboilers is our affair, and of no concern to you. And as for my little train and my ceremonial guard, surely you are aware of how perilous it is to travel the outlands without protection."

Smelt glared.

"Why are you here, Ambassador?" Washington asked, stepping forward.

"And who are you?" Goethe asked.

"I am Ambassador Rutherford Washington, representative of the Crankshaft clan."

"You have no right to be here," Goethe snapped. "Ragtag clans are of no interest to the Founders. There is no place here for your kind—pirates and swindlers—at the negotiating table of the true clans."

Washington's back stiffened, but he said nothing.

Buckle raged at Goethe's dismissiveness, but he held his tongue. Right now the battle was between the Imperials and the Founders.

"Then I shall ask," Bismarck blurted, eyes flashing, but infinitely better at hiding his emotions than his father, "why are you here?"

"Ah, straight to the point, are we?" Goethe said as he handed his folded gloves to Wallach. "Even before you offer me tea?"

"There is no tea," Bismarck said.

"Pity," Goethe replied. "I was anticipating a brilliant cup."

"What do you want?" Bismarck asked.

Goethe sniffed. "I have tried to keep the tone of this meeting pleasant, but it appears such a wish, faced with insulting accusations, a lack of tea, and the aggressive tone of your voices, is not a possibility. Fine. As you wish, Chancellor. The Founders clan is prepared to make the Imperial clan an offer of friendship."

"Friendship?" Valkyrie repeated, as if the words stung her tongue.

"Yes, friendship, my lovely Valkyrie," Goethe answered. His aide handed him a leather satchel, from which he drew a wax-sealed parchment scroll. "A pact of nonaggression and preferred trade that will reforge our association during these difficult times."

Buckle did not need to read the scroll—and neither did the Imperials—to know it was nothing more than a sugarcoated sham. Things were about to get ugly.

"On whose terms?" Valkyrie asked.

"The terms are laid out in the agreement," Goethe said, offering the scroll to Smelt. "And I assure you, much to my own personal surprise, they are quite advantageous to you."

"Are these terms negotiable?" Smelt asked.

"No," Goethe replied. "Such a document, once ratified by the Founders parliament, is irreversible."

"We would demand to negotiate our own terms," Smelt said.

"Not possible," Goethe replied, still trying to hand the scroll to Smelt, who so far had made no attempt to take it.

"And if we refuse this 'deal'?" Bismarck asked.

"Break the seal and read it first, at least, I would highly recommend," Goethe said.

"As a sovereign clan, we present our own terms, Ambassador," Smelt said.

Again, Goethe thrust the scroll toward Smelt. "I urge you to reconsider. A rash action could prove highly unfortunate for you and your people."

There was a long pause. The still air glittered with disrupted marble powder.

Goethe stood there, still offering the scroll, the insult of its rejection visible in his face. Buckle enjoyed that.

"You know that we are no easy target, Ambassador Goethe," Smelt said.

"And that is why we urge you to join us, Chancellor," Goethe replied. "Together we can form a mutual defense that will ensure the survival of both of our clans, and potentially win us more territory in the bargain."

"We are not interested in war," Smelt said coldly. "But we know you are gearing up for invasion."

"You should not trust spies," Goethe replied coldly.

"As much as you trust yours," Smelt answered.

Anger flared across Goethe's face, and he waved the scroll like a schoolmaster. "Do you think me a fool, Chancellor? Do you think Isambard Kingdom Fawkes a fool? Do you really think we do not know of your clandestine meetings up in the mountains, of your secret alliance of rogue clans to the east, your girding for war? The Grand Alliance—ha! You have signed your death warrants. And do not think that the offending Gallowglasses, Tinskins, and Alchemists shall be given clemency from their crimes either."

"I do not know what you are talking about," Bismarck said, but Smelt clutched his son's arm.

"We shall all suffer the same fate as the Brineboilers, shall we?" Buckle said venomously. He could hold his tongue no longer, and he wanted to knock a hole in Goethe's condescending smugness.

The anger disappeared from Goethe's eyes; he sighed, never acknowledging Buckle. "Securing your trust in the least trustworthy clans shall only bring you to ruin, Chancellor. They shall surely fail you once fire and blood is in the air. Think about that."

"We Crankshafts are with the Imperials as well," Buckle said. "And we fail no one."

Goethe looked at Buckle as he might look at a fly he was about to squash. "The Crankshafts?" he said with a laugh.

"If all you did was come here to force your will upon us, take your scroll and go," Smelt said. "We have no need of your one-sided *terms*."

Goethe glared. "I recommend that you quickly reconsider. For you should surely know that the Founders are of a strength and capacity far exceeding your own, even grouped in an illegal coalition, and that if you resist you shall be overrun, and the more strenuously you resist, the more your people's backs shall bleed for it."

Buckle's hand shot to his sword handle. He wanted to rage, to howl his indignation, to be in the thick of it. But he stilled himself.

Valkyrie stepped forward, shaking with a fury that showed in her body, but not in her voice. "You, Leopold Goethe, you are no ambassador. You are the mouthpiece of a war machine, and your words are designed to sow fear. But hear this—your bloody machinations shall fail you, for your treachery reaps only hatred and resolution."

Goethe looked at Valkyrie, not with hatred, but the way a man looked at a wounded horse just before he shot it. He turned and jammed the scroll into the open hand of a half-chiseled statue beside him, then grimly drew his white gloves from his pocket and tugged them on. "So be it," he muttered. He turned for the exit but suddenly halted, lifting his chin to look up at the ceiling. "And you—I know you," he said.

"Know who?" Bismarck snapped.

Buckle looked at Sabrina. Her eyes shone with fright, her throat shifting with an odd swallow.

Goethe laid his gaze upon Sabrina.

"You most certainly do not know me, sir," Sabrina replied, her voice defiant.

Goethe laughed. "Do not play games with me, Sabrina—it is Sabrina, is it not? Or did you change your name on the outside? I remember you. Yes, I *remember* you. You are a Fawkes, a Fawkes with hair more scarlet than Isambard's himself."

Gasps filled the room. Buckle's chest tightened up so fast he barely could breathe. The opaque layers surrounding Sabrina's carefully guarded past were being peeled away—if Goethe was to be believed. And the mustard in the pudding was that Buckle did believe him, not so much from his assertions as from the haunted look on Sabrina's face.

"My name is Sabrina Serafim," Sabrina said evenly, her face now as hard as granite.

"Serafim? A nice choice of name, Sabrina Fawkes, but it cannot hide your face, or that magnificent scarlet hair," Goethe said, pressing her harder. "I do not know what lies you have told your new clan, if the Crankshafts are the ones you call your masters now, but we are the same generation, cousin. We grew up together as children, you and I—do you not remember me? I am hurt. And what of your twin sister, with hair as red as yours, each of you the spitting image of the other? I know that she wonders every day where you might have gone. It shall break her heart if you have forgotten her."

Sister. That made sense to Buckle. The steampiper woman he had fought on the *Pneumatic Zeppelin*, the doppelgänger, could have been nothing less than Sabrina's twin. But Leopold Goethe's *cousin?* Buckle's mind raced. It surely was a lie. But then he realized what it was about Goethe's appearance that unsettled him so. Goethe had graceful, soft, low-lidded eyes, eyes with a distinct Asian character.

And Sabrina had the same exact kind of eyes.

"Once again, I must respectfully suggest that you are mistaken," Sabrina answered, her jaw clenched. "I do not know you, sir. And I have no sister."

Buckle knew that Sabrina was lying, but her past was her own business, mortifying as it appeared to be, and Buckle would be damned if he would stand aside while any member of his crew was interrogated by Leopold Goethe. "Enough!" Buckle shouted, striding forward. "You have delivered your message, and your answer has been given, Goethe. Be off with you."

"Silence, you bastard dog of a bastard clan! This is a Founders affair!" Goethe seethed.

"It is time for you to go, Ambassador," Smelt announced.

"I have not been given an acceptable answer," Goethe said, calming as he smoothed out his coat sleeves.

"You have your answer," Smelt said.

"I came here, old man," Goethe replied, "as an act of kindness. I came here to offer you a path away from your own destruction. You do recall, Chancellor, that even though we Founders have not lately enforced our suzerainty over you, you have never been declared independent—you are still our colony. I shall make my offer one last time. I pray that you shall swear to lay down the arms you have raised against us."

"You may go on your way, Ambassador Goethe," Smelt replied with a cool voice. "And you may tell your tyrant that the Imperial clan has cast our lot with the Grand Alliance, and we shall be visiting you soon."

Goethe laughed. "I admire your wolverine spirit, Chancellor, though in the end it shall earn you nothing more than a burning city and a trip to the gallows."

"We shall see," Smelt said.

"Very well. I have done all that I can do," Goethe said, turning on his heel to leave. He motioned for Sabrina to follow him as he passed her. "You are with me. Come!"

"I most certainly shall not," Sabrina said, surprised.

Goethe halted in front of Sabrina. "You are the blood and flesh of the Founders clan. The choice is not yours to make. You belong to us. Come with me."

"I would rather die," Sabrina snarled.

"By the claim of the crimson blood I am your master," Goethe said, and snatched Sabrina by the arm. "Take her!" he shouted to the steampipers, who immediately advanced.

Sabrina wrenched free of Goethe's grasp, whipping out her sword. Buckle had already lunged, the gleaming silver length of his blade hovering in front of Goethe's nose.

"To arms!" Rainer shouted.

A swishing clatter rang out as the Imperial cavalrymen yanked their swords loose from their scabbards. The twenty steampiper officers drew their pistols as one. Rainer and Albard leapt in front of Smelt, swords drawn, shoulder to shoulder.

Everyone held still in the tense silence, eyeing the gleaming swords and pistol muzzles. "I say," Buckle said dryly. "The negotiations seem to have taken an unfortunate turn."

―LX―

BY THE CLAIM OF THE
CRIMSON BLOOD

"YOU HAVE NO CLAIM UPON my sister," Buckle snarled at Goethe. "Her loyalties are her own."

"*Your* sister?" Goethe said, his eyes widening before he unleashed a dark, insidious smile. "I see she has worked her treacherous wiles upon you, Captain. But you are mistaken. She is the blood of the Founders, and as such, she belongs to the Founders."

"The Crankshaft navigator is here as my guest and under my protection," Smelt said, stepping forward. "I shall not have you or anyone taking her against her will."

"Then we have a problem, Chancellor," Goethe announced. "For I shall not leave without her."

"You *shall* leave without her," Buckle said. "And leave you will. Now."

"It would be most tragic for you if this situation came to blows, Chancellor," Goethe said, ignoring Buckle.

"You dare not fire upon us!" Bismarck snarled.

"I must do what I must. And where would your poor Imperial clan be after that?" Goethe asked. "With their chancellor and his vaunted children all dead. They would be lost sheep without a shepherd, easy prey for the wolves."

Smelt stepped alongside Buckle. "Leave my city, sir. Or draw your sword."

"No need," Goethe answered. "My death is meaningless in the scheme of things, Chancellor. You or your Crankshaft captain may well run me through, if either of you can move faster than a musket ball, yes, but once the smoke clears you shall be dead, and Sabrina Fawkes shall be returned to the Founders."

Sabrina Fawkes. The name stabbed Buckle in the heart. Sabrina Fawkes.

"I cannot allow it," Smelt said loudly. "The young woman is coerced."

Another long pause, heavy as lead, weighed down the atmosphere of the room.

Buckle rammed his sword home in its scabbard. He would not have another sister, regardless of her name, taken from him by the Founders. Not as long as he still breathed. He saw a way out. It was not a good option, but better than a hailstorm of bullets and blades. "I take great personal umbrage and insult when you lay your hands upon my sister, Goethe," he said. It was not a subtle tactic. Goethe would see what he was trying to do. But by the requirements of honor, he would be powerless to stop it.

Sabrina certainly realized. "Romulus, no!" she blurted.

"Personal umbrage? A duel? With you?" Goethe laughed. "Do not be foolish, Captain. I would cut you to pieces."

"Captain," Sabrina pleaded. "I can fight my own battles."

"Pistols or blades?" Buckle asked Goethe.

"Blades," Goethe replied quickly, his laugh fading into a serious grin. "Gentleman's Rules, of course."

"Gentleman's Rules. It is done, then," Buckle said, unbuttoning his coat. "If you prevail, Serafim goes with you. If I prevail, she is free and the matter is settled." Buckle was lying. Even if Goethe won—assuming Buckle was still alive—Buckle would board the *Pneumatic Zeppelin*, bomb the Founders train off the tracks, and take Sabrina back. Goethe was very, very far from home.

"Very well, then. I am in the mood for a bit of sport," Goethe said, his eyes brightening at the prospect of action.

The steampipers and cavalrymen lowered their weapons as Buckle, Goethe, and Wallach strode out to an open patch of floor under the chin of the stallion statue.

"I shall act as the captain's second," Valkyrie said, stepping into place alongside Buckle.

Buckle undressed down to his waistcoat—avoiding Sabrina's angry stare as he disrobed—and handed his top hat and coat to Valkyrie. He drew his sword from his scabbard as Valkyrie held it out for him, the finely sharpened metal ringing in the silence.

"Good luck, Captain," Valkyrie said aloud, then leaned to whisper in Buckle's ear. "Know this—if you fall, I shall not allow your navigator to be lost. That train shall never leave the station."

"Thank you, Princess," Buckle whispered back, swinging his saber back and forth rhythmically, sensing its balance, warming his muscles to the weight of the long steel. "But it shall not be necessary, for I am devastating with the blade." Buckle stepped out onto the dueling ground, testing how his boots might slip in the dust on the floor stones.

Goethe stood at a workman's table with Wallach holding his coat, cloak, and scabbard, also assessing the swing of his double-edged rapier. He looked fit and lean in his tight-fitting white waistcoat, a gold pocket-watch fob glittering at the pocket.

Smelt stepped into the center of the floor. "This duel is to be fought according to the Gentleman's Rules, as agreed upon by both parties. When one man is unable to continue, being either incapacitated or dead, the winner shall be declared. Cross swords!"

Buckle and Goethe strode out onto the floor, circling one another, their swords gleaming in the air between them. Intense study of one's opponent kept one calm and steady, Buckle knew. He watched how Goethe held his sword, the angle of the blade he might favor. Buckle's confidence in his swordsmanship was immense—but he was also smart enough not to underestimate Leopold Goethe.

Enough damned pussyfooting.

Always the aggressor, Buckle attacked, his boot soles squeaking across the powder-sloshed marble. Goethe held his ground, one hand tucked behind his back, looking bemused, sword low, as Buckle lunged. Goethe raised his rapier at the last instant, nonchalantly parrying Buckle's first swing.

"Really, Captain?" Goethe chortled. "Subtlety and the counterfeit stroke glorify the art of the blade, not the wild cutlass-hacking of a drunken boarder."

Buckle advanced on Goethe, slashing and shoving, attempting to roll him back on his heels, but the duke never allowed him the opportunity. Their swords leapt back and forth, spewing sparks when they clashed, the harsh clangs echoing off the high walls of the cavernous terminal. Goethe was murderously quick, quicker than Buckle, but Buckle was a physically stronger man, with better finish to his moves. Buckle eased back on his attack; such useless thrashing was going to wind him.

Seeing his chance as Buckle disengaged, Goethe feinted high and spun low, his blade tracing a wide arc, aiming to saw Buckle off at the knees. Buckle leapt over the swipe, slashing his saber at Goethe's sword arm, but Goethe was dastardly quick, again deflecting the cut. Goethe whipped his sword up and across Buckle's descending blade; it was a small, slick move, but it offered a mortal blow—if Buckle had not jerked his head back. If his boots had slipped ever so slightly on the powdery marble, he would have been killed. The razor-sharp tip of Goethe's steel whipped past Buckle's windpipe, slicing away a bit of his beard under the chin.

Buckle sprang back, sword weaving in front of him. That was far too close. That was what you got for dropping your guard.

Goethe smiled, looking a touch bored, a shiftless gleam of joy in his blue eyes. "Let me ask you, Captain," he asked, his voice sudden and unreal in Buckle's ears. "Just which sister is it you are fighting for?"

"What?" Buckle asked, his battle-soaked brain not comprehending.

"He is trying to rattle you, Romulus," Sabrina shouted. "Do not listen to him!"

"This navigator of yours," Goethe continued. "The red-headed Founders lass you are deluded into thinking is some sort of relative. Sister? She is not your flesh and blood. But you, you, Romulus Buckle—you have a *real* sister, do you not?"

Elizabeth. Buckle blinked.

And that blink was almost, very nearly, the end of Romulus Buckle.

Goethe's rapier flashed. Buckle caught the lightning-fast glint of the blade and raised his sword to meet it—but he knew he had not been quick enough. Jumping back, he arched his spine, head and hips jerked forward, and Goethe's blade passed his stomach. Goethe's sword tip ripped a mother-of-pearl button away from Buckle's waistcoat, and it skittered away across the floor stones.

For an instant, Buckle thought he had escaped unscathed.

But then he saw little droplets of his bright-red blood spray across the white marble chest of the stallion statue, and he cursed himself.

–LXI–

MERCY FOR THE WICKED

THE WOUND WAS NOT A bad one—a surface slice across Buckle's forearm, just below the elbow—but the psychological advantage of first blood was powerful. The ripped edges of his shirt sleeve dripped red. By all rights, Buckle should have been gutted.

Buckle spun away, hefting his sword in his hand as he and Goethe circled one another again. Goethe smiled at him.

"You bleed, Captain?" Goethe announced. "Perhaps you wish to beg for mercy now, while your major parts are still attached?"

Buckle's thoughts whirled in his head. If Goethe knew of Elizabeth, if he knew that Elizabeth was Buckle's sister, then he must know more.

Goethe lunged. Buckle clamped his teeth, slashing back and forth as Goethe advanced, slowly closing. His desire to kill Goethe would do no one any good. He had to disarm the man, cripple him, demand what he knew of Elizabeth. But Buckle also sensed that Goethe was far too proud to talk, and if he did, his words would be lies.

Buckle was not going to kill Goethe; he would chop the damned blackheart's toes off.

The fighting mind kicked in, overtaking Buckle smoothly, easily, as it always did; the ancient Roman war machine in his brain calculating, studying Goethe's technique in ways only one swordsman might estimate another. Goethe was quick, experienced, well-trained, but he had not kept up a demanding practice, and so he was also predictable, enslaved to the tactics of the textbook.

It was time to set the trap.

Buckle set to, bulling forward, swamping Goethe in a flurry of flashing blade strokes. Goethe deftly parried, but that was what Buckle wanted. Buckle eased up just a hair, lessening the force of his blows, dropping his guard a fraction, offering Goethe the telltale signs of a man beginning to tire.

Goethe took the bait, as the textbook required he should; he shifted to the attack, surging forward. Buckle let Goethe almost get inside his guard, then caught Goethe's blade with the edge of his steel, holding it as the blades slid against one another in a tumble of sparks. Buckle hunched, as if overwhelmed, bringing Goethe in even closer, then wrenched Goethe's sword arm high and shouldered him in the chest, straightening him up. Now inside Goethe's guard, Buckle whipped his saber low, slashing the tip across the top of Goethe's right boot, splitting the polished leather open like a mummy's mouth.

Blood welled up and out of the jagged crevice of the cut; Goethe howled, more with rage than hurt, and tried to fling Buckle back, but Buckle was too close. Buckle hooked his leg behind Goethe's left knee and flipped him backward.

"Charlatan!" Goethe shouted as he toppled back, taking a wild swing with his rapier as he fell. Buckle ran his sword into the space between Goethe's hand and his sword guard and ripped the handle away, sending the rapier bouncing across the floor. Two of Goethe's fingers went with it.

The rapier rolled to a stop with a clatter, the two severed fingers, still inside the white fingers of Goethe's glove, quivering on the floor. Goethe lay still—the entire room had fallen utterly still—propped up on his elbow, grasping his wounded hand, glaring at Buckle as blood poured down his white gloves. A pink puddle oozed out from beneath his right boot, his blood mixing into a thick paste with the copious stone powder. Goethe's eyes showed little pain. They were calm, superior, reptilian.

"Where is my sister, you blackguard?" Buckle snarled, holding the bloodstained tip of his saber in front of Goethe's eyes. With every fiber of his being, he wanted to throttle the vile Goethe, to feel the cartilage of his windpipe convulsing in the vise of his bare hands.

"Duke!" the steampiper officer shouted, his nineteen men surging with him as he hurried forward.

"Hold!" Goethe bellowed. The steampipers halted. He looked at Buckle again. "Why, Captain, I only know the rumors. It nearly worked, would you not say?"

"Tell me," Buckle said. "Or die." For all the world, Buckle wanted to kill Goethe, but he also knew that he would not. Goethe knew it as well.

"Please, Captain" Goethe smiled. "We both know you will not."

"The duel is over!" Smelt yelled, striding out onto the floor, Albard close at his side.

Buckle lowered his sword, surprised at how heavily he was breathing, and took a step back.

"The decision goes to Captain Buckle of the Crankshafts," Smelt announced. "The navigator Sabrina Serafim retains her freedom." Smelt turned to Goethe. "Ambassador, you are not welcome here. Pack up your steampipers and your ultimatums and go."

"My condolences, Chancellor," Goethe said as Wallach and the steampiper officer rushed forward and raised him, dripping blood from hand and boot, to his feet. "You have made a choice that you shall soon deeply regret."

"Go," Bismarck said.

With Wallach and the steampiper officer each supporting an arm, Goethe hobbled toward the door, leaving behind a trail of bloody boot prints. He gave Sabrina a smile as he passed her; she met his gaze, glowering. "Beware, Captain," Goethe shouted over his shoulder as he limped away, "Sabrina Fawkes is a disgraceful scrap. She shall betray anyone unfortunate enough to place his trust in her. You have been warned."

–LXII–

AIRSHIP ON FIRE

SABRINA HAD SAT BESIDE BUCKLE on the ride back up the cliff road, very close at his shoulder. She had not said anything during the rocking, rattling carriage ride. He had just tried to ignore the sting in his arm, ignore the revelation of her true name, and he found himself enjoying her closeness. They had earned a break. The bloodied Leopold Goethe and his steampipers were on their way home, the armored locomotives chugging in reverse back down the mountain in heaves of steam and smoke.

Smelt, Rainer, and Washington talked urgently about war strategy and diplomatic maneuvers for the entire ride, limiting the opportunity for anyone else to speak. At one point, Sabrina had gripped Buckle's gloved hand in hers, tightly, though she did not turn her head to look at him.

Buckle had liked the squeeze of Sabrina's hand on his, her expression of thanks, and a silent request that, despite Goethe's terrible words, Buckle never lose faith in her, however damningly dark and murky her family past—the family of the Fawkes bloodline, apparently—might appear to be.

Buckle also noticed, though not directly, Valkyrie reading his interaction with his navigator, her blue eyes moving from their laced hands to their faces.

Upon the arrival of the motor carriage and its heavy escort at the old town hall, the doors swung open and the group was ushered by the cavalrymen into a broad corridor that bore the pleasant musk of old wood and lamp oil. They quickly arrived at a grand entranceway, a marble-floored, pillared hall facing two towering timber doors—now bolted shut and guarded by four soldiers gripping blackbang muskets and eyeing the new arrivals nervously. A sweeping twin staircase ran up to a grand balcony with a balustrade of carved wooden horses; a story above it, its folds highlighted by soft sunlight streaming down through coal-hazed skylights, hung a white-and-black Imperial flag on a spike-headed staff, flanked by eight regimental banners. The flag was severely torn and bloodied—surely there was a legendary story behind that swath of battered linen.

Bismarck collected a friendship scroll and a folded Imperial banner for presentation to Vladik Ryzhakov, the leader of the Spartak clan.

Then the world fell off its axis again.

"Chancellor!" a household cavalryman shouted from the balcony of the town-hall staircase. "An airship approaches from the west! It is on fire!"

"Quickly! To the signals post! This way!" Smelt shouted, already racing up the stairs with Valkyrie, Bismarck, Albard, and Rainer on his heels.

Buckle followed at a run, with Sabrina and Washington alongside.

Reaching the top of the stairs, Smelt turned down a long hallway with blue carpets and long lines of stuffed elk heads, all adding a molting stuffiness to the fire-warmed air, dull with the odors of old hide and taxidermy glue. A bell rang outside with a deep, bounding peal.

They emerged onto a snow-drifted balcony where an Imperial signals officer stood in a dark-blue uniform, binoculars pressed to his eyes as he peered high to the west. Shouts echoed back and forth below, yelled from the pale-gray walls, towers, and metal-shingled rooftops. The city was planned, a neatly designed work of geometry with its unswerving ring roads and boulevards, but its sprawl stopped abruptly at its eastern wall, which topped the cliff face, the white-purple mountains barely visible in the haze far beyond.

Buckle hurried with the others to the rail and peered up through the cold, crisp afternoon air. A brisk breeze was running from the north, and it jangled the rope clasp of a hollow iron flagpole as the Imperial standard flapped above.

The signals officer threw out his arm, pointing. "There she is, high to the west, Chancellor. About a mile out, heading straight for us."

"I see her, Lieutenant Jannick," Smelt replied as Valkyrie handed him her binoculars.

Buckle spotted the black dot of the airship against the overcast—its long trail of dark-gray smoke made it easy to find—then drew his telescope and caught it in his glass. It was a small airship—the single set of glassy glitters suggesting a single gondola—and the red and yellow gleams along her flanks spoke of a serious fire.

"The scout airship *Troy* is escorting the damaged arrival, three hundred feet above her, Chancellor," Lieutenant Jannick said. "The zeppelin on patrol, the *Pneumatic Tirpitz*, is en route from the south."

"City defenses are on alert, Chancellor," Albard said.

"Very good," Smelt replied, concentrating on the sky.

Buckle lowered his telescope. With a fire like that aboard, Buckle doubted that the airship would make it to New Berlin. But the crew was not initiating a crash dive, making no attempt at an emergency landing to save their own skins—they were coming on straight and fast, their propellers whirling at high speed despite the dangers of funneling oxygen into loose hydrogen inside the burning envelope.

"Why do they not get to ground?" Sabrina asked. "If they do not get to ground quickly, they are finished."

"I don't know," Buckle replied. A weird shiver visited his stomach. Whatever message the desperate crew was bringing, it could only speak of catastrophe.

Sabrina sucked in a little breath of air. "It is Spartak. It is a Spartak airship."

"Yes, you are right," Jannick replied. "I see the double eagle on the port flank."

"The Russians?" Washington muttered incredulously. "Coming to us?"

Buckle raised his telescope to his eye again. The approaching airship, a corvette of perhaps three hundred feet, was showing the Spartak double-headed eagle emblem on her port-side envelope.

Of course it was the Russians, Buckle thought grimly. Spartak was the biggest bear in the room, from the Founders' perspective. Yes, the Tinskin fleet was probably bigger, but the Founders surely sensed that they could manipulate them. Spartak, on the other hand, was a notoriously difficult outfit to parley with. With their invasion already under way in Brineboiler territory and their resources irreversibly mobilized, it made sense to strike Spartak now, before they were ready, before the Founders lost the last advantages of surprise.

It was bad that Buckle could see the airship's flank. If she was coming on at full speed, trying to make New Berlin before the fire consumed her, then a broaching to, a sudden swing of the nose, was a disaster. She was either too damaged to control, or the bridge crew was dead. Buckle lowered his telescope, not wanting to see what was about to happen up close. The battle for survival aboard the Russian airship was already lost.

The airship exploded, the bulk of her stern vanishing in a brutal, brilliant flash.

Jannick gasped.

The burning fragments of the airship fell slowly for an instant, until her last gasbags blew up inside the bow—and then she fell in a plummet of fireworks. Great pieces of burning envelope skin and gondola tore away; a gush of water sparkled briefly as the blue ballast reservoirs split open under the collapsing superstructure.

Buckle and the others stood in silence as the Russian airship fell to earth. Such was the end for so many zeppelineers. Buckle did not fear it, but it was difficult to watch. It was just difficult to watch. The fiery wreck dropped behind a mountain ridge and disappeared from view.

Why had the captain of the Russian sky vessel believed that his mission to New Berlin was so urgent that he would gamble that his flame-engulfed zeppelin might last long enough to reach the harbor?

"This does not bode well," Smelt said slowly. "We must contact Spartak with absolute haste. We must find out what is going on."

"Agreed!" Washington blustered.

"I fear the Founders already may have pounced, Chancellor," Buckle said.

"Messenger pigeon!" Sabrina shouted, her eye still pressed to her telescope. "Messenger pigeon coming in!"

Buckle swung his glass back to the sky. It was not necessary—the flapping V shape of the pigeon was already close at hand, not three hundred yards off, approaching from the direction of the now-destroyed airship. The bird had a red-and-black Spartak flash on its belly and the red ribbon of a loaded scroll case rippling at its leg, a last message scribbled from the hand of a Russian zeppelineer now dead.

–LXIII–

MESSAGE FROM A DEAD MAN

"THE BIRD IS IN," BUCKLE said, watching the distant parapet as a pair of handlers under a homing target immediately scooped up the bird. The handlers' signal lamp was already burning, the edges of its case spilling a phosphorous glow; they started sending signals almost immediately.

"Founders invasion," Albard said slowly as he read the coded flashes of light, standing on the signals platform with his binoculars. "Rostov overrun."

Rostov overrun, Buckle repeated in his head. Rostov was the Spartak clan's southernmost stronghold, a port, and a big, well-fortified one. If the Founders had actually taken it, then this was no skirmish.

"Grand Boyar Ryzhakov requesting immediate Imperial assistance," Albard continued. He lowered his binoculars, looking to Jannick. "Acknowledge, Lieutenant."

"Yes, Captain," Jannick answered nervously, flipping the operating handle of his signal lamp, the casing issuing a hot stink as the shutters snapped up and down.

"There you have it," Bismarck muttered. "The war has begun."

War. The word shuddered down Buckle's spine. The inevitable had happened. He felt a surge of apprehension, followed by nervous exhilaration. He looked at Sabrina, whose face was soft but profoundly solemn as she looked back at him. Buckle smiled at Sabrina; he wanted it to be a reassuring smile, but he feared it might be rather grim.

"But, Spartak appealing to us?" Albard questioned. "We have been in a skirmish war with them for more than a decade."

"By invading Spartak, the Founders have driven the Russians to you," Buckle said.

"Yes," Smelt replied. "But our fleet is not yet ready for war."

"We can send a vanguard, a token of our support," Valkyrie offered. "The *Pneumatic Tirpitz* is on its way and will be here within the half hour. We can send her."

"And the *Lucerne* is bunkering," Colonel Rainer said. "On an accelerated schedule, she can be up in an hour."

"I cannot send two of our war zeppelins off and leave New Berlin exposed," Smelt said. "We could well be in for a Founders visit ourselves."

"Especially since we sent Leopold Goethe home with his toes and fingers in a bag," Bismarck added, winking at Buckle.

"We can recall the *Beowulf*, but she is patrolling the northern approaches," Rainer said. "She is more than two days away at best speed."

"Send for her immediate recall," Smelt ordered.

"The *Pneumatic Zeppelin* is rigged and ready," Buckle said. "We can be away immediately."

Smelt gave Buckle a hard look. "Spartak has requested Imperial support, Captain Buckle. The Crankshafts are not compelled to act."

"I believe we are, Chancellor," Buckle replied.

"Do you speak for the Crankshaft clan, Captain Buckle?" Smelt asked, turning his eyes from Buckle to Washington.

Washington stepped forward. "Captain Buckle does not, but I do. The captain has the right instinct. We are with the Imperial clan, and where you must fight, so must we. Our combined presence shall also surely impress the boyars of Spartak, and secure their willing participation in the Grand Alliance."

Smelt made no effort to hide his relief. "Very well. It seems, as it always does in diplomacy, that external events are making many of our decisions for us."

"May I play the devil's advocate a moment, Chancellor?" Rainer said. "We must also consider that possibility that this is a trap. If Spartak has gone over to the Founders, sir, then this frantic call for assistance is a perfect trap."

"No, Colonel," Smelt replied. "I know Vladik Ryzhakov. Well, I knew him a long time ago. That old bear would never submit willingly to the Founders, not to mention sacrifice one of his aircrews in a sham."

Valkyrie stepped forward. "We must go."

"Father, give me the *Cartouche*," Bismarck said. "With her I can get to Muscovy well ahead of the warships. It is imperative that Spartak knows we are with her as quickly as possible."

"Very well," Smelt said. "Tell Captain Snyder to assemble the *Cartouche*'s crew and make his way with all best speed to Muscovy. I shall send the *Pneumatic Tirpitz* after you, once she arrives here. But I cannot spare more, for I fear New Berlin may soon be under attack from the Founders as well."

"The Russians have plenty of war zeppelins," Washington said. "What they wish is to confirm your support."

Bismarck hugged Valkyrie, and she kissed his cheek. "Be careful, sister."

"And you, brother," Valkyrie said. "Be cautious—the Founders will be on their way."

"Cautious, but never faint of heart," Bismarck replied. He turned a serious eye to Buckle. "Take good care of my sister, Captain Buckle. Our hopes and dreams lie with her."

"I shall protect her as one of my own, sir," Buckle answered. "You have my word."

Bismarck smiled. Buckle glanced at Smelt, who looked like an old man in that moment, a tall, gaunt old man placing one hand on Valkyrie's shoulder and the other on Bismarck's. "Be brave, my children. Be brave!"

Bismarck shook his father's hand and hurried away with Rainer at his side.

Valkyrie patted her father's cheek, then turned to Buckle. "Let us fly," she said, striding out the door. Buckle, Sabrina, and Washington quickly followed her down the hall of antlered elk.

Rest one more moment, my zeppelin, Buckle thought, for I am coming, coming to fire up your furnaces, run out your guns, and take you to war.

PART THREE

THE BATTLE OF MUSCOVY

–LXIV–

THE CAPTAIN'S TABLE

THE MEAL WAS OVER, BUT Captain Buckle still wanted to talk. Sabrina watched him, ruddy-faced from laughter, thrice ready for the havoc of battle, an oiled cog ready to click into whatever gear was in action. His empty plate and grinning face stood in sharp contrast to the haphazard and nervous smiles worn by others at the Lion's Table, whose visages were pinched and serious over their barely touched bully beef and potatoes. Ambassador Washington seemed the most unsettled by Buckle's enthusiasms. Valkyrie—sitting where Max should have been—was nonplussed. Ivan, Surgeon Fogg, and Sergeant Salgado of the marines joined in Buckle's bravado, soaking it into themselves. Howard Hampton was also present, given a plate once the serving was done, and passing most of his beef to Kellie under the table.

"What can we do now but live forever, despite ourselves?" Buckle laughed. "Lads and ladies, we have defeated the kraken. What other thing could possibly strike fear into one's heart after one has smelled the breath of the kraken? We are immortal now."

"Infamous is more the term I would use," Surgeon Fogg said, grinning.

"By the skin of the dog," the marine sergeant Salgado groaned. "I would have given my firstborn and my second to have been out there with you!"

"Perhaps the time requires a more serious approach," Sabrina said, oddly distressed by Buckle's upbeat mood. Even the captured steampiper helmet, a bit of a macabre centerpiece in the middle of the table—fished out of Buckle's locker by Ivan—seemed to be suggesting a more solemn approach to the mission.

Buckle slapped Ivan's good shoulder—Ivan was seated on his left—and Ivan spilled his grog. "A crew fights best when it is happy, Sabrina," Buckle said. "And they are happy when their markers are paid and their stomachs are full."

"Damn it, Romulus," Ivan moaned, wiping rum off his chin.

Buckle laughed again. Sabrina watched him. He appeared a bit stupefied in his looseness, but he had barely touched his own glass. He was fired by a heat of expectation, and confident, for he was no captain if he did not overflow with confidence when action loomed. Buckle leaned back or lurched forward in his chair, as the conversation demanded, the great nose window of the *Pneumatic Zeppelin* ablaze with the illumination of the western afternoon clouds, the sun a molten forge at his back.

"Unfortunate, though. Old Valentine will lose that leg," Fogg said.

"Yes," Buckle replied, somber for a moment. "But what a story he has to tell at least, eh?"

"The beastie pretty much took a piece out of each of us," Sabrina said, poking her fork at her potatoes and turning a cold chunk over, leaving an uneven grease spot of condensation and butter on the china. "May the dead rest in peace." She said the last bit and she felt it, but her heart was not quite in it at the moment. They were hurtling toward Spartak at seventy knots, furnaces and propellers roaring, altitude one thousand feet, visibility excellent, a light crosswind coming south by southwest, compensating for drift. They were perhaps twenty minutes out from Muscovy, and the bridge crew should really be on the bridge.

She did not understand Buckle's dillydallying.

"Do not fret, Sabrina," Buckle said, reading her mind. "We are finishing up. Not a good idea to leave the junior lieutenants and midshipmen in charge on a battlefield, is it?"

"No, Captain," Sabrina replied. "I am itching for action, is more of the matter."

"Action, harrumph!" Washington—overcautious old Washington, the hoary legend, the stick in Buckle's craw—complained as he cleared his throat at the same time. "Battle? This is most aggressive, coming in at full speed."

"There is no other way to arrive, Ambassador," Buckle answered, still grinning at Sabrina. "There may be Founders in the clouds."

"I agree," Sabrina offered. "If the Founders are there, then our only chance is to blast them before they blast us."

Washington placed his knife on his plate with a loud *click*. "May I remind you, Captain Buckle and First Lieutenant Serafim, that regardless of whatever situation we find, even if there is an engagement under way, we are bound to stand off and observe until the matter is resolved."

"Stand off and observe," Buckle repeated with a disapproving tone. "What an unfortunate set of words."

"Stand off and observe, yes," Washington pressed. "The *Cartouche* is ahead of us to deliver our message of alliance. The

Pneumatic Tirpitz is only an hour behind us. We are here to show the Crankshafts as a part of the Grand Alliance, not to fight in the Imperials' stead."

"If we are all members of the same alliance, are we not then bound to fight for each other?" Fogg posited. Sabrina liked Fogg; if he had not been a surgeon, he would have made for a fine zeppelin officer.

"If the documents were signed and sealed, of course," Washington replied. "But the Russians have made an offer to the Imperials only. We have no sense of what they may offer us as terms."

"They are under attack, Ambassador," Buckle said quickly. "The fat is in the fire. A plea for assistance has come at great price from the battlefield. The time for negotiating fine points is over."

"That is not your decision to make, Captain," Washington answered.

"If the Russians are attacked, I shall not stand off, sir, with all due respect," Buckle said.

"Damned right," Sabrina said, earning a glare from Washington in so doing.

"Cheers to that," Ivan grumbled, tapping the metal fingers of his glove against his glass.

"Stop it, Ivan," Sabrina said. "Bloody annoying."

Ivan stopped tapping.

Washington folded up his napkin and placed it on the table. "I know you, Captain Buckle, you and all of our young lions. I have known you since you were brought in to us, a brat at Calypso's knee, and while your independent streak has always been one of your greatest assets, it has also been one of your greatest challenges. It bears repeating that although we may have just inked an alliance with the Imperial camp, we have no such commitment to or from Spartak. And we are not—we are *not*—in a state of war with the Founders."

"Well elucidated, Ambassador," Buckle replied. "I think we all know Balthazar's position on the matter."

"I say we blast the Founders out of the sky before they blast us," Salgado offered. Sabrina feared the sergeant might offer up a toast—he was an egregious toaster. "Why keep the gloves on when war is inevitable?"

"Because we need the time, Sergeant," Washington responded. "We are not prepared for war. We need time for the alliance to organize and assemble. There is a possibility, though perhaps remote, that the Founders might allow us some space if we do not provoke them."

Buckle was on his feet; Sabrina felt the anger rising in his mood. "If Spartak is destroyed, if the Imperials are destroyed, then all of our organizing and assembling will not save us."

"I expect you to obey Admiral Balthazar—your father's—wishes, sir," Washington replied.

"My father—" Buckle started, then bit his tongue.

Realizing that the argument was about to take a negative turn, Sabrina hopped to her feet, and in the same moment Fogg did the same, their chair legs scraping across the deck.

"I think we are all finished here," Sabrina announced pleasantly.

"Yes," Fogg concurred. "My thanks, Captain, but I must be on my way to finalize preparations in sick bay."

"We should make our way to the bridge, sir," Sabrina added quickly. "We should be within sight of Muscovy's eastern outposts in a matter of moments."

Buckle turned around to the window platform, folding his hands behind his back as he scrutinized the towering vault of the sky. "Very well. I thank all of you for your gracious attendance. Please report to your stations."

Everyone offered a chorus of "Thank you, Captain" and filed out of the cabin—everyone except Sabrina and Washington.

"Captain Buckle," Washington began.

"Please confine yourself to your quarters, Ambassador," Buckle interrupted. "In the remote possibility of action, you are best protected there, under the armor line of the envelope."

"Captain," Washington pressed.

Buckle reached up and tapped his pearl-colored fire horn—the one he had brought back with him from the Tehachapi Mountains—so it swung lazily on its leather strap at the side of the window. "That will be all, sir," Buckle said harshly, watching the arc of the horn.

Washington glanced at Sabrina, and she saw many things in his eyes—frustration, worry, regret. "Thank you for the lovely meal, Captain," he said quietly, and made his exit.

As soon as the door shut behind Washington, Sabrina turned to Buckle. "You should be more gracious with him, Romulus. He is an elder, after all."

"I take it that you are of the same mind as I, Sabrina?" Buckle asked.

"If you mean how to approach the Founders? Yes," Sabrina replied. "They are nothing if not creatures of treachery. Do not trust them to respect treaties or statements of neutrality."

Buckle turned around, his eyes alive with their wild expectation again, and snatched up his hat. "Come with me, Serafim," he enthused. "I doubt we are going to want to miss a second of this one."

Sabrina followed Buckle out the door, bubbling with a bloodthirsty expectation and dread that she was not accustomed to. If there was any sort of fight to be had that day, it seemed likely that Romulus Buckle would soon have the *Pneumatic Zeppelin* in the thick of it.

The Seasonal ball, with all its silk and joy and yearnings, seemed like a thousand years ago.

~LXV~

RUN OUT THE GUNS

"Crew at action stations, Captain," Sabrina announced.

"Very well," Buckle replied, standing on the bridge with Kellie seated at his toes. It was all beginning to feel real now. He could smell a hint of bloodlust on Sabrina, a thread of the gung ho in her voice. It was odd. She and Max were normally the calming hands on the wilder tendencies of his tiller...but, then again, soon the clouds might be raining blood.

"Visibility remains excellent," Sabrina continued. "No sign of the *Cartouche*."

"Aye," Buckle answered, detaching his telescope from his hat as he stepped over the dog and into the nose alongside Sabrina and Welly, who already had their glasses trained straight ahead. There was no reason to expect to see the *Cartouche*; the fast Imperial scout ship was probably already docked in Muscovy by now. Buckle scanned the horizon, with its undulating brown-and-white mountains, and the hazy glimmer of the dark-purple sea beyond. Muscovy, one of Spartak's southern strongholds, had yet to be sighted. If Rostov had truly been captured by the Founders, then Muscovy would be the next target.

The bridge was silent for a moment, in a way that Buckle enjoyed—filled with the unbroken, reassuring drone of the forward maneuvering propellers, and the steady rip of the wind running through the rigging and against the massive envelope overhead. The guns were ready, the crew tense. Since the day Buckle had won the captaincy of his zeppelin, this was the first moment she felt like a war machine to him.

"Bridge! Airships sighted!" the lookout cried down the chattertube. "One point off the starboard bow! Silhouettes and smoke!"

"Good eye, nest!" Buckle shouted into the chattertube. Finally the barrelmen had seen something first. He peered into his telescope and heard Sabrina suck in air at his shoulder.

"Sighted!" Sabrina said. "Two airships, no, make that three, at thirteen hundred, just northwest of the city."

Buckle caught the small dots in his eyeglass and, flipping down the trigger on his magnifying lens from his hat, could make out three big war zeppelins, the middle one bracketed by smoke, the tiny flashes of cannon muzzles sparkling along their gondolas.

"We have got an engagement," Buckle shouted. "Battle stations."

"Battle stations!" Sabrina shouted into the chattertube. "All hands to battle stations!"

"Gunner to the turret," Assistant Engineer Geneva Bolling shouted, leaving her station alongside Valkyrie to clamber into the hammergun pod just behind the helm.

"The stronghold is afire, sirs," Welly said.

Buckle swung his glass to the ground—the view was rapidly improving, with the *Pneumatic Zeppelin* coming on so fast. He saw great columns of black smoke, drifting westward, low across the earth, flowing from the pale-brown walls of Muscovy.

"Aye, she is burning up," Buckle muttered under his breath.

"Mortar barges to the south of the city!" the lookout shouted on the chattertube.

Buckle swung his lens to the south and quickly found the lumbering, squarish envelopes of two mortar barges, the Founders phoenix visible on their flanks, bombarding the city with their huge guns.

"No sign of an escort with the mortar barges, Captain," Welly said.

Welly was right. The slow-moving mortar barges should be protected by a fighting sloop or scout, but he could not locate any other airship nearby.

"Watch for him. He is surely there," Buckle said. Already the scenario felt slippery. Either the Founders were very sloppy, or he was charging into a trap.

"Aye," Sabrina said, swinging her telescope at Buckle's side.

Buckle observed the three war zeppelins battling it out over the city. The middle vessel was a big Spartak warship, holed and afire, bracketed on both beams by two Founders war zeppelins of similar size. The Russian was doomed—doomed unless Buckle joined the fray.

"All ahead flank," Buckle shouted.

"All ahead flank, aye!" Valkyrie repeated into the chattertube as she cranked the chadburn dial, ringing the bell. The engine room shouted its response as the stokers hurled coal into the fireboxes. The propellers drove up to a higher roar, the overdriven boilers rattling so hard that they vibrated the airship's decking.

"Run out the guns, Mister Considine!" Buckle shouted into the chattertube.

"Run out the guns! Aye, Captain!" Considine answered from the gunnery gondola.

Buckle figured that all three of the war zeppelins ahead had him outgunned—the *Pneumatic Zeppelin*'s armament of four twelve-pounders on the gun deck and a long brass four-pounder bow chaser were respectable, but just average. Her hammer-gun and the handful of swivel guns on the roof did not add much punch in a scrap between heavies. But Buckle knew that his gun crews were crackerjack—they would make every shot count.

"Mister Windermere, take us down to two hundred. Fifteen degrees, down bubble. Crash dive."

"Aye, Captain," Windermere replied, spinning the elevator wheel, depressing the *Pneumatic Zeppelin*'s massive fins. "Down ship! Crash dive!"

"Hydro! Vent twenty percent," Sabrina shouted. "Across the board."

"Venting twenty percent, aye!" Nero replied, cranking the master wheel on the hydrogen board.

The *Pneumatic Zeppelin* plunged, nose level on an even keel. The stomach-lifting suddenness of her drop exhilarated Buckle, with all her unhappy creaking and groaning as she exceeded her specifications for rate of vertical descent. Buckle was daringly testing her constitution. He was not worried, not one whit.

Kellie yelped, circling around Buckle's knees—she did not like crash dives overmuch. Buckle patted the dog, feeling the hard edges of her vertebra through his gloved fingers as his mind's eye observed his zeppelin from outside, checking her trim and line. He was going to duck down, come in low and fast. It was not hard to spot a zeppelin, but the best way to approach an enemy unobserved—especially when that enemy was preoccupied in an air battle—was low against the ground, from behind, and as fast as the devil might let you lash your boilers.

"Captain Buckle, I must insist," Washington barked at Buckle's back. "Battle stations? We are on an ambassadorial mission!"

Washington. The kraken wound on the back of Buckle's neck prickled painfully. How did Washington get on the bridge? He should have posted a guard on his door.

"Not now, Ambassador," Buckle said, then leaned into the chattertube. "Gunnery! Double-shot your guns!"

"Double-shotted, Captain! Aye!" Considine's voice careened back up the tube.

Buckle raised his telescope to his eye. The battle above was emerging in detail as the *Pneumatic Zeppelin* closed the gap. The Russians built big warships, ponderous behemoths with heavy cannons, famous for their ability to absorb copious amounts of punishment. That durability was something the Spartak zeppelin badly needed at the moment, for the two Founders war zeppelins flanking her were hammering away with broadside after broadside, the flashes of the individual cannons now visible as tiny red licks of flame, instantly followed by rivers of black powder smoke that drifted under their keels.

"The Russian is being peppered, Captain," Sabrina said at Buckle's shoulder. "Not a good place to be alone."

"No," Buckle answered. He swung his glass south of the Muscovy stronghold to the two mortar ships as they lofted massive, phosphorus-coated bombs into the city. Where was their armed escort? Surely they had one. Then he found her, flying so low that her gondola was near skimming the treetops, inching along to the west of the mortar vessels; she was a sloop, small, sleek, and fast. "There you be, you slippery little rat," Buckle said, then shouted, "Escort beyond the barges. Armed sloop low and in the hover."

Buckle scanned the earth, half-expecting a Founders armored train to be steaming up the old rails, its huge cannons far larger than any found on the weight-limited airships, but no locomotives steamed into view. "Keep an eye out for locomotive smoke, mates!" Buckle said.

A glimmer of light on a distant ridge caught Buckle's eye. He trained his lens upon it—fire burning in the trees, difficult to make out in the distance. But he recognized the long, oval shape of the flames: the wreck of a small airship. The *Cartouche*; somehow Buckle was sure it was the *Cartouche*. He glanced back at Valkyrie, who had her head down over her station. There was no point in telling her now. There would be time for sorrowful confirmations later.

The mortar barges were easy pickings, but Buckle passed them up—he wanted the big fish. He was certain the two Founders war zeppelins had yet to see him; he still held the advantage of surprise. The slug-like fixed-carriage mortar barges posed no threat in the *Pneumatic Zeppelin*'s rear, though the Founders sloop commander, if brash enough, might make a run at her. The lookouts would keep an eye on that gnat.

"Two hundred and fifty feet," Sabrina reported.

Windermere spun his elevator wheel back to its neutral position as the *Pneumatic Zeppelin* pulled out of her dive. "Leveling out to two hundred, aye."

The heavily forested ground flooded past below, splotched with white clearings. Buckle felt the zeppelin return to level in his stomach, her decks creaking and the girders overhead groaning, the canvas envelope rippling with the sharp snaps of a flag in a wicked wind.

"Two hundred," Sabrina announced.

"Maintain speed and chase the bubble," Buckle said softly. "Two degrees starboard."

"Two degrees starboard, aye," De Quincey repeated, nudging the helm wheel.

"Riggers, skinners, and snipers on the ratlines," Buckle said. He could now hear the low, rumbling thumps of the mortar ships as they launched their horse-size bombs on the city.

Suddenly Washington was at Buckle's flank. "Captain Buckle, I demand a word."

"Impeccably bad timing, Ambassador," Buckle said, hiding a sudden infuriation at having the squawking old Washington in his ear. "Please return to your cabin, sir."

"I shall not retire. I demand a word," Washington pressed.

"The sloop has seen us, Captain," Wellington reported. "She is coming round!"

"Stay the course," Buckle answered. The sloop could not carry more than a few four-pounders, and the *Pneumatic Zeppelin* was well out of her range. "Prepare for up ship, rapid ascent."

"Aye, Captain," Windermere said.

"We are at war with no one, Captain Buckle," Washington blurted.

"We are engaged, sir!" Buckle snapped. "Now kindly retire from my bridge!"

Washington's eyes flashed. "Break off your attack immediately, Captain, or I shall relieve you of command!"

The words shocked Buckle, though he did not show it. "Surely you jest, sir," he said.

-LXVI-

AN ACT OF WAR

A CLAN AMBASSADOR HAD NO real authority over a zeppelin captain in the field; the man was exasperated, indignant—and out of line. The bridge crew whirled their heads about to glare at Washington with hostile eyes; even Valkyrie looked on with disapproval.

"You presume too much authority here, Ambassador," Buckle said curtly.

"Turn around," Washington pressed. "Turn around, Captain, while we still have time to disengage."

"I shall not," Buckle answered. "We are committed."

"Admiral Balthazar expressly forbade engagement with the Founders. If we are not attacked we must not attack. We must not provoke," Washington continued, breathlessly.

Buckle felt a nasty surge of fury beneath his skin. Who was Washington to need remind him of the words of his own father? "If Spartak is lost, then all is lost."

"The admiral's orders are specific and binding. Turn back," Washington ordered.

"Leave my bridge this instant, sir," Buckle said.

"This is an act of war!" Washington exclaimed, his eyes wide, his face flushed a purple-tinged red. "You have no right to declare war on your own for the clan—no right!"

"Corporal Nyland," Buckle ordered. The corporal, a burly fellow who obviously relished being a marine, his brown eyes young over a great blond mustache and sparse but well-groomed muttonchops, jumped forward from his post at the stairwell.

"Sir!" Nyland said.

"The ambassador is confined to his quarters. Kindly remove him from my bridge," Buckle said.

"Yes, sir," Corporal Nyland replied; he turned to Washington. "Let's move along, sir. There's a good fellow, sir."

Buckle turned his back on the damning gaze of Washington's eyes as Nyland ushered him away. Forget Washington. He stepped forward into the nose bubble to scan the sky. The *Pneumatic Zeppelin* was now hurtling in full view between Muscovy and the startled crews on the mortar barges. The Founders sloop had swung her bow to the south, her engines straining for speed and altitude, her captain abandoning the fat barges as he took his ship on the run; it seemed the fellow lacked the brass balls necessary to take on the much larger *Pneumatic Zeppelin*. The sloop's signal mirrors flashed at the war zeppelins high overhead, but Buckle doubted that the big ships would see the warning.

"You should not expose the Imperial princess to such danger," Washington shouted, grabbing at the railing as Nyland bulled him politely up the staircase. "Your duty is to carry her and me to negotiations with Spartak, not start your own private little war!"

Valkyrie straightened up from the engineering boards, the lift of her chin lengthening her form. "Chief engineer is on her battle station, Captain," she said.

"Thank you, Chief Engineer," Buckle replied, then turned and yanked down the viewing apparatus of the "giraffe," a periscope containing a long series of mirrors that ran in a crooked tube all the way up to the zeppelin envelope's domed nose window. The device lost a lot of light in the transmission of the reflections, the images usually soft and muddy and easily knocked out of alignment, but it gave the piloting crew a view of the sky above the bow envelope, which they otherwise could not see.

Buckle turned the giraffe's focus ring and found the three war zeppelins, their ellipsoidal silhouettes black against the gray sky, eleven hundred feet above and immediately in front of them. The two Founders airships still maintained their favorable positions on both sides of the Russian—which meant that they had not yet seen the sloop's warning mirrors, nor come to realize a Crankshaft zeppelin was close at hand under their keels.

"Speed?" Buckle asked.

"Running at seventy-one knots, sir," Sabrina replied. "I estimate the ships engaged above are running at forty."

"When we catch them, propulsion," Buckle said to Valkyrie, "match their speed."

"Aye," Valkyrie said.

Buckle calculated his acceleration against the *Pneumatic Zeppelin*'s best rate of ascent; he wanted to pop up on the stern of the port-side Founders sky vessel, rake her from aft to fore with bow chaser and broadsides until she fell, and then, hopefully with some element of surprise still remaining—there was a good chance that the massive bulk of the Russian airship might block the view of the port-side zeppelin's fate from her sister—swing behind the Russian and hammer the stern of the second Founders airship with another round of raking fire.

The enemy rarely was kind enough to accommodate one's battle plans, however.

"Ready to up ship. Rapid vertical ascent," Buckle ordered. He could smell the gunpowder now, the acrid cordite of the blackbang, and his mouth watered, he wanted to be in the dustup so badly.

"Ready up ship! Rapid vertical ascent!" Sabrina repeated.

"Ready up ship, aye," Windermere replied.

Buckle's hands tingled as he squeezed the giraffe's leather handgrips, trying to keep the overhead zeppelins in view as his vessel charged them from below. His shoulders ached with excitement, and he took deep, calming breaths that no one could see. He was not afraid, but a crew would pick up on a quivering word or twitch, any sign of a captain's fear, and instantly be disheartened; they all knew that he, the dashing young Crankshaft captain, had never faced the likes of a real war zeppelin before, never mind three of them.

Buckle was confident. As far as he was concerned, he already had the sloppy bastards by the throat. "Helm! One point to port," he ordered.

"Aye!" De Quincey shouted. "One point a'port!"

Buckle leaned into the chattertube and shouted, "Number-five gun!"

"Aye, Captain, number five!" came the response from Howard Hampton. He was posted at the envelope nose-dome hatch, just inside the Axial corridor and only a foot away from the giraffe periscope's lens, and he was the only member of the bow-chaser gun crew who could hear orders on the chattertube. The other four gunners had run the long four-pounder out onto its turret on the bow pulpit and, despite the windscreens and iron barbette, would be near deafened by the torrents of wind.

"Tell Mister Banerji he gets the first shot," Buckle yelled. "But tell him to wait until we level out."

"First shot and level, aye Captain!" Hampton replied.

Buckle leaned back to the giraffe's eyepiece. He pressed his weight down into the bottoms of his boots, nailing his feet to the deck. "Chase the bubble on the way up, Mister

Windermere," he said. "I want a level firing platform when we arrive behind that Founders devil."

"Aye, Captain," Windermere replied, stretching out his fingers as he kept his palms planted on the elevator wheel.

"The mortar ships have pulled anchor and turned about off our port beam, sir," Sabrina said. "Turned tail and run."

"Good," Buckle answered. "Keep an eye out for that sloop. He might try to bounce us once we are engaged, but I doubt it."

The overhead silhouettes inched back into position inside Buckle's eyepiece. "Up ship!" he shouted. "Rapid ascent!"

"Up ship! Up ship!" Sabrina bellowed.

"Up ship!" Windermere grunted, whirling the elevator wheel with every ounce of strength in his shoulders, his gloved hands slapping the spokes as he snatched them through swing after swing.

Valkyrie stepped alongside Nero, slapping hydrogen feeder valves as he cranked his ballast wheels. The roar of water cascading from the scuppers joined the rumble of the engines and propellers and the resounding rattle and groan of the gigantic zeppelin as she catapulted up into the sky.

Buckle held on to the giraffe periscope, lest the force of the ascent drive him to his knees. Everybody was half-bent, holding on to something. Kellie had already curled up inside her cubby, chin on the deck, looking a bit dismayed.

"Three hundred and sixty feet," Sabrina yelled, watching the spin of her bronze altimeter as the sky rushed downward outside the nose-dome window. "Rapid ascent of fifteen feet per second and accelerating."

"Piece of cake!" Buckle shouted at Sabrina over the din.

"Just peachy!" Sabrina replied.

–LXVII–

THE BOW CHASER

MIDSHIPMAN DARIUS BANERJI WAS THE captain of gun crew number five, in charge of the long four-pounder that served as the airship's bow chaser. He crouched in the bow-pulpit gun turret, one hand gripping the lip of the iron barbette, the other on the brass cannon's cascabel. A freezing torrent of wind pummeled Banerji and his three-member gun crew as the *Pneumatic Zeppelin* rocketed up into the sky. Banerji was a slight fellow, and in their exposed position, the rush of wind battered every inch of his heavy coat, threatening to tear away his helmet and goggles.

It was quite something to be perched on the very nose of an airship on a rapid ascent; it was exhilarating, the sky enclosing them in a bottomless gray, as the dark shapes of the enemy war zeppelins grew larger and larger overhead, their gunnery gondolas spitting fire, their cannons shivering the air with deep-throated booms.

"Stay crackerjack!" Banerji shouted at his gun crew, who nodded at him from their crouching positions, packed in the small spaces between the gun carriage and the pulpit rails, wrapped in sheepskin coats, their bright red puggarees flapping on their helmets. The sponger was the ship's apprentice engineer, Lionel Garcia, a good friend of Banerji's from the midshipman's mess. The loader was the burly chief cook, Perriman Salisbury. The new man, the winder, was a mystery to Banerji, though his eyes looked steely enough; he was Adrian Pasternak, the new mechanic and the replacement for Henry Stuart, who had been killed by the kraken. Pasternak, strong looking, with burn scars on his forearms and throat, was reported to have been an excellent gunner aboard the *Hood*, the Crankshaft scout ship from which he had transferred, but Banerji relied little on prior reputation when it came to his gun crew.

There was one more soul out on the bow with them, perched on the curving bowsprit platform on the port side: a marine, Robin Bogdanovitch, crouched with her hands over the flintlock of her long-barreled musket, ready to fire.

Banerji glanced up. The zeppelins battling overhead were less than 250 feet away, and approaching fast. The *Pneumatic Zeppelin* was in position to tuck her nose right up the arse of the port-side airship. They might get a warm reception, a raking blast in return, if the Founders zeppelin had a stern gun. Banerji would ignore any stern chasers, no matter. Captain Buckle was going to land him point-blank on the enemy's backside, and it was his job to fire a devastating rake.

Banerji was terrified, his heart racing like a mad horse, tears welling in his eyes inside his goggles, but he knew that he was made of the stuff that stood fast in the face of danger; it was remarkably easy to do when other men were watching him, waiting for his decisions, their lives in his hands. "Steady, boys!" Banerji shouted. "Just a few moments, now!"

Something else drove Banerji this day, burned inside him. He had failed Captain Buckle by allowing the saboteur to escape him. *Failed* his captain. It chewed up his gut every time he thought of it. But he would be damned if he neglected his duty again now. No matter what the Founders threw at his little garrison on the tip of the *Pneumatic Zeppelin's* nose, his shot was going to be perfect.

Banerji glanced back and saw Howard Hampton, the powder boy—the captain had asked that he be addressed as a gunner's mate—poised just inside the hatch of the towering glass-and-cast-iron nose window. Howard had his ear close to the chattertube hood and the brass pipe of the giraffe periscope neck beside it; he cradled a velvet-and-leather canister containing the next powder charge, which he had carried up from the forward magazine. He looked pale and frightened, but resolute.

Banerji smiled at Howard. Howard's eyes brightened and he smiled back. So far, things had gone swimmingly. The gun crew had arrived on their action station promptly, flung the chocks, tackle, and tompion aside, and run out the gun with by-the-numbers gusto. The long brass cannon was loaded, primed, and ready to fire—a single ball, for the four-pounder did not perform well double-shotted. Garcia, the sponger, had one hand clamped over the barrel's touchhole so the wind could not suck out the fine-grained primer powder while he had his back to it, using his mass to shelter the slow match burning in its bucket. Perriman held a cannonball he had just rolled out of the shot locker, and Pasternak waited at the two winder wheels, one wheel for barrel elevation and depression, the other for turret traverse.

They were just under the fighting airships now, within pistol shot, coming up shockingly fast, no more than fifteen seconds away. Banerji could see the rigging patterns on the undersides of the gondolas, and their next volleys of cannon fire were loud, casting slender rivers of black smoke streaming away overhead.

Banerji doubted he would have to worry about aiming the six-foot-long barrel at all—he was certain that Captain Buckle would plant him straight on the keel line of the target, the perfect position for his dreaded raking shot, sending his three-inch cannonball, a cast-iron round spinning with burning phosphorus, rocketing through the length of the entire zeppelin at one thousand feet per second.

A raking shot was your best bet to pop a zeppelin with a single bang. The cannonball, throwing sparks and phosphors as it glanced off catwalks and girders, created so many holes in the hydrogen gasbags, in one side and out the other, that it stood a good chance of defeating at least one of the self-sealing rubber stockings and releasing a sure-to-be-ignited geyser of hydrogen.

The *Pneumatic Zeppelin* lurched with a great heave, rapidly slowing her ascent, and the weightless sensation made Banerji feel like he might puke the beefsteak and cinnamon pancakes Cookie had made everyone for breakfast. The air was suddenly a flood of dark smoke, awash with the acrid stink of blackbang gunpowder and the eye-stinging issue of steam boilers and superheated oil. After a moment of choking, they were up and out of it.

Banerji worried that somehow he was unprepared, even though he knew his gun was in perfect order. "Ready to fire!" he screamed as they humped up behind the mountainous white-brown-gray stern of the Founders war zeppelin, her five massive bronze propellers disemboweling the air with eardrum-splitting force.

They were so close that, for an instant Banerji feared the tip of the *Pneumatic Zeppelin*'s jib boom might be chopped away. But they leveled out clear above the screws, the harsh rush of the wind subsiding in his ears, and he was now staring into the stern window of the gigantic arse of the Founders zeppelin—the *Industria* was her name, clearly stenciled in silver across the stern arch board of her engineering gondola.

A musket ball banged off the iron barbette just in front of Banerji's face, the flash of sparks near blinding him for an instant. He saw a Founders crewman, dressed in black, standing in the center of the stern window, hatch open, gripping a smoking musket.

Bogdanovitch's musket cracked. The Founders crewman dropped his musket and fell away into the dark interior.

"Bravo, marine!" Banerji shouted. He peered down his gun barrel, though there was no need to aim—it was pointed straight down the *Industria*'s axial line, where, thank the Oracle, there was no stern gun waiting to pot them. "Fire!" Banerji shouted.

Shielding the slow match as he yanked it from its tub, Garcia eased it across the barrel's vent field and jammed the flame down into the touchhole.

The touchhole flashed. The gun erupted with a heavy *boom*, hurling scarlet-and-yellow flame and bits of fiery wad from the muzzle. The carriage recoiled, flung backward like a mad rhino along the turret rails, passing under Banerji as he leaned over it.

The oncoming wind snatched the muzzle smoke and hurled it into their faces before carrying it away an instant later. Banerji saw the shot shatter one of the *Industria*'s big rear windowpanes upon entry—satisfyingly close to the round center pane—followed by a small but bright white flash, as the ball hurtled through the inside of the airship. Whether the flash had been a momentary hydrogen breach before the rubber stockings stoppered the hole, or a ricochet off a metal girder, Banerji did not know.

"Stopping the vent!" Banerji shouted as he plugged the smoking touchhole with his vent piece. He hoped that his crew did not hear in his voice the obvious twinge of disappointment that their shot had not popped the enemy. "Reload!" he howled.

⊸LXVIII⊷

HARD A'STARBOARD!

ROMULUS BUCKLE HAD NOT SEEN the course of the bow chaser's raking shot through the *Industria*. But he did see her drop—not much, ten feet perhaps—the telltale sign of a sudden loss of hydrogen pressure.

"Heel! Hard a'starboard!" Buckle shouted.

"Hard a'starboard!" De Quincey shouted back, heaving the helm wheel to the right, the deck instantly threatening to roll as the airship's port-side maneuvering propellers turned and wound up. Windermere was busy on the elevator wheel, for it was difficult to keep the bubble level in a rapid rotation at high speed.

The looming backside of the *Industria* swung to the left as the *Pneumatic Zeppelin* heeled sharply to the right, turning at a good rate. De Quincey would bring the Crankshaft twelve-pounders to bear on the *Industria*'s stern to deliver a broadside rake with the bigger guns. Buckle caught a nose full of black-bang smoke as it flowed in over the gunwales. It stung his eyes and nose, and exhilarated him. The nasty stink of battle, of cannons pouring loose their red-hot iron and flaming wad, both braced and beckoned him.

Buckle saw the *Industria*'s steam exhausts pillow violently and her propellers flash at a faster rotation as more power was applied—the first sign of an evasive maneuver from her captain. He had not disengaged, had not broken away instantly once raked. It was sloppy work. Fatally sloppy work.

Snapping a toggle on his chattertube hood, Buckle spoke directly to the gunnery gondola. "Mister Considine, once we have them on the beam, you may fire at your discretion."

"Aye, Captain!" Tyler Considine's booming shipyard fore-man's voice quickly bounced back up the tube. "We'll have at them, sir!"

"Be ready to depress to follow her drop, if her captain is worth any salt at all!" Buckle added.

"Aye!" Considine replied.

"Altitude thirteen hundred," Sabrina said.

"Ready ahead all flank," Buckle said calmly.

"Ready ahead all flank, aye," Valkyrie repeated.

Buckle stepped to the port gunwale, sticking his head out-side as he kept the stern of the *Industria* in full view.

"Captain!" Sabrina shouted. "Snipers, off the beam!"

"Occupational hazard, Lieutenant," Buckle shouted back. The massive stern of the Russian war zeppelin was on his right, her guns still blazing. He eyed the *Industria*: with her emergency steam power applied and the *Pneumatic Zeppelin* slowing as she turned, she was increasing the distance them, but not enough to matter to the guns. One hundred to 150 feet was still point-blank range to a twelve-pounder, more or less.

The *Industria* began to ascend, her scuppers pouring great cascades of ballast water, waterfalls sparkling in the late-after-noon sun, as the great zeppelin began to lunge for altitude, to escape on the rise.

But it was too late.

Buckle understood the *Industria*'s dilemma; although her rubber stockings had withstood the four-pounder's raking shot, the airship was still in dire condition. Surely there were hydrogen leaks—even if small ones—and the captain had to assume that he now had volatile pockets of gas pooling under his roof in amounts larger than his venting system could immediately disperse. Dumping ballast was the safest tactic, but it was also the slowest.

De Quincey and Windermere slowed their manhandling of the rudder and elevator wheels, and the maneuvering propellers brought the *Pneumatic Zeppelin* nicely steady as she ascended level with the fleeing *Industria*'s stern.

"We are abeam!" Buckle shouted, the freezing wind on his cheeks, barely aware of the little flashes of the Founders sniper muskets on the *Industria*'s roof.

The sound of the two twelve-pound cannons firing in unison from the gunnery gondola 250 feet aft of Buckle erupted with a low, muffled, heartwarming *ba-boom*. Two streams of glittering yellow-white phosphorus ripped between the *Pneumatic Zeppelin* and her target. Two holes appeared in the stern of the *Industria*: one shattering the port side of her stern window, the other punching a small black hole in the envelope beside.

Buckle winced. It was difficult to witness that kind of a hit, even inflicted upon an enemy. In his mind's eye, he saw the two cast-iron balls hurtle through the guts of the zeppelin, cutting gasbags wide open, shattering the ligatures of the rubber-stocking mechanisms, tearing away rigging, shearing high-tension wires into slashing whips that could easily cut a man or woman in half, and such things were nowhere near the worst of it. Any frame girders or supports in the path of the cannonballs would be smashed apart, taking elements of the envelope with them, the jagged edges of the shorn metal plunging into the gasbags. The cannonballs would continue, roughly parallel to the Axial corridor, sending up huge sprays of sparks wherever they might hit metal, shrugging off waves of phosphorus as they passed through the massive caverns within the gasbags they punctured. For humans they brought nothing but agony, either in the splintering shrapnel of pulverized wood and iron that shredded limbs, faces, and spines or, for those physically unscathed, the terrifying realization of the incineration awaiting them in the inescapable pop.

And within a second the pop came.

Buckle raised his arm to shield his eyes. Two huge explosions racked the *Industria*, the force of the ignited hydrogen and air funneled outward by her compartment blast shields, belching surging eruptions of bright-yellow fire out into the sky. The heat hurt Buckle's face, so close was his zeppelin to the conflagration.

The *Industria*'s amidships gunnery gondola, sundered by a blast immediately overhead, broke away from her pins and dropped loose of the airship frame—she hung for a terrible moment, her brass-and-copper armor gleaming in a hammock of its own rigging and cables. The ropes and wires snapped, and the gondola dropped silently away, flashing in the muted sunlight as it spun into the void.

The *Industria* lurched, heeling oddly to port, smoke spewing from the burning edges of her gaping envelope holes. She began to drop away, falling into a slow, uncontrolled spiral.

Buckle observed the plunge of the *Industria* coldly, with a detached blend of horror and satisfaction. A cheer rose on the bridge, joined by a howl from Kellie. Buckle did not join in; he ducked inside, secretly angry with the instant of self-congratulation, of inaction.

"All ahead flank!" Buckle screamed. "Helm, bring us across the Russian's stern as tight as you dare! Bring me on that second Founders' arse as quick as the devil, Mister De Quincey, you blackjacket hound!"

~LXIX~

ASTERN THE *CZARINA*

Sabrina took a firm hold on her drift-scope handles as the *Pneumatic Zeppelin* surged forward with the wind at her back, sweat-drenched stokers hurling coal into her overheating engines, her turbines spinning so hard their vibration threatened to rattle loose the deck bolts, her driving propellers winding up to a screw-bending pitch. Sabrina felt the raw power of the zeppelin surge through her from the madly creaking deck, fueled by the cacophony of groaning, screeching, and grinding sounds the airship made when suddenly pushed so hard.

Sabrina ignored the protestations of the airship, for she knew every noise sounded the way it should.

Within the piloting gondola, the driving wheels whirled. Orders and reports sounded back and forth, but Sabrina barely heard them, peering out the nose dome as she was, watching the *Industria* corkscrew away in flames. Burn in hell, she thought. Burn.

The stern of the huge Russian war zeppelin loomed to port. She saw the arch board of the Russian airship and the name *Czarina* upon it, a name she had heard before. The *Czarina* was battered, leaving a wide trail of gray smoke in her wake, now and again streaking with black when she fired her cannons, and her propellers—six big bronze monsters—were in danger of fouling in a whipping mass of trailing ropes and wires blown away from the airship body, and now foundering in her slipstream.

The *Pneumatic Zeppelin*, advancing at an angle to just clear the *Czarina*'s stern, was making up the ground she had lost in her broadside swing—the distance between her port beam and the *Czarina*'s rudder was no more than a cable's length as it was—and Sabrina's airship was closing the gap far more quickly than she would have anticipated. The *Czarina* had slowed, now making no more than twenty-five knots. Was she badly damaged? Had her boilers taken a hit? Or could the Russian captain have cut back his engines, knowing the Founders zeppelin would match him, thus allowing Buckle's airship the opportunity to charge the enemy's vulnerable tail?

Balthazar had often expressed his admiration for the dogged, selfless courage of the Russians. If so, it was an excellent tactical move by the Spartak captain, but his airship would pay the price for keeping the Founders glued to his flank.

The piloting gondola passed through the wall of smoke pouring back from the *Czarina*, momentarily blinding Sabrina. She ducked her head and held her breath against the gusts of furnace-hot, ember-laden smoke as they poured in through the open ventilation ports. They were gone in a couple of seconds, when the *Pneumatic Zeppelin* escaped the trail.

"We are directly abaft the *Czarina*'s stern, Captain!" Sabrina shouted. "Forward lookouts report the Founders zeppelin, the *Bellerophon*, still in position to her starboard side!"

"Aye!" Buckle replied.

Sabrina could not yet see the *Bellerophon* beyond the bulk of the smoking *Czarina*, but the forward lookouts could. Still in position, eh? The *Bellerophon*'s captain, either too preoccupied with the *Czarina* or simply unable to see past her mass and smoke to witness what was unfolding on the opposite side, had left his sky vessel a sitting duck for the *Pneumatic Zeppelin.*

Sabrina eyed the *Czarina* as they passed, her six huge driving propellers chopping slow, gleaming in the dull sunlight, the rear of her engineering gondola a mass of pipes and vents, like the devil's factory of the *Pneumatic Zeppelin.* The *Czarina's* envelope was badly singed and holed, but the white-gray smoke streaming out of some of the rents suggested that although she had fires aboard, her crew was beating them down with hoses.

Sabrina saw a group of men, dressed in rust-colored or olive leather jackets, clustered in the stern window of the *Czarina.* It was not a circular, domed structure as in most airship designs, but rather a square box of glass, like a greenhouse set in a projecting frame of wood that was beautifully carved and gilded. Sabrina's eyes widened—in the center of the stern window, glass firing port flung open, stood a large cannon muzzle; a stern chaser had been run out, an iron twelve-pounder, closely attended by its crew.

Sabrina suddenly wondered whether the Russians considered the Crankshaft airship a friend or foe. Surely they had seen the *Pneumatic Zeppelin* blast the *Industria* and come on past them to ambush her partner? Buckle had given them his exposed flank while his guns were being reloaded. If he had been mistaken, if they had not marked him as a friend, then they were in a very bad state of affairs. To her relief, she saw the Russian gun crew waving their hats, furry ushanki and sailor caps with blue ribbons; she thought, though it was surely impossible, that she heard the vague, faint howls of their cheering.

"Signalman!" Buckle shouted back at the signals room. "Ensign Fitzroy!"

"Aye, Captain!" Jacob Fitzroy shouted, poking his head out of the signals cabin, with Meagan Churchill's head alongside.

"Flag the Russians! Signal to disengage and down ship immediately!"

"Aye, Captain! Disengage and down ship!" Fitzroy yelled, ducking back into the cabin with Meagan.

"Founders vessel disengaging, accelerating on the level!" Sabrina shouted.

The *Pneumatic Zeppelin's* piloting gondola cleared the stern of the *Czarina* to reveal the towering cream-colored rump of the second Founders airship, the *Bellerophon*, her canvas holed and crawling with snipers, her six propellers spinning up to gleaming whorls as she surged forward. She was damaged, with black holes in her skin—one had punctured the huge emblem of the silver phoenix on her flank, potting the head. She looked as if she had suffered horribly under the *Czarina's* big guns.

The *Bellerophon* was a graceful beast of a machine, equal in length to the *Czarina* and *Pneumatic Zeppelin*, but sleeker in diameter, carrying a vastly more complicated rigging system, with masts, yards, and sails furled at her nose and stern. Five gondolas gleamed with green-rusted copper plating under her belly, two of them lined with gun ports.

The *Bellerophon's* captain had finally realized his situation. He was charging to cut in front of the crippled and lumbering *Czarina*—and from the way his airship lunged at the bit, she looked damned fast—attempting to place the bulk of the Spartak airship between him and the *Pneumatic Zeppelin* until he could improve his position. It was a good maneuver. The *Pneumatic Zeppelin*, passing astern of him at high speed, could not match his turn to port—her momentum would sweep her wide.

The hammergun under the piloting gondola opened up on the *Bellerophon* with its harpoons, pounding with its low *chunk chunk chunk*—fired by Assistant Engineer Bolling instead of Max, who normally would have been in there. Sabrina suddenly missed Max with an unexpected pang.

"Fitzroy! Any response from the Russians?" Buckle shouted.

"No response yet, sir!" Fitzroy shouted back from the back of the gondola, where he and Meagan had run out the flag hoist.

The gunnery gondola, having now cleared the *Czarina*, fired a double-shotted broadside at the fleeing *Bellerophon*. The four cannonballs punched a tight cluster of holes in the enemy envelope, but to no apparent effect.

"Black-eyed devils!" Buckle cursed. "All ahead standard. Rotate. Hard a'port, Mister De Quincey. Come about and bear on the Russian!"

The bridge rang with the sounds of the chadburn bell and officers responding. Sabrina leaned over Welly, peering into the glass point of the nose, gripping the instrument panels of the navigator's station as the airship swerved violently to port, eyes glued to the escaping *Bellerophon* as she started to disappear behind the *Czarina*'s bow.

The *Pneumatic Zeppelin*, thrown into a severe rotational turn at high speed, vibrated violently. Superstructure girders screamed. Wires and ropes snapped and popped overhead, slashing away in high-pitched whistles. Two instrument tubes shattered on the bridge, leaking little waterfalls of greasy boil water. Sabrina glanced back to see De Quincey and Windermere both hauling over their driving wheels as hard as they could, snatching at the wheel spokes, both steaming with sweat that stained their heavy jackets at the necks and sleeves.

"Superstructure is overstressed, Captain!" Valkyrie yelled. "Pneumatic joint pressure is off the scale."

Sabrina grinned. Valkyrie was not yet familiar with Buckle's propensity to push everything beyond its limit. He believed that the *Pneumatic Zeppelin* was indestructible.

"She can take it," Buckle answered. "You Imperials make fine airships." Sabrina knew that Buckle would be damned if he was going to lose his position on the *Bellerophon*'s tail. There was no telling if the Spartak captain had seen their signal to disengage, and no telling if he would be willing to accept it. Buckle was asking the Russian, after taking a beating at the hands of the *Bellerophon*, to drop out of the fight while Buckle, set up with a near-perfect attack position, went for the glorious kill.

Buckle could not wait, or the *Bellerophon* would escape him. The Spartak captain had already slowed to bait the *Bellerophon* into a vulnerable position—surely he would drop off to allow the trap to close.

The rattling and shaking *Pneumatic Zeppelin*, her maneuvering propellers screaming as they pitched up to maximum on their nacelles, swung around at a dizzying rate, straightening out to bear on the stern of the *Czarina*.

"All ahead flank!" Buckle shouted. "Straight at the Russian!"

Valkyrie rang the bell. The *Pneumatic Zeppelin* surged forward.

"Collision course, Captain!" Sabrina shouted.

"Aye! Collision course," Buckle replied, watching the great mass of the *Czarina*'s envelope hurtling toward them, the double-headed eagle symbol a burst of gold on her dark-gray flank. The Spartak airship was still holding her course and altitude. And the *Bellerophon* had utterly disappeared behind her. "Hold fast!"

Sabrina looked back at Buckle. He stood with his hands behind his back, shoulders slightly hunched, eyes lowered, looking for all the world like a bull about to charge.

Always pushing everything—and everyone—beyond their limit, Sabrina thought as she braced for impact.

―LXX―

THE CHRYSALIS

"ROMULUS!" MAX SCREAMED. BURSTING FROM the snowstorm, her horse near berserk with fear, she saw the sabertooth charging him.

She jerked her jouncing musket level and it boomed in her hands. She saw the huge beastie's head snap away, the eyes on the right side of the head disappearing, the spray of green blood in the blizzard. The sabertooth's lifeless body crashed into Buckle, rolling over him.

"Romulus!" she screamed, hurling the musket aside and unholstering her pistol, reining the horse to a stop just before it trampled Buckle where he lay, flattened in the snow, lying in a ghastly bed of ice-coated human bones. "Captain! Get up! You must get up now if you can!" She grabbed at the reins of Buckle's tethered horse, but they would not yank free.

Buckle was up, on his feet, pistol and torch in hand.

Both horses shrieked—loud, terrified whinnies. The sabertooths were on the prowl. Max swung her pistol around.

A locomotive hit her in the back, a heart-stopping mass of fangs and claws. She was falling, the horse was falling, in a blur of darkness and snow. Somewhere in the awful thud of the landing, in the blinding blow to her head on the ice and the suffocating lungful of snow, she felt the bite sinking into her shoulder, the foul heat of the monster's breath on her neck, the claws ripping her flesh.

She fought back in the agonizing blackness. She fought back by hating the beastie.

A pistol blast flashed, illuminating the lids over her eyes, the nearness of it concussing her ears.

A great weight fell upon her, pressing the last traces of air out of her lungs, squeezing the blood out of her mouth.

"Captain, go. Leave me."

***

"Miss Max!" Miss Max!" the weak voice of Cornelius Valentine poured into the dark snowstorm surrounding Max. "It's just a bad dream, girl. Just a bad dream."

Had she just been screaming? Wailing? She could not tell. Her mouth was open and she was breathing hard. And her cheeks were wet. Doctor Lee had removed her aqueous-humor-filled goggles—there was no need to moisten her eyes while she slept.

"You awake, Miss Max?" Valentine asked.

Max opened her eyes. It was evening, perhaps—the light at the window curtains was dim and gray, though the night lanterns had yet to be lit. She tried to move. She could, but to do so made every muscle ache terribly. She held still, shifting her eyes so she could see Valentine in the reflection of the silver water jug on her bedside table.

"Yes," Max rasped, her voice sounding like it came from somewhere nearby. She focused her aching eyes on Valentine's mirrored reflection. He was situated on the opposite side of the middle aisle, perhaps four beds down. A privacy curtain was set up at the head of his bunk, but no one had drawn it. Max could see the disheveled outline of Valentine's long hair about his pale face on the pillow, the long ridge of his body under the infirmary sheets—and the flat place on the bed where his right leg should have been.

"No doubt we both will have nightmares for a while. We've both had a bit of a rough go up on the mountain," Valentine muttered. "You havin' your run-in with the sabertooths, and I with the kraken."

Max heard Valentine's words, but they jumbled when she tried to understand them. She caught a glimpse of the powder-blue hummingbird egg and the butterfly chrysalis Buckle had brought for her, nestled on the table. Beside them, she saw the yellow gleam of the sabertooth-claw bracelet he had fashioned for her.

The sight of the claws made Max shudder. Despite the pain, she raised her arm and pushed Romulus's bracelet behind the water jug, where she could no longer see it.

Buckle. Max could not remember where Buckle was. But the alarm twisting in the pit of her stomach when she thought of him tortured her. She closed her aching eyes, but the darkness there was full of floating flashes.

"We are quite the pair," Valentine said, shambling in his own morphine haze. "Both broken, both having a piece of us bit off by a beastie. You'll be fine, Miss Max. But me, me—they drum one-legged dogs out of the air corps straight away."

Max opened her eyes again, forcing the nerves and worry away, and focused on the chrysalis. Her brain washed clear as a mountain stream, though swept along as a floating leaf, without control. What kind of engine drove the brainless worm to build its own sarcophagus of silk and bury itself alive? she mused.

What kind of biological engine, what magnificent impulse of genetics, transformed the worm into the butterfly?

Such were the mysteries of the universe that occupied Max when she had time to indulge them—not the hunt for mathematical solutions.

But in math she now saw a sanctuary. A quiet cloister in the storm. A path to escape the pain.

Valentine was talking again, but Max lost track of him. She gave in to her Martian instinct, careening through an endless galaxy of numbers. The formulae rolled back and forth in her brain, numbed as it was by the morphine, and she kept losing track of her computations.

She had known of the immortality equation all her life. She had never been interested in it. Who would be interested in an unsolvable trick of digits? She was familiar with the Martian penchant for mathematics and numbers, but she was only half Martian, and that characteristic did not seem to be a part of her makeup. She was excellent at math, but it did not *intrigue* her.

Until now.

If only her memories of the chamber of numbers were something more than morphine-soaked blurs.

-LXXI-

COLLISION COURSE

BUCKLE READ THE SWING OF the deck; the *Pneumatic Zeppelin* was running fast, gaining immense speed out of her turn. He was in imminent danger of ramming the *Czarina*, yes. But he was not going to lose the *Bellerophon*.

"I do not think the Russian captain saw your request, Captain," Sabrina said, far too calmly. "Ten seconds to impact."

"Prepare for emergency ascent," Buckle said. "Prepare to dump all ballast."

"Aye, aye!" Nero answered, gripping the red velvet handles of the emergency ballast-release levers over his head. Valkyrie moved to the ballast boards, placing her hands on the hydrogen feeder wheels.

The twenty-story-high envelope of the *Czarina* rushed perilously close, rapidly filling the nose dome window like a mountain cliff.

"Up ship!" Buckle shouted. "Emergency ascent!"

The cry of "Up ship!" sounded around the gondola. Nero slammed his ballast levers down like a madman, Windermere spinning his elevator wheel with equal urgency. Valkyrie slapped the hydrogen valve controls up and open, flooding the gas bags to higher pressure.

The *Pneumatic Zeppelin* lunged upward, her nose raised, arching for the sky above the *Czarina*'s envelope. Suddenly they were above her, the long, broad length of her canvas back, a small planet hurtling beneath the nose window, passing mere feet below the keels of the Crankshaft gondolas and the blades of their propellers, the Spartak skinners and snipers running and throwing themselves flat before they disappeared behind. "Level off!" Buckle shouted. "We shall soon have the angle, sky dogs! Look sharp!"

"There she is!" Windy exclaimed as the *Pneumatic Zeppelin* hurtled out over the forward port quarter of the *Czarina*'s roof. The *Bellerophon* came into view just below, racing to port, the long, massive bulk of her envelope pale against the darkening earth.

With the *Bellerophon* in his sights, Buckle was in no mood to squander his chance. It seemed too easy. If he could, with his vastly superior tactical position, he would cripple the *Bellerophon*, board her, and take her as a prize. The Founders warship would make a desperately needed addition to the armada of the Grand Alliance.

They had cleared the *Czarina*. "Down ship!" Buckle shouted. "Emergency dive! Mister Windermere, put me level, and Mister De Quincey, put me on that devil's stern!"

"Aye, aye!" Windermere and De Quincey replied.

"Jettisoning hydro!" Nero announced, winding the valve wheels.

Buckle felt his mind firing as the *Pneumatic Zeppelin*, plunging, decks rattling, wind wailing in her rigging and over her gunnels, bore down upon the enemy. The *Bellerophon*'s captain was turning in to the *Pneumatic Zeppelin*, hard a'port, attempting to defeat Buckle's angle. Bad airmanship, clinging to a failed tactic, Buckle thought.

Both of the *Bellerophon*'s gunnery gondolas released a simultaneous port broadside—from the muzzle flashes it looked to be three cannons apiece—but the severe traverse of their barrels, probably cranked hard up against the aft frame of their gun ports, sent the shots just wide, the cluster of caterwauling cannonballs hurtling past the port side of the *Pneumatic Zeppelin*'s piloting gondola in glittering phosphorescent trails.

Kellie barked, emerging from her armored cubby. "In, girl!" Buckle snapped, and the dog scurried back in.

Buckle studied the discharge of the guns, never taking his eyes off the *Bellerophon* and her gunnery gondolas, wreathed in rivers of smoke. It would take the port-side Founders gun crews three minutes to reload—if they were any good at all. No matter. In two minutes, Buckle would have ripped off the *Bellerophon*'s wings, grappled her close, and leapt to board her.

"Hard a'port, Mister De Quincey," Buckle ordered. "Line up his flank on our starboard beam, sir."

"Aye, Captain," De Quincey responded.

"Starboard guns double-shotted and ready to fire, Cap'n!" Considine's voice rang breathlessly from the chattertube hood.

"Guns doubled and ready to fire," Valkyrie repeated.

Buckle leaned into his chattertube. "Gunnery! We shall broadside the engineering gondola to starboard. Take out their propulsion!"

"Broadside propulsion, aye!" Considine replied. Sabrina's head snapped toward Buckle, her green eyes wide under the chestnut curve of her bowler. She knew what he was up to. It was no time to attempt to take a prize, Buckle knew, and she disapproved. Ah, well, Sabrina often disapproved.

~LXXII~

BROADSIDES

THE *PNEUMATIC ZEPPELIN* WAS LABORING hard to port now, as De Quincey pinned the rudder wheel over, bulling the airship around onto the *Bellerophon*'s port flank, to match her turn as she tried to outrun them.

"Turret! Prepare to fire into the propellers!" Buckle yelled into the chattertube.

"Propellers, aye!" Geneva Bolling replied from the turret below.

Buckle felt the *Pneumatic Zeppelin* roll slightly into her port-side turn. It was only a degree or so, a small hedging of the deck under his boots, but one degree off zero bubble was a measurable discrepancy he did not want his gunners having to compensate for. "Mister Windermere," Buckle boomed. "Hold her steady as you please. Chase the bubble, sir—keep the platform steady."

"Aye, sir!" Windy answered, rocking his elevator wheel back and forth with his eyes on his inclinometer bubble in its ornate glass tube in front of him. "Zero level, aye!"

"Stern observer reports the Spartak airship has descended, Captain," Sabrina announced. "In pursuit of the *Industria*."

The mighty *Bellerophon*, not yet up to full speed and handicapped by extensive damage sustained from the *Czarina*'s guns, seemed to crawl as the *Pneumatic Zeppelin* hurtled down upon her. Buckle heard Banerji's bow chaser cannon *thump*, a distant, round wallop high above on the nose.

"Steady as she goes, lads and ladies," Buckle said, folding his hands behind his back and squaring his feet at his station, with the master gyroscope floating in its great metal-framed glass orb in front of him.

Buckle eyed the length of the *Bellerophon* as the *Pneumatic Zeppelin* closed in on her—she was a big war bird, but up close she looked worn, her skin mottled and stained, her copper gondolas encrusted with green oxidization. Sniper muskets flashed here and there from the envelope, trading shots with the Crankshaft skinners and marines.

A wild spattering of sparks and flame burst out of the *Bellerophon*'s high port-side propeller nacelle, the one being hammered by a glittering stream of harpoons from the *Pneumatic Zeppelin*'s hammergun; one of the steel points must have sunk home in the mechanism and jammed it. The propeller quickly tore itself apart in a scream of wrenching metal, kicking up and out of its seating and nearly tearing the entire nacelle loose of the main frame before it seized up and toppled over, smoking, motionless, ruined.

"Nice shooting, turret!" Buckle shouted.

The *Bellerophon*, her propulsion out of balance, began to yaw to port as the propellers on that side were overdriven by the opposite flank. The result enhanced the rotation of the *Bellerophon*'s turn, swinging her stern away from Buckle and bringing her gunnery gondolas around for a better broadside.

"Curse the luck!" Buckle snapped. "Helm, hard a'port! Keep us on his beam!"

"Aye, Captain!" De Quincey said, whipping the rudder wheel around, excitement flowing through his voice with the timbre of a plucked violin string.

The *Pneumatic Zeppelin* swung hard to port, coming around so she once again ran parallel to the *Bellerophon*, who had straightened out her course.

"Get us close, helm," Buckle said.

"Aye, Captain," De Quincey replied.

"Gunnery—ready for a broadside to starboard!" Buckle said into the chattertube.

"Aye, Captain! To starboard!" Considine responded.

The *Pneumatic Zeppelin* caught up with the *Bellerophon*, the flanks of their envelopes no more than one hundred feet apart, the *Pneumatic Zeppelin*'s nose at the amidships of the Founders sky vessel, her guns lined up with the enemy's aft engineering gondola.

"Match speed!" Buckle ordered.

"Matching and maintaining speed, Captain!" Valkyrie replied, her hand on the chadburn handle.

"Closer, Mister De Quincey, damn your hide! Bump ribs with the charlatan!" Buckle yelled; he dashed to the starboard gunwale, thrusting his head out into the freezing wind, anxiously awaiting the sound of his own guns.

Buckle glanced back to see the *Pneumatic Zeppelin*'s two starboard twelve-pounders fire. The red-yellow flashes of their cannon muzzles slapped the air, their puffs of smoke and burning wadding snatched away in the slipstream between the two gigantic machines. He felt the force of the muzzle blasts shove the airship aside. The cannonballs sliced between the *Pneumatic Zeppelin* and the *Bellerophon*, and while one missed, hurtling off into the sky in a descending arc of rapidly dissipating phosphorus, the others struck the target.

Three twelve-pound cannonballs tore into the *Bellerophon*'s engineering gondola, ripping through its copper plating and blowing out terrible holes on the opposite side in great flashes of burning oil, armor shards, and shattered wooden boards. Fire instantly rose in the breaches. Sparkling water cascaded down from above, likely from a ballast tank burst open by a wrench of the airframe. The entire gondola began to shudder, as if every piece of machinery within her had gone off its tracks. Within moments, the shuddering stopped.

"Another propeller has shut down, Captain!" Sabrina shouted. "Their number one, closest to us, port side!"

"They've stopped all engines!" Windermere shouted.

"Aye!" Sabrina affirmed. "All propellers are shutting down!"

"Slow and match speed! Bring us alongside. Grappling position!" Buckle shouted, watching the *Bellerophon* as she rapidly slowed.

"Grappling position?" De Quincey repeated, his eyes widening. "Aye, Captain."

Buckle saw the massive propellers rotating down to a lazy stall under the port-side stern of the *Bellerophon*. With her propulsion center severely damaged, the *Bellerophon* could not escape him; her choices were now to surrender or fight it out. Buckle figured they would choose the latter.

"Grappling position, sir," Windermere said. "Up ship fifty feet, sir!"

"Aye!" Buckle nodded. It was best to board high, out of reach of the maximum elevation of the enemy's gondola cannons. "Order boarding parties to assemble on Eagle deck, by division."

"Pardon me, Captain," Windermere asked, incredulous. "We are to board her?"

"Yes, Mister Windermere—I mean to board her and take her."

–LXXIII–

BOARDING PARTY

"HERE WE ARE, MATES!" BUCKLE shouted robustly at the dozens of faces clustered on the Eagle deck catwalk: expectant, determined, fearful faces, pinked by their hasty charges up the ladders, ratlines, catwalks, and stairwells, their red puggareed helmets near brushing the underside canvas of the *Pneumatic Zeppelin*'s roof as it rippled overhead, the tops of the massive hydrogen gasbags heaving on both sides, their laces of metal and rubber stockings spiderwebbed across their massive backs. Muskets, pistols, and cutlasses from the weapons lockers gleamed in the half-light, alongside axes, hatchets, and boat hooks. "The war is upon us!" Buckle continued. "The war is here. Either we fight them here, in the sky over Muscovy, or we fight them in the streets of the Punchbowl. It is they who have chosen this path, but it us Crankshafts who shall determine where it ends!"

Buckle raised his sword. The crew responded with a throaty, nervous, energy-rousing cheer.

"Fight them, lads and ladies, fight them knowing that it is they who bombed us at Tehachapi, who destroyed our airships and murdered our innocents. We turn our fire and sword upon them now. Now it is our turn to take one back!"

The boarders responded with a wholehearted "Hurrah!"

"And watch out for tanglers." Buckle grinned. "I have been known to forget about the beasties now and again!"

Nervous laughter and guffaws bolstered the crowd.

Buckle swung up onto the amidships observation-nacelle ladder. "Keep your divisions together. Stay close to your officers. Discharge your weapons at the point of attack, then close as quickly as possible hand to hand. Bring the fight to them, mates. Have at them, the cursed Founders dogs, and I guarantee you the *Bellerophon* is ours!"

The crew responded with wild, bloodthirsty cheers as Buckle planted his helmet on his head and sprang up the ladder. Valkyrie was close at his heels, her Imperial rapier at the ready. Buckle had not wanted her to accompany him, had not wanted the princess so exposed to the extreme peril of a boarding attempt, but she had been regally adamant, stating her case with one boot on the bridge stairwell and her scabbard in her hand. The second officer's place was with the captain, according to the rules of engagement, she had informed him, with her calm, infuriating correctness, should he choose to join the boarding party.

At least Buckle had convinced Valkyrie to replace her Imperial pickelhaube with the Crankshaft pith and its red puggaree, lest the crew mistake her blues for the enemy in the confusion of the fight.

Buckle hurled himself up the ladder and scrambled out the low forward hatchway of the amidships observer's nacelle. He barely felt any pain in his legs, already burning from the physical exertion of charging up fourteen flights of stairs and ladders, for he was now driven by adrenaline. The sudden openness of the sky fueled him, the ceiling of the world aglow in a blanket of dimpled, high-altitude clouds illuminated by the falling sun's incandescent colors of molten gold.

The freezing wind was thick with the stench of blackbang powder. Buckle coughed as he scurried forward along the spine board, passing his scattered skinners and marines, the fluttering canvas of his great airship's roof dwarfing him on both sides. There was no need to bend low against the wind—the *Pneumatic Zeppelin* was running slow, perhaps fifteen knots, as her massive canvas back slowly edged closer to the monstrous hump of the smoking *Bellerophon*, not more than one hundred feet to starboard. The *Pneumatic Zeppelin* was higher than the *Bellerophon* by perhaps thirty feet, hedging her bulk above the maximum inclination of the *Bellerophon*'s main guns.

The *Bellerophon*'s envelope was an anthill, crawling with defenders assembling to repel the coming attack. The musket of a Founders marine, perched on the *Bellerophon*'s roof, flashed with a *boom*, and the whistling ball passed just over Buckle's head as he stopped beside a grappling cannon.

"Snipers, Captain," Valkyrie shouted over the wind at Buckle's back. "I would suggest you keep your head down, sir."

Buckle glanced back at Valkyrie as she stood on the spine board, tall and blond and jarringly conspicuous in her Imperial powder blues amidst the tans and reds of the Crankshaft crew members. She was a lioness among wolves, and by her mere presence, gripping her long, gleaming silver sword, she dominated the hardy air dogs scrambling about her, assembling at their action stations or hastily unwrapping the oilskin covers of the pepper guns and grappling cannons.

"Assemble by divisions! Man the grapnel launchers!" Buckle shouted. He was counting the numbers of Founders crewmen collecting on top of the *Bellerophon*, the flashes of their marines' muskets offering tiny white bursts here and there along the long sweep of the envelope. "You might duck a touch yourself, Chief Engineer," Buckle replied to Valkyrie. "You make for quite a target in that uniform."

The Crankshaft boarders grouped at their stations at the bow and amidships. A marine named Cartwright—conspicuous in his gold-buttoned red coat and white pith—knelt clear of the gathering ranks and, after carefully aiming, fired his long-barreled musket. Buckle saw the phosphorescent trail of the ball zip toward the *Bellerophon*, but it missed whatever target the marine had marked it for.

Buckle eyed the distance between the *Pneumatic Zeppelin* and the *Bellerophon*, which was no more than seventy-five feet now. Windermere and De Quincey were laying them alongside perfectly. The huge Founders airship, her skin holed and streaming with smoke, looked intensely battered—the guns of the *Czarina* had perhaps crippled her even more badly than Buckle had first estimated.

The battle was already under way, with muskets blazing on each side. A Founders crewperson, a woman in a gray coat, fell away from the *Bellerophon*, dropping into the gaping void between the towering flanks as they crept toward each other.

"Founders' dreadnaughts, ha! She's a big old coal bucket!" Ivan shouted, arriving at Buckle's shoulder in a great huff, his metal face piece and goggle gleaming under his ushanka and second set of goggles. Ivan gripped a monstrous cutlass in the hand assisted by his clockwork arm, a pistol in the other.

"Ivan!" Buckle exclaimed. "I failed to notice your name on the boarding-party lists."

"And a damned shameful error it was, sir!" Ivan answered, testing the edge of his blade with his thumb.

"Just do not get yourself killed," Buckle snapped. "I have no desire to contend with Holly Churchill regarding the loss of your sorry hide." Buckle's words worried him a bit, for Meagan Churchill was also somewhere on the roof with them.

"Do not worry about me, Captain." Ivan laughed, tapping the metal plate on his cheek. "I can walk through bomb blasts with little more than a dent these days."

"Well, while you are at it, why do you not join Ensign Yardbird and lead the bow division across?"

"Aye!" Ivan grinned, and took off toward the bow at a run, dodging crewmen as they perched in wait for the attack.

"Ready the hooks!" Buckle shouted, his order passed along by his officers and midshipmen to the stern. He saw Darcy, the olive-skinned boar of a boilerman, manning the handles of the forward grappling cannon. "Ready to have at 'em, Mister Darcy?"

"Aye, Captain! Aye!" Darcy yelled back, his wide, white-toothed smile made even more dramatic by the roundness of his chin.

A musket ball punched through the envelope skin near Buckle's boots, leaving a small, black, smoldering-rimmed hole. The musket battle continued as pistols, with their higher-pitched cracks, joined the fray. A few bodies dropped on both sides.

"We are within pistol shot!" Valkyrie shouted. The whale-like roof of the *Bellerophon* was no more than fifty feet away, with the bottomless crevasse of air between the two zeppelins darker than the evening sky. Buckle could see the faces of the Founders crew, pale in the weak light, teeth bared as they hurled insults, or strangely calm as they aimed down pistol and musket barrels.

"Fire grapnels! Fire all harpoons and hooks!" Buckle howled, and his officers echoed his order down the line.

Time to grab hold of the tiger's tail.

~LXXIV~

GRAPPLING HOOKS

THE SIX GRAPPLING CANNONS FIRED, with shallow hippopotamus-belly-flop *whumps,* the charges on the barrels sending the fifteen-pound grappling hooks in high arcs, their ropes trailing over the top of the *Bellerophon.*

Buckle paced along the spine board. "Retract! Bring us in!"

The grappling cannon operators yanked back the retracting levers at the base of each gun, which sent up screaming blasts of steam as the pneumatic winches below began recovering the lines. The grapnels caught hold of the *Bellerophon,* their sharp claws hooking into canvas and rigging, lines snapping taut with the tension of the winches.

The *Pneumatic Zeppelin* rocked to port with a lumbering groan as her steam-driven machines drew the great masses of the two zeppelins together in a slow, sideways glide. The gap was quickly down to twenty feet, the *Pneumatic Zeppelin* being cinched down from her higher position, coming more level with the back of the *Bellerophon.*

Buckle lifted his sword into the air overhead. Bullets zipped past like bees. "Steady! Steady!" he shouted at his boarders—about forty in number, more than half the zeppelin's complement—all bent at the knee, leaning forward, muskets and pistols poised. He eyed the Founders aircrew across from him, similar in number, their independently discharged guns and pepper cannons quiet on the hasty reload—the Founders had wasted much of their shot at too great a distance. They crouched on the roof or hung on the ratlines, swords and pikes glittering in the sunset, a frozen tableau hung in a translucent void, holding their breath just before the two gigantic zeppelins collided.

"Fire pepper guns!" Buckle screamed. The two forward pepper cannons—small guns packed with canisters full of grape shot—erupted in an irregular volley. Knots of the Founders crew staggered, men and women screaming at terrible wounds, the dead, perhaps three or four, falling, gratefully silent.

"Fire weapons!" Buckle shouted. Forty Crankshaft muskets and pistols discharged as one, the line of muzzle flashes bright in the darkening evening. The ranks of the Founders staggered. The Crankshaft boarders laid down their firearms and rose, knives, axes, pikes, and swords gleaming in their hands.

The *Pneumatic Zeppelin* and the *Bellerophon* crashed together, their flanks meeting below where their envelopes were at their fattest, two mountains of canvas, ropes, and iron trundling into each other with a rumbling shake and a roar of bending metal. The airships bounced apart, perhaps five feet, and slammed into each other again, this time staying tight, pinned by the winches, creating a vertigo-inducing chasm between.

A low howl rose in Buckle's throat, ending in the bellow of "Attack!" He charged, sprinting down the slope of the starboard zeppelin roof, and just as the canvas fell away, threw himself into the air with a great leap, sword raised, pistol pointed directly in front of him. He dropped, for the spine of the *Pneumatic Zeppelin* was a good fifteen feet higher than the back of the *Bellerophon*. In midair he fired his pistol into the face of a Founders crewman, a short, stubby fellow clinging to the ratlines, who was waiting to impale him on some kind of pike. The Founders man plummeted away. Buckle landed on the sloped port side of the *Bellerophon*'s roof, bouncing on the canvas skin; he snatched at the ratlines, tossing aside his empty pistol.

Sword high, Buckle climbed as his crew flung themselves across the gap, their flying leaps silhouetted against the glowing clouds, swarming the *Bellerophon* in a din of screams and hurled orders, of clashing swords and pistol shots, their shouts near lost under the whistling wind and the moans of the airships grinding at their flanks.

Buckle snapped his head toward the bow just in time to catch sight of a Founders rigger swinging for him on a rope, bouncing along the skin like a demented spider with a long sword.

Buckle raised his second pistol, but a single shot rang out from behind. The Founders rigger bent over at the stomach, toppled off his line, and fell only a few feet, his lifeless body hanging upside down, his boot entangled in his line.

Buckle glanced back to see Sergeant Salgado perched on the *Pneumatic Zeppelin*, musket smoking, offering him a wide grin. His grin disappeared. He jumped to his feet, desperately drawing his pistol. "Captain! Look out!" he screamed.

Buckle looked up. A Founders officer, dressed in black with silver piping on her collar and sleeves, was charging down at Buckle from above, leading with her saber, flanked by two *Bellerophon* crewmen—stokers, by the looks of their blackened faces and leather coveralls—both gripping smithy hammers.

Salgado's pistol cracked. The whistling ball missed, leaving a tiny hole in the canvas between Buckle and the Founders officer.

Buckle fended off the officer's sword thrust with his saber; he raised his pistol and fired it point-blank into the woman's chest. The force of the ball slammed her backward, her cap spinning away to reveal short-cropped orange hair streaked with gray—her body bounced off the envelope and catapulted limply down upon Buckle, rolling into his legs and slamming him face-first into the canvas, before tumbling off into the chasm below.

Buckle tried to arrest his fall, landing hard on the angled skin that stank of mold, the iron frame beneath delivering a bruising blow to his abdomen. He had no time to catch the breath that had just been slammed out of his lungs—the first Founders stoker was on him, swinging his hammer in a low arc, aiming to bat Buckle's skull off his shoulders. Buckle was up, thrusting his saber to deflect the hammer blow, and as the man's momentum carried him forward, Buckle smashed the side of his head with his pistol butt, probably cracking the skull, and the man somersaulted past, rolling away.

The second stoker was on Buckle an instant later. Buckle brought his saber up, but the man's powerful swing slapped the sword out of his grasp, the blade plunging into the canvas and sticking there, out of his reach. The stoker laughed, swinging his hammer again. Buckle threw himself flat to avoid it, but the stoker kicked him in the jaw, and he rolled down the ratlines. Buckle looked up, half stunned, and saw the flash of a dagger in the stoker's hand as he leapt upon him.

The stoker suddenly jerked still. A silver flash burst out of his chest, splattering Buckle with blood. The man's eyes rolled up white. Valkyrie stepped out from behind him, planting her boot on his back to kick him off her blade, sending the body over the side. She leaned down and offered Buckle her gloved hand. "I heard you were notorious for falling off airships, Captain Buckle."

"An odd time to find your humor, Princess," Buckle said, not sure if he had any teeth left in his mouth or not.

~LXXV~

THE *BELLEROPHON*

VALKYRIE YANKED BUCKLE UP ON his feet. He retrieved his saber and they clambered up to the crest of the spine, where the hand-to-hand battle was now in full swing. The numbers might have been close, but it seemed as though the half-pirate Crankshafts were already gaining the upper hand. Salgado and his marines remained perched on the higher roof of the *Pneumatic Zeppelin*, potting the Founders officers as fast as they could reload and aim again.

Buckle and Valkyrie waded into the fray, catching a group of Founders off guard as they held the foremost section of the bow. Buckle stepped over the facedown body of Regina Ford, a somber but competent member of his propulsion crew, her blood running in rivers that pooled in the depressions of the topside canvas. He closed ranks with hydroman Murray Collins and stocking man Sylvester Turpin, both hardy veterans and near surrounded on their edge of the roof.

Buckle glimpsed the flash of Valkyrie's red-and-gold-laced blue cuff at his side as she deftly wielded her blade. She was fighting one stride behind him, covering his back, in the same fashion Max or Sabrina would have.

Hurdling a grappling line, Buckle cut down an enemy crewman—nearly chopping the poor fellow in half—before he was rushed by a Founders officer in a well-tailored uniform with cuffs resplendent in silver lace; he was a strawberry-haired youth with blue eyes and a red-whiskered mustache, oiled to curl at the tips. The strawberry-haired officer handled his sword well—Buckle was hard-pressed to hold him—but he did not keep his adrenaline in check and swung too high and too hard, allowing Buckle to lunge under his guard and dispatch him by running the point of his sword deep into his innards. The Founders officer cried out and dropped, curling up in a ball as Buckle stepped over him.

The forward roof of the *Bellerophon* was a killing ground. The deck was awash in blood and fallen rigging, littered with bodies both motionless and crawling, while the zeppelineers still standing trampled them. Men and women screamed in agony as swords and axes bit into their bodies and broke them, followed by the vengeful, animal cries of the victors, howling up their courage.

With the bow section lost, the surviving Founders backed up, retreating slowly in good order toward amidships, exacting a toll with sword and pike on the Crankshafts who charged them.

Buckle heard a chorus of "Hurrah, musketeers!" on his left, from the roof of the *Pneumatic Zeppelin*. It was uttered by the second wave—the port-side gun crews and the remaining boilermen and stokers—led topside by Wellington Bratt and the boatswain Richard Aubrey, bringing nearly a dozen fresh Crankshaft muskets and cutlasses to the fight. Welly shouted "Ready ranks!" and his division lined up near amidships, directly opposite the clustered Founders defenders.

Shoving his way forward in the mass of Crankshaft boarders, Buckle waved his saber above his head and shouted. "Founders!

Lay down your arms and you shall be spared! Surrender!" Buckle's response was a well-aimed pistol ball that whizzed just past his skull, the streak of its phosphorus mere inches from his eyes.

"Aim!" Welly screamed. The musketeers lifted their dozen rifles as one.

The Founders defenders cringed, perhaps fifteen of them still standing, still fighting, but now with one eye on the Crankshaft firing squad on the opposite roof: they compacted, which was the wrong response to the danger, but all their officers were down.

"Crankshafts!" Buckle yelled as loudly as he could. "Stand fast! Do not move forward! Stand fast!"

Buckle's crewmen eased back, and a small gap appeared between the attackers and the Founders.

"Fire!" Welly yelled. The small line of muskets boomed in a burst of black smoke and snake-tongued orange flames. Phosphorescent trails streaked into the tightly bunched Founders—many crumpled, some motionless, others screaming as they gripped bloody legs and arms—shattering the glass bubble of the observer's nacelle.

Buckle expected the Founders to break, to retreat, to drop down the nacelle hatchway in a panic, crashing down upon one another on the landing below. But they did not. They closed their ranks and stood their ground. Not one offered to surrender. Not one begged for mercy.

"Have at them!" Buckle bellowed, and the Crankshaft boarders around him surged forward, closing in, bloodthirsty after the casualties they had suffered, overwhelming the remaining handful of Founders even as they swung their weapons about them.

The last Founders crew member left standing, a small woman wearing the leather belts of a rigger, threw her sword, a spinning flash of silver, into the mass of advancing boarders before a pistol ball cut her down.

"Form up!" Buckle shouted, a furious animal pleasure working in his brain as he hurried aft to the nacelle, stepping over bodies, fallen weapons, and dark splashes of blood. "Secure the roof, Mister Bratt!" Buckle shouted across the gap. "Transfer the wounded and prisoners immediately!"

"Aye, Captain!" Welly responded; his gunners and stokers were already leaping across, fastening gurney clamps to one of the grapnel ropes to establish transport for the severely wounded. Buckle saw Meagan Churchill among them, for she was part of the number-two gun crew, and her right hand was dripping with blood, though whatever the nature of the wound, it was light enough for her to ignore it.

Ivan saluted Buckle as he strode past in the crowd. "Nice to see you still alive, brother," he said with a grin.

"And you, brother," Buckle said.

"The amidships hatch is locked down, Captain," Darcy announced as he tugged powerfully at the observer's nacelle hatch. "It is locked."

"No matter," Buckle replied. Even if the hatchways were thrown wide open, Buckle would not have used them. He would never give the defenders below the luxury of being able to predict the points where his attackers might penetrate. His boarders would cut their own entrances into the fabric roof and drop in via those, avoiding whatever traps the defenders had surely set underneath the hatchways.

"Each division, fore and aft of the nacelle! Cut two doors on the spine, here and there!" Buckle ordered with points of his sword; hydroman Murray Collins, his face and pith helmet splattered with blood, tossed him a loaded pistol. Both Darcy and the engine officer, Elliot Yardbird, took up position with axes as their boarding groups collected around them.

Buckle grinned at the overheated, blood-spattered faces. "We have them, lads and ladies. So shall we?" Buckle clamped his knife between his teeth and took a good grip on his pistol and saber. Buckle nodded at Darcy, who quickly chopped a large, square opening in the envelope skin.

Buckle took a quick look down into the ragged rat hole, unfortunately dark compared to the incandescent evening sky. He glimpsed the bright trails of a few loose fireflies and the barely visible lines of a catwalk grating. There was no telling what might await him down in the shadows.

Leaning forward, Buckle dropped in.

~LXXVI~

SCUTTLED

BUCKLE PLUNGED DOWN INTO THE *Bellerophon* with questions haunting the back of his mind. Why had the Founders defenders been locked out on the roof? Even with the access hatches screwed down, anyone with a cutlass or axe could hack a door into existence with a few deft strokes of the blade. It made no tactical sense: the structure of a zeppelin provided an excellent defense in depth; to order a last stand on the roof—the most exposed position—was almost criminal.

Unless, unless, the captain had sacrificed part of the *Bellerophon*'s crew to buy himself time. If so, then their blood had purchased him a few precious minutes.

Buckle landed like a cat on the grating, letting his knees absorb the impact of the eight-foot drop. He stayed low, coiled, advancing with pistol and sword so the crewmen following him did not land on his back. The catwalk was similar to the *Pneumatic Zeppelin*'s Eagle deck, with the great curved tops of the gasbags heaving quietly on both sides, their black humps laced with spidery stocking lattices.

Visibility was rotten. It was difficult to see much of anything in the *Bellerophon*'s dark, hazy attic. The roof canvas had a barely perceptible glow—imparted by the last shreds of evening light—and intermittent buglights burned brightly here and there, leading away to a great distance down the catwalk, where occasional yellow streaks of stray fireflies corkscrewed between. Smoke and superheated steam had formed a fog under the roof, assaulting Buckle's nose and eyes, rancid with the foulness of overheated iron and oil, powder smoke, and doped canvas consumed by fire. No doubt there was hydrogen in the mix as well.

Buckle let the vile air hurt him, accepting the discomfort. He sensed that the catwalk was empty of defenders. He heard them in the darkness, racing away, their boots clanking down the labyrinth of stairwells and ladders below, dousing lanterns as they retreated.

The Founders were not defending the center of their airship, a strange tactic considering how furiously they had battled on the roof. The height advantage meant everything in a boarding attempt—to lose the upper decks essentially meant losing the fight.

Valkyrie was at Buckle's back now, coughing, with more members of the boarding parties dropping in ahead and behind.

Buckle pulled his knife from his teeth and sheathed it in his belt as he headed for the main stairwell landing. He needed to get down to the keel deck, where he could seize the piloting gondola and take control of the ship. Quickness was his greatest ally, for once his boarding party was winding down deep into the *Bellerophon's* rib cage, they would surely be outnumbered by the Founders crew. He could not give the enemy time to reform and attack in force.

Ivan, Yardbird, and their boarding division appeared from the murk ahead.

"The bridge!" Buckle shouted. "We must make the bridge immediately!"

"They have turned tail, Cap'n!" Ivan said with a rough cough, flushed, brandishing a pistol.

"Stay together! Stay on me!" Buckle shouted.

"Aye," Ivan replied, his goggles reflecting a fire or lamp somewhere behind Buckle, aglow like an owl in a dark forest.

"Hurrah!" Buckle shouted, racing down the stairwell, his boarders following him through the haze in a clatter of boots and jangling weapons. The interior of the *Bellerophon* was a hellish wreck, bashed apart by Russian cannonballs: stairs and catwalks were blown to pieces, their mangled metal gleaming in the flickering light of scattered fires; shorn ropes and rigging dangled at every turn, swinging in the scalding blasts from broken steam pipes and burst valves.

Buckle arrived on a broad landing—the *Bellerophon* did not seem to possess a uniform Castle deck, but rather a complicated series of small catwalks—turned, and descended another long set of stairs to the Axial deck below. The air was much clearer here, the damage less extensive, and still—halfway down the zeppelin—not a single Founders crewman to be seen. Buckle paused, his eyes darting. The Founders should be swarming, leaping from cubbyholes and platforms with blades flashing, marines firing close-range pistol shots, a steampiper on the fly, something.

Buckle could still hear the low racket of boots on the run across the decks beneath, and such abandonment was unnerving.

To hell with it. If the Founders wanted to organize a last stand on the keel, where Buckle could assault them from above, then they had done no more than choose their place to die.

Buckle advanced slowly on the next stairwell, taking a moment to regain his bearings and allow his boarders to reassemble behind him. The innards of the *Bellerophon*, her envelope infested with smoldering holes, breathed and groaned like the belly of a wounded monster that had swallowed them. Trickling patches of fire were all that were left of far larger conflagrations, beaten down by the fire hoses that now lay cast off on the deck, water sputtering from the nozzles and pouring through the gratings in glittering streams.

The cannons of the *Czarina* had inflicted considerable damage upon the *Bellerophon*'s gasbags, which had been severely punctured, their rubber-stocking mechanisms stretched beyond capacity and in tension flux, quivering so violently that they emitted an odd, high-pitched hum.

She was broken up, yes—but she was salvageable, still quite a prize.

Buckle glanced back at his boarders as they followed at a crawl, looking back and forth, weapons gripped tightly, unsure of what sort of trap they might be charging into. Valkyrie's cool blue eyes met his, and he thought he caught a victorious gleam in them. Buckle increased the rate of his stride. His boarding could not lose its momentum. A huge platform was just ahead, the top of a main stairwell leading down into the *Bellerophon*'s launch bay, a huge compartment just aft of the great airship's beam.

A sudden barrage of orders, delivered harshly, echoed up from the launch bay. With the cries came the sounds of axes slamming hard on wood, followed by the high-pitched pops of ropes snapping.

"On me!" Buckle shouted as he sprinted down the Axial deck. It only took ten seconds to reach the platform rail overlooking the massive launch bay. Buckle saw the zeppelin's cigar-shaped launch resting at her berth five stories below, her decks loaded with black-coated crew members, the wind and darkness of the night streaming under her exposed keel, her hull lit by lines of sparkling buglights.

The launch bay suddenly echoed with the loud *bang* of metal levers and clamps snapping back. The launch dropped. She plunged silently, straight down, the wind making an eerie, unearthly sound as it roared up and over her envelope skin that fluttered emptily over unfilled hydrogen bags. The launch fell away from the warm-orange touch of the buglights, and took on the blue-gray glow of the moonlit night, darkening by degrees as it descended closer and closer to the earth.

Buckle stared, bewildered. Had the Founders really abandoned the *Bellerophon*? Had they relinquished possession of a precious war zeppelin with no more than one sharp fight?

"I'll be damned, the devils gave her up!" Ivan said.

"Captain!" someone shouted frantically from behind.

Buckle spun around to see his boarders backing away from Daniel Povenmire, the machinist, who had just pulled a grievously black, round bomb out of the maintenance box where it had been stuffed, its fuse burning a soft crimson. Povenmire yanked the fuse out of the bomb casing and stomped the smoldering hemp under his boot.

Faces whipped back to Buckle, all dawning with a grim realization. The colossal creaks and groans of *Bellerophon* now felt doomed.

"They've scuttled her," Valkyrie whispered softly, speaking in the way a sleepwalker might, as if from a dream, as if from not believing.

"Lucky for us the cowards used slow burners," Buckle said confidently, looking at his pocket watch. He had waltzed into a Founders trap—but the jaws had shut too slowly. "How long was left on that fuse, would you estimate, Mister Povenmire?"

"Can't be sure, Captain. Maybe two, two and a half minutes. Depends upon the quality of the hemp," Povenmire answered quickly. "I'm no expert on Founders ordnance, sir."

"Then let's get the hell out of here," Buckle said, already on the move. "Or the *Bellerophon* will blow up and take us and the *Pneumatic Zeppelin* with it."

–LXXVII–

SHACKLED TO A DEAD MAN

THE RACE BACK TO THE roof of the *Bellerophon* was a desperate scramble through a labyrinth of thickening smoke, steam, and fire. Buckle cursed at the twisted rails and missing staircase steps as he climbed, forcing his burning thigh muscles to propel his weight, his heart walloping in his chest, his face overheating, his lungs sucking in an assault of smoke—the choke was near overwhelming, but it would do not good for him to go tumble-down now. The damaged airship seemed to intentionally place her wrecked guts in the way, her loose ropes and wires tangling boots, loose blocks and tackle swinging to bash the skull, furious gushes of steam lashing the face, every inch ahead obscured by murk and darkness. Even the remaining buglights, hanging in diffused yellowish orbs, were fading into oblivion.

Yet they were almost to the Eagle deck now, and Buckle could see the dim orange light of lanterns at the forward observation nacelle overhead. He blinked streaming water out of his eyes and stared at the jouncing back of the crewperson in front of him—it was Ilsa Gallagher, and a spatter of blood mottled the white bandolier that swept from her left shoulder to her right hip.

"Almost home!" Buckle cried out over the rasping coughs and the boots ringing on the stairs. Buckle was the last man in the group, making sure no one was lost and left behind, while Valkyrie leapt like an antelope at the lead. She had just reached the now-brighter yellowish-orange observation nacelle. Crankshaft crewpersons knelt above on the roof, trying to leverage waffling firefly lanterns into the column of superheated smoke hurtling upward out of the broken glass, as from a locomotive chimney.

At the nacelle platform, Valkyrie leapt to the ladder, swinging up and out. Ivan stepped aside, shoving each crew member up in turn, not needing to urge them to climb any faster than they already were. The rush slowed to an agonizing stop in the miasma of barely breathable, skillet-hot air. Buckle tossed aside his helmet, wiped the sweat running from his forehead, and peered at his watch. His people had made the climb to the roof in forty seconds.

He had a minute and a half, maybe a few seconds more, before the *Bellerophon* blew. And that was if Povenmire had guessed correctly, and if there had not been bombs haphazardly lit all over the ship without any regard for uniformity of timing. Yet, Buckle thought as he shuffled forward in the line, jamming his watch back into the depths of his pocket, the Founders had proven so yellow that it was likely the bombers had waited until the last possible second to apply their matches to the fuses.

Drowning in the smoke, Buckle stopped his breathing, letting his heart pound in his chest as it ached to cough the lungs clear. He reached the nacelle ladder and Ivan reached for him.

"Captain!" Ivan yelled in the rushing air.

"Your turn!" Buckle howled back, and the gasp of air his body forced him to take with the shout near doubled him over with hacking.

Ivan grabbed Buckle by the collar of his coat and hauled him up the ladder after him. Waiting hands plunged into the pounding stream of heat and smoke and propelled Buckle up with such urgency that his boots barely touched the rungs. He fell free of the smoke column, stumbling into the cold, clear air, his lungs near freezing themselves solid as he gasped like a drowned man.

"She has been scuttled! Bombs!" Buckle heard Valkyrie shout with a raspy hitch in her voice, back toward amidships. "Disengage and boom off! We are shackled to a dead man! Cut the lines! Just cut the lines!"

The boarders leapt back across the gap to the flank ratlines and the wide, broad gray back of the *Pneumatic Zeppelin*, where Wellington and the boatswain, Aubrey, raced back and forth, chopping grappling lines with axes, and the second-wave crew was hastily drawing boom poles from their fastenings along the spine boards.

Buckle staggered over bodies, fallen weapons, loose helmets, and pools of blood. His coughing subsided and his eyes grew accustomed to the silver incandescence of the moonlight spilling through the clouds—an illumination much brighter than the inside of the *Bellerophon*.

"Captain!" Valkyrie shouted. "Time to go!"

Buckle turned to see Valkyrie wave him toward the port side of the *Bellerophon*. For a moment he thought that they were the last two aboard, but then he noticed boilerman Rodney Winship and the marine Cartwright, desperately yanking at the gurney wire, which had been strung across the gap between grappling-cannon posts on each airship. There was a body in the gurney, a wounded crewman.

Buckle raced along the roof with Valkyrie at his side, both dodging debris and strewn rigging. All the grappling lines but one had been cut, the crew members on the *Pneumatic Zeppelin* poised, boom poles in their hands, waiting for the gurney to pass.

"Launch the gurney and boom off, damn your hides!" Buckle shouted, his singed lungs stabbing as he ran.

"It's no use, Captain!" Winship yelled, stepping back from the gurney. "The lines are fouled!"

Buckle and Valkyrie arrived at the grappling-cannon post, Buckle tearing off his gloves as he tackled the Gordian knot of wires and rope at the base of the gurney. He felt the nudge of the booms pressing the *Bellerophon* to starboard, and heard the maneuvering propellers of the *Pneumatic Zeppelin* whirl up, the nacelles traversing to drive the airship away from the *Bellerophon*.

"It be just a damned fogsucker, sir!" Cartwright said, furtively glancing at the boom poles, pressing the muzzle of his pistol to the gurney wire. "He is not worth the risk, I say! Let him burn!"

Buckle saw the face of the man poking out of the burlap wrapping and leather bindings that secured him to the gurney—it was the strawberry-bearded Founders officer he had skewered, apparently still alive.

Buckle shoved Cartwright's pistol aside. "Go!" he shouted at Winship and Cartwright.

Cartwright spun and sprinted down the envelope slope, leaping across to the *Pneumatic Zeppelin*.

Winship hesitated. "He is near dead, sir! He is not worth the effort, sir!"

"Abandon ship, Mister Winship," Buckle snapped as he battled the dismaying tangle of wire and rope. "That is an order!"

Winship dashed away.

Buckle grunted, his eyes stinging, concentrating on pulling loose the contortions of the knot, denying himself his desperate need to look at his watch. Valkyrie stood across from him, looking over the gurney, quickly tying something up.

If Buckle had thought about it—if he had truly *thought* about it—he would have left the Founders man to die. But he was operating on instinct now, and his instinct would not allow him to abandon a wounded airman to a terrible fate.

That and the damned Gentleman's Rules.

The gurney came loose. Buckle pulled on the baying line, hand over hand, and the gurney lurched out into the gap between the two sky vessels as the crewmen on the other side hauled it across. "Abandon ship, Princess—that is an order!"

"Very well, Captain." Valkyrie nodded and leapt down the slope, jumping across to the *Pneumatic Zeppelin* as the crew, their bodies dark silhouettes against her mountainous spine, pulled her aboard and shouted, urging their captain on. But if the *Bellerophon* popped now, they were just as dead as he.

The *Pneumatic Zeppelin* and the *Bellerophon* separated with a shuddering rumble, pulling apart as the *Pneumatic Zeppelin*'s propellers wound up to screeching roars and she backed off the doomed *Bellerophon* with a thunder of ripping rigging and splintering tack. Buckle saw a crack of night sky open between the towering airships. Bodies—at least a dozen—and debris that had tumbled into the crevasse now fell through the widening gap, their black forms plummeting down to the void of the earth beneath, the ground dotted with orange fires.

As the massive zeppelins eased apart, the grappling cannon bent on its post, its line the only attachment left between the two vessels. Buckle grabbed the rope just as it snapped and held on, keeping the gurney suspended, though the weight of it began to drag him down the side. The *Pneumatic Zeppelin* crewmen hauled the gurney in, and Buckle released the rope as they secured it.

Buckle scrambled back up to the *Bellerophon*'s spine, avoiding her envelope breaches and hatchways, which were now expelled scalding columns of smoke and steam.

A chorus of encouraging howls came from the opposite roof. Buckle saw Valkyrie and Ivan hurrying along the deck, swinging themselves down the ratlines to extend their hands. The chasm between the two airships was opening up far faster than Buckle had anticipated, which was good for the *Pneumatic Zeppelin*, but bad for him.

Buckle sprinted down the port-side curve of the *Bellerophon*'s upper flank, watching the rift between the two envelopes grow ever wider as he ran. The *Pneumatic Zeppelin* was descending away, her roof now about ten feet lower than that of the drifting *Bellerophon*, and that gave him a better chance. Buckle tried to calculate the distance he had to fly as he dashed toward the maw of dark air between the two airships and then just gave up on the math—whatever the distance was, he had to make it.

Then the *Bellerophon* blew up.

The zeppelin heaved upward in a violent paroxysm. Buckle stumbled and kept going, headlong, as stupendous geysers of burning hydrogen erupted through the roof.

Buckle landed his boot on the edge of the envelope and launched, hurling his body out into the chasm that separated him from the *Pneumatic Zeppelin*. He saw the faces of Valkyrie, Ivan, and his crew staring at him, cringing at the furnace-hot explosions, their gleaming red eyes distraught.

He was witnessing them witness his own death.

Buckle sailed across the sky, thirteen hundred feet above the dark earth—and then he began to drop away, short, out of her reach, and the *Pneumatic Zeppelin* rushed up and away from his outstretched fingers.

The dying blast of the *Bellerophon*, a continental concussion of fire, slammed Buckle in the back.

‒LXXVIII‒

WHAT THE NAVIGATOR SAW

When Sabrina Serafim was furious, she did not like to show it. But she knew that Romulus Buckle could read it in her eyes. So to hell with it, she grumbled in her mind. He should know how angry she was with him, her captain who, walking beside her with his top hat cocked on his head and the back of his leather coat burned and black, had once again barely escaped a violent death. It was all in a day's work for him, apparently forgotten, with his boots now on Spartak ground, the dark night pulsing with the fires of Muscovy in the distance.

After the battle, the *Czarina* had signaled a desire to parley, so Buckle, the back of his coat still smoldering as he stood on the *Pneumatic Zeppelin*'s bridge, had followed the Spartak zeppelin to a mooring yard just south of the city. Sabrina had joined the negotiating party along with Valkyrie, Corporal Nyland, and two more red-jacketed marines. Ambassador Washington, having emerged from his cabin in a foul and standoffish mood, had joined them, demanding that he do all the talking with the Russians.

Washington led the group now, his strides forceful, his mist-puffs of breath and white lambskin greatcoat soaked with the yellow illumination of the lanterns swinging in the hands of the marines. They were walking down a path cut through a scattered forest grove, the tall arrowhead shapes of the fir and pine trees black against a cluster of burning buildings on their left. Steaming at three thousand feet under the moonlit clouds, the gondola lights of the Imperial war zeppelin *Pneumatic Tirpitz* twinkled, having been signaled by Valkyrie to go on patrol as soon as she arrived.

Sabrina's ears still rang with the tumultuous roar of the dying *Bellerophon*; the muffled quiet of the countryside, the soft crunch of boots in the snow, made her eardrums buzz harder. She glanced back: behind them the dark mass of the *Pneumatic Zeppelin* loomed, her gondolas a mere three feet off the ground, her skinners and riggers fast at the repairs, shouting back and forth across the great whale expanse of her envelope, which was scorched black along nearly the entire length of her starboard side. The skin-repair teams worked in small bubbles of yellow buglight mixed with the witchy orange gleam of the night lanterns.

Sabrina turned forward. The Russians were approaching, ten of them, their silhouettes dark against the silver-white moonlit snow, their forms made burly by greatcoats of animal skins and leather, their round, stern faces ruddy in the light of the torches they carried. They were advancing fast; two on the left were riding big, shaggy horses, with two wolfhounds loping at their gaskins. Two hundred yards behind the Russians, the *Czarina* hovered low, her fires extinguished, but her envelope holes still leaking copious amounts of smoke that lumbered in slow drifts to the northeast.

Beyond the *Czarina*, about two and half miles distant, the stronghold of Muscovy burned, her buildings and ramparts swamped in spectacular ribbons of fire. In the waves of light cast by the conflagration, Sabrina could just make out a road, a white strip leading northward into the wilderness; all along its length moved shadows, an army of overloaded wagons and straining horses, a population abandoning their fallen city, whose funeral pyre cast light but no warmth on their backs.

Sabrina shivered. The bitter cold did not bother her—it rarely did—but she felt an old discomfiture; with a revulsive sting she recalled the fashion in which Leopold Goethe had identified her in front of all the others. She was a Fawkes, yes, and she did remember Goethe, as a boy—his words must have inflicted immeasurable harm upon her life among the Crankshafts. No one had said anything to her about it, not even Buckle, but she knew it would eat away at them once they had time to think about it. The magnifying glass of suspicion would swing its jaded eye in her direction once again.

And Buckle would defend her from all comers, as he always defended her.

Sabrina was not one to idolize anyone, especially a man. But to her Romulus Buckle had become larger than life, once again cheating the swing of the grim reaper's scythe as it grazed his heels, a tale breathlessly related by midshipmen Charles Mariner and Alison Lawrence upon returning to the bridge after the destruction of the *Bellerophon*. Captain Buckle, risking his life to save an enemy wounded by his own hand and disembarking last—as any good captain must—had taken a doomed leap between the zeppelins as the *Bellerophon* incinerated in a mountainous blast at his heels. And it was the force of this blast, a concussion that near knocked down everyone on the roof of the *Pneumatic Zeppelin*, that hurled Buckle the extra distance he needed. He landed in the ratlines, the back of his leather jacket completely afire, and held on with one hand until the crew hauled him up and doused the flames.

Sabrina had seen the burning *Bellerophon* fall away, a giant body of fire folding in upon itself, transforming into a skeleton raft of flames as it plummeted toward the earth. Thirteen hundred feet down, it crashed into the trees of the snowbound gray-white mountains, where what was left looked more like an insignificant forest fire than what had once been a magnificent flying machine.

At that moment, Sabrina had once again been certain that her captain was dead. She had done what the situation had demanded; once the news of the scuttling had boomed down the chattertube, she had ordered the grappling lines cut and the maneuvering propellers traversed to starboard, so she could disengage from the *Bellerophon* at best possible speed.

When the report came that Buckle was not yet aboard, Sabrina had hesitated, waiting one more moment, risking the entire ship for its captain. Just after she had commanded that the propellers be thrown into maximum rotation, the bombs had gone off, and she immediately ordered the firing of the starboard broadside into the *Bellerophon*, hoping to further hurl the zeppelins apart through blast and nonstabilized recoil.

A wall of flame rolled up against the piloting gondola in a sizzling roar, roasting the glass dome and sending a tongue of flame in over the starboard gunwale, before rolling away as quickly as it had come. The chadburn and helm wheel had been singed, the helmsman and Nero's bald head singed, the entire starboard side of the *Pneumatic Zeppelin* singed, but they had all ducked through it handsomely.

It was close to a minute after the blast before the news came down that the captain had survived. A gush of relief turned Sabrina's body to rubber. She was thankful for the elated cheers of the bridge crew, for no one noticed how she almost dropped to her knees.

"Here be those Russians," Buckle whispered into Sabrina's ear. The Spartak company was no more than thirty yards away now, and from the corner of her eye she could see Buckle grinning with some satisfaction under his top hat, its array of copper and bronze gizmos gleaming in the lantern light. "Burly-looking devils, eh?"

"Aye," Sabrina said stiffly, not looking in Buckle's direction, hoping her straight-ahead stare might express her anger toward him in a way he would recognize. Her intense feelings toward Buckle, swallowing her whole despite her vehement but silent protests, dismayed her. Her inability to shield herself from those feelings dismayed her. What had happened? Where was the unwavering commitment to her purpose that had consumed her life? When she had led the joint Crankshaft-Alchemist rescue mission inside the City of the Founders to free Balthazar, she had experienced an urge to slip away, to vanish into the shadows with her dagger in her hand and exact her revenge. But she did not do so. After being orphaned, after losing her dear Marter, after a near lifetime of brutality and being hunted, she had no longer thought herself capable of love. But she did love Balthazar. And now she feared that she was in love with Buckle.

Sabrina did not know how she felt about that.

She had always been in control of herself, and yet now, suddenly and without warning, her mastery of her emotions had failed her. It happened, for unfathomable chemical, visceral, and metaphysical reasons, whenever she entered a room that contained Romulus Buckle.

Damn you, Romulus, Sabrina thought. Damn you.

~LXXIX~

THE BOYAR AND THE CLOUD COSSACKS

Buckle, walking immediately behind Ambassador Washington, eyed the Russians with a grin. He could see their faces clearly now, illuminated as they were in the fluttering orange halos of their torches. Eight wore uniforms and Cossack fur hats—members of the *Czarina*'s crew—while the two horse riders looked like landsmen in their heavy fur cloaks and ushanki. It was easy to see, the sky a gleam of silver moonlight and the earth lit up by the terrible fires of Muscovy in her death throes, sending tides of red and orange eddying across the countryside as if the world were the inside of a potbellied stove.

A man of average height led from the center of the Spartak group, exuding a physical confidence that was easily read in the swagger of his bearing, bareheaded with black hair and a dense beard, wearing a rust-brown wool greatcoat with overbearing gold-and-red epaulettes gleaming on each shoulder. He was grinning widely, his eyes intense and a shade wild with the spark of recent action.

The dark-bearded man had to be the captain of the *Czarina*, and if so, a capital commander. He had withstood a bracketing by two Founders war zeppelins and then, dropping away holed and afire, still gamely dove to finish the *Industria*, which had somehow managed to regain control and was limping south-ward. The Founders sloop easily escaped him, but the mortar barges, bereft of their cowardly escort, had not been so lucky.

Buckle liked the Russian captain already.

Washington cleared his throat, a low, breathy sound over the crunching of many boots across the shallow, crystalline snow.

"Greetings, Crankshaft!" the Spartak captain shouted first, throwing open his arms. "All hail the sky warriors from the east! Bravo! A fight worthy of a mad badger!"

"It is an honor to make your acquaintance, sir," Washington said, and when he took the Russian captain's hand, he nearly lost his own, the powerful fellow shook it so hard. "I am Ambassador Washington, representing the Crankshaft clan."

"Nicholas Zhukov, boyar of Muscovy. Welcome to Spartak, Ambassador, though I cannot vouch much for her current con-dition," the captain said, raising his eyebrows, which resembled small squirrels, at Valkyrie. "I see Imperial blues among you, very lovely blues."

"Boyar Zhukov, may I present Princess Valkyrie Smelt of the Imperial clan," Washington said.

"We have come to assist, at your request," Valkyrie offered politely.

Zhukov gave Valkyrie a small bow. "Ah, yes—and in an Imperial-designed zeppelin bearing the Crankshaft emblem, no less," he said as his two huge wolfhounds came and sat on each side of him, their wolfish heads resembling the armrests of a throne. Zhukov gave Sabrina and her red ringlets a penetrating glare. "And a scarlet as a member of your contingent as well?" he mut-tered. "Strange days are upon us, I say!" Zhukov's eyes locked on to Buckle. "And are you, sir, the captain of the *Pneumatic Zeppelin*?"

"Aye," Buckle replied. "Captain Romulus Buckle, at your service, Captain Zhukov. I must compliment you and your crew—you fight like eagles, sir."

Zhukov flashed a smile with a set of big white-and-gold teeth as he brushed past Washington to shake Buckle's hand. "Bah! To hell with eagles. I fly like a tangler! And so do you, Captain Buckle!"

Buckle laughed as openly as did Zhukov, the Russian's breath a slightly rotten breeze of warm tobacco, sausage, and heavily creamed borscht pickled with vodka. Zhukov was near half a foot less than Buckle's height, but much fuller in girth, his mass accentuated by his unruly hair and beard, which seemed to block everything out behind him. His hand-shake almost yanked Buckle's shoulder bone out of its socket. Zhukov's expressive, ruggedly featured face made his age dif-ficult to measure. Buckle guessed he was in his early thirties, though he looked closer to forty.

"We go to war together, you and I, my friend, eh?" Zhukov said, just to Buckle.

"Yes, we do, sir," Buckle replied. It was rare that he instinc-tively trusted other men or women without knowing them at all—Andromeda had been another—but Buckle placed great faith in his gut feelings.

"Ahem!" Washington cleared his throat. "I do not wish to appear abrupt, Boyar Zhukov, but we need to establish our situ-ation quickly."

"Our situation, sir," Zhukov said, "is that we are with you and you are with us, whether we like it or not. Our Rostov strong-hold has been overrun—with two pocket zeppelins captured at their moorings, damn me to hell—but we blew up the rail-way tracks and stopped the armored trains at Krasnaya bridge.

And the Founder fools overextended reaching for Muscovy." He lifted his hand and crushed the air in a fist. "Their attack has shattered upon the rocks of our resolve."

"But your city is blown to pieces," Washington said. "This is an unsustainable position."

"Muscovy is lost, temporarily," Zhukov said. "Our people are retreating north over the mountains, to Santa Inez. The *Czarina* is to steam to Archangel, where our fleet now assembles. Our outposts have signaled that the Founders are advancing north as we speak, but their zeppelins are crawling to keep pace with the trains. We have a fat forty-five minutes to make good our escape."

"We are with you, Boyar Zhukov," Washington said. "You have asked for assistance from the Imperial clan and she has come, bringing our Grand Alliance with her. Crankshaft blood has been spilled alongside yours. The Founders invasion must be stopped."

"Not stopped, Ambassador—destroyed," Zhukov said. "And who are the members of this Grand Alliance?"

"Along with Crankshaft and Imperial, we have the Alchemists, Gallowglasses, Tinskins, and Brineboilers," Washington replied. "And I am certain we may add Spartak's signature to the list, in the spirit of mutual defense and friendship."

Zhukov paused, a torrent of thought in his eyes. The wind sighed through the group, gently rocking the lanterns and calming the horses who had been stamping the snow and jangling their tack, continually turning their big, dark eyes toward the fires of the city. "Our alliance is a foregone conclusion under the circumstances, a pact signed in blood this day. But the Brineboilers are already..."

Zhukov was cut off by the *boom* of a gigantic explosion inside Muscovy, a blast that rattled the earth and sent a colossal ball of flame roiling a thousand feet above the city, a fireball illuminating the world like a small sun before it vanished. Startled at first, Buckle stared at the catastrophe with the detachment of exhaustion. He knew what it was—the stronghold magazine, hundreds of barrels of blackbang powder going off at once. The sky glittered, a brilliant display of a billion bright-red cinders raining down like burning snow. The ashes of Muscovy.

"They have had at us, the Founders devils!" Zhukov snarled as he peered upward. He then cast a serious gaze upon Washington. "The Tinskins," he said, showing his teeth with disgust. "Unconscionable rats."

Washington nodded. "I believe the threat of mutual destruction will keep them in line—for the time being."

"Never trust them," Zhukov said. "Now, we must make way."

"The *Pneumatic Zeppelin* must return home immediately," Washington said. "But I urgently request passage aboard the *Czarina* to Archangel. I must have an audience with Grand Boyar Ryzhakov."

"Of course, of course. He shall be in Archangel with the fleet," Zhukov answered, allowing his eyes to take another approving, lustful measure of Valkyrie.

"We should—" Washington started, but he was cut off by a vicious cheer near at hand to the west.

Buckle cocked his head to the side, peering through the black bars of the trees to focus on the small group of buildings, ruined and afire—most likely the result of a wayward Founders mortar—about thirty yards away. A mob of Russians had gathered around a large gallows, streams of flame licking its posts and crossbeam, encouraging a hangman as he lowered a noose around the neck of another man on the scaffold, a crooked cripple, whose head was covered by a dark canvas bag.

"They are hanging a spy." One of the Spartak horsemen laughed, his voice thick with drink. "Old as the hills, a fog-sucker, addled as a moonchild. And he had some devil robot with him."

"I approved no executions on the drumhead," Zhukov said, but he made no move to stop the proceedings.

The old prisoner cried out, his shaking voice carrying across the snowbound earth. "Who saves old Shadrack?" he wailed. "The Oracle be eternal, yea—but who saves old Shadrack?"

"Stop!" Buckle screamed, hearing his howl in his ears before he was aware of having uttered it, realizing he had bolted forward toward the burning gallows before he was aware of giving his body a command to move.

–LXXX–

THE BURNING GALLOWS

THAT ROMULUS BUCKLE WAS ABLE to save the wretched hide of old Shadrack was a near-run thing. He charged into a small square surrounded by bomb-gutted, burning buildings, where the gallows towered like the spire of some terrible, fire-ringed church. A sea of heavy-lidded, death-dealing faces turned to Buckle; the Spartak clanspeople had dispatched a good tally of "spies," judging from the stack of dead bodies piled like cordwood at the edge of the square.

Buckle shoved his way into the crowd. The grumbling mass, their sense of revenge boiling, glared at his foreign clothes and closed in, grabbing, sticks and fists raised. Buckle would have found himself in considerable trouble if Zhukov's two horsemen had not arrived at a gallop, robes flying and pistols drawn, ordering a halt to everything.

The mob stood silent, still clutching Buckle, the fires crackling, the horses stamping uneasily, the prisoner motionless on the gallows. It seemed to take forever for Zhukov and the others to arrive.

"Why, Captain Buckle, do you step in on behalf of the accused?" Zhukov asked as he hurried up along the road, red-faced and puffing, Washington, Sabrina, Valkyrie, and the others close at his heels.

"I believe he is a Crankshaft with whom I am acquainted," Buckle replied. A lie, perhaps. But if it was Shadrack, if it was the same man whom Buckle remembered as a boy, then it was surely possible that he was a clansman.

"A Crankshaft here?" Zhukov sputtered. "Wearing Founders black?"

Buckle eyed the prisoner on the scaffold platform, his head still obscured by the hood, his bones poking against the oversize black Founders prison-guard uniform that hung on his body as if upon an undersize hangar.

"I cannot explain his current predicament. I must see him, Captain," Buckle said, shrugging off the now halfhearted grips of the clanspeople who had seized him.

"Bring the prisoner down," Zhukov ordered.

The hangman, a portly toad with perfectly styled black hair and a frightened sneer, removed the noose and propelled the accused man down the steps in a series of tugs and shoves, keeping him upright by jerking on the ropes that bound his hands behind his back.

"Remove this man's hood," Buckle said to the hangman as he brought his victim to the foot of the steps.

The hangman eyed Buckle with contempt. "Who are you, stranger, to spit orders at me? Perhaps you are no more than a spy, like the rest!"

The crowd murmured its approval of the suggestion and edged in with refueled menace. Buckle was in no mood for dallying; the heat of the fires stung the already fire-pinked skin of his face and back, his jaw hurt like hell, and the kraken-sucker wound on the nape of his neck felt like it was full of razors. He tore away the hood, nearly taking the prisoner's head off with it.

The crowd howled its vicious disapproval.

"Enough, good people!" Zhukov bellowed at the mob. "Let the mystery be solved!"

The crowd cringed and stepped back.

The hood slipped out of Buckle's hand. Under an explosion of tangled white hair lit up by the gallows flames, out of the gaunt, skull-like, tight-skinned face, bulged the huge, wild, bloodshot eyes of Shadrack, peering straight up into the heavens.

Shadrack gasped as if he had not taken a breath for a hundred years. His forehead purpled about the temples and he lowered his terrible eyes, fixing them on Buckle. He smiled, a near-toothless, fanatical smirk, oblivious to the stink of death about him.

"You have saved old Shadrack, boy, as he knew you would!" Shadrack sputtered, his voice quavering but loud. "I was waiting for you here. Waiting. It is difficult to wait. Even when one is told to wait. Difficult. Who saves old Shadrack? Ah, the question has twice been answered—perhaps even thrice! You, sir, have saved old Shadrack!"

"You do know this moonchild?" Zhukov asked.

"Yes," Buckle replied.

"And I know you, Romulus," Shadrack said, his eyes focusing normally on Buckle, his mind freed from something that had long tormented it, but only for an instant. The crazy glare returned, snatching his sanity away.

"Release the prisoner," Zhukov ordered. One of his officers cut Shadrack's bindings away.

A Russian woman, a lovely young girl with a face contorted by rage, flung a finger at Sabrina and screamed. "A scarlet! A redhead as red as blood! A Founders bitch! Hang her! Hang her!"

The voices of the mob rose to a bloodthirsty roar. Zhukov, clambering up on the stairs, cut it off. "Silence, you fools!" Zhukov bellowed. The young woman dropped to her knees as Zhukov glared at her. "Which one of my officers has organized these executions? Where is my officer?"

The mob responded with a terrified silence, heads down. The fires crackled, matched by the crimson embers raining down from the sky, reinforcing the atmosphere of Zhukov's dangerous displeasure.

"A lynch mob? How dare you? How dare you! I am Zhukov, the boyar of Muscovy, and only I can sentence a citizen to death! The city may lie in ruins, but the rule of law is still upon you, and I am the rule of law!"

Zhukov calmly turned to one of his officers and pointed at the hangman. "Hang this traitor immediately," he said.

"No!" The hangman shrieked, sobbing. "Please, Boyar—I seek mercy! Mercy!"

It was too late. Two of Zhukov's officers snatched him up, lifting his boots off the ground, and carted him up the steps.

Zhukov slapped Buckle on the back as an old drinking friend would. "My apologies to you, Captain Buckle, that you were forced to witness such disarray. You may take your man with you, of course."

"Saved! And I have brought the answer for you!" Shadrack shouted with a ferocity that made both Buckle and Zhukov jump. "I am commanded to bring you the answer, and I have brought you the answer!"

"What answer?" Buckle asked.

"Elizabeth," Shadrack replied.

-LXXXI-

THE MELTING POT

BUCKLE STARED AT SHADRACK. THIS was the man who had helped his father fight off the sabertooths that night long ago in the Tehachapi Mountains. Surely, perhaps, somewhere in that shambling brain, now plunged into the whirl of insanity, the truth still lurked. The truth of what had happened to Buckle's parents. And *Elizabeth*.

Buckle found nothing to trust in the bulging, crazed eyes. But Shadrack had to know *something*.

"What nonsense is this?" Washington groaned, stepping forward. "Oh, no, no, no!"

"Who is Elizabeth?" Valkyrie asked.

"Captain Buckle's blood sister," Sabrina whispered. "Missing and believed dead."

"It is nothing!" Washington blustered. "A myth about the captain's lost sister."

"Elizabeth," Shadrack muttered. "We must..." His voice trailed off, along with his mind.

Buckle grabbed the old man by the shoulders, trying to make him focus by staring into his swimming eyes. Whatever the old jabberwock knew, he was going to either coax or throttle it out of him. "What do you mean when you say the answer is Elizabeth?"

"I know where she be, or will be," Shadrack mumbled. "It is difficult, the knowing, for it is dark to me."

Buckle would have shaken Shadrack like a wet rag if he had not feared the rickety old skeleton would fall part.

"Where?" Buckle asked rapidly.

"Atlantis," Shadrack said quickly, matter-of-factly, as if he knew he must spit it out before his brain betrayed him again.

"Of course!" Washington said. "The maddest place she could be tucked into. Captain, it is time to go. The Founders will be upon us shortly. You must return home to Balthazar at best speed."

Barely listening to Washington, Buckle chewed on the name, unable to take his eyes off Shadrack, whose mouth now worked soundlessly. Atlantis? The mysterious clan city long hidden under the western sea? What damned reason would the Atlanteans have to keep Elizabeth?

"Why Atlantis?" Buckle asked.

"Why not?" Shadrack chuckled.

"Do not play three-legged riddles with me," Buckle snapped.

Shadrack nodded gravely, his jaw shuddering, not from fear but from some awful tic. "If you go there, she will be there, when you go there."

"Captain!" Washington exclaimed with exasperation. "This is intolerable. We must abandon the lunatic and depart."

Zhukov laughed.

"If Elizabeth is in Atlantis," Sabrina said softly to Buckle, "we could never reach her. No one knows the way into the underwater city."

"No one knew the way into the city of the Founders, either," Buckle replied.

"No one is going to Atlantis," Washington said.

"Not going?" Shadrack shrieked, his emaciated, sinewy arms twisting under the fabric beneath Buckle's hands. "Do you not see what old Shadrack has done? What answer old Shadrack has given you?"

"What answer?" Buckle asked. "I know you. I *know* you. From the cabin on the mountain. You were there with us, with my father, Alpheus, at Tehachapi."

"We must go!" Washington howled.

"Of course I know you, little fellow. That is why I brought Penny for you," Shadrack pleaded, his eyes welling up with tears. "Penny Dreadful—she knows the way! She knows the way!"

"Who is Penny Dreadful?" Sabrina asked.

Shadrack's weak brain collapsed. He stared up at the red rain of cinders and mumbled incoherently.

Penny Dreadful? Hopefully this person was sane.

Buckle spun to the crowd. "Was there someone with this man? A girl? Speak up!"

"Tell this officer what you know, if you know anything," Zhukov ordered.

The young woman stepped forward, shaking. "When we captured the spy—when we found him, he was in the company of a beastly little automaton, one of the old Atlantean machines."

"And where is that automaton now?" Buckle asked the woman.

The woman turned a frightened glance toward Zhukov. "They tossed it in the melting pot."

"Where?" Buckle snapped, grabbing the woman by the arm. She pointed a quivering finger at a small foundry build-ing across the square. The outer wall was collapsed and Buckle saw a group of clanspeople within, collected around a crucible furnace fired up with glowing red coke.

Buckle dashed forward, hearing the sharp *thump* of the gallows trapdoor behind him. The Muscovy hangman had met his doom.

It only took a matter of seconds for Buckle to reach the foundry, charging over the rubble of the wall and into waves of stinging heat flowing out through rows of cupolas, molds, and hydrogen collectors. Four Russians in leather aprons were shoveling more coke into the furnace, while a dozen more peered down into the melting pot, their faces glowing with an eerie dance of red and amber light.

Buckle saw the Penny Dreadful, a metal robot constructed in the bulky form of a nine-year-old girl, lying in the bottom of the bowl like a discarded doll. It was a ghastly looking iron, copper, and bronze thing, strange in its metalwork and the foreign art of its forging. Its feet were fashioned into high-laced boots, its skeletal legs disappearing under a pinafore of shimmering, cloth-like metal. Octagonal glass bubbles lined both sides of the torso, cold and dark. The arms, designed to look much more human than the legs, ended in beautiful multijointed hands. The automaton's neck, poking up out of its brass lace collar, seemed to approximate human anatomy, as if the metal skin concealed metal muscles and ligatures. The face, a stylized representation of a young female, slept, its mouth a black hollow, the nose small, the eyes hidden behind bronze lids with copper eyelashes pressed shut over smoothly polished cheeks. It had hair, a flowing, industrial version of hair, thousands of tiny copper strands braided along each side of the skull and hanging down to the shoulders.

The Penny Dreadful robot looked dead. The edges of it that touched the crucible sizzled, throwing sparks as the metal softened, preparing to melt against the rising heat.

"Remove the automaton!" Buckle shouted. "Get it out of there immediately!"

"And who the hell are you?" One of the Russians laughed unpleasantly. "Another foreigner? How about we toss you in the pot with the machine and find out what you are made of?"

Buckle reached for his pistol.

"That will not be necessary, Captain Buckle," Zhukov said, stepping in through the collapsed wall with Valkyrie and Sabrina at his back. "Now! Take the robot out of the pot!" he ordered the Russians. "And with alacrity, you swine!"

The Russians hastily collected their steel tongs in their heavily gloved hands, took hold of the Penny Dreadful by head and ankle, and dragged it, smoldering and smoking, up and out of its crematorium. The four men shifted the robot—it was apparently lightweight, despite its appearance—to a table and dropped it there. One of the smiths threw a bucket of water across the body, the liquid exploding in a hissing blanket of steam as it cooled the red-hot edges of its metals.

Buckle stepped over the smoldering figure of the automaton. Up close, the metalwork was worn but elegant, though melting had occurred on the heels and rump, as well as the elbows and the right side of the head, where the intricate surfaces were now smoothly rippled.

It was too late, Buckle despaired. The Penny Dreadful and the secrets it might contain, if any at all, were probably lost.

"If you want the melted robot, Captain, you may have it," Zhukov said, giving the Penny Dreadful a disapproving glance. "Though it is not much of a reward for the man who is most certainly the savior of myself and the *Czarina.*"

Suddenly, the Penny Dreadful awoke. A soft yellow illumination pulsed in the region of the heart, coursing outward along hundreds of tiny liquid-bearing glass tubes to the arms and legs. The glow traveled up the neck and into the skull, swirling within, the fringes of the eyelids spilling newly kindled brightness.

Buckle leaned over the Penny Dreadful. "Do you hear me, machine?" he asked.

The bronze eyelids flicked open with a *clank*, revealing two glass orbs with copper irises full of swirling, sparkling, lemon-gold incandescence. The eyes whirled to Buckle with such exactitude that he jerked back.

"Who are you?" the Penny Dreadful asked, in a voice surprisingly similar to that of a human female child.

"I am Captain Romulus Buckle. Who are you?"

"Why, I am Penny, Penny Dreadful, of course."

Buckle stared into the bizarre little-girl face, hearing the automaton's gears and springs winding and clicking inside the skull. "Penny Dreadful, do you know the way to Atlantis?"

"Of course I do," Penny Dreadful replied brightly. "I was born there, after all."

~LXXXII~

THE PENNY DREADFUL

CAPTAIN BUCKLE STRODE INTO THE cramped chart room at the rear of the *Pneumatic Zeppelin*'s piloting gondola, Ambassador Washington hard on his heels. Buckle was greatly annoyed, and even more displeased when he saw Howard Hampton and Penny Dreadful—the half-girl, half-metal goblin—sitting in the chairs, both patting Kellie. Kellie looked a bit unsure about the robot, but she was not inclined to turn down a good scratching, from a human or otherwise.

"This is not your mission," Washington said. "Captain, you go too far."

Buckle turned back to face Washington. There was little free space in the cabin, and it was dark—it took a moment for his eyes to adjust from the rich green boil illumination on the bridge. His face was close to Washington's, his right leg pressing against the Penny Dreadful's iron knees.

"It is an opportunity, sir," Buckle whispered back. He could hear the bridge crew relaying orders in preparation for liftoff. He desperately wanted to be out on the deck with them. "With the invasion under way, every clan is in peril. The people of Atlantis shall understand this."

"The people of Atlantis," Washington said, punching the word *people* in an unfriendly way, "care for no clan but themselves.

They are absolutely neutral. Have you given thought to the fact that you shall not be able to find their city under the sea? The Atlanteans have no door to go knocking on, and I doubt they shall be popping up to greet you."

"Penny Dreadful knows the way in."

Washington uttered an unformed, frustrated sound. "This bashed-in automaton the Russians were about to melt down for scrap? You are going to risk this airship and the lives of your crew chasing the mumblings of an ancient robot and the insane prisoner who led it here?"

Buckle said nothing. He thought of Shadrack, who had vanished after the group charged to the rescue of Penny Dreadful. It irked Buckle to have lost the old man; he had so many questions for him. Buckle looked at Penny Dreadful, who returned his gaze with her shimmering eyes. Howard Hampton looked uncomfortable, not wanting to be trapped in a small room with an angry ambassador and a defiant captain.

"It is your duty to return home," Washington pressed. "You can no longer afford to jump every time some rusty bucket of bolts starts yammering about your poor, dear sister."

Buckle locked eyes with Washington. "My sister is important, but I shall bring Atlantis into the Grand Alliance."

"Do not lie to me, Romulus," Washington whispered, almost sadly. "I have known Balthazar all of his life and I love his children, you and Elizabeth included, as a blooded uncle might. And you know this. But Elizabeth is dead, Romulus. The Founders killed her at Tehachapi. Whispers and rumors will never bring her back, and if you chase her ghost in the night now, you will achieve nothing but your own death and the death of every crew member aboard the *Pneumatic Zeppelin*."

Buckle was at the battle station in his brain, a place where all bomb blasts and insults passed by him like water in a river, clear and unscathing. He looked into the passageway, where the stained wood planks gleamed with the bioluminescent green glow of the boil lamp overhead. Normally, he would have agreed with Washington and returned to a safe Crankshaft harbor. But Lady Andromeda's words from the night before never left him; they haunted him. *You must find a way to rescue Elizabeth. Elizabeth is the key to winning this war, the key to all of our futures. She must be rescued at all costs.* Never in a thousand years would Buckle have thought that he would trust a foreign clan member so utterly as he trusted Andromeda. For an instant, he tried to doubt himself and his belief in her words, but his forced uncertainty did not stick, passing in a heartbeat.

Elizabeth was the key to *everything*.

But Washington would never believe it.

And Buckle knew Elizabeth would be in Atlantis. He *knew* it. "I can bring the Atlanteans to us, sir, and win the war in so doing." As he spoke, he heard the rumble of horse hooves arriving on the ground below the gondola.

"Such overconfidence is dangerous, Captain," Washington countered, taking a deep breath. "Think of your position. With the Russians retreating north to Archangel, you are alone with the Founders coming up from the south. If you strand your airship over the sea, you cut yourself off, putting the Founders between you and home. I guarantee you the Founders shall take advantage of that mistake. The Atlanteans shall not rise to meet you, sir. You will be greeted by nothing but black ocean, and, once the Founders fleet surrounds you, it shall become your grave."

"I assure you I shall find a way," Buckle said evenly. He could not tell Washington what Andromeda Pollux had told him, but he trusted Andromeda so much it actually frightened him. The recovery of Elizabeth was the paramount mission. Without her, according to Andromeda, the Grand Alliance would lose the war, and that would only be the beginning of the evil that would rise.

Washington sighed, his anger dissolving, looking older and more haggard than he had when his face had been tense with argument. "So many things have happened before, Romulus—so many things you do not know. The world is not so cut and dried as you think."

"Captain?" Valkyrie leaned into the cabin doorway.

"Yes," Buckle replied. Valkyrie looked good, looked sharp. She had just learned of the destruction of the *Cartouche* and her brother's death fifteen minutes before; Buckle had asked her, with all the sympathy a man could muster, if she might wish to spend some time alone in her cabin. She had refused him, stating that the *Pneumatic Zeppelin* required her chief engineer on the bridge, and she would do her mourning later. If she wanted to remain in the thick of it, Buckle would allow her to do so.

"The *Czarina* has sent a mounted escort with a horse for the ambassador, sir," Valkyrie said.

"It is time for you to go, Ambassador," Buckle said.

Washington sighed, then offered Buckle his hand. Buckle shook it warmly. "Good luck to you, Captain," Washington said.

"And to you, sir," Buckle replied. He had great respect for Washington. He was sorry to send him away like this.

"Please follow me, Ambassador," Valkyrie said. "And we shall be ready to be away in five minutes, Captain."

"Aye," Buckle said.

Washington followed Valkyrie out into the passageway. "A horse?" he grumbled. "It has been a hundred years since I have ridden a horse. My goodness."

Buckle placed his hand over his mouth and ran his fingers along his cheeks to the point of his whiskery chin. Kellie, Howard, and Penny Dreadful lifted their faces to him, the eyes of the boy and dog shining, alive with their own life force in the weak light, while the gold-yellow orbs of Penny Dreadful gleamed with power quite unhuman. "How are we doing in here, Howard?" Buckle asked.

"Just fine, Cap'n," Howard replied, sounding rather joyful that the tension in the air was gone. "Penny here, she knows some quite extraordinary word games, sir."

"She does, does she?" Buckle asked.

"I am always good at learning things," Penny Dreadful said, folding her hands in her lap with the light click of metal on metal.

Kellie, released from her scratching, trotted out the door, brushing against Buckle's knees as she passed. Buckle suddenly felt uneasy. Washington was right. It was insane to place all his eggs in one basket, a basket woven by a madman and carried by a somewhat-melted robot. He suddenly missed Max, having her at his side, always a paragon of objectivity, always ready with wise advice even if he did not want to hear it. "You are certain you can get us to Atlantis, Penny Dreadful?"

"Oh, quite, Captain," Penny Dreadful replied. "Please, do not worry."

"Have you been having any mechanical problems?" Buckle asked. "I do not know how long you lay in the crucible. Perhaps I should have my chief mechanic take a look at you."

"I feel extremely hale, thank you," Penny Dreadful replied.

"You were not functioning when we found you," Buckle said.

"I had shut myself down," Penny Dreadful replied.

"And why was that?"

"Is it not obvious, Captain?"

"Humor me," Buckle replied. "I am not much used to conversing with machines."

"Because they were about to melt me," Penny Dreadful said, something resembling a sob rising in her voice. "And I did not want it to hurt."

Hurt? Buckle thought. In what way could a machine feel hurt? "Ah, well, I am glad you are well, Miss Dreadful, and that we were able to rescue you from any hurt."

Penny Dreadful's mouth formed an odd smile, and her eyes burned a little brighter. "And for saving my life I am eternally grateful, Captain Buckle. Be sure of that. Metal people never forget, you see." She tapped her head with an iron finger in a childish fashion that Buckle found disturbing.

"Very well, then," Buckle replied. "How about I escort you out onto the bridge, and you can help my navigator find the hidden city of Atlantis?"

"Oh, Captain," Penny Dreadful said with a giggle, slipping off her chair and skipping past Buckle, her iron shoes clomping heavily across the deck. "Things are not hidden if you know where they are!"

~LXXXIII~

THE GRAVEDIGGER

Max awakened, released from Buckle and sabertooths both. Her brain battled the morphine even in her sleep. It was late—she could tell by the brightness of the infirmary lanterns and the darkness of the window curtains. Tyro's iron lung wheezed with its constant beat, and though she could not see Valentine, she sensed that he lay fast asleep in his bed.

Max tried to move—tried to lift her head, an arm, a finger—and failed. Pain stabbed her neck and back. She ignored it.

The infirmary nurse walked past, holding an empty syringe, its glass gleaming in the light of the lantern flames. She was a middle-aged woman with a bored face and little yellow flowers sewn into the collar of her medical smock.

Max could not remember the woman's name.

She was suddenly frightened. Not for herself, but for Romulus Buckle. For the *Pneumatic Zeppelin* and her crew. Buckle had refused to tell her things, bad things. The airship and her crew were in mortal danger—she was sure of that. But there was more to fear. Something unknown, something even more terrifying than the prospect of war.

Something slithering beneath the known world.

She should be there, with them, guarding them.

When she was small, she could remember standing in the snow in front of her parents' house. Someone had killed a timber wolf, and the creature's body lay in the back of a wagon. She and Tyro stared at the dead animal, having edged up to it until there were mere inches away from its face.

The dead wolf stared at them with its lifeless yellow eyes, which were frozen open. Its mouth was open, too, the dark tongue lolling out over the jaw, framed by the rows of big, dirty, yellow teeth.

The fangs frightened Max. The dead animal smelled awful, of old carrion and rancid blood. She wanted to retreat, but Tyro would have teased her. Tyro had reached into the mouth and grabbed the tongue. Max had never forgotten that moment.

She closed her eyes, and she was in the chamber of numbers again. Her Martian unconscious, fueled by her dreams, had revisited the place and rebuilt it for her, piece by piece, carving brilliant details out of her murky memories, *working the problem.* The candle flickered on the table—she could smell its old, oily paraffin.

The numbers would not leave her alone. The crowded formulae on the walls kept returning to her unbidden. Perhaps she had absorbed the mystery of it, the obsession, somehow, when she lay in the chamber, near death.

Without willing it, she kept reviewing the calculations, flipping them upside down, inside out, the morphine constantly dragging her in and out of her lines of thought, zigzagging her brain.

She smelled burning wood and Fassbinder's Penicillin Paste. The formulae shifted, transformed, evolved into something else. The caterpillar in the chrysalis broke free, a butterfly.

Suddenly the never-ending flow of numbers stopped. It almost made sense. She was a hair's breadth, a decimal point, from solving it. The immortality equation. She gasped, fearing that in the next moment the morphine would wash over her and she would lose track of the long line of winding calculations she had just done.

She needed to record the numbers. Without them, she might never be able to find her way so close to the solution again.

She reached for her pencil and paper. She had requested them at one point, and Doctor Lee had accommodated her, placing them on her bedside table.

She lifted her arm and, shaking like a leaf, stretched her fingers toward the paper.

And then she froze.

Someone had arrived in the infirmary.

Someone, or *something*.

Heavy steps approached along the aisle. Max's heart started pounding. Disinfectant-laden air rushed in and out of her nostrils. She strained against the limits of her vision, but she could not see what was coming.

But she could sense him. Heavy as the end of time. Effortless as the fall of night.

The pencil and papers flew off the table, as if struck away by an invisible arm, the papers falling to the floor like leaves, the pencil rolling away in a small, high-pitched trundle.

The footsteps stopped. It was standing at the foot of her bed.

Max peered down and saw him.

The Gravedigger.

It was he, his face barely visible in the darkness, but his form silhouetted in the lamplight, the tall, black-winged Martian who had met Max at the entrance to the Edifice of the Dead and refused her entry, cast her away.

Max's heartbeat almost choked her, it was racing so fast.

Was she dead?

The Gravedigger spoke, his voice weary, layered with warning, but without malice. Max felt his hot breath on her cheek, too—at least she thought it was his breath, even though he was seven feet away. That surprised her. She had always thought that the Gravedigger's breath would be cold. "You are special, because you are one, and you are the other. Two minds live within you, two souls, two prisms with which to understand the universe." He paused, and she saw a frightening blue glow rise in his black eyes. "You are too close. The answer you seek would bring you nothing but misery. Turn away from the equation and never return to it again. I have warned you."

Max's vision fluttered as her pounding heart overtaxed her greatly weakened body. Her wounds burned like fire. Flinging her eyes wide open, she saw that the Gravedigger was gone.

She did not know if he had ever really been there.

Darkness squeezed out the light.

She fainted.

-LXXXIV-

TO ATLANTIS

The *Pneumatic Zeppelin* had stopped, briefly, to allow the Imperial princess a moment to stand watch over the burned wreckage of the *Cartouche*, the tomb of her brother, Bismarck, and his Imperial crew.

Buckle climbed down the rope ladder from the piloting gondola's hull-access hatch. The zeppelin was terrain-moored on the sweeping flank of a mountain ridge, anchored twenty feet off the ground in rough territory, and a fresh breeze was making her strain at her hawsers.

Buckle's boots landed on hard-crusted snow and frozen grass; he immediately strode toward Valkyrie. She was about seventy-five yards away to the north, her slim figure clearly visible against the smoldering skeleton of the *Cartouche*, crumpled like a red-hot spider crushed under the heel of a giant boot.

If the very world itself had been at peace that morning, there was no doubt that she was at war tonight. The colossal fires of Muscovy still raged far away to the northeast, still casting whirlwinds of fiery red embers high into the sky. Across the mountain ridges were scattered the burning pieces of the *Bellerophon*, the *Industria*, and the two Founders mortar barges. Only the ocean seemed untouched in its great, impenetrable blackness. And it was into that blackness Buckle knew he must now go. Far out there, somewhere, where sharks and sea-monster beasties roamed the depths, lay the fabled city of Atlantis. Elizabeth was in Atlantis, if old Shadrack was to be believed, and he would get there, if Penny Dreadful knew the impossible way in.

Buckle had cast his lot with the asylum inmate and the defective robot.

But if Elizabeth was in Atlantis, he had to find her.

He had to.

Buckle slowed to a stop ten feet behind Valkyrie and paused respectfully, one hand resting on the pommel of his sword and the other on the butt of his pistol.

Valkyrie did not move, but she knew it was time to go.

The armored trains and war fleets of the Founders were coming.

Valkyrie glanced over her shoulder at Buckle and looked at him. Her eyes, silvered by the moonlight, were wet.

Buckle removed his top hat. "Princess, if I may—I cannot describe to you our sadness at your loss of your brother and his crew. You are our crewmate, and we are now given to you as you are to us, through battle and blood, and the entire ship's company offers its condolences."

Valkyrie did not respond immediately. She gazed down the snowbound mountain to where its ridges plunged into the sea. The ocean breeze rocked a handful of her fine blonde hairs that had escaped their pinnings back and forth about her cheek and neck. "This wind shall worry us as we try to make headway to the west," she said.

"Aye," Buckle replied.

The wind rose, spurring the fires as they slowly consumed themselves on the shattered wreckage of the *Cartouche*, their whitish-orange illumination slowly dying against the pale-silver moonlight.

"I thank you and the crew for your sympathies, Captain," Valkyrie said. "You are most kind."

Buckle nodded, then turned to face the sea as well. The cold wind hummed, giving voice to the void, bringing with it the thunder of the waves breaking upon the white-frothed, iridescent line of the beach. Sea lions barked to the north, far away. Ice-coated tree branches rubbed together, issuing a musical tinkle, joined by the occasional, fragile shattering of falling icicles.

The *Pneumatic Zeppelin* creaked louder on her ropes, the breeze fluttering her canvas with the sound of birds' wings, whispering to Buckle that she was unhappy being earthbound and begging him to fly. Buckle heard it. So did Valkyrie.

Valkyrie removed her right glove and knelt, picking up a handful of gray ashes from the snow; she let them stream through her stained fingers.

"I can give you another minute," Buckle said.

"No," Valkyrie whispered. She stood and turned to Buckle, drawn up to her full length, her beautiful face stern, her eyes dry. "I have said my good-byes, Captain. Thank you." She placed her Crankshaft pith helmet with its red puggaree on her head. "Let us go and get your sister."

Buckle smiled grimly at Valkyrie, and for the first time, he saw her smile back—a smile cocooned in sadness, but an honest one.

They strode back up the ridge to the *Pneumatic Zeppelin*, her huge ellipsoidal shape looming against the night clouds. She was running dark—with interior buglights and night lanterns only—so the Founders lookouts could not espy her from afar.

"Please get the lead out, sirs," Ivan urged impatiently from the base of the rope ladder. "Or have you forgotten about the fogsucker armada on its way?"

"Just make sure my engines work, Mister Gorky," Buckle replied.

Ivan sighed, his metal arm and faceplate gleaming, his magnifying goggles making his eyes look overlarge and buggy through the glass. Buckle had asked Ivan, as they prepared to meet with the Russians, if he wished to accompany them—the Spartak clan was his original bloodline. Ivan had refused, saying that though his heart was Russian, he had no desire to shake hands with the bastards who had abandoned him on the streets of Archangel, where Balthazar, visiting on a trade mission, had found him, a filthy infant in a basket, riddled with the carbuncle plague and left in the gutter to die.

Ivan lifted his goggles and gave Valkyrie a respectable bow as she arrived under the ladder. "Princess, my sympathies," he said.

"Thank you, Mister Gorky," Valkyrie answered. "You are most kind."

Buckle clambered up the rope ladder. When he entered the access hatch in the deck of the piloting gondola, he was nearly bowled over by Kellie, as she excitedly dashed about, and found himself at the metal feet of Penny Dreadful, her yellow eyes peering down at him, glowing with the reflection of the bioluminescent green boil.

"Captain is aboard!" De Quincey shouted, looking back from the helm.

"Up ship, if you please, Miss Serafim!" Buckle ordered as he climbed onto the deck and leaned back into the hatchway to offer his hand to Valkyrie. She took it, her long, ash-stained fingers wrapping securely around his as he swung her up.

"All sentries aboard! Prepare to away!" Sabrina shouted into the chattertube hood. "Lift anchor!"

Buckle hauled Ivan up the hatch and then strode to his station. Sabrina tipped her bowler to Buckle and returned to her position in the nose. The bridge was alive, boil glowing in every glass tube, sphere, bubble, and orb, imparting its familiar, otherworldly illumination.

Buckle felt both ebullient and anxious, and let his crew carry out their familiar tasks without any need for his orders. Voices sounded from the ratlines above and the keel deck behind as the anchors were secured home, the mooring lines winched in and coiled into the rope wells, the marine sentries numbered and aboard, and the ballast and hydrogen wheels cranked and poised.

"All hands aboard. Ready to up ship, Captain," Sabrina said.

"Up ship, five hundred feet," Buckle ordered.

"Up ship, five hundred!" Sabrina shouted into the chattertube.

Buckle felt the wonderful weightlessness of his huge airship as she escaped the earth.

"We are away," Sabrina said. "Guns are loaded, tompions in. Sixty-eight souls."

Sixty-eight souls, Buckle thought. Five killed, ten wounded—three seriously—in the battle with the *Bellerophon*. "All ahead half," he ordered.

"All ahead half, aye!" Valkyrie repeated, clapping the chadburn dial and ringing the bell.

"All ahead half, aye!" Yardbird responded from engineering, ringing the daughter bell.

Buckle folded his hands behind his back as the ascending *Pneumatic Zeppelin*'s turbines launched her driving propellers into gargantuan, chopping whirls. "Helm, bear due west."

"Bearing due west, aye!" De Quincey answered, turning the rudder wheel a few tocks.

The propellers whirled up to a comfortable hum as the airship smoothly accelerated. Buckle heard the slow whoosh of the water ballast pouring from the scuppers, and felt the upward surge of the extra press of hydrogen into the cells. The snowy mountain ridges fell away below the nose dome as the *Pneumatic Zeppelin* rose, filling the night horizon with the great expanse of overcast sky and the black mass of the ocean.

Buckle turned and looked at Penny Dreadful, the little-girl machine, who stood behind the ball turret of the hammergun, her eyes glowing under their copper lashes. She looked at him but did not speak.

"I have our speed at twenty knots against the headwind, Captain, correcting for drift," Sabrina said, looking back at Buckle from the nose. "What is our destination?"

"Why, you know our destination, Navigator," Buckle said wryly, as he looked down at the dark, glittering, endless sea. "We are headed to Atlantis."

THE END

ACKNOWLEDGMENTS

Every novel is a labor of love, and there are many wonderful people who have shared this journey with me. I am fortunate to be the son of Richard and Janet Preston, my stalwart patrons, whose inexhaustible love and support have always fueled my sense of who I am and what I must do. I am lost without my wife and eagle-eyed reader, Shelley, whose love, positivity, and enthusiasm keep me afloat, and our two daughters, Sabrina and Amelia, who inspire every word I write. I must also thank my sisters, Marsha and Joanna, and all of the family and friends who have lavished me with encouragement along the way.

Special thanks go out to Julia Kenner, a tremendous writer and friend, who generously opened doors for the first manuscript. I must also thank Trident Media Group and my first agent, the fantastic Adrienne Lombardo, who championed the first book and believed in Romulus Buckle as much as I did. Heartfelt thanks go out to my new agent, Alyssa Eisner Henkin, my brilliant caretaker, who is currently constructing ambitious plans for our future. I also owe a huge debt of gratitude to my wizardly and most patient editor Alex Carr and everyone on my 47North team, and also to my incomparable development editor, Jeff VanderMeer.

I must also express my thanks to Kellie, a little dog whose memory, in some lovely, wonderful way, inspired the writing of this steampunk series.

ABOUT THE AUTHOR

 RICHARD ELLIS PRESTON, JR., IS fascinated by the steampunk genre, which he sees as a unique storytelling landscape. *Romulus Buckle & the Engines of War* is the second installment in his new steampunk series, The Chronicles of the *Pneumatic Zeppelin*. Richard has also written for film and television. He lives in California and haunts Twitter @RichardEPreston.